About the Author

...eld writes contemporary women's fiction, mainly set
...vourite county of Lancashire where she lives on the
...the moors with her husband, daughter and cat. Her
...ovel won the Romantic Novelists' Association Joan
...n Award for new writers.

...not writing or reading, Kate enjoys walking in the
...shire countryside, Pilates, visiting historic houses and
...s, and volunteering in her village community library.

THE
MAN

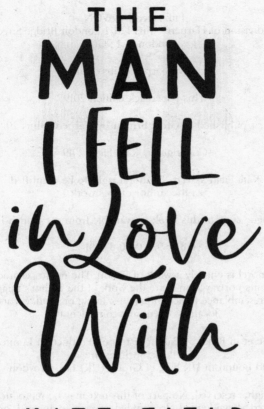

I FELL in Love With

KATE FIELD

avon.

Published by AVON
A division of HarperCollins Ltd 1 London Bridge Street
London SE1 9GF

www.harpercollins.co.uk

This paperback edition 2019

First published in Great Britain by HarperCollins 2019

A catalogue copy of this book is available from the British Library.

ISBN: 978-0-00-831781-2

This novel is entirely a work of fiction. The names, characters
and incidents portrayed in it are the work of the author's imagination.
Any resemblance to actual persons, living or dead, events or
localities is entirely coincidental.

Typeset in Birka by Palimpsest Book Production Limited,
Falkirk, Stirlingshire
Printed and bound in UK by CPI Group (UK) Ltd, Croydon CR0 4YY

MIX
Paper from
responsible sources

FSC
www.fsc.org

FSC® C007454

This book is produced from independently certified FSC™ paper
to ensure responsible forest management.

For more information visit: www.harpercollins.co.uk/green

To Stephen – because it would be rude not to

Chapter One

Spotlights swept over the hotel ballroom, illuminating a magical party scene. Christmas decorations twinkled with glittery brilliance; ladies in their finest gowns mingled with men in gorgeous black tie, cheeks flushed by wine and conviviality; and by the side of the stage, in a space unexpectedly lifted from the shadows, my husband held hands with another man.

'Who's that with Leo?' my friend Daisy whispered. Daisy had a figure friends would call petite, and enemies dumpy; she must have had a more limited view than I did. 'I quite like that sexy bald look. He's divine.'

But he wasn't. He was real – horribly, unquestionably real. Those fingers entwined with Leo's were made of skin and flesh, blood and bone, just like mine. And though their fingers dropped apart as the beam of light settled on the stage and pooled over the edges to where they stood, it was too late. I had seen. Most of the guests, expecting nothing more interesting than a display of luxury raffle prizes, would have seen. Friends, family, colleagues, and fellow school parents were all here tonight, attending this charity dinner at my instigation.

Every corner of our lives cracked apart with this one swift blow.

'Mary?' Daisy said, as I became aware of a rustle of whispers, of curious gazes landing on me; humiliation scorched my skin. 'What's going on?'

I couldn't reply. I looked at Leo, and Leo looked at me, the rest of the room forgotten. This man had been my best friend for twenty-five years, ever since the glorious summer day when the Black family had moved in next door. He had joined thirteen-year-old me as I sat on our front wall watching the removal men, desperately hoping that tucked away amongst the chairs, tables and white goods, they might produce a girl to end my lonely days. There had been no girl; but as Leo had consoled me by emptying a new tube of Fruit Pastilles to find my favourite green one, I had known there would be no more loneliness.

He had become my boyfriend when I was fifteen; my husband when I was twenty; the father of my children when I was twenty-one and twenty-three. So what was he now, when I was thirty-eight? I had a split second to decide, but it was enough. I read the terror, the anxiety and the appeal on his face, and there could only be one answer. He was what he had always been – my dearest friend – and that could never change, whoever's hand he held.

I stepped forward on legs that felt like stiff pegs, and met Leo halfway. I drank in every detail of his face – white and frozen above the deep black of his dinner jacket, but still a face I knew better than my own – and then leaned past him and kissed the cheek of the stranger who had held Leo's hand – the hand that had belonged to me, and my children, for so long. Exclusively, I had thought.

'How marvellous to see you,' I said, borrowing my mother-in-law's favourite word, as if I could borrow her sangfroid too, and with it bury the overwhelming terror of being a public spectacle that I had inherited from my own mother. 'You're just in time for the raffle! Daisy, do you have any tickets left for . . .' And here my brightness wobbled. Who was he? Leo and I shared everything, including our friends. How could he know someone well enough to link his flesh with theirs, without me even knowing their name?

'Lovely to meet you,' the man said. 'I'm Clark.' He held out a ten-pound note to Daisy. 'I'll take some tickets.'

'Leo?' Daisy asked. He glanced at me, blinking rapidly in his best dotty professor way, as if the complexities of buying raffle tickets were beyond him. I had seen that expression a thousand times; how could he be so familiar and so unfamiliar all at once?

'Don't we already have some, Mary? Did I see some pinned to the fridge?'

'Yes, I bought some last week.' They had been stuck on the fridge next to photos of our children, photos of us, and invitations to things we were supposed to be doing together. My heart wept at this casual reminder that though his hand may have so recently been linked with Clark's, his whole life was linked with mine. 'But you can get some more.'

3

He did, just in time: Daisy had barely crammed the corresponding tickets into the raffle drum when her boss, our local MP, took to the stage to start the draw. I won nothing, as usual, so I'd wasted my time daydreaming about the star prize: a two-night romantic spa break in a boutique hotel near Windermere. I screwed up my useless tickets, while on stage the MP continued his appeal for 'green 246'. Then Leo called out, sounding baffled but delighted.

'I've won. I'm green 246.' He held his ticket aloft, and smiled his charming smile – the one that always looked as if it had been surprised out of him – at first Clark, then me, then the room at large. He went up to collect his hotel vouchers, but as he made his way back to where I stood beside Clark, a drunken whisper rose from the crowd of acquaintances around us.

'A romantic break! Which of them do you think he'll take?'

Leo froze, paralysed with shock. He wasn't used to this; people weren't nasty in Leo's world – it was a gentle, courteous place. He looked at me – me first, this time – with a wordless appeal that he had no right to make but that I couldn't refuse. I linked my arm with his, and we walked out, gathering our mothers on our way. My family was everything. It was us against the world, even when that world was no longer what I had always assumed it to be.

I paid the babysitter on automatic pilot, hardly knowing what I said as she peppered me with questions about the food, the venue, the company . . . That one made me pause. What did she know? Had news spread already?

As soon as she had gone, I dashed up the stairs and popped my head round Jonas's door.

'Hey, Mum.' He spoke without taking his eyes off the TV screen, where a gruesome Xbox battle was underway. 'Have fun?'

'Yes, we did! We all had a great time!'

'What, even Granny Irene? What did you do, drug her sherry?'

I kissed the top of his head, the thick black hair exactly like mine, and moved on to the next room to check on Ava. Her light was off, and in the sliver of brightness spilling in from the landing, she looked my innocent angel again as she slept, not the tempestuous teen who often took her place. I watched her sleeping for a minute, as I had done so many times before, but never with such a sore heart. What was she going to wake up to? What future would unfold when I returned downstairs? I was tempted to go to bed and avoid it – I had spent a lifetime ignoring difficult truths; it was my stock-in-trade – but Leo's quiet 'Mary?' drifted up the stairs and pulled me back down.

I made two large gin and tonics, sloshing an extra measure of Tanqueray into my glass. Leo had switched on the lamps in the living room, framing us in a romantic glow entirely inappropriate for the discussion we were about to have.

'What's going on?' I asked, sitting down opposite him so I had a clear view of his face.

'I'm having a relationship with Clark,' Leo said. There was no hesitation, no prevarication. He met my gaze unflinchingly as he spoke. 'I met him two years ago, but it only developed in February.'

He said something else but I didn't catch it, too busy ignoring the implications of 'developed' and scrolling back through the year, hunting for signs I'd missed. I couldn't see any. We'd plodded on as normal: Easter with the family, summer in the house we always rented outside St Ives, school and university terms ending and beginning. Only Jonas's GCSEs had broken the pattern this year – or so I'd thought.

And then Leo's choice of word hit me. Relationship. Not sex, not affair, not fling. Leo valued words too highly for it to have been anything but a deliberate selection. A relationship was more than physical, and more than friendship: it was a deep, emotional connection. I scrolled back through the year again, this time looking for signs of my own deep connection with Leo, other than as colleagues, co-parents and housemates. I couldn't see any. How had I been so blind?

'Are you leaving?' A tremor rippled through the words.

His voice said, 'Mary . . .' His face said, yes. 'Not before Christmas,' he added, granting a short reprieve – but until when? Boxing Day? New Year? Spring?

I took a long slug of gin while I tried to fathom out what I should say next. Perhaps it would have been easier if it had been another woman. I could have ranted; I could have demanded to know what she had that I didn't. But the standard lines didn't apply in this case. It wasn't so much a rejection of me, but of my entire sex. That gave me no comfort.

'Why didn't you tell me? Why let me find out like this? And in public . . . You know how much I hate being gossiped about . . .'

'Tonight was an accident. We've discussed what to do many times, but this was never part of the plan. I'm sorry, Mary. I didn't know how to tell you. I couldn't find the words.'

'From a professor of English Literature, that's quite some confession. You had centuries of words to choose from.'

Leo's words stung, right through my skin and deep into my bones. At some point, in secret, they had discussed me, and how to break the news of their relationship. How could I not have known? Leo wasn't made for deception; surely the guilt would have stained him somewhere, like nicotine marks on the fingers of a secret smoker? I studied him, but there was no change: the fluffy brown hair, the soft skin, the wise hazel eyes, the tortoiseshell glasses – he was just the same. He still looked like my Leo, and sounded like my Leo.

'How could you do this? We had a deal. After Dad . . .' I stopped. I hadn't cried since I was eight years old; not since the day I had returned home from school and found that my adored daddy had gone, never to be heard of again. I wouldn't start now. 'You know how much loyalty means to me. On the first day we met, when we sat on the wall outside this house, I told you everything and you promised that you would never let me down. You promised again when you proposed.' I took off my engagement ring and waved it at him, the diamond twinkling joyfully in the lamplight. '"I will follow thee to the last gasp with truth and loyalty." You had it engraved on my ring.'

'I know. I meant it.' Leo took my hand. 'I love you. That hasn't changed. But with Clark . . .' He looked up, and even before he spoke I saw the wonder, the excitement, the jubilation in his eyes, too bright and overwhelming for him to disguise. 'The day is more luminous when he's in it. Life is more exhilarating. I crave his company like an addict. We've never had that, Mary. If you'd ever felt what I have with Clark, you'd understand why I can't give it up.'

It was an extraordinary speech for a man to make to his wife. Every word hurt. And they hurt most because I couldn't deny them. Our marriage was good and strong, solid enough to have lasted to the end if there had been no Clark. But it hadn't been based on exhilaration and cravings. My chest burned with a surge of jealousy: not that Leo felt this way about Clark rather than me, but that he had those feelings at all.

'Fuck, Leo, what do we do now?'

He dropped my hand.

'You don't swear!' he said, goggling at me – as if that one word had been the biggest surprise of the night.

'And you don't screw men. We've both learned something this evening.'

It was a cheap shot, and I regretted it when Leo's face cracked with grief. This wasn't an overblown TV drama, or a scandal to be sensationalised in the *Daily Mail*. It didn't matter that Leo had fallen in love with a man rather than a woman. I wasn't going to scream, or beg him to stay, or plot revenge. Real life was more complicated than that. I didn't hate Leo. I hadn't instantly stopped loving him. I wasn't sure I ever would. But there was one thing I was sure of: I couldn't let Jonas and Ava repeat my childhood. They would not lose Leo – even if that meant we all gained Clark.

After an awkward hesitation at the top of the stairs, we shared our bedroom as usual. I wasn't ready to shut him out tonight; wasn't ready to accept this new reality yet.

Leo's phone buzzed with an incoming text while he was in the bathroom. I was already in bed, too twisted with anxiety to sleep. It buzzed again, and stamping down my conscience, I shuffled across the mattress and picked it up.

'Just spoken to Mum. I can't believe you've done this to Mary.'

It was from Ethan, Leo's younger brother. Ethan had been away on a French exchange when the Black family moved in next door. Although he was more my age, by the time he returned, I was already a limpet on Leo's rock and nothing could have prised us apart. He had lived in New York since the early days of our marriage, and rarely came back. If even he had heard the news from a different continent, how widely would my humiliation have spread at home?

I dropped the phone, slid over to my side of the bed, and longed for the day to be over.

Chapter Two

We agreed the remaining lifespan of our marriage over mugs of tea in bed the following morning – a whispered discussion, so we wouldn't disturb the children. Once we had spent mornings trying to muffle quite different sounds.

I couldn't fault Leo for his honesty now, however much it hurt to hear it. He was clear from the start: it was a case of when, not if. He would leave, whatever I said or did. He wanted to be with Clark. Come the New Year, he would be sharing cups of tea and God knew what else in bed with Clark. He was sorry, and I believed him, but he was relieved and excited too. How could he not be? A new life and new adventures lay before him, while I was left holding together the tatters of our old life.

We told the children later that morning, and it was an experience too horrendous to dwell on. They weren't prepared for this. Leo and I never rowed, because it wasn't in his character and I had taken pains to repress it in mine. Jonas, sixteen years old and usually so laid back in true Black style, was appalled at Leo's treachery, but I couldn't let them take sides. I ended up defending Leo so enthusiastically that anyone would have thought I'd fixed him up with Clark myself.

Ava was my main concern, fourteen going on forty, and too much mine: I was terrified that I would have passed on something in my DNA, so that she would blame me just as I had blamed my own mum for the breakdown of my parents' marriage. But she had also inherited my skill of bottling up her emotions. She listened to us in dry-eyed, stony-faced silence, until eventually she announced, 'You do know you've ruined my life, don't you?' and flounced out, thumbs already flying over her phone.

I'd hardly had time to catch my breath when I spotted my mother, Irene, loitering outside the kitchen window.

'Are you free?' she asked, poking her head round the back door.

'Yes, it certainly looks like it. Absolutely free and single. Thanks for reminding me.'

Mum chose to ignore this, and pulling out a chair, installed herself at the table. Clearly this wasn't a flying visit.

'What was all that business about last night?' she asked, cutting straight to the point. 'It must have set everyone talking when you rushed us out like that.'

'I think they were probably more interested in Leo being gay than the fact that we left before the dancing.'

'Leo isn't gay,' she said, in the manner of a foreman of the jury, pronouncing a not guilty verdict. 'Remember when we went to see *The Sound of Music* at the Palace. He hated it.'

'Of course! That's all right then. I'll tell Jonas and Ava it was a mistake, and Leo can make his apologies to Clark. Thank goodness you sorted that out for us.'

'There's no need to be sarcastic. I'm only trying to help. If that's how you spoke to Leo, it's no wonder he had his head turned.'

But I hadn't spoken to Leo like this. I'd never shouted at him, never nagged, because I'd seen my mother treat my father that way, had lived through the consequences, and had never forgiven her. I thought I'd been a model wife. How was I to know that eventually Leo would want a model husband?

'Don't you think you've let yourself go?' Mum continued. 'You're never out of those jeans. When did you last have your hair cut? Or shave your legs? I noticed you were wearing thick tights last night.'

'I don't think hairy legs can be an issue,' I said. But here was one of the downsides of our living arrangements. Mum had given her house to me and Leo when we married, and had moved into the garage, converted and extended to suit her. It had been an extraordinarily generous gift, and had allowed us the luxury of a mortgage-free life. Not a Mum-free life, though. From her vantage point at the bottom of the drive, she missed nothing: her curtains looked like they had a nervous complaint, they twitched so often. And we certainly didn't have the sort of relationship where proximity was a good thing.

'A dress and a haircut aren't going to fix this.'

'What's going to happen? Is he going to give up this man, now he's been found out?'

'No.' I put down my mug. I'd already drunk enough tea this morning to keep Tetley in profit for a year. 'Leo will stay for Christmas, then move in with Clark.'

'But that's only a few days away! What about the children? He'll want to stay for them, surely?'

'Apparently not. I'm not worth staying with, even for their sake. Like mother, like daughter.'

I ignored Mum's pained expression and slumped down on a chair.

'But I won't keep them apart. Leo will still see them as often as he can.'

'Mary . . .' Mum looked as if she wanted to say more, but let her words trail off with a sigh. 'How did they take the news?'

'Jonas was cross, but he'll come round. He's a Black.' Mum nodded. The Blacks were a different species to us. If a family of Martians had moved next door to us all those years ago, they couldn't have seemed more alien or more exotic in comparison to our life. 'But Ava . . .' I shrugged, not from indifference, but because my worries were too heavy to distill into words. 'I'm not sure she'll ever forgive us.'

'She will.' Mum reached out and patted my knee, in one of those embarrassing moments of affection she occasionally attempted. 'And you'll be there for her, come what may, won't you? It will all work out. You didn't turn out too badly, did you?'

Now I really was worried.

It was inevitable that I would end up next door, in the house still occupied by Leo's mother, Audrey. She was the perfect mum: warm, happy, supportive; always ready with a hug, always knowing when to speak and when to listen. Since the day the Blacks became our neighbours, I had probably spent more time at their house than my own, irresistibly drawn to the whole family.

I called her name as I opened the back door, and she dashed into the kitchen, and folded me in her arms – something my own mother had singularly failed to do.

'Oh, Mary,' she said, pulling back to look at my face. I knew it wouldn't look as bad as hers: there were no tears on her face, but the pink and puffy eyes testified that there had been recently. 'I don't know what to say. Let's have some gin.'

I would have resisted – I had to pick up Ava from the riding stables later – if Audrey hadn't looked so much as if she needed one. We took our glasses through to the living room, a haven of calm neutrality, in contrast to the serviceable dark patterns that I had grown up with, chosen by my mother so that they wouldn't show the dirt. Audrey put her glass down on the side table beside her chair, next to a framed photograph of her husband, Bill. Bill had died four years ago, devastating us all.

'Are you furious, Mary? Will you ever forgive him?'

I sipped my gin while I thought what I could say.

'I'm not furious.' I stopped. How did I explain this to Leo's mum? I couldn't forget Leo's description of his feelings for Clark. He had been right. We had never shared that. Our friendship was deep and precious, and sex had been exciting at first, when we had been hormonal teenagers, new to the act, but that had faded long ago. Our relationship had been contented, companionable, steady – safe. It was exactly what I had chosen. But if Leo had now discovered there was something more, how could I begrudge him his choice?

'He said he didn't go out looking for this, and I believe him,' I continued. 'He fell in love. I'm not sure it's possible to prevent that, is it?'

'No. Although sometimes it's not always possible to have the love you want.' I assumed she was referring to her loss of Bill, and reached out to take her hand, but she shook her head. 'Sometimes sacrifices have to be made. There are other people to consider.'

'What good would it do to force him to stay for Jonas and Ava? They won't benefit from an unhappy father. That's not what you want for Leo, is it?'

Audrey sighed.

'This isn't what I wanted for any of you. You know that, my darling, don't you? You've always been as good as a daughter to us. If I had known it would end this way . . .'

'How could you have known? This has taken us all by

surprise, probably even Leo.' I perched on the arm of Audrey's chair. This had shaken her more than I had expected; there was no sign of her usual effervescent self. 'You realise that this won't change anything between us, don't you? You can't get rid of me. I'm going to be coming around here as much as I always have, drinking your tea and eating your biscuits. Although it may be more gin than tea for a while,' I added, finishing my glass.

'I'll buy a few more bottles. In fact,' Audrey said, finally flashing a smile, 'I can ask Ethan to pick some up for us in duty free. Have you heard that he's coming back?'

'No.' Leo hadn't mentioned it; he rarely mentioned Ethan at all. 'When will he be here?'

'He's flying back tonight. His Christmas plans fell through so he's decided to come home. Isn't it the most marvellous news? Ethan is exactly what we all need to perk us up.'

It was obvious that something was wrong with Ava as soon as I saw her emerge through the gate at the stables, jodhpurs stained in muck, boots filthy, grooming kit dangling forlornly from her hand. The teenager who had stalked through the gates with self-conscious confidence this morning had shrunk to a child with a bowed head, pink nose, and staring eyes that were defiantly holding back tears.

'What's the matter?' I met her halfway across the car park, anticipating tales of injury and an emergency trip to the doctor.

'Nothing. I'm fine.'

I wasn't falling for that.

'No, you're not. What's happened?'

'Nothing. Just drop it, okay?'

'It clearly isn't okay. Have you hurt yourself? Have you fallen off?'

'No. I'm not a baby. I can ride a horse without falling off.'

She was busy giving me the teenage glare when one of the girls from her year at school sauntered into the car park, and smirked in our direction. I hustled Ava away and into the car.

'Has Jemima upset you?'

'No.' Ava took off her hat and puffed up her flattened hair. I waited, refusing to switch on the engine until I'd heard more. Ava broke first. 'She said something about Dad. It doesn't matter.'

'Said what about Dad?'

For once, I must have stumbled on the magic tone of voice that compels teenagers to obey.

'About how horrible we must be if he's had to turn gay to get away from us . . .'

My heart was torn between sympathy and indignation. I grabbed the door handle.

'Come on. We're going to set her straight on a few things.'

'No!' Ava held onto my arm so I couldn't leave the car. 'Don't make a scene. Everyone at school will hear about it. Please!'

I let go of the handle, and watched as Jemima rode past in the front seat of a top-of-the-range Mercedes. I was no more keen on a public scene than Ava, but it was galling to let her get away with such vile comments, especially when I suspected there was more Ava wasn't telling me.

Ava sat in silence, twisting her whip in her hand, not looking at me.

'You know it's not true, don't you?' I asked. 'Whatever she said. It's prejudiced and small-minded and ignorant. Dad doesn't think like that. He loves us.'

'Is he really leaving?' There was a thinly disguised wobble in Ava's voice.

'Yes.'

'I don't want him to go.'

'Neither do I.'

'Then can't you stop him?'

And there was my little girl, trusting eyes turned on me, expecting that I could sort out the problem, and somehow repair the rift that Leo had created in the family. Could I? Should I? It was an impossible situation. I couldn't see any way that I could make both Leo and the children happy; no way that everyone could have what they wanted. How could I insist to the children that they should never settle for second best – that they were marvellous people and could have whatever they wanted – and then prevent Leo leading by example?

'I think we have to let Dad do whatever will make him happy,' I said. 'You'll still see him as much as you want.'

'No, I won't. He won't be there when I go to bed, and he won't be there when I wake up.'

She was right; and how much worse would it be for me, going to sleep and waking up with an empty expanse of bed at my side, beginning and ending each day with the reminder that I had failed? That despite everything I had done, every instinct I had suppressed, every burst of temper I had stamped down, every ambition I had given up, it hadn't been enough? That in the end, my genes had caught up with me, and delivered the fate I had been determined to avoid since my mother had driven away my dad?

It turned out that I'd been wrong, on that day when the Blacks moved next door all those years ago, to think that my loneliness was over. It had been a reprieve, that was all. Leo moved into the spare bedroom that night; he thought it was appropriate now the children knew, less of a mixed message for them. We'd had occasional nights apart before, but he had never seemed so far away as he did now he was on the other side of the internal wall. I could still hear his snores, but only faintly; couldn't hear the funny snuffle he made, half snore, half sigh, when he was deeply dreaming. Usually I would stretch out, glory in all the extra space. But today the bed felt hard and cold and just plain wrong – a pretty accurate reflection of my whole life right now.

Sunday lunch was traditionally a big affair in our house: three generations, three courses, and sometimes three bottles. It was a chore – Leo was useless in the kitchen, and left me to do it all – but the reward was seeing all my family gathered close, reinforcing our bond, however bumpy the previous week had been. There was no Sunday lunch this weekend. Some bumps were too high to smooth away with a roast chicken and chocolate sponge. Leo had gone to pick up his brother Ethan from Manchester Airport, which we all accepted as the excuse for the abandoned lunch.

With time weighing on my hands, I decided to take the dog for a walk, despite the freezing December temperatures and the mist hanging so low it cocooned my head like a balaclava. Dotty was officially Ava's dog, a gloriously mad goldendoodle that we had travelled to South Wales to buy for her tenth birthday; but since her obsession with dogs had become an obsession with horses barely six months after Dotty's arrival, it was generally me who had to look after her.

I didn't mind today: the opportunity to tramp the fields around Stoneybrook, our village located deep in the Lancashire countryside, letting the fresh air sting a trail down to my lungs and the cold numb every sense, was exactly what I needed. It was good to exchange hellos with normal people, who had normal lives, and who knew nothing of mine. Or I hoped they didn't – but as the walk went on, my paranoia grew. Was there something suspicious in that smile, something judgemental in that look? Was I being scrutinised for signs of trauma? Then, as we were on the home straight, squelching through the field that backed onto our house, a greyhound and its owner caught us up: my fault for dawdling, reluctant to get home.

I knew the owner, a tall, stocky man in his early forties: he was a teacher at Broadholme school, where Jonas and Ava were pupils, and had taught Jonas art in his first couple of years – a vague connection we acknowledged with a nod and a smile if we ever passed on our walks. I was more wary of acknowledging him today. There had been a group of teachers at the Christmas charity dinner. What if he had been one of them? Was he sneakily weighing me up, curious about the woman who had driven her husband gay? I hunched down into my scarf, and quickened my pace, tugging on the extending lead, but Dotty had other ideas. She pounced on the greyhound as if they were long-lost best friends; a manic, wagging, bouncing bundle of fluff, while the greyhound gazed nobly into the distance, refusing to acknowledge her.

The man – Owen Ferguson, I remembered, from two excruciating parents' evenings, when we'd all had to fake enthusiasm for Jonas' artwork – smiled and tipped his head towards Dotty.

'Quite a handful, I imagine?'

'Yes.' I examined his words for hidden layers of sarcasm or innuendo, but couldn't detect any. 'She certainly throws herself at everything with unchecked enthusiasm. Literally,' I added, as Dotty leapt up at the greyhound again. 'Sorry. Dotty! Come here!'

She ignored me; my voice had a unique pitch that neither dogs nor teenagers could hear. Owen whistled and the greyhound sauntered immediately to his side.

'Impressive,' I said, tugging the lead to drag Dotty back. 'Do you use that trick on the children too?'

'No, they'd never hear it over the ear pods.' His smile flashed up, a deep, brief smile that reminded me of Leo. 'I need a klaxon to round them up.'

I smiled back, but it faded quickly, and I couldn't think of anything else to say.

'Are things . . . okay?' Owen asked. I nodded, once, and he repeated the movement back at me, which could have looked odd, but was strangely comforting. 'Good.' He bent down and ruffled Dotty's head. 'Goodbye, Dotty. I expect we'll see you around.'

He headed off diagonally across the field towards the village, while I went straight on to the kissing gate that opened onto the road a little way down from our house. As Dotty stopped to water the bottom of a telegraph pole, Leo's car approached and pulled onto the drive. He got out and slammed the door, a rare sign of temper for Leo. Seconds later, the passenger door opened and Ethan emerged. It must have been two years since I had seen him, but he had scarcely changed: hair as thick and blond as ever; immaculately dressed despite a seven-hour flight; confident, athletic movements, even in the way he pushed the car door shut and hauled his suitcase from the boot. It would be impossible to guess, from looks, character, or temperament, that these two were brothers. I watched as they paused in front of the car. Raised voices carried towards me, the words muffled by the mist, but the anger behind them clear; and then Ethan turned and looked right at me. Leo followed his gaze, and after one final heated exchange, they stalked off in different directions, Leo to our house, Ethan next door.

Chapter Three

Clark was joining us for Christmas lunch. It had been my idea, and I still wasn't sure if it was the best or the worst one I'd ever had. But I wanted Leo to be with the children for one last Christmas – wholly with us, body and mind, not sneaking off to make furtive phone calls, or leaving before the pudding in an attempt to split his day between us. So Clark had to come; and the delight on Leo's face when I issued the invitation clarified things for me. It was the best idea for him, and the worst one for me.

The present opening was a subdued affair, despite the jolly Christmas music, the defiantly twinkling fairy lights, and glasses of Buck's Fizz all round. It all went on too long: I had overdone it during a manic spending spree the day before, as if somehow a bigger stash of presents could compensate the children for the impending loss of Leo. They were pleased; they smiled; but it wasn't the carefree joy of previous Christmases. I couldn't see how we would ever get that back.

I had agonised over whether to buy a different present for Leo. In my usual efficient fashion, I had ordered his Christmas gift months ago: a handmade pair of silver cufflinks, each one in the shape of a miniature book, engraved with the title of his favourite novel by the Victorian author Alice Hornby, Lancashire's answer to Charlotte Brontë. Leo had spent his academic career studying Alice's life and work, with me as his eager research assistant; he had already published an annotated edition of her novels, and his biography would be launched in a few months, the culmination of a lifetime of work for both of us.

The cufflinks had seemed the perfect present, and in many ways, they still were. But would he want to wear them, and be constantly reminded of me, and all we had achieved together? I gave them to him anyway, and the delight on his face was almost as great as when I had invited Clark for Christmas. And though I had braced myself for a boring gift from him – because, after all, he had known that our time was almost up and could have shopped accordingly – I should have known him better. He gave me a necklace, with a thick round pendant made of green Murano glass, which reminded me at once of that green Fruit Pastille he had found for me on the day we met. There were tears in his eyes as he watched me open the box, and his hands trembled as he fastened the clasp around my neck. And though I recognised that it had been chosen to mark the end, I knew that it promised a beginning too.

'A bit late to be making an effort, isn't it?' Mum said, when she toddled across from the garage with a bottle of cheap sherry for me, wine for Leo, and a Terry's Chocolate Orange each for Jonas and Ava. 'Is that a new dress?'

Of course it was: another emergency purchase yesterday. Clark was coming. I wasn't going to meet him properly for the first time in the same dowdy skirt and blouse I'd worn for the last four years.

'A new necklace too?' she carried on. I fingered it: the glass pastille was comfortingly smooth under my finger. 'Who's been buying you jewellery?'

'One of my lovers dropped round with it early this morning.'

'From Leo, is it?' Mum asked, ignoring what I'd said: clearly the pitch of my voice was inaudible to pensioners too. 'Has he dumped the boyfriend then? You should take him back. You'll struggle to find anyone else, in the circumstances.'

I turned and led her into the living room, without giving her the satisfaction of asking which particular circumstances she had in mind. My age? My looks? My crabby mother living in the garage, overseeing my every move? Leo drew her over to the sofa, distracting her with his quiet, charming conversation, while I hovered in the doorway, wondering how on earth I was going to survive without him.

Audrey and Ethan were next to arrive. Audrey looked stunning in a red wrap dress, blonde hair piled into a sophisticated messy bun, and yet still managed to hug me and say I looked beautiful with impressive sincerity. Ethan was . . . Well, Ethan was Ethan, no more and certainly no less than he had always been. He had lived a charmed life, and now even age was favouring him; his face had perhaps filled out a little, but it suited him; the confidence that had once seemed a size too big now fitted him like a jacket tailored to the millimetre. With my confidence so recently shattered, I felt oddly flustered to see him again; so much so that when he leaned forward to kiss my cheek, I opened my mouth to wish him a merry Christmas instead, twitched my head, and somehow managed to catch his kiss perfectly on my parted lips.

'And a happy Christmas to you too, Mary,' he said, laughing, and all at once we were teenagers again, partners in fun, and I couldn't help laughing along with him; the first time I had laughed in days, it felt.

Ethan's arrival brightened the mood for a while; his liveliness was infectious. Jonas and Ava were fascinated by him, and by the selection of hoodies, rucksacks and other paraphernalia that he insisted all the coolest New York teens were wearing. I could have kissed him again, deliberately this time, when I heard Ava's laughter drifting into the kitchen, and Jonas sounding more animated than usual as he explained to Ethan the intricacies of one of the Xbox games we had given him for Christmas.

'It's a shame they see so little of him,' Audrey said, echoing my thoughts as she joined me in the kitchen. 'You should have gone to visit him in New York. His apartment in Brooklyn is the most marvellous place. You would love it.'

We should have gone, and I had suggested it often enough, but Leo had a seemingly inexhaustible well of reasons why we couldn't. First the children had been too young, then he didn't want to interrupt school, or something was happening with his career, or the weather would be too hot or too cold, or the cost of the four flights was out of our reach . . . We had even missed Ethan's first wedding because Leo had decreed that six-month-old Ava was too small and noisy to travel so far. It was lucky that his second marriage had been to an English girl, and had taken place in Northumberland, as by that time Ava was seven and she would have been even noisier if she had been denied her chance to be a bridesmaid.

But it occurred to me, belatedly noticing Audrey's use of the past tense, that we wouldn't ever go to New York now – not the four of us, at least. Leo might take the children one day – possibly with Clark, though the details of that foursome were too painful to dwell on – but I wouldn't go. My connection with Ethan was over, the chance of free accommodation in New York lost with it. Not only Ethan – my link with Audrey had been pulled apart too. All the fine threads that criss-crossed between our families, binding us together, had been sliced through by Leo's hand – by Leo's hand holding Clark's hand. Whilst it might be insignificant to him – I only had Mum, and it was unlikely he would be sorry to escape her – the prospect of a severance from Audrey was only marginally less painful than losing Leo.

'You won't be tempted over there, will you?' I asked. 'Now that Leo isn't around to keep you next door . . .'

'I'm not going anywhere,' Audrey replied, taking my hand. 'You were never just Leo's wife to us. You must know that.'

I did, at heart, but it was easy for the doubt to creep in: the rejection by Leo was so fundamental that it was like the first in a chain of dominoes, and as soon as our marriage tumbled, I expected them all to fall.

The doorbell rang. Audrey clung to my hand as we heard Leo's footsteps clack along the tiled floor towards the front door – going at the perfect, steady pace, with neither unseemly haste nor false reluctance. It had gone quiet in the living room, so the sounds from the hall carried through to us with no competition: the rattle of the keys; a muffled exchange of words; a low laugh, from Clark, I guessed; and then a moment of silence. Dear God, were they kissing? Were they kissing in my hall? My chest began to burn with the effort of not breathing, as I strained to work out what was happening.

Audrey squeezed my hand, a sharp, painful squeeze, and gave me one of her rare stern looks.

'You can do this,' she said, and she removed my pinny, tidied my hair and steered me in the direction of the hall.

I couldn't look at Leo; didn't want to know if happiness was shining from his face, or see lips that might have recently been kissed by someone other than me. Instead I fixed my attention on Clark. He smiled – a nice smile, open and friendly – and stepped forward.

'Happy Christmas, Mary,' he said. 'It was kind of you to invite me.' He held out his hands, an exquisite bouquet of flowers in one, and an expensive box of chocolates in the other. 'These are just a small thank-you.'

For what? For giving him Leo? It was a very small thank-you for that.

'A thank-you for the meal,' Clark added, appearing to read my thoughts.

'You're welcome,' I said, ridiculously polite. What next? Send them up to our bedroom with my blessing? 'I'd better hide them away. You might want them back once you've tasted the food.'

Leo laughed, as if this was the wittiest thing he'd ever heard; although I suppose he had just been marooned with my mother.

'Come in and meet everyone,' he said, and ushered Clark into the living room, with me trailing behind like an ancient bridesmaid. The room was already silent when we entered, but the silence seemed to thicken as all eyes swivelled towards Clark; all eyes except Ethan's. He looked at me, eyes the colour of a hazy summer sky, scouring my face first before turning to study Clark.

Leo made hasty introductions.

'Mary's mother Irene, Ava, Jonas, my brother Ethan . . .'

No one moved. And then Audrey, lovely Audrey, in her cheery red dress, came dashing in and rescued us all from our torpor.

'Don't forget me,' she said – positively trilled – and without a second's hesitation she pulled Clark into a hug and kissed both of his cheeks. It was exactly the way she had greeted me when Leo had first introduced me, with enthusiasm and delight, apparently oblivious to the chaos of a house move going on around her. Now she was oblivious to the awkwardness around her – or perhaps she wasn't, and this was her way of dealing with it. Whichever it was, it worked. Ethan rose and shook Clark's hand, Ava and Jonas mumbled a greeting, and Mum inclined her head to acknowledge his presence. And Leo looked so proud – of Clark, of Audrey, of all of us – that I had to dash into the kitchen to get a grip on my emotions, terrified that the achievement of not having cried since my dad left thirty years ago might be about to come to a loud and messy end.

Christmas lunch was a triumph in a culinary sense, despite my having siphoned off a bottle of Prosecco for my own use, whose contents vanished with mysterious speed. A combination of alcohol and Audrey helped smooth the rough edges off the awkwardness we all felt; with the exception of Ava, who wasn't allowed a drink, and my mother, who was genetically programmed to wallow in awkwardness wherever she could find it.

It was impossible not to notice the parallels between this and my first meeting with the Blacks all those years ago; impossible not to think how bizarre it was that I should witness my mother-in-law getting to know my replacement. We learnt that Clark was forty-one, the same age as Leo;

that he had two parents, two sisters and four nephews. We found out that he was the Donor Communications Manager for a famous children's cancer charity based in Manchester, a job that he described with humility, enthusiasm, and compassion. We heard that his hobbies were films, cycling, and cooking. But above all else, I discovered that he was an intelligent, amusing, lovely man. I liked him. I had no idea if that made things a thousand times better or a million times worse.

After dinner, Ava pulled out the box of Trivial Pursuit for the traditional game of everyone trying to beat Leo. I ducked out this year, letting Clark take my place, and went to tidy the kitchen, finding simple pleasure in restoring order in the one area I could. Noise and laughter floated down the hall.

'What are you doing?'

Ethan followed me into the kitchen and pushed the door shut.

'Tidying up.'

'I don't mean in here.'

I knew exactly what he meant, knew what he was going to say, and it was one of the reasons why I had spent the whole of Christmas Eve out shopping, so that there was no danger of this conversation taking place. I grabbed a pile of cutlery, and fed it into the dishwasher with as much rattling as I could manage.

Ethan touched my arm.

'Mary.' I ignored him. He grabbed the cutlery from me,

threw it in the basket and slammed the dishwasher door closed. 'What's the matter with you?'

'With me?' That riled me. How was any of this my fault? 'Nothing.'

'That's my point. Leo's about to leave you, and you look about as bothered as if you'd run out of milk.'

'Of course I'm bothered! I don't want him to go. Would you prefer it if I stayed in bed and cried into my pillow? Or if I shouted abuse at him and cut up all his suits? Do you think that would help Jonas and Ava?'

'It might help you. It might show Leo that you do actually care, and that he has something to stay for.'

'Me being me isn't enough to make him stay, is that what you're saying? That I've driven him away? Thanks for that vote of confidence.'

'That's not what I meant . . .'

'And what makes you qualified to give me advice on relationships, with your two failed marriages and string of ex-girlfriends?'

Perhaps I had gone a bit far with that one – his second wife had been unfaithful, according to Audrey – but what right did he have to stand in my kitchen, berating my indifference? I knew some people would find my reaction odd, but I thought Ethan knew me better.

'I know exactly what you're doing. You block out things that are difficult, pretend they're not happening. It's what you've always done.'

'That's not true!'

'What is it then? Some grand sacrifice for Leo? You love him, but you're letting him go? Listen to me, Mary. It's not heroic or noble to do that. It's the wrong choice. If you want something enough you should carry on fighting for it, even if you get knocked down a thousand times, and no matter the collateral damage. Don't condemn yourself to a life of loneliness and regret.'

He gazed at me then, and it was as if he'd ripped open that confident jacket, and shown me someone entirely different underneath. I didn't know what to say, and was spared having to say anything when Leo walked in. He looked from Ethan to me, and back to Ethan.

'What are you saying to her?' I had never heard Leo's tone so sharp.

'The truth.' Leo's head jerked back as if Ethan had struck him on the chin. 'I told Mary that she needs to fight to keep you.'

'Do you have a problem with Leo being gay?' I asked. There had always been tension between these two, but this level of animosity was new.

'Not in the slightest. I only have a problem with him deciding he's gay now, years after marrying you.'

'I haven't made the decision. I met Clark, and I can't ignore what I feel for him.' Leo stared at Ethan. 'You can't help who you fall in love with. *You* should understand that.'

And Ethan, whom I had never before seen lost for words, simply shook his head at Leo and walked out.

Chapter Four

The envelope arrived on a cold day in late March during the Easter holidays, landing on the doormat with a thud that I heard from the kitchen, and which seemed to shake the entire house. I didn't need to open it to know what was inside. I didn't want to open it and make it real. I left it on the hall table, pulled on a coat, hat, and wellies, and took Dotty for a walk.

The footpaths around the village were quiet as I trudged through the slushy remnants of the snow that had fallen earlier in the week. It was mid-week: work would have deterred some of the usual dog-walkers, the bad weather many of the others. But Owen Ferguson emerged from the front path of a neat stone terrace as I passed, and hesitated, as if deciding whether to force his company on me or to turn in the opposite direction. I smiled and he must have made up his mind, as he fell into step beside me as we headed towards the centre of Stoneybrook.

He was wearing a black beanie hat, very much like one I had bought for Leo a couple of years ago. It suited him. His greyhound was wearing an extraordinary hot pink quilted coat, with a zebra print trim.

'It wasn't my choice,' he said, acknowledging my vain attempt to disguise my surprise. 'I inherited it.'

'A dog jacket? That wasn't a generous legacy. Lucky you had a dog it fits.'

'I inherited the dog too. It was a complete package.' He quickened his pace to keep up with me; Dotty was either eager to complete our circuit and get home, or determined to beat a greyhound. 'My neighbour adopted her from a greyhound rescue charity, but then was diagnosed with a terminal illness. I agreed to take on Lucilla.'

'Lucilla?' I tried not to laugh: it was a perfect name for the aloof animal, but I couldn't imagine Owen calling for her in the park.

'She won't answer to anything else. Or wear any other coat.'

'What colour did you want her to wear? Navy blue like the Broadholme uniform?'

He grimaced. 'Anything but that. Are your children not with you for the holiday?'

'Ava's at Pony Club, and Jonas is revising with a friend,' I said. 'Do you have children?'

'Two boys. They live with my ex-wife in Scotland. I'll have them next week.'

It occurred to me, then, that I had misunderstood Owen's question. He hadn't meant were Jonas and Ava with me *today*; he had meant were they living with me this week. It was the question of a divorced parent – from one to another. It didn't

36

matter whether I'd opened the envelope or not. I was one of them now.

'I think someone's trying to get your attention,' Owen said, and gestured towards the semi we were passing. Daisy was standing in the front window, banging on the glass and then beckoning inside with both arms.

'It's Daisy. Mrs Flood,' I added, in case he needed her parents' evening name to place her. 'I'd better see what she wants. Enjoy the rest of your walk. And enjoy next week with your boys if I don't see you before then.'

'I will.' The words were heartfelt, and his face transformed at the mention of his children, in the same way that Leo's did. I pulled Dotty back down the street and walked up Daisy's front path. Daisy opened the door before I was halfway there.

'I need your tongue!' she cried, in a voice of loud melodrama that must have carried as far as Owen, as he turned and looked back at us before walking on. 'Mine's exhausted, and I still have over two hundred envelopes to lick.'

Daisy and I had been friends for years, since our daughters had started in Reception class at Broadholme at the same time. She had a part-time job working as an admin assistant for our local MP, who spent a lot of money on printing leaflets saying how fabulous he was, leaving him with no money left for self-seal envelopes. It was a thankless job – quite literally, as I had seen for myself that the MP barely knew Daisy's name – and it paid a pittance, but she needed every penny. Her ex-husband had backed her into a financial corner, offering to pay for their daughter to stay on at Broadholme only if Daisy accepted a meagre maintenance payment for herself. I was lucky, by contrast; something I tried to convince myself every day.

'What's all this in aid of?' I asked, picking up one of the leaflets that lay in a pile on Daisy's dining table. 'The general election is over a year away. I hope he isn't going to bombard us from now until then.'

'Of course he is. We're a marginal seat. This is his new idea. He's going to send out a newsletter every two months to remind the voters about how much he does.' I made a mental note to avoid Daisy's house in two months' time. 'Was that Mr Ferguson I saw you with?'

That was the thing about Daisy: she looked a fluffy airhead, but had an amazing mind for detail. It was either one of her most endearing or her most annoying character-istics.

'It was.' I stuffed and licked my first envelope, hoping it might deter Daisy from further questioning. No such luck.

'Sorry, was I interrupting something?' she asked, grinning. 'You needn't have come in if you were busy.'

'If I'd known that this was all you wanted me for, I'd have stayed with Owen,' I replied, grimacing at the taste of the cheap glue.

'Owen? Since when did you reach first-name terms?'

'We've bumped into each other dog walking a few times.'

'I always knew you were a dark horse, Mary Black. Under that calm, unflappable exterior, there's a whacking great man magnet, isn't there?'

We both laughed at that: Daisy knew perfectly well that I had been with Leo forever. No one had ever asked me out, or propositioned me, or made a pass or whatever it was called now. Not even Leo: as teenagers, we had drifted into something more than friendship, and I had been the one to push it to the next level.

'Owen's not bad looking,' Daisy continued. She held up one of the leaflets, on which she'd carefully drawn a moustache, beard and horns on a photograph of her employer, and smiled as she pushed it into an envelope. 'It's a shame he's so tall. We'd look ridiculous together. You should definitely consider him. He's an art teacher, so you know what that means. He can do great things with his hands.' She laughed. 'Or has he already taught you that?'

'Of course not. I'm married.' I thought about the envelope sitting on my hall table. 'Half married.'

'Half married?' Daisy paused in her licking. 'You don't mean the decree nisi has been granted already?'

I nodded. 'Clark has some extremely efficient solicitor friends. Apparently we're lucky that it's all gone through so quickly. At least, I presume it's gone through. There's a letter from my solicitor at home. I couldn't face opening it.'

'Oh, Mary.' Daisy reached across the table and squeezed my hand. 'Ignoring it won't make it go away. Why did it have to be so rushed? You've hardly had chance to get used to the idea. It's not like Leo to be so unfair.'

'It's not Leo's fault. I agreed to it.'

He had asked for a divorce two days after Christmas, on the day he had left our home and moved in with Clark. He didn't want to be an adulterer for any longer than necessary; his relationship with Clark deserved to be more than an extra-marital affair. He had been generous with financial arrangements; I had been generous about sharing the children. I had signed all the paperwork and returned it promptly, in my usual calm and efficient way.

'There's nothing to stop you seeing Mr Ferguson, then, is there? Or someone else. Have you thought about online dating? I can help you fill out a profile, if you like. It will be fun!'

'About as much fun as peeling off all my nails one by one. It's too soon.' I didn't add that it would always seem too soon.

'Too soon? Come off it. Leo was seeing Clark while you were still married. You're being positively patient.' She with-drew her hand and scooped up another pile of leaflets. 'It's been three years since James left me. Loneliness doesn't become any easier with time, trust me on that. You might not be ready to look, but don't walk round with your eyes closed, okay?'

Leo was waiting in his car when I finally arrived home with Dotty. She leapt on him as he got out, wagging her whole body and licking every part of him she could reach. Perhaps if I had ever greeted him like that, he wouldn't have needed Clark.

He followed me into the house and immediately picked up the envelope from the hall table. The printed stamp from the solicitors' office gave away what it was.

'You haven't opened it.'

'Not yet, I . . .' No excuse sprang to mind. I didn't lie to Leo. 'Is it about the decree nisi?'

'Probably. It was granted yesterday.'

I couldn't avoid it any longer, and it didn't seem so bad with his gentle eyes watching me. I tore open the envelope, and there it was in black and white: confirmation that we were halfway to being divorced.

Leo took the letter from my shaking hand, dropped it on the table, and drew me into a hug. It was the closest physical contact we'd had for months.

'Oh, Mary,' he murmured against my hair. 'I'm sorry. I never imagined we would come to this. You deserved better than me.'

'No. I wouldn't change a thing.' I leant into him, feeling the soft squishiness of his chest, inhaling the scent of the Johnson's baby shampoo he had used for as long as I had known him. I tightened my arms round him, and enjoyed the moment: but it was comfort I felt, not desire. Leo was a safe and familiar world. I missed it.

'Will you be okay on your own tonight?' he asked, pulling

away. 'I can come back for Jonas and Ava in the morning instead.'

'No, they're looking forward to seeing you.' And to not seeing me for two days, at least as far as Ava was concerned. I could do no right in her eyes at the moment. 'Besides, I won't be on my own.'

'You won't?'

It was too gloomy in the hall to see Leo's expression, so I was sure I must have misinterpreted the tone of his voice. He had no reason to be jealous, and even less reason to be cross.

'Daisy has invited herself round for a drink later,' I explained. I reached the study door and threw it open, so that the bright light filled the hall. Leo smiled.

'It could never be a single drink with Daisy. Don't let her lead you astray.'

'I can't afford to let her lead me astray.'

Leo let that go with a soft sigh. Even without a mortgage on this house, it had been hard to divide the wage from Leo's university job between two households. I had no independent income: the research work I did for Leo's academic studies filled much of my day and left no time for paid employment. I worked for love – of the subject, as much as of him. I had started off by supporting Leo's obsession with Alice Hornby's novels, but had soon come to share it, and I couldn't give up the work now, however awkward it might be. We had spent years writing the new biography, with the prime intention of spreading the word about how brilliant Alice was. Now the stakes were raised: we needed the book to be a financial success too.

The study was exactly as it had always been: one large desk in the centre of the room, with chairs on either side, one for Leo and one for me. A battered sofa filled one wall, stuffed bookcases the others. I had hated this room growing up; my mother had used it to store all my father's belongings, giving me false hope for years that she had known he was coming back. As soon as Leo and I moved in, I had hired a skip and thrown away everything that had been his or theirs. Now it was my favourite room in the house.

Leo sat in his chair and set up his laptop. We had a couple of hours to work before the children arrived home.

'Is everything ready for the launch?' he asked. The biography was being published in a couple of weeks, and the publishers were marking the launch with a party at the Manchester Central Library.

'Yes. Here's a first draft of your speech.' I pushed a sheaf of paper across the desk. I always wrote Leo's speeches for him. He was brilliant when giving a university lecture, but his style didn't suit a public event so well. 'I've arranged for Claire to look after you on the night, so she'll make sure you're in the right place and give you a nudge when it's time to give your speech.'

'Claire?' Leo looked up from the paper.

'From the publishing company. You've met her before. Luscious red hair and 1940s curves . . .'

Leo still looked blank. It had been a comfort in the past, his complete indifference to other women. Little had I known.

'But why do I need Claire? You normally do that.'

'I won't be there.'

'Why not? Is there something on at school? We arranged this months ago.'

That was exactly the point. We had arranged it months ago, at a time when I, at least, thought we were contentedly married. For a professor, he could be incredibly dense.

'I've attended in the past as your wife. You have a new one now. A new partner, that is.' I picked up a paperclip and started untwisting it. 'Clark will be going with you, won't he?'

'He'll be there. I need you too.' Leo eased the paperclip from my fingers. 'You deserve to be there. This book would never have been written without you. It's as much yours as mine.'

The front cover told a different story: it only bore his name, just as the annotated novels had done when they were published. I hadn't minded before – or not much. We were a team, and he was the public face of it. So why did a tiny niggle of resentment rise and stick in my throat now?

'Okay, I'll come. And the party at Foxwood Farm too?'

'Of course. That was your idea. You must be there. Will I need a speech for that?'

'No. I'll pick a short passage for you to read from the biography. Lindsay, who's organising the event, wants it to be an informal celebration of all things Lancastrian: literature, music, food, drink. The press will be there, as she's hoping to drum up more business as a party and events venue. Hopefully we'll have some un-Lancastrian weather, so we can use the courtyard outside as well as the main barn.'

Leo fought but failed to hide a grimace. It had taken a great deal of persusasion to convince him to support the event at Foxwood Farm, even though it was on the outskirts of the village; I hoped he wasn't thinking of backing out now he would have to travel up from Manchester. He didn't enjoy the brazen commerce of launching a book, and preferred to focus his attention on the academic side, leaving me and my lower sensitivities to deal with the business elements. Luckily I loved the promotion aspect, but I was going to have to work even harder this time.

'After the official launch, I'm going to tour around local independent bookshops to see if any are interested in stocking it, or even holding an event with you, a signing or something like that.'

Leo pulled his face again.

'Will they want an academic book?'

'Don't call it that. We agreed we weren't going to market it as an academic book. It will appeal to the general public too. That's why we worked so hard on getting the tone right.'

It's why *I* had worked so hard on the tone, ignoring Leo's flights of academia: having read too many turgid biographies during my degree, I was determined that Leo's wouldn't be one of them. And we'd got it right, I was sure of it: Alice

Hornby, the quiet gentleman's daughter who had written passionate novels of love and desire from the secrecy of her bedroom, had come to life in our book, strolling through the paragraphs, her voice echoing with every turn of the page and her scent lingering above the words. It was a romance as much as a biography, designed to make readers fall in love with Alice as Leo and I had done.

'I know you'll do your best,' Leo said. 'If anyone can sell Alice, you can.' He smiled, acknowledging our shared passion, but my response was half-hearted, too conscious that it was the only passion we now shared; in truth, the only passion we had shared for years. 'But while you're doing that, we need to start on our next project.' His smile withered. 'I've agreed to write that book I was asked to consider a few months ago – the one about Victorian writers. How society influenced them, and how they influenced society.'

'But I thought you turned that down!' He hadn't been keen on the idea at all. The brief had been to include at least three chapters on the Brontës, which was like asking a Manchester United fan to spend a season promoting Manchester City.

'I didn't take it up. We were busy finishing Alice's book at the time. Circumstances have changed now.'

'You mean we need the money.' There was no other expla-nation: it was literary prostitution, and it was devastating to see Leo caught up in it, even if part of me whispered that he had brought it on himself.

'It would certainly help. From now on I will have to accept

whatever I'm offered. If only we could find Alice's lost novel! That would change all our fortunes.' It was the enduring mystery of Alice Hornby: four books had been published, but a few surviving records had dropped tantalising hints that she may have worked on another, that no one had ever seen. Leo sighed. 'But after all our years of searching, what are the chances of that?'

Chapter Five

'Isn't this exciting?' Audrey said, as we hurried across St Peter's Square as fast as our heels allowed. The party to celebrate the launch of Leo's book was taking place in the newly refurbished Manchester Central Library. Although my invitation hadn't mentioned a plus one, I invited Audrey anyway, to avoid that awful moment of turning up alone. Her comment felt more like a rallying cry than a real question, and I made no response other than a smile and a nod that could have meant anything. 'I love the chance to dress up.'

She had certainly pulled out all the stops, brightening the usual grey Manchester evening with an electric-blue dress that would have made me look a frumpy Tory wife, but which Audrey carried off with panache. In contrast, my reliable grey dress – my equivalent of the little black dress, as black hair, Black name and black clothing made me feel like a pallbearer – seemed a predictably dull choice.

'Chin up,' Audrey said, linking her arm in mine. 'Tonight is a celebration. This book is going to be a tremendous success. I couldn't be prouder of both of you. I'll need bubblegum on the soles of my shoes tonight to stop me floating to the ceiling with happiness.' She laughed and drew me closer. 'Keep an eye on me. What with the news about Ethan, no one will blame me if I get a little tipsy tonight, will they?'

'Of course not.' No one could ever blame Audrey for anything. She was universally loved. 'What news about Ethan?'

'Hasn't Leo told you? Ethan has a job to do in London for two or three weeks – don't ask me what, you know I haven't a clue what he does – and then he's going to take a sabbatical and come home for a few months. Isn't that the best news? Both my boys with me again.'

It seemed heartless to prick her bubble by pointing out that technically Leo wasn't with her anymore – or not as he had always been, living next door.

'Why's Ethan coming back?' I asked. 'Has he exhausted all the women in America now?'

'Mary!' Audrey's glance of mock severity was probably deserved. Sometimes I was prone to forget that she was my mother-in-law, and not a friend. 'Ethan isn't like that. Deep down, he has the most wonderful, loyal soul.' She dragged me up the steps and into the library. 'Whatever gave you the idea that he played around?'

'Leo used to tell me about Ethan's girlfriends. It was a different name every time they spoke. Sometimes I wondered if Leo was actually jealous of Ethan's single life . . .' Audrey patted my hand. 'When is he coming?'

'Probably July, and you must help me persuade him to stay until Christmas. Wasn't it fun to have him here last year?'

Christmas hadn't been fun from where I was standing, but I suppose that wasn't Ethan's fault. I couldn't see what use I would be in persuading him to stay, either, but luckily Audrey was distracted.

'Isn't this marvellous?' she said, gazing around in obvious delight. 'Is that the arts man off the television?'

I took a mental backseat and let Audrey rattle on as we made our way to the room where the launch was being held. I'd only been involved in the discussions at an early stage, so was eager to see how everything had been arranged, and I wasn't disappointed. Alice Hornby dominated the room, just as she should. The one authenticated painting of her, a full-length image of her sitting at a desk, writing, had been blown up onto a canvas that filled one wall. Extracts from her novels and letters, in her own painstakingly neat handwriting, hung on vertical banners on each side of the room, and Leo's book was displayed on a table in the centre. Behind the table, Leo and Clark stood side by side, arm brushing arm, chatting to a journalist I recognised from *The Times*.

I helped myself to a glass and winced as the dry champagne settled on my tongue. It would have been Prosecco in my day: Leo knew I preferred it. And as I downed half the glass, determined not to read any significance into the replacement, Clark caught my eye, smiled, and nudged Leo. Leo looked over at us, raised his hand in greeting, and carried on his conversation. That hand may as well have slapped me across the cheek.

'Let's mingle,' Audrey said, tugging my arm again. If she carried on like this I would be covered in bruises by the end of the night: external ones, to match the internal ones. 'Who do we think looks most approachable? What about the group by the window?'

She kept this up for the next half hour, as we toured round the guests, singing the praises of Leo, Alice, and the book. Leo and Clark were circling the room in the opposite direction, but before our paths could cross, Claire from the publishing company tapped her glass for attention, and after a gushing introduction, Leo delivered his speech. He carried it off brilliantly, his lovely mellifluous voice caressing each of the words I had written for him. Everyone laughed, sighed, and nodded at the right moments, and I was about to lead the applause when Leo fiddled with his glasses, a sure sign of his discomfort.

'I can't let the moment pass by without acknowledging the contribution of one special person,' he said. This wasn't in the speech. Was he going to declare his devotion to Clark, in front of all these people? In front of me?

Audrey and I were lurking at the back of the room. Even so, Leo found me through the crowd of smartly dressed people. He smiled, and I knew that I shouldn't have doubted him.

'There is nothing in life so satisfying as a shared passion,' he said. Audrey took hold of my hand, clearly having less faith in Leo than I had. 'This book would not be the success it is without the encouragement of my wonderful helpmeet, Mary

Black. Mary, this book is dedicated to you, with eternal thanks.'

The second that followed seemed to stretch for hours, as no one knew quite how to react. Audrey saved the moment.

'How marvellous!' she cried, and raised her champagne glass. 'To Mary Black!'

As the applause died down, Leo made his way towards us and Audrey melted away into the crowd.

'You changed the speech,' I said.

'I only added the words that you were too modest to write.'

Too discreet, not modest: we never publicly acknowledged how large a contribution I made to Leo's work. 'Encouragement' wasn't the word I would have chosen.

'Tonight seems to have gone well,' I said. 'Everyone I spoke to loves the book. There should be some glowing reviews at the weekend.'

'I'm told there will be half a page in *The Times*. We'll convert the nation to Alice lovers yet!'

'And hopefully make some money in the process,' I added, wishing that I didn't always have to be the practical one, keeping a firm grip on the strings of his balloon, stopping him getting carried away with academic enthusiasm. It was the job I had done for years, never questioning our roles. I wondered what it would be like to have someone anchoring my strings, letting me fly high.

'Mum's enjoying herself, isn't she?'

'You know she loves seeing your success. And she's thrilled about Ethan coming back.'

'How do you know about that?' Leo's voice was unexpectedly sharp. 'Has he contacted you?'

'No, why would he? Audrey told me earlier. She's hoping he'll stay until Christmas.'

'Christmas? No, he won't last so long. He was made to be the single man about New York. You should come round for dinner,' he said, unexpectedly changing the subject. 'Clark is an excellent cook.'

'Tonight? I had a snack earlier with the children.'

'No, not tonight. Come round properly, for a dinner party. Clark,' Leo said. I hadn't noticed Clark creep up, and forced myself to smile. 'Tell Mary that we'd love to have her over for a dinner party.'

'Of course we would.' Clark's smile was undoubtedly genuine. It was infuriatingly impossible to dislike him. 'Nothing formal. Supper with a few friends. Why don't you two fix a date and I'll see who else is free?'

'Marvellous,' I said, hiding my true feelings behind Audrey's favourite word again. 'I'll look forward to it.'

It wasn't entirely a lie. I was curious to see Leo's new home. The children had stayed over, but there was only so much information I could pump out of them. And I supposed I should be grateful now for any opportunity for a night out. An invitation from my ex-husband and his gay lover might be the best offer I had all year. It hit me, as the smartly dressed people swirled around me, the exotic cocktail of perfumes wafted past my nose, and excited chatter swept by my ears, that this might be my farewell performance on this stage. I had always been invited to these events as Leo's wife. Where did that leave me now?

As I glanced around the room, searching for Audrey, my eyes were drawn to all the things I had ignored before: the reassuring touch on the small of a back; the secret smile exchanged across the expanse of the room; the speculative wink received with an encouraging blush. My radar was on high alert: I sensed relationships at every stage in all corners of the room. And I had never felt so alone in all my life.

'Did Dad say anything last night?' Ava asked the next morning, as she waved a piece of toast around, never quite bringing it within biting distance of her mouth.

'Yes. He gave a speech about Alice Hornby. It went well.'

Ava tutted, rolled her eyes, and dropped the toast onto her plate.

'I don't mean about that,' she said, fourteen years of accumulated disgust throbbing in every word. 'Did he mention the sleepover?'

'What sleepover?' My own toast fell to my plate. I wasn't going to like it, whatever it was; I knew by the way Ava was flicking her mousey hair in an artificially nonchalant way. She might look like a Black, but her character had been cut from the same cloth as mine. I glanced at Jonas, but he had his earphones in, and gave a shrug that either meant he hadn't heard, or didn't want to get involved. He resembled me, but his temperament was entirely Leo. It was hard to say which of them had the better deal.

'I thought I'd invite a few friends for a sleepover, probably on the Bank Holiday weekend. Chloe can come,' Ava said, knowing that I wouldn't disapprove of Daisy's daughter, and instantly making me worry who else she might want to invite. Surely not boys, at fourteen? My heart thudded at the very idea.

'That's great!' I said, smiling too brightly in my relief that it was nothing worse than a sleepover. 'We can rent a film and I'll make popcorn and pizza . . .'

'No need for that.' Ava had twisted her hair so tightly round her finger that when she let go, it stayed in a ringlet. 'We won't be here. We're going to Dad's.'

'Dad's?'

'Yeah, Clark said it would be okay.'

'Clark?'

'It's his flat too. They have two spare bedrooms.'

So our one spare bedroom was no longer enough. My eyes flicked around the kitchen, taking in the relics of a family breakfast: toast crumbs on the worktop; a sticky trail of honey leading from the jar to the sink where the knife had been dumped; a couple of stray cornflakes on the floor; a puddle of milk on the table. And that was only as far as I could see: if I turned around, I would spot the pile of abandoned shoes, the coats and blazers thrown over the furniture, and the school books in a muddled heap, and not in school bags as I had requested last night. Of course Clark's flat would be preferable to this. But I loved it here, whatever state it was in. My happiest memories were here, papered on the walls and blooming in the garden: memories of my father, before my mother drove him away, and memories of Leo and the children, before I had driven him away. One throwaway remark from Ava had prodded all my bruises: that was life with teenagers. I was a parent, not a human being: I wasn't allowed to feel.

'It's a long way for everyone to go,' I said, foolishly believing this was an innocuous remark. But that was another reality of living with teenagers: no remark was unarguable.

'No, it's not. If you drive us, it will only be an hour. And at least there's something to do there.'

'At Clark's? What can you do that you can't do here?'

'We can go shopping, obviously.'

'Shopping? With Dad?'

'On our own. We don't want Dad. He's got less fashion sense than you. We don't want to go to Marks & Spencer or somewhere like that.'

I discreetly felt the back of my top, making sure the M&S label was tucked down. It was rare that I had the advantage over Leo, especially where Ava was concerned. But then I stopped the thought, shame prickling across my chest. It wasn't a competition. How could I be so disloyal as to feel a flicker of pleasure that for once I wasn't the most embarrassing parent?

I stood up and began the usual morning routine of nagging

and chivvying, in the vain hope that we might leave the house on time. Jonas chucked a few things in his rucksack, picked up an apple, ran his hands through his hair and was ready. Ten minutes later, Ava was still upstairs, titivating as my mother would have said. I bellowed up the stairs, sounding too much like Mum for comfort.

Ava stomped down after the third bellow. Her black eyeliner was so thick it looked like she'd applied it with a permanent marker pen, but I knew better than to start that discussion when we were pushed for time.

'I've not finished my hair!' Ava grumbled, standing a few stairs up from the bottom so that she could glower down at me more effectively. 'Look at it!' She grabbed a chunk and waved it in my direction. 'I haven't straightened this side. The kink is still there. I'm going to look hideous all day and it's all your fault!'

Ava and her kink were legendary in our house: no one else saw it, but it caused her endless angst. And of course it was my fault, even though my hair was ruler straight, and if Ava did have a kink, it undoubtedly came from her Black genes; everything had been my fault since the day Leo moved out, and most of the time before that. The next stage in the familiar tirade was to blame me that she had inherited Leo's mousey colouring, rather than my Celtic black hair and green eyes. Sure enough, Ava opened her mouth to begin the argument, but I bit my tongue, and whisked her and Jonas out of the house without another word.

It was no surprise that by the time we turned up at Broadholme, there were only a couple of minutes left before registration.

'We were never late when Dad brought us,' Ava pointed out. That was too much. Leo had done nothing but drive the car, oblivious to everything I had done to get the children from their beds to the car door. But before I could retaliate, Jonas patted my arm.

'Chill, Mum,' he said. 'We're here now.'

I nodded in response to these wise teenage words, and to make up for my near grumpiness, I used my pass to enter the teachers' car park: the pass was a perk of being on the PTA, although we were only meant to use it when we attended meetings. While the children took forever to gather their stuff, I loitered in the disabled space, engine running like a furtive getaway driver. Three loud knocks shook my window. I pressed the button to open it.

'Mrs Black, you know I should give you detention for abusing your PTA pass.' Owen Ferguson peered in at my open window, a warm smile making a joke of his words. 'I hope you have an excellent excuse.'

'Can I blame the dog? That's the traditional excuse, isn't it?'

'It is. Whose homework has Dotty eaten?' Owen smiled across at Jonas, who shrugged, and at Ava in the back, who flushed pink and avoided eye contact. 'I'd love to hear how missing homework can explain your presence in the teachers' car park.'

I laughed. 'Okay, you've rumbled me. Dotty is innocent. We were running late, that's all. There's no hope of escaping that detention, is there?'

'Oh, I don't know about that. Perhaps we could discuss it over an after-school drink?'

An after-school drink? What on earth did that mean? An instant coffee in the staff room with a borrowed mug, or a proper drink in the pub in the evening? Did he mean just the two of us? Alone? A date? I'd never been on a date in my life. The moment stretched. Embarrassment stole over Owen's face. Jonas and Ava were staring at me; I didn't need to see them to know that. The ghost of Leo hovered over my shoulder. Owen's head was framed in the rectangle of the window, gentleness and kindness engraved on every feature. How could I be anxious about anyone who reminded me so much of Leo?

'A drink sounds great,' I said. 'Let me know when you're free.'

Owen looked surprised, but then smiled with more pleasure than my agreement could possibly deserve.

'I will do.' He tapped his watch. 'Come on, you two, time for registration.'

He wandered off, but despite his warning, there was no movement from within my car.

'Mum!' I turned to see Ava's wide-eyed, stricken face. 'What are you doing? You can't go for a drink with Mr Ferguson.'

'Why not?'

'He's a teacher!' Ava said this with the expression and tone of voice that might have been justified if she was outing Owen as a cannibal. But I could still feel the warm glow from his smile, making me defiant.

'So what? I'm pretty sure he's a man as well.'

'Urgh, that's just gross.'

'What is?'

'You and Mr Ferguson . . . kissing.'

'We're not kissing.' Of course, I immediately started thinking about kissing. Could I kiss Owen? His lips were plumper than Leo's. Would that feel odd? The whole idea of kissing other lips seemed odd. I had never expected to do it, had never wanted to do it, except once, in one mad, extraordinary moment . . . Heat rushed across my skin. 'Let's see how the drink goes first.'

Jonas pulled out one earphone, and grinned.

'Go on, Mum,' he said. 'He'll be lucky to have you.'

Ava reached across from the back seat and punched him on the shoulder.

'Shut up. It's embarrassing. She's too old for all that.'

'I'm only thirty-eight.'

'Exactly!'

'Dad's forty-two.'

'But he's not going out with one of my teachers! What will my friends say? It will be so embarrassing. I can't believe you're doing this to us. You're so selfish.'

Ava got out of the car, slammed the door, and stomped

off without saying goodbye. Jonas loitered, passenger door open.

'It's okay,' he said, gazing at me with eyes that were just like mine, only without the bags and wrinkles. 'You deserve some fun. She'll get used to it.'

I didn't believe either statement, but leaned across the handbrake and kissed his cheek. He submitted before pulling away and strolling into school. I waited in the car park until he was out of sight, grateful that while I had lost so much, I still had my lovely, peace-keeping boy.

Chapter Six

A few years ago I set up an informal 'meals on wheels' service for the older residents of the village, so early the next week, when I was left with an extra meal at lunchtime, I dropped in at Audrey's house to see if she wanted it.

'Audrey!' I called, as I pushed open the door with my shoulder, balancing the plate of food in my hands. 'It's only me! One of the old dears went out shopping and forgot I was coming, so I have . . .'

The plate fell to the ground, bouncing on the lino and sending vegetables rolling. Audrey was lying on the floor, half in the kitchen, half in the hall. She was wearing her pyjamas and slippers; a mug lay on its side on the hall carpet beyond Audrey's head, surrounded by a brown stain; there was another stain on the kitchen lino, spreading from beneath Audrey's legs. The smell of rich morning urine filled the room.

'Don't come in, Mary.' Audrey's voice was faint, weakened by fear. A sheen of sweat shimmered on her face, around eyes that were enormous and terrified. Audrey, my lovely, lively Audrey, looked as if every second of her sixty-five years had stamped their mark on her all at once, adding ten more years for good measure.

'What's happened?' I asked, stepping over some stray broccoli, and kneeling at her side. Her left arm was tucked underneath her at an awkward angle. I took her right hand, rubbing it between mine, trying to add warmth. 'How long have you been here? Since breakfast?'

'I tripped over the door plate . . .'

The door plate between the kitchen and the hall had been loose for months. I had told Leo before Christmas, and he had promised to fix it – but as usual, I hadn't wanted to nag. Why hadn't I pressed him? Why hadn't I fixed it myself? Was it because somewhere in my head, I hadn't accepted that this post-Leo world was real?

'Where are you hurt? Can you tell?'

'My arm. Mainly my wrist. I can't lean on it to get up.'

'Don't try. I'm calling an ambulance.'

I started to stand, but Audrey clutched my arm. Her grasp was as feeble as a child's.

'No. I can't go in an ambulance like this.'

I nodded, understanding exactly what she meant. I ran upstairs to her bedroom and picked out a fresh pair of knickers and pyjamas. It was an effort to put them on, as I feared exacerbating injuries or causing Audrey pain; she closed her eyes when I inched down her knickers, and I stopped, terrified I might be damaging a broken hip, but she insisted I carry on. It never occurred to me to be embarrassed. I would walk on hot coals rather than undress my own mum, but this was Audrey. Nothing was too much for her.

I couldn't change her pyjama top, as I couldn't risk disturbing her arm.

'I don't match!' she said, with a hint of her normal self.

'I don't expect the paramedics will mind,' I replied, putting down the phone after calling for an ambulance. 'We'll tell them that it's the latest fashion: mismatched pyjamas as daywear. In fact, if I'm quick, I could go and put on some random nightwear too, to establish the trend.'

That raised a weak smile, which was better than nothing, and while we waited for the ambulance I followed Audrey's instructions and washed her face, applied lipstick, and spritzed her with perfume. I tried ringing Leo, but he was on voicemail, so I left a message. Then all I could do was wait.

We seemed to spend hours in A&E, but at least when Audrey was finally seen, the news wasn't as bad as it might have been. Audrey had suffered a Colles fracture, which meant that she'd broken the bone in her left arm just above the wrist. It was a clean break, and didn't need surgery, but she would be in a plaster cast for up to six weeks, and she could have residual stiffness for up to a year. For a fiercely independent woman, who was prone to think herself half her actual age, it was hard to accept, and I turned my back, pretending to read a poster while Audrey shed some discreet tears.

'Has Leo not telephoned?' she asked, while we waited for confirmation that she could go home.

'Not yet. I've left a couple of messages.'

'What about Ethan? Have you let him know that I'm fine? I would hate for him to be anxious.'

'I haven't told Ethan.' It hadn't crossed my mind. What use would he be, in New York? 'I don't have his number.'

'What time will it be over there? About lunchtime? Do call him. He'll tell me off if he finds out days after the event. Take my phone and give him a ring. Make sure he knows that I'm right as rain, and there's no cause for panic.'

Reluctantly, I took Audrey's phone and went outside, squeezing past the smokers balancing on crutches at the entrance of the hospital, to find an empty bench. Ethan's number rang out, and I scuffed my feet under the bench, hoping for voicemail.

'Hello, Mum! I wasn't expecting to hear from you today. What are you up to?'

I had to lift the phone away from my ear: the love that poured from it, coupled with that familiar Lancashire accent with a New York twist, caught my breath in a way I hadn't expected.

'Mum? Are you there?'

'It's Mary.'

'Hello, Mary Black! What are you doing brightening my day?' And then his tone changed as realisation dawned. 'Mary? Is something wrong?'

'It's all fine, but Audrey wanted me to let you know that she fell over today . . .'

'How bad is it?' Ethan interrupted. His voice was raw with fear. I wished this job hadn't fallen to me. Leo should have been the one to tell him – if only Leo had returned my calls. 'No varnish, Mary. Is she okay?'

'She will be. She's fractured her wrist – her left one, so she'll still be able to use her right hand. Although not for a few days. She's bruised her knee, so will need a stick for a while until that settles.'

'Can I talk to her?'

'Ring her in a couple of hours. I'll have taken her home by then.'

'You will? Where's Leo?'

It was an innocent-sounding question, and I had an innocent answer ready. But I kicked at the gravel under my feet, reluctant to give it.

'I haven't been able to speak to him yet. He's probably at work.'

The silence stretched until I thought we might have been cut off. That 'probably' wouldn't have convinced Ethan; he must know that it was after five over here.

'Will you look after her?' Ethan said at last. 'I know I've no right to ask now, but . . .'

'You don't need to ask. She's my friend. Of course I'm going to look after her.'

'Let me know if she needs anything.' He paused. 'You're a star, Mary Black. You know that, don't you?'

I didn't; I lived with two teenagers. Far from being celestial, most days I felt as important as something they'd trodden in. But Ethan had a way of making the mundane sound extraordinary, and the extraordinary sound magnificent. I had forgotten quite how potent he could be.

We had been home for a couple of hours before Leo called back, and then, at least, he drove straight over. Audrey had fallen asleep, lying on the sofa in front of the television, worn out by the drama of the day and the drugs given to her by the hospital.

'Where have you been?' I hissed at Leo, as he hovered in the doorway, looking at Audrey. The irony wasn't lost on me, that I sounded more like a jealous wife than at any time during our marriage.

'I had no university work today, and Clark took the day off, so we . . .'

I held up my hand; I didn't want to hear what they had been up to.

'Didn't you have your phone? What if there had been an emergency with the children?'

He had the grace to look guilty, but I was too highly wound today to let it go.

'You can't cut us off completely, Leo. You've only loosened the strings, not untied them. You still have a family, and sometimes we need you.'

'I appreciate that. I'm not trying to cut you off. When I

made plans with Clark, I couldn't have known there would be an emergency today.'

'There could be an emergency any day. That's the point. They're unscheduled. You need to keep your phone on when you're not teaching, or at least check your messages occasionally. If you're so keen not to be disturbed, I promise I'll only ever ring if it's a matter of life or death.'

'Life, death, or literature.' He smiled, trying to make amends by resurrecting an old joke we had shared, but I wasn't ready to soften yet.

'Audrey needed you, Leo. She wanted to see you. The fall has shaken her more than you realise. I had no trouble contacting Ethan, and he's on a different continent and time zone.'

'Ethan?' Audrey snuffled and stirred as Leo raised his voice. 'When did you speak to Ethan?'

'This afternoon.'

'Do you often ring him?'

'No. Why would I?' I sat down, across the room from Leo, confused by the look he was giving me and the sudden interrogation. 'I don't even have his number. I called him because Audrey asked me to. What's the problem?'

'There isn't one.' Leo sat down next to me. His hair was soft and fluffy, as if he'd recently had a shower, but there was no smell of Johnson's baby shampoo. Instead, when I leaned closer, pretending to adjust the cushion behind me, I was struck by an exotic aroma that made me think of expensive hotels – not that I had much experience of those. 'But you're clearly wound up,' Leo continued. 'I hope he hasn't said anything to aggravate or upset you. At least you won't have to see him again. Don't they say that one of the greatest advantages of divorce is being able to drop the in-laws?'

I wouldn't blame him if Leo thought that: I'd often be happy to drop my mother, preferably from a great height. But while I had rarely seen Ethan over the years of our marriage, it was painful to think that rarely might turn to never. Our connection went beyond my marriage; Ethan had been a good friend, an integral part of my growing up, as essential as Leo, in a different way. We had been in the same year at school, and had almost gone to the same university until Leo had proposed when he graduated from Oxford and persuaded me to change to Manchester so we could stay close together.

'Ethan's not the problem,' I muttered, but Leo was watching Audrey and didn't appear to be listening.

'Don't worry about Ethan,' he said, patting my hand as if I were his maiden aunt. 'I'll speak to him and make sure he leaves you alone.'

Chapter Seven

Audrey was a terrible patient, every bit as bad as I expected: not because she was demanding, but because she refused to make any demands. I had to go round earlier and earlier each morning to try to catch her before she attempted to dress herself; if it carried on, there would barely be a gap between putting her to bed and getting her up.

Leo came over on the Friday afternoon following Audrey's accident, and worked in the study so that I could have the afternoon off to visit a couple of bookshops. I had compiled a list of shops within a thirty-mile radius, and intended to visit them all over the coming weeks to see if any would be interested in an author event with Leo to promote the Alice Hornby biography. My enthusiasm was trampled when the first shop turned me away almost immediately, but the owner of the second shop agreed to attend the Foxwood Farm event the following weekend and meet Leo before deciding whether to invite him to hold a signing. Now I had to hope that Leo rose to the occasion.

Neither of the children would agree to come to the Foxwood Farm Lancashire Evening, and as I still wasn't used to appearing anywhere on my own, I invited Daisy to join me. The rain of the morning had finally broken to reveal a dazzling blue sky, and the temperature had risen from coat to cardigan warmth, so I walked through the village to collect Daisy at her house. She opened the front door before I was halfway up the path, and quickly pulled it shut behind her.

'You can't come in,' she said, dispensing with the customary 'hello' and starting up the path with her bag in tow. 'The house is a tip. Chloe is at her dad's this weekend, so I'm having a sneaky sort out of all the old clothes and toys that she'd never let me throw away if she was here.'

'You should have said. I would have offered to help.'

'I know you would.' Daisy followed me through the gate and left it swinging at a forlorn angle. I went back and closed it. 'But I only really wanted to clear out a few things. You'd have blitzed the house like a military operation. You'd have shot me at point blank range for suggesting something had sentimental value.'

'That's unfair. I would have tried diplomatic negotiation first.' I smiled, but Daisy's words stung. The 'efficient and capable' label was so firmly sewn onto the back of my neck that I couldn't imagine the world held a pair of scissors sharp enough to cut it out.

Foxwood Farm was situated at the southern edge of the village, a pleasant stroll away in the spring sunshine. The farm was looking magnificent, decorated for the event with flags and bunting showing the red rose of Lancashire. It was too early in the year for real roses, but tubs and flowerbeds filled the farmyard and pansies, tulips, and azaleas danced in a brilliant display of colour. As the weather had turned fair, the cobbled courtyard outside the main barn where the event was taking place had been scattered with bales of hay covered in furry sheepskin rugs to make benches, and old crates covered in crisp white cloths provided makeshift tables. Large braziers stood around the edge of the area, already flickering with flames that would light up the area as darkness crept in. Although we were on time – being efficient and capable, I was never wilfully late – a decent crowd was already milling around in the evening sunshine, colouring the air with conversation and laughter. I reached out and grasped Daisy's arm, sent off-balance by an unexpected shot of loneliness.

'Let's get a drink,' Daisy said, and dragged me inside. It was quieter here, apart from a small group gathered in front of a table that was set out as a bar. There was an impressive display of Lancashire drinks: real ale with weird and wonderful names from a micro-brewery a few miles away; sloe gin and blueberry vodka from a farm in a nearby village; and a delicious selection of soft drinks from Fitzgerald's, the famous temperance bar. I picked up a glass of wine.

'That's French.' Daisy pointed disapprovingly at my glass. She had chosen a pint of beer, an incongruous sight in her dainty hands, but she carried it off; she was one of those naturally pretty women who could carry off anything. Beside her petite blonde figure, I looked like the Grim Reaper's warm-up act. If we weren't such friends I would never have stood within ten feet of her. 'You're not being loyal to the spirit of the evening.'

The glass hovered halfway to my lips, as my values battled with my need for wine. Luckily Lindsay, who had organised the event, was nearby and solved my dilemma.

'We used a Lancashire wine merchant,' she said. 'It was the closest we could get.' I drank half my glass, conscience clear. Lindsay smiled, and leaned across to kiss my cheek. 'You deserve that wine after your hard work this afternoon. The display looks great.'

Lindsay gestured over to one corner of the barn. The central space was set out with chairs ready for the entertainment to begin, and each performer – not a word I had dared use to Leo's face – had been allocated an area to display their work around the sides. Leo's table was a shrine to Alice Hornby. The famous picture of her stood on an easel in the centre, surrounded by glass boxes containing replicas of some of her personal items: a tiny pair of outdoor shoes, complete with battens; an ivory fan; a purse embroidered with miniature birds, which we believed Alice had sewn herself. One box held a couple of pages of a draft of her most famous novel, *The Gentleman's Daughter*; her handwriting was as familiar as my own, and thrilled me every time I saw it. A discreet pile of Leo's book lay at the rear of the display, along with postcards and bookmarks bearing some of Alice's most beautiful quotations. I had also added some leaflets about the

Alice Hornby Society, which Leo and I had started ten years ago in a bid to connect fans of her work and promote awareness of her writing.

'Is Leo outside?' Lindsay asked, glancing at her watch. 'We're starting with the rock choir soon, and Leo's on after that.'

'I don't know where he is.'

'Have you lost him?'

How could I reply to that? I had lost him, but in a more permanent way than Lindsay meant. Amazingly, and despite my conviction that the whole world must be talking about us, it seemed that there was one house in Stoneybrook where the gossip had not yet spread.

'We're not . . .' Above the chatter around us, the clink of my wedding ring against my glass was deafening. I couldn't finish the sentence. I finished my wine instead. Daisy gripped my hand.

'Mary and Leo are divorced,' she said, leaning towards Lindsay and lowering her voice. 'Leo lives in Manchester now. He may be delayed by traffic.'

She stopped there, giving only half the news; the rest would be obvious soon enough. And the sympathy in Lindsay's eyes, when she pulled me into a brief hug, was quite enough to bear without witnessing her reaction to the rest of it. How long would it be before someone looked at me without pity or curiosity? I longed for a life of quiet anonymity again.

The rock choir were halfway through their set of songs by North West artists, and were belting out an arrangement of

Elbow's 'Open Arms' which moistened even my stubbornly dry old eyes, when Leo sauntered in with Clark. I slipped out of my seat and met them at the back of the barn, horribly conscious that many members of the audience were watching us.

'Hello,' I whispered, dragging up my public smile, and kissing them each in turn. Leo still didn't smell like my Leo, and he had cut his hair much shorter, losing the fluffiness that had characterised him for the last twenty years. The new look suited him. 'You're in perfect time. The choir has one more song after this, and then it's your turn. I've marked the passage that you're reading.' I delved into my handbag and pulled out a copy of the book, adorned with Post-it Notes. 'And try to squeeze in a mention of the Alice Hornby Society. I've left some application forms on the display over there.'

Leo turned in the direction I was pointing.

'It looks wonderful, Mary, well done. You never let me down.'

Those words, which would have once meant so much, could only ever be bittersweet now. Loud applause for the choir shattered the awkwardness of the moment, and I motioned to Leo to go to the front, while I resumed my seat next to Daisy. Clark remained standing, leaning against the wall, his attention wholly on Leo.

Lindsay welcomed Leo, and then Leo made a few opening remarks and began to read from the book. I had chosen a lively passage, describing a prank that Alice and her sister had played on their hated governess, and which had gone on to form the basis of a scene in her most famous book, and the audience laughed as I had hoped. But I was hardly paying attention to the words, too transfixed by Leo. He didn't smell like my Leo; he no longer looked like my Leo; and he performed for the audience in a way that my Leo would never have done. He was relaxed, smiling, comfortable in himself as he had never been in the days of our marriage. There was no doubting why. Whenever his gaze swept the room, it always lingered over Clark.

The applause when he finished was as rapturous as it had been for the choir, and way beyond anything I had expected. I rose from my seat, propelled by pride, heedless of the fact that no one else was giving a standing ovation until Daisy yanked me back down.

'He was great,' Daisy said, with undisguised surprise. 'He made me want to buy the book, and Lord knows there have been times when I thought I might go insane if I heard the name Alice Hornby again.'

'You're a philistine. She is the world's greatest writer.'

'Don't waste your breath on me. I won't read anything unless it has a glossy cover and celebrity interviews.' She looked over at Leo, who had now joined Clark. They were talking, heads bent close together, tightly bound to each other even though they weren't touching. 'He's changed. He looks . . .' She screwed up her eyes, studying him. 'Free.'

That was it, exactly. Perhaps because Daisy hadn't seen Leo

for a few months, the alteration was obvious to her. Leo did look free: free of care, free of pretence, free of being someone he was not. Free of me. Our stars had been aligned for so long; but his had now risen to a height that seemed well beyond my reach.

A performance poet came next, entertaining us in a traditional Lancashire dialect, followed by a popular local folk band, before supper was served – Lancashire hotpot, served with pickled red cabbage, which was simple but delicious. I was one of the last to be served, distracted by talking to the bookshop owner who had previously promised to attend, and by that time many of the guests had wandered outside to enjoy their food. Carrying my plate of steaming hotpot, I headed the same way, trying to find Daisy. She was never easy to spot in a crowd, but I located her at last, talking to a tall blond man who had his back to me. His head was tilted down towards her, exposing a stretch of tanned skin between the collar of his shirt and his exceptionally neat hairline – a perfect horizontal line that my finger itched to trace. I must have drunk more than I thought, because as I stared at his neck, my lips tingled with an inexplicable urge to taste that warm skin.

Heat raced through my blood, carrying with it the echo of a long-forgotten memory. My feet wouldn't move, either forwards or backwards. And then Daisy glanced in my direction, waved, and her companion turned and smiled. My lungs seized with horror, shame, and sheer wrongness as I realised that the stranger who had stirred the unfamiliar desire, reminded me of the passion that I had chosen to live without, wasn't a stranger at all. It was my brother-in-law, Ethan.

In my frantic haste to return to the barn, I crashed into a man in the doorway, sending a lump of red cabbage somersaulting onto his pale shirt. Efficient and capable? I had never felt less.

'Mary?' The man took hold of my arm and steadied me. It was Owen. I hadn't known he was coming tonight. He smiled and I relaxed. 'What's the matter? You look like you've seen the proverbial ghost.'

'Sorry,' I said, fighting to return to normal. 'Look at your shirt.' I picked off a clinging shred of cabbage. A pink stain remained. 'I have something that will get that out, if you let me have it.'

'Now? You'd like me to take my shirt off here?'

'No, of course not . . .' It took me a moment to realise he was joking.

'Don't worry. I can wash my own shirt.'

'Can you?' Leo had never touched a washing machine, as far as I knew.

'Shall we start again?' Owen let go of my arm. 'Hello, Mary, it's good to see you. Come and sit down and eat your hotpot.'

There was something so gloriously mundane about that sentence, that I let him steer me over to some empty chairs. He chatted about Lucilla and school, and the brilliance of the rock choir, while I picked at my food. I thought I'd lost my appetite, but Owen was such restful, easy company that my plate soon emptied. He took if off me and stood up.

'Another wine or would you like a coffee?'

'Wine, please.'

He threaded his way to the bar, squeezing past people with polite diffidence. There was something solidly reassuring about his broad back and sturdy waist. Light brown hair lapped over his collar; no sliver of exposed neck there to catch women unawares. Panic fluttered in my chest. It hadn't been Ethan, surely? He was in New York. Audrey had mentioned him yesterday, doing something or other in New York. He wasn't supposed to be in the country until July, so he couldn't be here, right now, at Foxwood Farm, and I couldn't be fantasising about his neck. It was impossible, and it was wrong. Unnatural. Undesirable. Undesirable desire. I was in danger of becoming hysterical.

'This isn't what I had in mind when I suggested we should have a drink together,' Owen said, handing over my wine. 'We're under scrutiny.'

'Are we?' I looked around, expecting to see Daisy watching, but instead found Leo gazing our way.

'Your ex-husband?' Owen indicated Leo, and I nodded, unable to say the word that would acknowledge that 'ex'. 'You're still on good terms?'

'Yes. We'll always be friends.'

'Friends?' I frowned, unable to read Owen's tone, and wary of making a wrong assumption about what he was asking. This was a whole new world to me: men had only ever been men, not potential boyfriends or partners. I didn't know the rules of this game, or understand the language in which it was played. Owen helped me out. 'I'm a simple soul, Mary. I like you. I don't like complications. If it may prove to be a temporary split . . .'

'It won't.' No one could see Clark and Leo together and have any doubts about that.

'And that other man?'

I turned to where Owen indicated, assuming he was referring to Clark. My stomach heaved, and not in reaction to the hotpot. It *was* Ethan. Ethan was here, tonight, in Stoneybrook, not in New York. So that reaction earlier had been to Ethan . . . I applied my mental blinkers, shutting out that thought.

'Ethan. Leo's brother.'

'I suppose it will take time for them to accept you have separate lives now.' Not just them. I smiled, an automatic rather than meaningful gesture, but Owen leant forward. 'Are you still up for that drink? Perhaps without the minders?'

Even I couldn't misunderstand that. I hesitated, feeling as if the room had fallen silent, and every pair of eyes and ears were waiting for my response – including mine. My gaze wandered over Owen's face, past honest brown eyes, a straightforward smile, and on to a delightfully ordinary neck.

'Yes. What about Tuesday?'

'Are you trying to get squiffy, Mary Black? The music isn't that bad.'

Warm breath blew against my ear, and I turned to face

Ethan. He still wore the smile of the thirteen-year-old boy I had first met: confident, cheeky, effortless.

'I love the music. The arrangements are amazing.'

A trio of young men were playing jazzed-up versions of old Lancashire songs with extraordinary energy and vigour. It was a mesmerising performance, and had drawn in most of the people who had remained outside after supper. I had been queuing at the bar when they started, and had been too entranced to move away.

'The arrangements? Or the handsome young men in dinner jackets?' Ethan laughed. 'You always were much more cultural than me.'

'Surely not even you can have lived in New York for so long without some culture rubbing off. You have Broadway, the Met, the MOMA . . .'

'And the New York Yankees. Much more my thing. There's more drama in a baseball game than in any Broadway play.'

'Have you ever been to a Broadway play?'

'Yes. Don't look so surprised. I made it all the way through *The Phantom of the Opera*, and I'd only had two beers. I needed more than two to recover afterwards.'

He laughed, and it was impossible not to join him. This was good; this was normal. I hadn't looked at or thought about his neck once.

'What are you doing here?'

'Mum gave me her ticket. She thought one of the family should support Leo.'

'Did you hear him?'

'I arrived just in time and lurked at the side.'

'I didn't notice you.'

'No. You never did notice anyone else when Leo was around.'

That was true; or perhaps it would be more accurate to say that I had chosen not to look. Except once . . . but I mustn't think about that.

'I actually meant what are you doing here, in England. Audrey said you were coming over in the summer.'

'I brought it forward. I wanted to see how she was.'

'And how is she?' I asked, poised to be offended if he suggested in any way that I wasn't looking after her properly.

'She's great.' He smiled, reading me far too well, even after all this time. 'I knew you'd care for her. But you shouldn't have to. She's our responsibility.'

Briefly he rested his hand on my arm, softening the rejection that his words might have given.

'I don't give a stuff about whose responsibility it is,' I said. 'I do it out of love. You won't stop me.'

'Then we'll do it together. I'll be your humble servant, Mary Black.'

He clicked his heels together, and bent over in a deep bow, flicking a glance full of mischief at me as he did. Then his face and body straightened as he looked over my shoulder. 'Hello, Leo.'

'Ethan.'

'Great performance earlier.'

'Thank you.'

I swivelled from one to the other. They weren't close – they were too different for that – but this clipped formality was new. Had something happened between them? Leo clearly wasn't surprised to see Ethan here, although he hadn't told me that he was coming home.

'Mary, I've spoken to Clark, and we wondered about next Friday,' Leo said.

'Friday? Do you want to do something with the children? Because Ava has maths clinic after school . . .'

'No, not for the children. For the dinner party.' I had forgotten all about it. Leo had mentioned the dinner party at his book launch a few weeks ago, but hadn't raised the subject since then. 'You'll be free, on a Friday night, won't you?'

'Yes, I suppose so.' Of course I was. When did I ever do anything? Tuesday, I remembered with a jolt. I was going out on Tuesday too, on my date with Owen. Where might that lead? I brushed my hair off my face, conscious that Leo and Ethan were watching me. A memory raced into my head, only a snatch but so clear that I shivered, feeling again the cold night air, the soft rain tickling my cheeks, the heat of a bonfire on my skin, and the gentle touch of a hand brushing aside my hair. . .

'Friday,' I repeated, fixing my gaze on Leo. 'That would be lovely.'

Chapter Eight

'Come on, Daisy, you read the glossy magazines. What's the dress code for a dinner party with your husband and his gay lover?'

'It's never come up in a magazine I've read.' Daisy stared into my wardrobe. She'd been doing this for the last five minutes, as if by the power of her stare she could replace all the clothes with new ones. 'When did you last buy anything new?'

'1998.' For a moment, I thought she believed me. Were my clothes that bad? 'Stop pulling that face. You're acting scarily like my mother.'

'Not even Irene would wear this.' Daisy pulled out a paisley print dress, which I had probably last worn in the difficult months after Ava's birth, when I still thought the tummy and droopy breasts were temporary afflictions. 'Do you have a wardrobe full of fashionable clothes in another room?'

'What about the grey?' I pulled out the usual jersey dress. Daisy wrinkled her nose.

'To say it's on its last legs would be a compliment.' She rifled through the rail, which took about five seconds. 'You do realise, don't you, that one of the advantages of divorce is that you have an extra half of a wardrobe to fill with new clothes?'

'I bought a new dress for Christmas. But Clark has already seen that. I don't want him to think I only have one decent thing. And why do I need new clothes? I never go anywhere.'

'This is your second night out in a week.' Daisy settled down on the bed, making herself comfortable in a way that didn't bode well. Sure enough, she began an interrogation. 'Talking of nights out, are you going to tell me how it went with Owen on Tuesday?'

'It was fine. Nice.' Terrifying, if she wanted the entire truth.

'What did you do?'

'We went to the Inn at Whitewell and had a couple of drinks.'

'That was a long way to go. Good choice though. Very romantic.'

'Very private. He wanted to avoid any students or parents.' Or any husbands or brothers-in-law.

'And you had fun? It was a success?'

'I suppose so.'

I removed my jeans and T-shirt, and took the grey dress off the hanger, ready to put it on. Daisy looked me up and down, and went over to the chest of drawers.

'Have you no decent lingerie?' she asked, rooting around my underwear. 'Leo must have bought you some for Christmas or birthday presents.'

'No. He generally bought books.'

Daisy held up a saggy bra and granny knickers.

'Fond of grey, aren't you? Please don't tell me you still wear these monstrosities. Although those things you have on now aren't much better. See how different it could look . . .'

She heaved up my bra straps, fighting gravity. As she did, the bedroom door opened and Jonas walked in.

'Mum . . .' He stared at the sight in front of him – and what a sight it must have been for an innocent young boy. 'Not you as well,' he muttered and backed out. Daisy laughed.

'You need a lock on that door. What if you'd been in here with Owen?'

'We've only had one drink!' I pulled on the grey dress, ignoring Daisy's disapproving tut.

'Two drinks,' she corrected. 'And surely a kiss?'

'No! Well,' I conceded, 'a kiss on the cheek.' It wasn't where Owen had aimed for, at the end of the evening, but I had chickened out and turned my head at the last moment.

'Oh, Mary, you're hopeless. You've devoted so much time to studying Alice Hornby that you're acting like a Victorian virgin. You're allowed to have sex with a man who isn't your husband.'

'Being allowed to do something doesn't mean I want to. Anyway,' I continued, turning away from Daisy's sympathetic expression, 'whether Alice Hornby died a virgin is one of her greatest mysteries. There's a letter . . .'

'Spare me the lecture. You didn't go on about her to Owen,

did you? You've spent so long in a bubble with Leo that you've forgotten not everyone is nuts about the Hornby woman.'

'I can't not mention her. It's my job.' I opened my jewellery box, took out the green pendant necklace that Leo had given me for Christmas, and fastened it round my neck.

'Colour! At last!' Daisy said, nodding in approval. She probably wouldn't have approved if she had known where it came from, or that I was wearing it as a gesture of loyalty to Leo. 'We're going shopping before your next date. There will be another, won't there? You haven't scared him off with your prudery?'

'As you've seen, removing my clothes would have scared him off far more effectively than keeping them on. We're meeting to walk the dogs tomorrow, if the weather's fine.' I spritzed perfume, brushed my hair and dug out my smart pair of heels. 'I can't put it off any longer. Will I do?'

'Even in that dress, you look gorgeous.' Daisy hugged me. 'Remember – you're a single woman, not an abandoned wife. Go dazzle.'

Leo met me at his new front door, looking smart in chinos that I had bought him and a shirt that I hadn't. We kissed cheeks politely – such a versatile gesture, capable of bookending the start and end of a relationship. His cheek was soft under my lips, so soft that I suspected it must be the effect of moisturiser. I had to hand it to Clark – he had smartened Leo up in a way that I had never managed.

'This is nice,' I said brightly, following Leo into a large space that served as living and dining room. Huge floor-to-ceiling doors opened onto a balcony overlooking the Bridgewater Canal. Inside, the room was pale, shiny, and minimal, all blond wood, white furniture, chrome, and glass. I couldn't imagine Jonas and Ava staying here. Did they have to shower and put on one of those boiler suits that TV detectives wear, so they didn't contaminate the place? I cringed at what Clark must have thought of our house at Christmas; but still, I wouldn't swap my cosy chaos for this place. Six months ago I would never have dreamt that Leo would either.

Clark came in from the balcony, where he had been talking to two men and a woman I didn't recognise.

'Hello, Mary. We're glad you could come.' Only I seemed to feel any awkwardness over that 'we'. 'Come and meet the others while Leo gets you a drink.'

He led me out to the balcony and introduced his colleague, Pete, and wife Liz, and Andrew, an old friend from university. A few minutes later the final guests arrived, another married couple who had once been guests at my house, and who clearly had no idea what to make of me now being a guest like them.

As Leo and Clark had work connections with the two couples, it was inevitable that I would fall into conversation with Andrew.

'Incredible view, isn't it?' he said, leaning against the balcony rail. I nodded, while making a mental note to tell Jonas and

Ava never to do that. In fact, perhaps I should sweep the whole flat for potential hazards. 'I assume you're a friend of Leo's as we've never met before. Do you work with him at the university?'

'No, I . . .' Why had this not occurred to me, that I might need to explain my presence? I had been too vain, supposing that everyone would know who I was – that my reputation would have gone before me. How demoralising, to discover that Leo hadn't thought me worth mentioning. And how aggravating, a rebellious part of me argued, that he hadn't thought to smooth the evening for me by pre-warning the other guests. Caught on the hop, I had nothing to offer but the truth. 'I'm his wife.'

'Leo's wife?' Andrew stared at me as if he'd just noticed that I had green scales and a horn. 'You're the last person I'd have expected to see here. Lower down the list than Elvis.' He laughed. 'Good for you. Not many wives would have been so tolerant. Mine certainly wasn't.'

'You mean you're . . .' I trailed off, not sure what the PC word to use was.

'No, absolutely not. My ex-wife was intolerant about much more minor things than that. Leo's had it easy.'

We both glanced over at Leo. He and Clark were watching us, but swiftly looked away and started talking.

'That wasn't suspicious, was it?' Andrew said. 'Do you think we might have been set up?'

'Set up?'

'Hadn't you noticed that all the other guests are couples?'

'No.' Or rather, I had, but I hadn't attached any significance to it – certainly not the type that Andrew was suggesting. The idea that Leo might have tried to set me up with a blind date was preposterous. Wasn't it? I gazed over at Leo again, and he smiled and gave me a nod – the sort of encouraging nod I had seen him give the children a thousand times.

'No such thing as a free dinner,' Andrew said. 'Shall we get it out of the way and then we can enjoy the rest of the evening? No offence, Mary, but I didn't come here looking for a partner, and I don't think I've found one.'

It was hard not to take some offence at being rejected after I'd spoken less than a dozen words. Perhaps Daisy had been right about the dress. But that was besides the point – the point being, what was Leo doing, trying to pair me off with this stranger? Before I could go and tackle him, Clark called us in for dinner. It wasn't a surprise when I was ushered to a seat next to Andrew.

'Fancy seeing you here,' he said with a grin.

Andrew had been right: removing the awkwardness from the start meant we could talk about what interested us with no pressure about how we were being perceived. Of course I ended up talking about Alice Hornby, and my plans to visit as many bookshops as I could in Lancashire to plug Leo's book and arrange publicity events.

'My cousin owns a bookshop in Bickton,' Andrew said. 'Wilsher Books. Is it on your list?'

'Near the bottom. I'm starting with the closer ones first, and don't they specialise in children's books?'

'Yes, but not exclusively. I'll give you Janey's number. Tell her I insist she meet you.'

I handed over my phone, and Andrew tapped in the details. Leo watched from the other end of the table. I waited until he went into the kitchen at the end of the meal, then followed and closed the door.

'Is this a blind date?' I demanded. 'Are you trying to fob me off with Andrew?'

'I wouldn't say fob you off,' Leo said. He smiled, but that charming, innocent smile wasn't going to work this time. 'We thought you might get along. He's a good man.'

'I don't care if he's an amazing man, or even Superman. Why would you think that I'm looking for a date?'

'I don't want you to be on your own.' He took my hand and stroked across my tense knuckles. He had probably touched me more since becoming gay than in the last year of our marriage. 'I'm well aware that it's my fault you are on your own. If I can help change that, I will.'

'By finding me someone else.' Not by coming back himself. 'You're not my pimp. Don't demean yourself by acting like one.'

'Mary!' I pulled back my hand and turned my head away so that I didn't have to see the hurt expression on his face. He had hurt me more. How could it mean so little to him, to imagine me with another man?

'Doesn't it bother you?' I snapped, unable to let the point drop. I might as well show him my true nature. What use was pretence now? 'Would you not care if I went home with Andrew tonight, let him kiss me in all those places that only your lips have ever touched, let his bare skin glide over mine, let him put his . . .'

'Don't.' His voice wavered; tears glittered in his eyes. 'Yes, it would bother me. It wrenches my heart to think about it. But so does the alternative – that you would never know companionship or happiness again.'

I hugged him, slotting into my space as if I had never been away, and that's how Clark found us. He put his hand on Leo's shoulder, and the simple affection in the gesture made me pull away.

'Shall I go?' Clark asked.

'No.' For a moment Leo leant in towards Clark so their shoulders brushed. He managed a smile. 'I haven't progressed far with the coffee.'

'I'll do it. Mary, will you help?'

Laughter drifted in as Leo returned to the guests. I waited, watching Clark fill a tray with smart coffee cups, wondering why he wanted me to stay behind. We had never been alone before.

'Mary . . .'

'Don't,' I interrupted, suspecting from his tone of voice where this was going, and not wanting to hear it. 'Don't apologise.'

'I can't. I'm not sorry. I adore Leo.' He shrugged, not in an insolent, careless way, but rather emphasising how helpless his feelings were, how powerless he was to contain them. And I was glad – how could I not be – that Leo was so well loved. Glad, and searingly jealous.

'But you need to know,' Clark continued, 'how difficult this has been for him. He fought his feelings for so long. He talked about you constantly, how wonderful you are, and how he'd found more contentment in marriage than he'd ever expected.'

Contentment? It was the way I would have described our marriage too; and yet it sounded so inadequate when held up against adoration, against the strength of feeling so achingly obvious between Leo and Clark.

'I didn't encourage him. I didn't set out to break up your marriage. He needed to make the choice himself, which way he wanted to go. It's taken him a long time to acknowledge who he is. But he's still who you knew too. He loves you as much as he ever did.'

'And I love him.'

'I know. That's what I want to say. Don't stop, will you? He needs us both.'

Clark held out his hand and I took it, but rather than shaking it, he covered it with his other hand, as if we were sealing a pact. And perhaps, in a way, we were: a pact to make this strange new family work, for Leo's sake, and for Jonas and Ava. As if to emphasise the point, Clark mentioned the children over coffee, asking my advice about what they might like to do at the weekend.

'Where are they tonight?' Leo asked. 'With Irene?'

'No. Jonas insisted they didn't need a babysitter, but I asked Daisy. Mum was busy. She was expecting a visitor. I think it might have been a man.'

'A man? Irene?'

Leo's reaction was exactly how I imagined it would be – we had joked for years about Mum's lack of interest in men since my father disappeared. He smiled at me, his expression full of surprise, amusement, and mock horror, and in that moment, he was mine again: the boy who had joined me on the garden wall, and who had carried me through the teenage years with steady arms and unwavering loyalty. But it wasn't true: he wasn't mine. I had seen that tonight, in every glance and every touch he had exchanged with Clark; the way his voice softened with love when he spoke to him; the way they fed off each other, prompting jokes, nudging out stories, bringing out the best in each other. The flat had absorbed him too: the photo of Audrey and Bill that had once graced our house now stood on a shelf; his keys and phone lay in an oak bowl that I had given him as a birthday gift, now enjoying a new life here; and perhaps the most distressing sight – the hideous pottery coaster that Jonas had once made, bearing the misspelled legend, 'World's Gratest Dad', sitting on a coffee table beside Leo's current book. This was where Leo belonged. This was his life now, and I was his past. I was an expert at blocking out reality, but I couldn't ignore it any longer.

The evening had been long enough. I guzzled my coffee, burning my throat, and popped to the bathroom before leaving. As I returned to make my excuses and say goodbye, Andrew's voice rose over the smooth soul music that had been playing in the background all evening.

'Have you set a date yet? Or are you going to leave us all behind and do it somewhere sunny?'

'Is someone getting married?' I asked, blundering into the conversation.

The room fell silent, save for the crooning voice of Marvin Gaye. Clark took hold of Leo's hand.

'Mary . . .' Leo said.

It was obvious, of course, and I didn't even have alcohol to blame for my slow wits. Who else could Andrew have been talking to, when the other two couples present were already married?

'Mary,' Leo said again. Happiness radiated from his face, though the bones of his knuckles stood out in sharp prominence as he gripped Clark's hand. 'It's me. I'm going to marry Clark.'

Chapter Nine

I closed the front door softly behind me, and kicked off my shoes so that my heels didn't clatter on the tiled floor. The television mumbled in the living room, and I opened the door, never needing to see Daisy more. But Daisy wasn't there. Ethan was sprawled on the sofa, long legs stretching across the room, Dotty curled up at his side. He looked over his shoulder and smiled.

'What are you doing here? Where's Daisy?'

'Joe asked me over to play Xbox, so I said she might as well go home. You don't mind, do you?'

I shook my head. At any other moment, I would have been thrilled: Jonas had once tried to involve Leo in his games but it had been a disaster never repeated. But I couldn't take that in now. I'd expected Daisy. I hadn't neutralised my expression or my feelings enough to see anyone else.

'Mary?'

Ethan sprang up from the sofa, causing Dotty to grumble, came over to me and manoeuvred me under a lamp. He studied my face so minutely that he could probably have earned a first-class degree in it by the time he spoke.

'What's the matter?'

Catching sight of my reflection in the mirror above the fireplace, it was obvious why he had asked the question. My eyes seemed to have taken over my face: two huge, dark pits of anguish floating on a pale moon, surrounded by a galaxy of black hair. I was washed out, black. My name had never suited me better, on a night when it felt no longer mine.

'Mary,' Ethan repeated. His hands were gripping my arms. 'What's happened?'

'Leo and Clark are getting married.'

His evident surprise was a relief. At least I wasn't the last to know.

'He told you tonight? At a dinner party?'

'No. I overheard it.'

I closed my eyes, but couldn't stop the scene replaying in my head. It had taken me a moment to process Leo's announcement, for my brain to verify what my ears had heard. Humiliation crawled along my skin again as I pictured the looks of sympathy swiftly flung my way, and imagined the conversations that might be taking place right now. *Can you believe she didn't know? . . . Did you see her face? . . . That was a more entertaining dinner than we expected!*

Ethan's expletives pulled me back to my own front room.

'I can't believe he's done this,' he said, removing his hands from my arms and taking a step back. 'No wonder you're distraught. It's so soon.'

'It's not that.' That aspect hadn't occurred to me, but he

was right. It was soon. Less than six months ago we had been living in this house as man and wife. And now . . . My breath shuddered. 'I've lost him.'

And then I couldn't hold back; thirty years of practice couldn't prevent the tears now. I cried, proper, heaving sobs that shook my body, scalded my cheeks, and fractured my breathing. Ethan gathered me into a hug, and when I didn't stop, scooped me up and carried me over to the sofa, where he held me for I don't know how long, until my tears and my body were equally exhausted. Gradually I became conscious of a solid, muscular chest beneath my head, so different from Leo's squishiness, and of an unfamiliar floral scent filling my nose. I pulled away, and slid along the sofa, putting as much distance as I could between us.

Ethan went to the kitchen and returned with a wodge of paper towels and two glasses of brandy. I blew my nose noisily, scaring poor Dotty.

'Did you think he would come back?'

'I don't know. I don't know what I thought.' I wasn't sure that I'd been thinking at all; I'd blocked the unpleasantness out, as usual. The months since the Christmas party, when Leo first appeared with Clark, seemed blurry and unreal, as if I'd been sleepwalking through them. How had this happened? How had I let Leo go, and not put up any resistance? 'What have I done?'

Dotty jumped on to the sofa, nuzzling her head against mine, her tongue licking the salty residue from my cheeks.

'This is what I was worried about. This is exactly why I tried to warn you at Christmas.'

'Well, congratulations for being so smart. You always have to be right, don't you?'

'Jesus, how can you think I would want to see you like this?' He jumped up, knocking his knee on the coffee table. 'None of this is right,' he said, bending over to rub his knee. 'He shouldn't have done this. I should never have . . .'

Floorboards creaked overhead as Jonas moved around his bedroom. Ethan stopped, and sat down on the other sofa.

'Do you want him back?' he asked.

It was an impossible question – pointless too. I could never have him back, that was clear from what I had seen tonight. I could ignore separation and divorce, but the sight of Leo's joy at living with someone else filtered through even my thick blinkers.

'I want things to be as they were.'

Ethan looked up at that.

'Why? Because it was perfect? Because you were happy?' He paused, waiting for a reply. He didn't get one. 'Or because it was safe, easy, what you were used to?'

I stared at him. Why was he saying this? One minute he had held me as I cried, and now it felt like I was under attack. His voice was gentle, but his gaze was ruthless.

'We were content.'

'Content? And was that enough? Leo said you'd not had a physical relationship for months. Is that true?'

'He had no business discussing that.' I stroked Dotty's head, wishing the sofa would swallow me up. Yes, it was true, and it was humiliating, and I hadn't expected anyone else to find out.

'So why would you want to go back to that? You must have known something wasn't right.'

'Why? There's more to a relationship than sex. Perhaps that's where you've been going wrong.'

I glared at him, but didn't find any anger in his face, only regret.

'Perhaps I have,' he said.

The credits rolled on the TV show, chirpy music shattering the strange, close atmosphere that hovered over us. Dotty yelped as my ring caught in her fur. It had been force of habit, getting ready to go out, to put on my engagement ring. My wedding ring was still in place too. I pulled them both off, bruising my knuckle trying to remove the wedding ring, and dropped them onto the coffee table. My finger looked oddly pinched without it, and the skin was shiny white, as if that one strip had been preserved from the ageing process.

Ethan picked up the wedding ring and rolled it in his fingers.

'Grandma's ring,' he said. We hadn't been able to afford new rings: Audrey had given us two old ones when we announced our engagement. 'What will you do with it?'

'Pass it on to Ava, I suppose.'

'I carried this ring with me everywhere for two weeks until

Leo put it on your finger. I honestly never thought it would come off.' Briefly, he closed his fingers over the ring. I didn't know what to say; I didn't recognise this thoughtful, melancholy Ethan. He smiled at me, a guarded smile, concealing whatever he was thinking. 'I'd better go.'

The next morning, I left the house to take Dotty for a walk a precise thirty minutes before Leo was due to pick up the children, intending to do a sixty-minute circuit and miss him. Ethan was the first to put a spanner in the works, dashing out of Audrey's house before I was halfway down the drive, and vaulting over the hedge with impressive agility. He didn't even have the grace to puff when he slid to a halt in front of me.

'Hello!' The sunny smile was back, as if the Ethan of last night was a figment of my imagination. 'How are you this morning?'

'Fine.'

'As bad as that?'

He laughed, and I raised the shadow of a smile. I looked like hell, or one of its residents: black hair did no favours to a pale, unslept face.

'Are you heading out? I thought you might have visitors.' He pointed to the road, where a car was parked a couple of metres past the end of the drive. I didn't recognise it.

'It probably belongs to a walker.' A terrifying thought sidled into my head. 'It wasn't there last night, was it?'

'It might have been. Why?'

I looked down the drive to Mum's garage. Her bedroom curtains were still closed, well past the time she was usually up and about.

'Irene?' Ethan laughed. 'Good for her. How long has that been going on?'

'I don't want to think about anything going on.' I didn't know what was worse: the fact that Mum might be having sex at all, or the fact that if she was, it proved she was more desirable than me. Where had she met a man? If it was a man – I should know better than to make assumptions like that anymore. My left thumb rubbed along the inside of my ring finger, as it had been doing all morning, like a tongue unable to resist probing the gap left by a missing tooth.

'Do you want company?' Ethan asked. 'I could do with some exercise. Mum seems to think I haven't eaten properly for eighteen years. At this rate, I'll need to pay for two seats when I fly back.'

'You're going back?' I spun around, trying to untangle Dotty's lead from my legs. 'I thought you were here for six months.'

'I'll stay for as long as I'm needed.'

That wouldn't be long the way Audrey was going: she had abandoned her stick already, and was coping remarkably well one-armed. I was wondering whether to agree that Ethan could join me – he certainly didn't need the exercise, as his T-shirt revealed only too well, but I needed the company – when Leo pulled onto the drive. He came over and stood beside Ethan, and I marvelled, as I had done so often in the past, how the same two parents could have produced children with not a single obvious feature in common. Ava and Jonas didn't look alike, superficially, but there was something about the shape of their chin and lips that marked a connection. With Leo and Ethan there was nothing: you could stare at them for days and not find so much as an eyelash the same length.

'Are you taking Dotty out?' Leo asked, bending down to stroke her head. She didn't respond; she had taken umbrage at his desertion, and no amount of strokes would win her over. 'Can it wait? I came early so we could talk.'

'A bit late, isn't it?' Ethan said. 'You should have talked to her before last night.'

'In hindsight, it was unfortunate . . .'

'Hindsight? Bloody hell, Leo, if you'd taken your nose out of your books for a second you'd have seen how obvious it was that this would happen.'

'Let's go back in.' I felt like banging their heads together; they were squabbling more than Ava and Jonas. They didn't know how lucky they were to have a sibling, even if they had nothing in common. 'Dotty can wait a few minutes.'

I turned back to the house, Leo following, but glanced back when Ethan spoke.

'Leo.' I expected more sniping, but I was wrong. Ethan put an arm round Leo's shoulder and gave him a quick hug. 'Congratulations.'

Smarting at Ethan's disloyalty, I marched into the house and sat at the kitchen table, keeping my jacket and shoes on. This wasn't going to take long. I couldn't bear it to take long.

Leo came up behind me and put his hand on my shoulder.

'I'm sorry, Mary. I'd rather you hadn't discovered the news that way.'

'What, in public? It's rather fitting, isn't it? At least there was a smaller audience for my humiliation this time.'

My stupid, weak heart ached a little at the misery on Leo's face when he sat down, but I ignored it. Last night I had grieved. This morning I was furious.

'Who proposed? Did you do it? Was it the proper bended-knee affair?'

'No. Clark proposed.'

That softened me, slightly. An image of Leo on his knees had tortured me all night. The image was drawn from imagination, not memory. His proposal to me had been a rushed question, blurted out in Audrey's back garden, several weeks after he had returned from Oxford after completing his degree. He had been acting so strangely that it was a relief when he proposed rather than dumped me, and I hadn't given a thought to the mechanics of it. I hadn't realised I missed the huge, romantic gesture until I had pictured him offering it to someone else.

'And have you set a date?'

'Probably September, so there's time for a honeymoon before term starts.'

'Honeymoon?' Another image I would much rather not have in my head. 'Presumably something more exciting than a B&B in Llandudno?'

'We had a special time in that B&B. I wouldn't change it. I have no regrets about a moment of our time together.'

'Then why end it? If it was so special, why aren't we still together?'

'Clark.' He lifted his hands from the table, empty of words for once, a circumstance so unusual that it spoke more powerfully than anything he might have said.

'And you couldn't have resisted? For the children? For me?'

'I tried. But things have seemed different ever since I turned forty. I may be halfway through my time. I couldn't continue denying who and what I am.'

'I see. That was quite some birthday present you gave yourself, wasn't it? Licence to do exactly what you wanted. Will you be so generous when it's my fortieth?'

Leo reached across the table and held my hand.

'You have benefitted already, can't you see? When did you ever challenge me like this when we were married? You only ever gave me half of yourself, as if you switched off a whole aspect of your character – your essential spark – when you entered this house. Did you truly believe I would have loved you less if you had disagreed with me sometimes?'

'My dad . . .' I began, but Leo interrupted.

'I know. You blame Irene for driving him away. But nothing she did should have driven him away from you.

105

If you hadn't been so reasonable, I would have fought to my bones to see Jonas and Ava. Either he was a weak man, and didn't deserve you, or there was more to his disappearance than you know.'

It was too much to absorb today. I had spent so many years loving Leo and resenting Mum, that I struggled to acknowledge that they were neither so good nor so bad as I had believed them. Leo rubbed his finger along the space where my ring had been until a few hours ago.

'You've taken off your ring.'

I nodded. I had already noticed that Leo had moved his to his right hand.

'It was time.'

'Time to move on?' When I said nothing, he sighed. 'Don't say it's no business of mine. I love you as much as ever. Your business will always be mine. You will be my best woman at the wedding, won't you? There's no one I would rather have by my side.'

With exemplary timing, Jonas and Ava clattered into the kitchen. They drew up short at the sight of us sitting at the table, Leo still holding my hand.

'What are you doing?' Ava said, looking from one to the other. 'Have you changed your mind? Are you back together?'

She tried to appear indifferent, but there was a glimmer of hope in her voice that she couldn't disguise. It almost set off my tears again.

'No, we're not,' I said, withdrawing my hand and standing

up. 'Dad has some wonderful news to share. He and Clark are getting married.'

'Married?' It was agony to see the emotion rippling across her face, but to know that acknowledging her distress by giving her a hug was entirely the wrong thing to do. At last she managed to settle on the familiar, surly expression. 'I won't be a bridesmaid. I'm not wearing a stupid frilly dress.'

'Are you okay, Mum?' Jonas removed one of his earphones – an extraordinary gesture of concern.

'Of course I am. Dad has asked me to be his best woman, so it's going to be a very special occasion, isn't it?'

Despite my most encouraging voice, no one looked at all convinced.

It was only later, when Leo had taken the children away for their weekend visit, that I remembered I had promised to meet Owen for a dog walk an hour ago. Before I could think better of it, I dragged Dotty down the road to the village, and knocked on the door of the cottage where Owen lived. There was no answer.

Should I leave it at that? Try again later? Send a text? I wished I knew what the rules were. I wanted to show that I'd made an effort – turned up, albeit too late. Rummaging in my bag, I found a pencil and an old Post Office receipt, and scribbled a message on the back.

'Sorry! Unexpectedly detained this morning. Complications – but all over now. Same time tomorrow instead? Mary.'

I stared at the scrap of paper, trembling in my fingers.

Should I screw it up, or push it through the letterbox? I hesitated so long it was a wonder the neighbours didn't call the police and report me for loitering. Time to move on, Leo had said. I shoved the note through the letterbox and walked away.

Chapter Ten

One advantage of Ethan's return was that while he kept an eye on Audrey I could resume my plan to visit local bookshops to drum up interest in the Alice Hornby biography. Initial sales figures had been encouraging, especially after a glowing review in *The Times* that had given me a secret rush of pleasure, even though my name wasn't mentioned anywhere. While we weren't going to make our fortune with a few dozen local sales, the more people we could interest in Alice, the more chance there was that the Alice Hornby Society would grow in number – if we had our way, one day Alice would be mentioned in the same breath as Austen and the Brontës, as one of the leading female writers of the nineteenth century. We wouldn't be satisfied until the BBC made an adaptation of at least one of Alice's novels.

Today I had arranged to visit the bookshop in Bickton that Andrew had mentioned at Leo's dinner party. It turned out to be a lovely double-fronted shop, and although one of the two rooms was exclusively for children's books – a gorgeous space with beanbags, tiny chairs, and even a wigwam filled with cushions – the other room held a good mix of fiction and non-fiction. It even passed the Hornby test: browsing the shelves while the owner was serving a customer, I spotted a copy of Alice's first novel, *The Gentleman's Daughter*, nestled amongst the classics. I moved it into a more prominent forward-facing space when no one was looking – or I thought no one was looking.

'You must be Mary,' Andrew's cousin, Janey, said, appearing at my side and putting the bookshelf back into pristine order. She laughed. 'Good attempt, but no deal. I can spot a book out of place from fifty paces. Alice Hornby stays where she is.'

'She needs a helping hand,' I argued, instantly warming to Janey and her sense of order, even if it did scupper my plans. 'It's unlucky she's a H. By the time shoppers have browsed past Austen, Brontë, Dickens, and the rest, they'll have no money left. I don't suppose you could be tempted to try organising books in order of first name?'

'It will never happen while I'm in charge.' She looked me up and down, and I must have passed muster, because she smiled again. 'Tea and biscuits?'

It was probably the easiest sales pitch I would face. Janey loved books, authors, and her shop, and was keen to do anything to promote all three. She was building a reputation for holding author talks and signings, and was happy to consider an event for Leo, if she enjoyed the book. I gave her the copy I had brought with me.

'Leo Black?' she said. 'No wonder you're so enthusiastic.

Husband?' She opened the back cover and inspected the photograph. It was one of my favourites: Leo had refused to have a formal photograph taken, and we had chosen a laughing shot of him in St Ives a few years ago. 'Lucky you.'

'Yes,' I answered without thinking, and then my thumb caught my empty finger, reminding me of my mistake. 'Ex-husband, actually. But I was lucky, and the enthusiasm is entirely genuine. It's a brilliantly written, warm-hearted book, and a fascinating account of Alice's life.'

It was one advantage of not having my name on the book as co-author; I could boast about how fabulous it was without modesty holding me back. I set off for home, glad that the meeting had gone so well, and proud of myself for acknowledging my divorced status for the first time. It was progress – a baby step, maybe, but better than nothing. And there was this thing with Owen too, whatever it was. We had walked the dogs on Sunday, and conversation had been easy and comfortable; he had the same laid-back manner as Leo, and so was familiar and new at the same time. I must have done something right, as he had made a tentative suggestion about meeting for dinner at some point. Dog walking was harmless; I could cope with dinner; it was the step beyond that worried me.

I was so busy wondering what I would do if Owen tried to kiss me – somehow the obvious answer, to kiss him back, wouldn't take root in my mind – that I missed a couple of instructions from the Sat Nav, turned left in the wrong place and found that instead of heading towards home, I was bowling along a thin country lane with high hedges; the sort of lane that enticed you deeper into the countryside, with a series of unmarked crossroads and no sign of civilisation in any direction.

Amazingly, after five minutes of plunging so deeply into the countryside that I feared it would take general surgery to extract me, the hedges turned into garden walls, the road widened to allow more than a cart to scrape by, and a whole village appeared from nowhere. Two pubs squared off from opposite sides of the road; in a row of shops converted from terraced houses there was a butcher, with all prices marked by the pound; a newsagent; and a hairdresser's that looked as if it had been last decorated in the sixties. Union Jack bunting drooped across every building. Most surprising of all, as I crawled through the centre, marvelling at the village that time forgot, was the sight of a bookshop at the end of the row.

I parked outside, and studied the shop properly. The inside of the windows was covered in yellowed plastic to protect the display from the sun: a bizarrely optimistic precaution for a shop in Lancashire. It made it difficult to see the books on display, but I could make out a Harry Potter and a Dan Brown, so the shop seemed to be in the right century, unlike the rest of the village. A gloriously traditional hand-painted sign above the window simply read 'Archer's'. This shop hadn't come up in my internet searches; I'd be astonished if it had any internet presence at all. I doubted they could attract a crowd of more than three to any event, or that I could persuade Leo to come here, but peeping inside was irresistible.

A lively jingle greeted my entrance; a proper old-fashioned bell was fixed to the door on an ornate iron spiral. The shop was bigger than it had looked from the outside, filling what would have been the front room and passage of two neighbouring cottages. Mumbled conversation and the sound of a boiling kettle drifted through from an open door in the back wall.

I noticed all this on the periphery of my vision, as my attention was caught by a wooden bookrest standing on the cluttered desk that served as a counter. The bookrest was filled with two copies of each of Alice Hornby's four novels: the beautiful green Virago paperback editions that had been published many years ago. They were the first copies of Alice's books I had owned, and I had adored everything about them, from the well-chosen portraits that graced the cover to the passionate stories inside.

'They don't write books like that anymore.' A lady in her sixties appeared through the rear door, mug in hand, and nodded towards the book I was holding. 'You could get a lovely matching set there. You won't find new copies of those editions anywhere else now.'

I could well believe it. They must have been published at least twenty years ago, which was a sad reflection on how often the stock changed in this shop.

'They are beautiful,' I said. 'I have battered old copies at home.'

'Time to replace them, perhaps?'

'I couldn't possibly. It would be like replacing my children. I've lived with them so long that they fall open at my favourite passages. Buying new copies would be as bad as going through nappy changes and toilet training all over again.' I put the book back on the bookrest and smiled. This was an opportunity I couldn't miss. 'Actually, I popped in here hoping to sell a book rather than buy one.'

'Oh yes?' The tone wasn't encouraging, nor was the way she folded her arms, an impressive move when she still had her drink in her hand. Undaunted, I ploughed on.

'It's great to meet another fan of Alice Hornby. My husband, Professor Leo Black, is the country's leading expert on her.' I deliberately dropped the 'ex' and added the 'Professor' to try to curry favour, but there was no sign of softening. 'Were you aware that he's recently published her biography?'

A strange whirring noise emanated from the open doorway, and the lady glanced over her shoulder.

'We had heard,' she said. But before she could say more – if she'd intended to – a wheelchair zipped out of the door behind her at some speed before coming to a smart halt beside the desk. At first glance, the wheelchair appeared to contain a pile of woollen blankets, but on closer scrutiny I made out a tiny person nestled in the folds. It was an old lady – I thought – with sparse grey hair and a face so wrinkled it looked as if she'd been left in a hot bath for decades.

Surprisingly bright brown eyes stared out at me from amongst the wrinkles.

'Careful, Bridie.' The voice was little more than a quaver, but the gaze didn't falter. The younger woman, Bridie, unfolded her arms at last and adjusted the heap of blankets.

'It's all right, Mum,' she said. 'Don't get worked up.'

What had I done? I didn't see how I could have alarmed either of them; looking ordinary was my stock-in-trade. I leaned over the desk, my hand outstretched.

'How do you do?' I had no idea where that sprang from. I'd never used the phrase before in my life, but it had a reassuringly non-threatening sound. Or it had to my ears – the old lady, on the other hand, shrank even further back in her chair. 'I'm Mary Black.'

'How'd you find us?'

'It was sheer luck; I missed a couple of turns from the Sat Nav and ended up in this village. I'm visiting local bookshops to see if any would be interested in taking Leo's book or for him to come for a talk or signing.'

'Muckraking,' the old lady muttered. It wasn't the reaction I'd hoped for. 'Fishing for gossip, that's all it is. Folk should be left in peace.'

'The book isn't like that,' I said, grasping from this that her objection seemed to be about the biography, rather than personal. Although as I'd written much of that book, it *was* personal. 'We couldn't be bigger fans of Alice. The book is a tribute to how wonderful she is, and what an amazing writer.

There's no muck. We spent years researching, poring over diaries and letters, and I talked to as many surviving relatives as I could find.'

'Relatives! They know bugger all.' The old lady snorted. 'Servants knew what was what in those days.'

'I know. I found the housekeeper's journal. We even know what Alice had for dinner on her twenty-first birthday. Isn't that incredible!'

The old lady didn't seem to share my excitement. I thought I heard a mumble of 'crumbs' – which certainly wasn't what Alice had for dinner – but it was lost under some kerfuffle with the blankets. Then, more distinctly, she said, 'Let the dead keep their secrets,' and with a final glare, she spun her chair around and disappeared into the back room.

'Can I tempt you with any of our books?' Bridie asked, as if nothing unusual had gone on. Perhaps this was the usual performance for customers. She plucked a paperback off a shelf at her side. 'This was shortlisted for an award.'

It was a thriller that had been published at least three years ago. I hated thrillers, but it seemed a small price to pay for having agitated an old lady, so I handed over my money and escaped before she could make me feel guilty enough to buy more.

Audrey and Ethan were in their front garden when I arrived home. Audrey was sitting in a deckchair while Ethan dug up a huge azalea that had died two years ago. I wandered over to the dividing hedge in response to Audrey's wave.

'How was your day?' she called. 'Have you sold oodles of books?'

'Maybe. One shop was interested.'

'Weren't you meant to be selling rather than buying?' Ethan stopped digging and rested on his spade. Sweat darkened the hair at the edge of his face, and his T-shirt clung to his chest. He gestured at the book in my hand.

'Oh, I couldn't help this. I didn't really plan to buy it,' I gabbled. My eyes wouldn't leave that T-shirt; I was having a Lady Chatterley moment. 'Would you like it?'

Without waiting for an answer, I tossed the book towards him – clear evidence of my discomposure, as I would never normally have mistreated a book that way. Despite my rubbish aim, Ethan stretched and caught it in one hand. He had always excelled at sport.

'Thanks.' He glanced at the book. 'Looks good. And I'm flattered that you now acknowledge I can read.'

This confused me, until I remembered an infamous argument we'd had once during which I may have flung the words 'ignorant' and 'illiterate' at him, and might possibly have suggested that he hadn't touched a book since the rubber ones he had used for teething. It was hardly gallant of him to remember such nonsense. He smiled, evidently enjoying my embarrassment.

'I didn't have you down as a gardener,' I said, attempting to change the subject.

'No? You shouldn't pin labels to people. You might find you can't see past them.'

He was infuriating. Leo never spoke in riddles like this. I turned to Audrey for some sanity.

'Isn't he doing a marvellous job?' she cried. 'That poor azalea should have heard the last rites years ago. What shall we replace it with? I fancy something exotic, don't you, Mary?' She laughed uproariously, carrying us along with her though we'd have been hard pressed to explain the joke. 'You'll come back to plant it for me, if you've gone, won't you?' she asked Ethan.

'I told you I'm not going anywhere until you're fit. It's only a viewing.'

'A viewing?' I repeated. 'Are you buying a house?'

'Renting. Maybe. I'm not welcome here.'

He grinned, and Audrey wagged her finger at him.

'I adore having you here. But tell him, Mary. He's a young man. He can't live with his mother. He'll never find a nice girl if he's hanging about here, will he?'

'Oh, I don't know, it never held him back in the past, did it? Girls have always sniffed him out like flies to dung.'

Ethan laughed and imitated Audrey by wagging his finger at me.

'Are you busy tomorrow?' he asked. 'Why don't you come with me to view the house?'

'Me? Wouldn't you rather take Audrey?'

'It's a marvellous idea,' Audrey said, wiping away my

objections before I could utter them. 'You've done wonders with your house. And you're constantly telling me that I should be resting.'

I was – and she was constantly telling me that she was perfectly fine, so what was she up to now? Whatever it was, I could see she wasn't going to be swayed.

'Fine,' I said. 'Where is this house? Somewhere ridiculously trendy, I expect, for an adoptive New Yorker?'

'It's on the other side of the village,' Ethan replied. 'Waterman's Cottage. Do you know it?'

Know it? I loved it.

'Waterman's Cottage? Down by the reservoir? It's my fortune house.'

'Your what?'

'My fortune house. The house I'd buy if I won or earned a fortune.'

Ethan shook his head, laughing.

'Are you really telling me that if money was no object, you'd buy a small house in the village where you've lived your whole life? When you could have the world?'

'My life is here. This is my world.'

Ethan smiled, but it was a smile I couldn't identify.

'I think it's time we made your world a little bigger.'

Chapter Eleven

Waterman's Cottage was perched on its own at the edge of the embankment that led across one end of the Stoneybrook Reservoir, and had spectacular views across the water. Only ramblers and dog-walkers ever went past, and the only neighbours were ducks, geese, herons, and the deer that roamed the woods on either side of the reservoir.

'I've not been down here for years,' Ethan said, as we strolled down the lane and the cottage came into view. 'I'd forgotten this place existed. It's an idyllic spot, isn't it?'

'Yes, but I wouldn't have thought it would appeal to you. A bit quiet after New York, isn't it?'

'The New York you've seen on TV. There's much more to it. I love going running in Prospect Park. You can get away from the noise and the crowds, and see nothing but country-side. It reminds me of home.'

He sounded almost wistful, which was a surprise, because I'd always assumed he disliked living around here. He'd certainly vanished to New York in a hurry; little more than three weeks after announcing his plan, he'd gone. Leo and I had only just made it back from our honeymoon in time to say goodbye.

'I didn't think you missed it here,' I said.

'Some things. More than you know.' He smiled, and the wistfulness was gone. 'Come on. The agent's waiting. I hope she doesn't mind Dotty.'

The estate agent adored Dotty – she was an irresistible dog when on her best behaviour – and offered to look after her in the garden while we looked around the house. I couldn't wait to see what it was like inside, and hovered eagerly at her shoulder as she unlocked the front door.

'You're like a greyhound keening to get out of the trap,' Ethan murmured in my ear. 'Steady on. I hope you're not going to be disappointed.'

'How could there be disappointment behind a door like this?'

It was an amazing door; an amazing building. The Victorians had clearly believed that even a functional building for a lowly waterman should be beautiful. It was built from huge rectangular stones, blackened with age, and at one end stood a two-storey tower complete with turret. The door itself was a massive wooden arch, with black iron straps. It swung open at last and I charged in.

It didn't take long to explore the downstairs, and we wandered around pretty much in silence; mainly because Ethan was busy with the practical man things, looking out for plug sockets and telephone points, and I was stunned into silence by how gorgeous it was inside. It was better than I could ever have expected: all golden oak floors and woodwork, open fires, and an extension made almost entirely of glass offering panoramic views that I could have gazed at all day.

Without waiting for Ethan, I headed upstairs and found two small but pretty bedrooms, a family bathroom, and the most incredible master bedroom I had ever seen. It was on the top floor of the tower, and glass panels had been placed in the flat ceiling so you could lie in bed and gaze at the stars. There was an open fire in one of the walls, and near it a free-standing roll-top bath.

'Quite a love nest in here, isn't it?' Ethan crept up behind me and stole my thoughts.

'I might have known that's what you were looking for.'

He grinned, the saucy grin that had won over every girl in our year at school, and I tried to chase away the image of him entertaining in that bath, bare skin against bare skin, glowing in the heat of a crackling fire. He kicked off his shoes and lay on the bed.

'You've got to come and look at this,' he said.

I perched on the edge of the bed and dropped my head back.

'Not like that.' Ethan laughed. 'You need to lie down to get the full effect.' I didn't move. Ethan rolled his eyes, grabbed one of the pillows from under his head, and placed it in the middle of the bed. 'There. Your virtue is totally safe now.'

'I never thought it was in danger!'

Feeling like an old prude, I pulled off my boots and lay down, being careful to stick close to the edge of the bed. I gazed up through the glass ceiling at the sky: it was like a living water colour painting, splashes of translucent white cloud chasing across a blue backdrop. It was hypnotic, and I felt more relaxed than I had done in weeks.

'Amazing, isn't it?' Ethan's voice broke the spell, and I turned my head to find his eyes fixed on me, such a bright blue that they could have been mirrors reflecting the sky.

'Irritating when the sun comes up at 4 a.m.,' I said, deliberately shattering the strange mood. Ethan laughed, making the bed vibrate in a disturbing way beneath me.

'Where's your sense of romance, Mary? Imagine lying here and being kissed awake by the soft touch of the rising sun. What could you do in those extra hours?'

'Clean the oven, scrub the toilets, finish the ironing, walk the dog . . .'

At last he looked away, and I watched the clouds again, but struggled to recover the peace I had found before.

'Why has this place been for sale so long?' Ethan asked. 'I can't believe it hasn't been snapped up.'

'The price, for a start. They wanted three-quarters of a million when it first went on the market.'

'Sounds reasonable, when you look at the location and the quality of the renovation.'

'Reasonable?' I goggled at him. 'You've lived in New York too long. I don't call it the fortune house for nothing. But that's not the only thing. A lot of people in Stoneybrook think it's an unlucky house. The couple who renovated it so beautifully fell out during the work, and divorced before they ever spent a night here.'

'Not a curse either of us need worry about.'

There was nothing I could say to that: it was true, and thoroughly depressing. The bed shook as Ethan rolled over and tossed aside the pillow between us.

'Sorry,' he said, putting his hand on my arm. 'That was tactless.'

My mobile phone rang, and I leapt off the bed to fish it out of my bag. Owen's number flashed up. I stepped out onto the landing to answer.

'Hello?' I whispered.

'Mary? I can barely hear you. Are you in the middle of something?'

'No. Nothing at all.' I glanced towards the open bedroom door. Ethan hadn't moved. I could hardly tell Owen that I had been lying on a bed with a man; and not just a man – Leo's brother. What had come over me? It was those hypnotic clouds: they had raced away with my senses. 'But shouldn't you be in the middle of something? Haven't you a class to teach?'

'It's a free period.'

'Aren't they for marking, not ringing me?'

'I don't set homework so close to exams. The students have enough pressure, don't they?' I smiled: it was the sort

124

of thing Leo would say. 'Besides, I'd rather talk to you than do marking.'

'That's good,' I said. It was a fatuous reply, but I wasn't used to people – men – saying nice things to me, and I was too aware of Ethan's proximity to say anything more.

'You sound distracted. Are you sure I'm not interrupting?'

'Sorry. I'm taking Dotty for a walk. You know what she's like.'

Owen laughed, such a warm, understanding laugh that I felt doubly guilty for lying to him.

'I do. You need all your wits about you. I won't keep you. I was reminded earlier that there's a PTA meeting tonight. I've been press-ganged to join. Are you going?'

'Yes, I'll be there.'

'Great. Would you like to go for a drink afterwards?'

The bed creaked loudly as Ethan moved.

'Yes, I'd love to. I'll see you later.'

I returned to the bedroom, my socks skidding on the wooden floor. I sat on the edge of the bed, brushed the dust off the soles of my feet, and put my walking boots on again. The mattress rocked as Ethan sat up. There was an odd atmosphere as we sat on opposite sides of the bed, back to back, putting our shoes on; as if it were the end of an affair, and we were about to return to our ordinary lives. I shook my head, casting off such stupid imaginings.

'Was that Leo on the phone?' Ethan asked, as we met at the bedroom door. 'Why didn't you tell him you were with me?'

'It wasn't Leo.'

Ethan paused, as if he were processing that thought.

'Are you seeing someone else? Already?'

Perhaps I was still feeling guilty about misleading Owen, but something about Ethan's tone – about that 'already' – rubbed me up the wrong way.

'What if I am? It's none of your business.'

'Perhaps not, but . . .'

'And what do you mean, already? It's almost five months since Leo left.'

'I know. I just didn't think you would have got over him so soon. Who is it?'

'No one you know.' I couldn't meet his eye. 'A teacher at Broadholme.'

'A teacher?' Ethan shook his head. 'What did you do, scour the local schools and colleges for a Leo substitute?'

I pushed past him and stomped off down the stairs, but Ethan ran down behind me and wouldn't shut up.

'You're not moving on, you're moving backwards. You know I'm right – I can see it in your face. You can't wheel this teacher in to replace Leo and pretend nothing ever happened.'

'It's nothing to do with replacing Leo! How could I replace him? I was with him for over half my life. No one will ever know me as well as he does.' Although he didn't know this me, this grumpy, argumentative me. But that was besides the point. 'Owen seems a decent, kind man. I like him. He's good company. What's wrong with that?'

126

'Everything! You're thirty-eight, not ninety! You should be having fun, excitement, adventure – a rich, colourful life, not settling for more beige.'

'How do I have adventures with two children, an ex-husband, a dog, a house, a mother, a mother-in-law, and a huge heap of responsibilities? Real life *is* beige.'

'And what does Leo think about this teacher? Does he know?'

'No. But as he's already tried to fix me up with one of Clark's friends, I shouldn't think he'll care. So you've no reason to object, have you?'

It was a rhetorical question, so I hadn't expected to see such a struggle on Ethan's face as he tried to work out an answer. He hadn't given one before the front door opened, and the estate agent tentatively peered in.

'How's it going?' she asked. 'Do you need more time?'

'We've had more than enough,' I said. 'Thanks for minding Dotty.' I plucked the lead from her hand and stalked off up the lane, leaving Ethan behind.

To their great disgust, Mum would be babysitting Jonas and Ava while I attended the PTA meeting; usually I had relied on Leo being home, and although Ava argued vociferously that they were too old to need a minder, I still didn't feel comfortable leaving them alone. I called at Mum's garage on my way back from Waterman's Cottage to check that she wouldn't mind hanging on a little longer while I met Owen for a drink.

I knocked on the door as usual and went in without waiting for an answer.

'Mum?'

The living area, a combined lounge and dining kitchen, was empty. I was about to check the bathroom when the bedroom door opened a sliver, and Mum appeared, wrapped in a silky dressing gown. She pulled the door closed behind her.

'What are you wearing?' I asked. The dressing gown was plum, with a Japanese-style pattern on it. I'd never seen her wear anything so colourful or so impractical.

'A dressing gown.'

'That's not the one I bought you for Christmas.'

'No, well, I'm saving that one for best.'

Now I was suspicious. The one I had bought her for Christmas was a fluffy old-lady affair, with a high neck and big buttons. There was no way anyone would think it better than the slinky number she was wearing.

'Why are you in your dressing gown in the middle of the afternoon? Are you ill?'

'I was having a bath. Stop being so nosy, Mary. I don't pry into your affairs.'

She didn't need to – she simply watched it all from her window. Not that I had affairs – or not the interesting kind, anyway. Mum tightened the belt on her robe, and as she did, the neckline sagged for a moment, revealing more wrinkled cleavage than I could ever have wished to see.

'What's the matter with you?' Mum asked. 'You'll turn the milk sour with that face.'

'It's the only one I've got.' I sighed. 'It's just something Ethan said.'

'I might have known. He always did stir you up like no one else. I was worried for a while . . .' She stopped, which was a rare thing: she didn't usually hold her opinion back. 'I mustn't keep you. Did you want something?'

'Only to see if you'd mind staying with the children for an extra hour or two tonight.'

'I suppose I could do an hour. Are you expecting the meeting to go on?'

'Yes.' Two lies in an hour! My conscience cracked under the strain. 'Actually, no. I thought I might go out for a drink afterwards. With one of the teachers,' I added, giving full disclosure.

'Yes, okay.' She obviously hadn't heard me, or else there would have been a million questions. She fiddled with the door handle behind her, and then suddenly she coughed, but it was a fraction too late. I had already heard it – the sound of movement in the bedroom behind her. Dear God, what would I have seen if I had walked in there earlier?

'Are you . . . ?' What word could I possibly use, that wouldn't cement the horrific images whisking through my head? 'Entertaining?'

'Is it so unlikely?' Frankly, yes it was. Apart from the obvious objections – she was old, and my mother – she had shown no interest in any other man since my dad vanished. What had this mystery man got that had won her over? On second thoughts, perhaps it was better not to know.

'That's great news,' I said, because, ignoring the revolting mental images, it could only be a good thing if she had something to occupy her other than finding criticisms of me.

'Yes, it is,' Mum said, and then she smiled and I caught my breath – because for an instant, this wrinkled, grey-haired woman had the look of the warm-hearted mum from my early childhood that I had all but forgotten about.

Chapter Twelve

We weren't rumbled until the very end of the PTA meeting, so close to making a successful getaway that I had mentally removed my gloves and balaclava.

The meeting had droned on for a couple of hours, while simple decisions were broken down into so many unnecessary details that the original question was buried under all the rubble. Our esteemed leader Marissa, never my greatest fan, had been a model of restraint, with only two pointed references in my direction: once when she had mentioned what a gay afternoon she'd had, and once when she had delighted in describing someone as a 'man's man' with an arch look at her cronies.

When the 'any other business' was finally exhausted, Daisy leaned over and whispered in my ear.

'Thank God for that. I think if I'd heard her say 'but' one more time, I'd have jumped over the table and head-butted her.'

I laughed.

'What day is it? I feel like we've been here for weeks. I'm desperate for a drink now.'

'Fab idea. Shall we sneak off to the Hat & Feathers? I could furtively round up a few of the others.'

'Oh . . . well . . . I suppose you could. I've already agreed to go with Owen.'

'You're going to the pub with Owen?' I don't know why I'd bothered lowering my voice; Daisy's excited shriek caught the attention of the entire room.

'What's this?' Marissa turned back from the door. She looked at Owen. 'Are we adjourning somewhere for drinks, Mr Ferguson?' She glanced at her watch. 'I can give you an hour.'

I couldn't believe I had risked catching my mother *in flagrante* just to spend another hour with Marissa.

'It's not group drinks,' Owen said. 'I'm going out with Mary.'

It was clear from the gasps, wide eyes, and flapping mouths that most of the other members of the PTA took this as a declaration of a relationship rather than of Owen's plans for the next sixty minutes. Even Daisy nudged me and bulged her eyes in a gruesome way that I took to mean she wanted further information.

'Well!' I'd never seen Marissa speechless before. I didn't know whether to be relieved or affronted: was it so unlikely that I would have a date? Even my mother had looked less surprised. 'That is interesting news! Of course we wouldn't dream of getting in your way.'

I groaned: the news would be all round school by tomorrow. Ava was going to kill me, unless the embarrassment killed her first.

*

'It's a two-minute wonder,' Owen said, apropos of nothing, after nearly an hour in the pub. I thought I'd hidden my anxiety about being gossiped over, and been a bright and cheery companion; obviously not. 'We're not interesting enough to make the headlines for long.'

That was true, but it was also utterly depressing. I couldn't help remembering Ethan's remarks. Were we too beige to be noticed? I glanced down: jeans and a grey jersey top. No colour there either. Had I always been so invisible?

My bonus hour was up. I picked up my bag and Owen followed me out to the car park. He waited at my side as I unlocked the car.

'Do you think it's time we tried something more than dog walks and snatched drinks?' he asked.

'More?'

'Come to my house one night. I'll cook.'

'One night?' What did that mean? How much of the night did he have in mind? My fingers were glued so tightly to the key fob that I inadvertently locked the car again.

'The kids are with me this weekend, but what about Friday or Saturday next week?'

'For the night?' I was being ridiculously skittish, but nerves and uncertainty were making me stupid.

'I hadn't planned that far ahead.' Owen's cheeks darkened, but curiously, instead of feeling more embarrassed, I was relieved and touched that he was finding this as awkward as I was. He was a good and kind man, just as I had told Ethan.

133

I liked him. Perhaps it was time I took the next step – added some colour to my dull life, made myself visible. I could do this, couldn't I?

'Let's say Friday,' I said, and I pressed a kiss to his lips and escaped before I could change my mind.

Ethan knocked on the kitchen door next morning, and strolled in without waiting for a reply.

'This is what you do when you have the house to yourself! I've caught you out.'

He had caught me having a cup of tea and reading a book at the kitchen table: a fifteen-minute break amid a list of jobs as long as both my arms. I was timing it with my watch. Eleven minutes to go. Even so, I had to justify myself.

'I'm thinking,' I said.

'Thirsty work, is it?'

'Yes.'

'Hungry work too?' He pulled out a chair, sat down and put a packet of Jammy Dodgers in front of me. Goodness knows where he had been hiding those: his clothes were too well fitted to allow any bulges to go undetected.

'What's that?'

'A packet of Jammy Dodgers.' He pushed them nearer to me. 'Also known as a peace offering. I was an idiot yesterday. Sorry.'

'Only about yesterday? Or does that sorry cover the whole thirty-nine years of being an idiot?'

'Don't push your luck.' Ethan laughed and ripped open the packet of biscuits. He took one and demolished it in two bites. He shoved the packet again so it nudged my hand. 'Get eating. They're your favourites, aren't they?'

'Yes. How do you know that?' I couldn't imagine Leo knowing that I had a favourite biscuit. Such mundane things passed him by, like how the toilet roll was miraculously replaced in the bathroom, and how there was a constant supply of clean socks in his drawer.

'They were the ones you always picked out of Mum's biscuit tin,' Ethan said.

He'd noticed that? Not only noticed – remembered it too, after all this time. I pulled my sleeve down over my watch, so I couldn't see my break coming to an end.

'Did you decide to rent the cottage?' I asked, taking a Jammy Dodger and nibbling around the jam centre: it was impossible to eat them any other way.

'Yes, until October.'

'I didn't think you'd resist that love nest.'

'Who could?'

'Not me.' Ethan waggled his eyebrows at me in a suggestive way, and I laughed, adding, 'Don't worry, next time you're on that bed I'm sure you'll have a much more appealing companion. When do you move?'

'Probably over the next couple of weeks. Mum's managing well now she doesn't need the stick.'

'She'll be fine. I'll keep an eye on her.'

'I know you will. That's one of the reasons I came over. Are you around next week to check in on her? I need to go to London for a few days.'

'Next week? Well . . . yes, of course I can be.' I thought I sounded convincing, but I didn't convince Ethan. It struck me for the second time today that he was more observant than I gave him credit for.

'What is it?' he asked. 'Do you already have plans?'

'Not definite ones. I wanted to go back to a bookshop I discovered the other day. There was something odd about the way the owners reacted to the Alice Hornby biography.' It had been bugging me ever since my visit to the Archer's bookshop. The more I thought about it, the more I wondered if they had some knowledge of or connection to Alice – though I couldn't see how, as I had spent weeks poring over her family tree and working my way through all the leaves and branches. 'It might be nothing, but I'd like to go back. I've no time this week, as Leo has emailed me a list of urgent research.'

'Okay. You do that on Monday, and I'll go to London on Tuesday.' And that was it – it was so easy. I wasn't used to my own wishes coming first, or, quite often, coming anywhere at all. 'And this Sunday you can come next door for brunch. I promised Mum the full works, New York style. Unless you're seeing your teacher.'

'I don't think so. Brunch sounds good.'

'Have you been seeing him long?'

'Not really.' I kept it brief, not wishing to spark another

136

row; although it was tempting to argue in the hope of more Jammy Dodgers.

'So it's early days? Quite casual?'

'I'm not planning a double wedding with Leo, if that's what you're asking. Or one at any time in the future.'

I stood up and went over to the sink, pouring away the remains of my tea. It was time to get back to work. Ethan was studying me too closely for comfort. His chair scraped across the floor as he followed me.

'Don't you think you'll marry again?'

'I can't imagine it.' I shrugged. Six months ago, I had believed in the whole 'death us do part' business. I would need some convincing to believe in that again. 'Will you? Surely two divorces must have shown you that you're not cut out for marriage.'

'I'd give it one more shot. But it would have to be with the right person this time.'

I laughed.

'Third time lucky? Good luck finding her. Wouldn't it be easier if we were all branded at birth with the name of the person we were destined to be with?'

Ethan should have smiled: it was the sort of nonsense we'd exchanged hundreds of times before. But he seemed to be considering the idea seriously.

'It wouldn't work,' he said. 'Because sometimes circumstances get in the way of even the most perfect match. And you need to allow for second chances. Sometimes there's a right person for one half of your life, and a right person for the other.'

I didn't want to dwell on any of that. There weren't enough Jammy Dodgers left in the packet to help me digest those thoughts.

'I'd better get on,' I said, and Ethan nodded and opened the back door. Before he could go, I called out. 'Ethan?' He looked back. 'Am I invisible?'

This time he did smile, but not in recognition of nonsense. He understood; I'd known he would.

'No,' he said. 'I can see you, Mary.'

The Archer's bookshop was as quiet as on my last visit, but this time old Mrs Archer was snoozing in her wheelchair behind the desk when I walked in. The shop bell didn't wake her, so I opened and closed the door a few times until I saw a glint as her eyes flicked open.

'Bridie!' Mrs Archer made a surprisingly loud and grating noise, rather like an infant blowing into a recorder for the first time. 'It's her!'

I wasn't as offended by this lukewarm greeting as I might once have been; in fact, I felt right at home. Ava had developed a habit of referring to me as 'her' since Leo moved out; that was when she deigned to acknowledge my existence at all. She hadn't spoken to me for several days, not since the news broke that I had gone out for a drink with Owen – apart from the initial accusation that I had ruined her life. I couldn't imagine what she would do when she discovered that I was having dinner at his house. Thank goodness we had Jonas to maintain some semblance of harmony at home.

Bridie came through from the back room.

'Hello,' she said, employing the more customary greeting, even if her tone and expression lacked a shopkeeper's usual bonhomie.

'Hello!' I sang back. It was hard not to overcompensate with cheeriness in the face of such overt suspicion. Mrs Archer pulled her blanket closer around her, as if she feared my smile might infect her with joy. 'Do you remember I came in last week to talk about my husband's biography of Alice Hornby?'

'We remember,' Bridie said. Mrs Archer snuffled. I took that as permission to carry on.

'I had the impression that you weren't keen on the idea.' That was an understatement and a half. 'I've brought a copy with me. I thought you might like to read it and then you can see for yourselves how respectful it is. No muck,' I added, for the benefit of the old lady.

I held out the book, but they recoiled as if it smelt of petrol and was making a ticking noise.

'Please read it,' I said, and put it down on the desk. 'All we want to do is raise Alice's profile, and introduce more people to the pleasure of reading her books. Why should Yorkshire and the Brontës have all the fame?'

At last I detected a glimmer of interest, and the temperature thawed by one degree; if I'd known that a bit of Yorkshire-bashing would do the trick, I'd have tried it last week. Bridie picked up the book – hallelujah! – and gingerly turned the pages.

'Oh Mum,' she said, stopping at a photograph, though I couldn't tell which one. 'Would you look at that?'

She bent forward to show her mother the picture and I peered over the desk. They were looking at a double-page spread, showing the oldest photograph we'd been able to find of Alice's family home and, opposite it, a picture of how it looked now. The modern photo had been taken at the annual meeting of the Alice Hornby Society; the house was privately owned, but the owners allowed us to meet in the grounds. The house had been updated so sympathetically, that it looked largely unchanged; but the gardens had been landscaped and the sunshine brought out all the vivid colours. Mrs Archer said nothing, but a tiny, knotty hand emerged from the blankets and turned over a few more pages.

'Do you know the house, or the Hornby family?' I asked.

'There's a connection through Mum,' Bridie conceded. Archer? It definitely wasn't a name that featured on the family tree, but I supposed it could be a remarriage that I had missed. I was burning with questions, but before I could get started, Mrs Archer snapped shut the book and retreated into a pile of tweed.

'We'll read it,' Bridie said, stowing the book away in a desk drawer. 'No promises, mind. Non-fiction isn't too popular around here.'

Nor was fiction, judging by the state of the shelves; I couldn't see any new gaps since my last visit. Even if they liked the biography, it seemed unlikely that they would ever sell a copy. But this had gone beyond sales now: there was some mystery here to do with Alice Hornby and the Archer family and I wasn't going to rest until I found out exactly what it was.

Chapter Thirteen

I wasn't chickening out of my date with Owen when Daisy rang, but I certainly had more than a few wobbles.

'Just making sure you're still planning to turn up,' Daisy said, knowing me too well, even though I had been careful to express nothing but enthusiasm all week.

'Yes, of course I am.' My indignation was pure bluster. 'I'm dressed and ready to go when Mum toddles over.'

'You mean when she tears herself from the arms of her lover?'

'Urgh, don't. That image isn't going to put me in a romantic mood for tonight.'

'Have you met this mystery man yet?'

'No, not even a glimpse. She must smuggle him in and out under cover of darkness, so that's not a good sign, is it?'

'Perhaps he's a toy boy half her age.'

'That would make him younger than me!'

'There you go. She might be afraid he'll take one look at you and switch to a younger model.'

I snorted at that, and wandered over to the window. There was a car parked on the road again, the same blue Ford that

I saw there most days. Whoever it belonged to, he was pretty keen to spend his time with Mum. I hardly ever saw her now, and when I did, she was unrecognisable: smiling, glowing, with newly dyed hair the colour of Caribbean sand, and smarter clothes. She was looking younger by the day, while I went the opposite way. But why should I be jealous? I was going out for dinner with a man, wasn't I?

'What are you wearing?' Daisy asked. 'You have made an effort, haven't you? I know, take a photo and send it to me and I'll check if it's okay.'

I did, though I wasn't planning to change, whatever she said. It had taken ages to decide on what I had on now: newish dark jeans and a midnight-blue silk blouse with sheer bell sleeves. At least it was a colour – not grey, or beige – although with my black hair it did make me look like a sorceress – or I hoped I looked like a sorceress, not a wicked old hag.

'You'll do,' Daisy said, when she phoned back. 'But take off the necklace. It's the one Leo gave you, isn't it? You can't be thinking about him tonight. Have you shaved your legs? Are you wearing proper lingerie, not those droopy grey things I saw before? Have you packed some condoms?'

'Oh God, I can't do this.' I sank on to the bed, feeling queasy, not so much butterflies but huge bats flapping away in my stomach. 'I don't know what to do. There's only ever been Leo. What if he looks different? What if he does different things? I'm going to make an idiot of myself.'

'No, you're not. Don't sound so terrified. You fancy him, don't you?'

'I like him.'

'That's not what I asked. When you see him, do you want to drag him somewhere private and tear his clothes off? Do you struggle to keep your hands off him? When you kiss him, do you forget everything else?'

'We've only been on dog walks and to the pub. And it's not really like that, is it, in normal life?'

'Yes. As far as I remember,' Daisy added, sighing. 'Wasn't it with Leo?'

'I suppose it might have been, in the early days.' My over-riding memory was of the awkwardness. After using the law to resist me for a long time, Leo had finally succumbed when, on my sixteenth birthday, I had thrown myself on him and put him in a position where he couldn't say no. Neither of us had had the first idea what we were doing. Leo had subse-quently taken the obvious course of buying a book, which had terrified us both so much that we left it to trial and error after that.

'Are you really telling me that you've never felt so overcome by passion that you lose all sense?' Daisy gasped. 'Oh Mary, is it because Leo's gay? Did you never have a proper relation-ship?'

'Of course we did. You have to believe he managed to overlook my femininity at least twice.' A whole new lorry load of worries rolled into my head. 'What if . . . you know

'. . . Owen can't manage it? I'm tying myself in knots, fretting about what might happen, but he might not even fancy me.'

'Mary, calm down. You don't have to do anything unless you want to, even if he cooks your dinner.' I nodded, pointlessly as she couldn't see me. 'And I think we can take it as a given that he does fancy you. Why else would he lure you to his house? To show off his spag bol?' She laughed. 'Irish nymphs with glossy black hair and emerald eyes are pretty rare in these parts. You'd be surprised by how many men fancy you.'

'None, now Leo's taken himself off that list?'

'Seriously, have you walked round in a blindfold all your life? Have you never so much as flirted with a man who wasn't Leo?'

'No,' I said – but I didn't say it quickly enough. There had been a fatal moment of hesitation, and Daisy was on it like a vulture.

'Mary?' I could picture Daisy's expression as clearly as if she'd been in the room: the surprise, the excitement, the curiosity. 'Who?'

'No one,' I said. I stood up as memories jostled to take root in my head, the reminders that I had once glimpsed the passion Daisy spoke of, had once come close to losing all sense. There was no reason why I couldn't find that with Owen, was there? Abandoning the flat shoes I had pulled out of the wardrobe, I picked up a pair of sexy heels instead. 'Mum's here. I've got to go.'

Owen hadn't made spag bol. He served up a proper three-course meal of salmon, tarragon chicken, and melt-in-the-middle chocolate pudding, which we ate at a candlelit table in his tiny kitchen. The obvious care he had taken to get the food and the atmosphere just right made me so tense that I was petrified I might bring back the delicious food at any moment. Gulping wine was doing nothing to steady my nerves, despite my best efforts.

'Coffee?' Owen asked, when I finally finished my pudding, unable to stretch it out any longer. I nodded, and watched as he opened the cupboard and reached past the regular coffee cups for oversized mugs. It obviously hadn't escaped his notice that I'd drunk more than my share of two bottles of wine. 'Go through to the lounge and make yourself comfortable.'

I tottered next door, wondering what he expected me to do: loll on the sofa as if I were at a Roman banquet, waiting for him to feed me after-dinner mints? I prowled around the room, inspecting the photographs of his children, the small collection of books, all on art, and the paintings on the wall. Owen startled me when he came in and I almost toppled forwards and banged my nose against the glass of the picture I was peering at.

'Sorry!' I said. 'I was trying to decipher the signature.' That was harder to say than I'd anticipated 'You painted this, didn't you?'

'Yes.' He acknowledged it without embarrassment or false modesty. I liked that. 'It's of Loch Shiel in the Highlands. We spent a few summer holidays there when the children were small.'

'It's beautiful.' I took the mug that Owen held out, sat down on the sofa and slurped the coffee. It was strong, and sobering even in two mouthfuls. 'Do you not go there anymore?'

'No. It's not the same going back on my own, and when I go away with the children they want shops and nightlife, not mountains and solitude.' Owen sat down beside me. 'What are you doing this summer?'

'We're going to St Ives. We go every year.'

'We?'

It took my staggering brain a moment to catch up with Owen's meaning, and when it did I felt mortified. I'd answered automatically – and of course I'd meant me, Leo, Jonas, and Ava, with the usual assortment of mothers and friends coming and going. I booked the house every August, ready for next year; and last August I'd had no reason to suspect that this year the tectonic plates beneath our marriage would have shifted and pulled us apart. I'd paid the deposit on booking; the balance would have been collected by direct debit by now.

'I don't know,' I said. Perhaps I looked as woebegone as I felt, because Owen shifted so that his arm lay across the back of the sofa, resting with gentle strength against my shoulders. I leaned back into it, soaking up what comfort I could. 'I'd not thought about holidays, and how they'll change. I suppose it will just be the three of us now.'

I lapsed into silence as I tried to imagine me, Jonas, and Ava rattling around the St Ives house for five weeks. Perhaps Mum would join us for a couple of weeks as she usually did – unless she made other plans with her mystery man. There would be no Leo, no Audrey – no break for me from the pressure of entertaining teenagers through the summer. But it might be worse: perhaps I would have a longer break than I could wish for. Leo and Clark might want to take the children away on holiday themselves, maybe somewhere more exciting than Cornwall. What would I do then, on my own?

My head drooped back on to Owen's arm, as if it couldn't support the dead weight of these thoughts any longer. Owen reached forward, took the almost empty mug from my hand, and put it down on the coffee table next to his. Hooking his arm around my shoulders, he pulled me towards him and kissed me.

This wasn't the sort of kiss he had given me before. Even I, with all my inexperience to draw on, recognised that this was a good kiss: that he was painting a passionate invitation with his lips. Like a fledgling bird, still not confident its wings would work, I put my arms around Owen, and it was fine: somewhere between the squishiness of Leo and the muscle of Ethan; comfortable and solid. I could cope with this.

But then, as I was busy thinking that this wasn't too bad – was, in fact, quite pleasant – I realised that Owen had moved his hands to the front and he was unbuttoning my blouse.

Cool air grazed my skin as he pushed the two halves aside, pulled down my bra, and dipped his head to my breasts.

His hair tickled my chin as I looked down. Panic flooded my brain. Was my muffin top too obvious? Was my bra too plain? Could he see my stretch marks from there? Had I eradicated every bit of body hair? I sucked in my stomach. How could I kiss him and hold my breath at the same time? Should I be making an appreciative noise? Was I rubbish at this already? Oh God, I was too old for this.

'Mary?'

'Yes?' I hadn't realised that Owen had stopped until he spoke.

'Just checking that you're still awake. You're very . . . still.'

Still? Did he mean stiff? Unresponsive? Frigid? Generally terrible at this? Why had Leo never told me? I wished I hadn't drunk so much, so my head would stop whirring. Or better still, I wished I had drunk more, so all these mortifying thoughts would drown and leave my mind full of lovely, peaceful nothingness.

'I . . .' I didn't know what to say, or do. Should I shove his head back down and try to be less still? Before I could decide, Owen pulled my bra back up, tucking my breasts in tenderly as if they were children going to bed for the night. He fastened my blouse, and once my stomach was safely covered, I let out a big breath.

'Owen, I'm sorry . . .'

'No need to be. Tell me – is it me or the timing?'

'Me.' He was looking at me with such kindness, such concern, that I couldn't bear to say anything else. 'I'd been with Leo since I was fifteen. I thought he was forever. I've no idea what I'm doing now.'

'You're doing fine, Mary.' He kissed me – a kiss on the lips, but quite different than before, tender not passionate. 'There's no hurry. Do you want another coffee?'

I shook my head. All I wanted was to be at home, muffled under six jumpers, smothered by two duvets, and as far from naked as it was possible to be. How did you look someone in the face – someone you didn't know all that well – when they had seen and tasted your breasts? Especially when it hadn't been a mutual unveiling: the humiliation of this aborted seduction was all mine. I was pretty good at ignoring reality, and a master in denying my feelings, but just at this moment embarrassment stained my skin like a whole-body tattoo, and I couldn't see beyond it.

'I think I'd better go,' I said.

'There's no need to rush off.'

'I don't want to keep my mum up late.' I glanced at my watch: it was barely ten. My shoes had fallen off, and I shoved my feet in them, my head spinning as it readjusted to the altitude.

'I'll walk you home.'

My attempt to protest was lost as I stumbled and crashed into the doorpost. Owen took my arm and steered me back to my house; the weather had turned since I had left, and the rain lashed us as we hurried along the road as fast as my heels would allow. Owen didn't hang about; as soon as we reached the top of my drive he kissed me and walked quickly away, shoulders hunched against the rain.

The blue Ford was parked outside, and a light shone through the curtains at Mum's garage, as her friend presumably waited for her to return. I unlocked my front door, slipped out of my heels, and crept around the downstairs, ready to tell Mum that she could go home – but she wasn't there.

The living room ceiling creaked, and laughter and mumbled conversation floated down. Was Mum with Jonas? It seemed unlikely – but so did the fact that not so many minutes ago I'd been flashing my boobs at a man who wasn't Leo. I padded up the stairs in my bare feet, and pushed open Jonas' door. He was sitting on his desk chair, games controller in his hand, and Ethan was beside him, sprawled on Ava's fluffy pink beanbag, his entire focus on a bloody shoot-out on the TV screen.

It was a minute before either of them noticed me, a minute in which I saw Jonas smile more than he often did during a whole day. Then Ethan groaned, tossed down his controller, glanced towards Jonas and saw me. He smiled, and that smile loosened my taut nerves so that I relaxed for the first time all day.

'Just in time to witness my annihilation,' he said. He stood up from the beanbag, in an athletic move that didn't involve my usual technique of falling onto hands and knees first. 'I'll beat you next time, Joe.'

'No chance.' Jonas grinned, and raised a hand in my direction. 'Hi, Mum. Don't drip on my stuff, will you?'

I backed out of his room and Ethan followed me downstairs. He grabbed the towel from the cloakroom and threw it towards me, but I was a hopeless catcher when sober and had no chance now, when I seemed to have at least four hands, all going in different directions. Ethan laughed, picked up the towel, and moved behind me to dry my hair, stroking the towel down from the crown of my head to where the damp ends clung to my shoulders. Standing in the hall, shivering as the tiles chilled my bare feet, it still felt weirdly more intimate than anything Owen had done that night. I snatched the towel off Ethan and stepped away.

'You're in London,' I said.

'Nope, I'm right here. I came back this afternoon.'

'What have you done with Mum?'

'Buried her under the patio. Did you want her somewhere else?'

Wide eyed, I stared through the kitchen door and towards the back of the house.

'She went home. She had company.' Ethan smiled. 'Are you drunk, Mary Black?'

'No. Yes. A little. Why do you always call me Mary Black?'

'It's your name.'

'Is it?' Why hadn't I thought about this before? I had only become a Black when I married Leo. Should I have stopped being a Black when he divorced me? Only yesterday I had bought something online, and automatically selected the drop-down option 'Mrs'. But I wasn't, was I? And I wasn't Miss Black – that was Ava. No one warned you that the side effects of divorce would be making themselves felt so long after the event. 'Should I not change it now?'

'No, keep it. It suits you. You should always stay as Mary Black.'

With his hands on my upper arms, two patches of warmth seeping through the flimsy fabric of my sleeves, he manoeuvred me into the living room and down onto the sofa.

'Water or coffee?' he asked.

'Water.' I shuddered, remembering the taste of coffee on Owen's tongue. I shut my eyes, but the embarrassment was too deeply ingrained to go away that easily. The next thing I knew, something fluffy tickled my foot and my leg jerked up.

'Watch out, Cinderella, you almost knocked my teeth out.' Ethan was kneeling in front of me, my slippers in his hands. He grabbed my foot. 'Your feet are like ice. I presume these are yours. Too small for Jonas, and far too uncool for Ava.'

'Thank you.' I mustered as much dignity as I could, but there was precious little left at this point in the evening. Where had the calm, unflappable version of me gone? Had Leo taken her away with him, and left this idiot in her place?

'Your mum said you were out with your teacher friend tonight.' I suspected Ethan was translating what she had actually said. 'Go anywhere nice?'

'His house. He made dinner.'

'Did he?' There was something off about Ethan's tone, but I couldn't figure out what. 'Good cook?'

'Yes.' I patted my stomach, which felt like a balloon hanging around my waist. 'I'll need extra dog walks to get rid of this.'

I reached for my glass of water, and looked up to find Ethan had joined me on the sofa and was staring at my stomach. Perhaps I shouldn't have drawn attention to how large it was. In his glamorous New York circle, anyone over size six was probably considered obese.

'Did you go out like that?'

'Yes.' Was I now obese and badly dressed? Okay, I had on fluffy slippers that an eighty-year-old might think old-fashioned, but from the ankle up I was presentable, wasn't I? 'It's not beige,' I added defensively.

'It's not fastened properly. Your buttons are done up wrong.'

I checked, and he was right – it would, I suppose, have been an odd thing for him to lie about.

'Have you just had sex with him?'

The baldness of the question, flung into what had been a comfortable silence, slapped me back to a degree of sobriety.

'What if I have? We're both single.'

'Only just. You weren't meant to leap into bed with the first man you met.'

'What was I *meant* to do? Meet in the presence of a chaperone and let him occasionally kiss my fingers? Times have moved on.'

'*You've* not. This isn't the way you behave.'

'What do you know about me? You're my ex-husband's brother, not my diary.'

'This has nothing to do with my relationship with Leo, only with you. I've known you as long as he has.'

One week less, but it was true; if Leo had been my rock growing up, Ethan had been my oxygen. His return to Lancashire had made me realise how much I had missed his friendship when he left for New York. He was watching me now, leaning forward so his arms rested on his knees, tension in his shoulders and disappointment in his face.

'Of course I didn't sleep with him,' I said. My head dropped onto the back of the sofa and I covered my face with my hands. 'It was probably the most excruciating experience of my life. We didn't get past unbuttoning my blouse. I can't do it. It's too terrifying, and too embarrassing. No one has seen me naked apart from Leo.'

'Not true.' He spoke quietly, but I didn't mistake what he said. I removed my hands, and looked at Ethan. He was leaning back against the sofa now, a teasing smile on his lips, dazzling blue eyes shining right into mine.

'What's not true?'

'I've seen you naked.'

I must have been much, much drunker than I thought. I stared at him, trying to understand.

'What? When? You haven't . . . we didn't . . .'

'You were the first fully naked girl I ever saw.' Ethan stretched out his long legs, and crossed them at the ankle.

'We were sixteen. Leo was away, and all the parents were out. You were sunbathing in the garden naked, and then you suddenly stood up and cartwheeled down to the end of the lawn and back again.'

I didn't remember, but I didn't doubt that I had done it. I had felt different that summer, the summer I turned sixteen. I was confident, excited. Exams were over, and I thought I'd done well; Leo was mine, properly mine since my birthday; the future looked glorious. What had happened? Where had the cartwheeling girl gone? *She* wasn't beige; *she* wasn't mortified at the idea of being seen naked. I longed to be that girl again.

'Where were you?' I asked.

'At my bedroom window.'

'And you watched? That's disgusting. I was your brother's girlfriend.'

'I was sixteen. You were naked. It was utterly not disgusting.'

I should have been embarrassed. I should have been mortified for the second time tonight, desperate to hide under those six jumpers and two duvets. So why wasn't I? Why did I feel . . . alive? As if electricity was flowing around the room, and had just shocked me back to life?

'I'm surprised it didn't scar you forever,' I said.

Ethan smiled. It was my smile, the smile he saved for me.

'I think perhaps it did.'

156

Chapter Fourteen

I was in the back garden, playing tug-of-war with a lawn-mower twice my age, when Leo brought the children back on Sunday evening.

'What are you doing?'

Hot, sweaty, and knackered, I was in no mood for daft questions.

'Ballroom dancing. I've picked a bloody awful partner.'

'Where's the gardener? Is he ill?'

'No, he's expensive.' Too expensive to afford now that Leo's income was divided between two households. He acknowledged that with a sigh.

'Can't Jonas do it?'

'He's probably more expensive.' That was unfair. I didn't always have to bribe him to do chores, unlike Ava, who wouldn't budge for anything less than paper money, but I'd been at pains not to make Jonas feel he was the man of the house and obliged to look after us. My CV was expanding daily with all the new skills I was learning. It would have been so much more efficient if Leo had given six months' notice of his intention to leave, so we could have paid to have some jobs done while we had the money.

'Are the children okay?' I asked, following Leo as he prowled around the garden, inspecting the flowerbeds. He was sure to find them a disappointment: my fingers were definitely not green, and I didn't dare pull anything up, as I couldn't tell between weeds and flowers.

'Yes, they had a good weekend.' Leo turned his inspection from the plants to me. 'Did you?'

'Yes.' Apart from the naked boob business with Owen, the naked cartwheel business with Ethan, and the naked terror of seeing either of them that had kept me trapped in the house until now. Dotty was sulking and I would have to take her on a long yomp tomorrow to make friends with her again. 'What is it? Why are you looking at me like that?'

'Ava said that you've been seeing a man.'

'Don't tell me,' I said, rolling my eyes very much as Ava might have done. 'She was grumbling about him being a teacher.'

'She may have voiced an objection of that nature.'

I laughed, and Leo smiled and took hold of my hand.

'Are you happy? Is it serious?' His gaze roamed over my face, as if he were looking for something. 'Have you . . .?'

'Have I what? Are you asking if I've had sex with him?' I snatched my hand back. 'What is it with you Black men? Why are you so obsessed with my sex life? It was bad enough when Ethan asked.'

'Ethan? When have you seen him?'

'He's living next door. It's hard to avoid him.'

'It will be better when he moves out. You're only like this when he's around. I'll have a word with him, and tell him to stop aggravating you.'

Like what? I wanted to ask. Grumpy? Argumentative? Myself? I stopped at the bottom of the garden, and looked back towards our house standing shoulder to shoulder with Audrey's, only a low fence separating them. I glanced at Ethan's bedroom window: no movement there today, other than the ghost of a sixteen-year-old, one who could have teased me mercilessly for what he had seen, but instead had kept his secret for over twenty years. Why had he done that?

'Don't say anything. It's not Ethan's fault. I can be bad-tempered whether he's here or not. You just never saw it because you were so easy to live with.' I linked my arm with Leo's. 'Have a word with that blasted lawnmower, if anything. It's easily as old and as irritating as Mum.' I led Leo over to the bench beside the pond. Hundreds of tiny tadpoles swarmed around in the water, just about visible through the murky water and the strange furry green things that were floating in it. Another job for my endless to-do list. 'Sit down for a while. I want to tell you about the strange bookshop I went to this week.'

I told him all about my bizarre visits to Archer's, and how I was convinced there was some connection to Alice Hornby.

'Family?' he asked. 'How did we overlook them? You were

meticulous in going over the family tree. You wouldn't have missed them.'

I squeezed his arm, touched by that vote of confidence.

'There are definitely no Archers on the family tree, even at a distance. I've checked again. But I had the impression that they might be related to the servants. I think the old lady knew the housekeeper's name. At the time, I thought she'd muttered "crumbs", but now I wonder if she actually said "Coombs".'

'It's possible,' Leo agreed. 'We checked the servants as well, though, didn't we?'

'Yes, but it was harder than the family. Mrs Coombs kept a record, but most of the housemaids were only listed by first name. It was impossible to track them down.'

'So this might be a whole new avenue of enquiry?' I nodded. Leo grasped my arm. 'What if they have mementoes of Alice? We mustn't raise our hopes as high as the missing manuscript – it's unlikely a servant would have been entrusted with that. But a letter, maybe? A note or a sketch? This is fantastic, Mary.'

It was, and even more fantastic, for me, was to see how excited he was, how enthusiastic about what we might discover. It was what had made living and working with him for so long such a delight; physical passion had always come second to our mutual fascination with Alice Hornby.

'I miss you,' I said, and I put my arms round him and hugged him close. 'I miss this.'

'I know.' Leo rested his head against mine, and we sat

160

nestled in each other's arms as late afternoon sank into early evening, and the sun moved behind our oak tree, casting shadow branches over our heads.

'I suppose I ought to feed the children,' I said at last, unfurling from his embrace.

'And I should go home.' He tried to soften that blow with a smile, but it was still enough to produce a dull pain in my chest.

We wandered back up the lawn and around the side of the house to where his car was parked in its habitual place next to mine.

'Hang on,' I said, as he opened the car door. 'We need to talk about the summer holidays. The St Ives house is booked for the usual five weeks. It's all paid for.'

'Is it? I assumed . . .' He hovered behind the car door. 'Of course we mustn't waste it then. What do you suggest? That we split the summer between us?'

'Well, yes . . .' That was a sensible solution, I supposed. More sensible than the mad idea that we could all go together as usual, with the addition of Clark. How had I believed that would work? That I could bear watching them together for five weeks?

'Clark can only have two weeks off in the summer. Why don't you take the house for three weeks, and we'll take two? Jonas and Ava will still have the full five. I'll check with Clark and let you know which dates would suit us.'

And then he was gone, leaving me on my own again.

*

Mum called round later that night, marching in through the kitchen door as if she still owned the place. It used to drive me mad; now I could hardly believe how my mood brightened at the prospect of adult company, of any sort.

'Tea?' I asked, winded by a slug of guilt when she looked surprised at the offer. It was how I would have greeted Audrey, not my mum.

'I'm on my way out. But thank you, Mary.'

She was dressed to go out, now I looked at her properly: a colourful print dress that I had never seen before, court shoes with an inch-high heel, and a seductive shade of red lipstick.

'I saw you in the garden earlier, with Leo,' she said, straightening the towels that were hanging on the rail of the range cooker. 'In a close embrace.'

'Yes.' How did she do it? In two sentences she had riled me again, implying I had done something wrong. It had been extraordinarily generous of her to give me this house, but I sometimes thought a mortgage would have been less of a burden than a lifetime spent under scrutiny.

'Is there a chance, do you think, that you might get back together?'

'No. It's too late for that.'

'It's never too late. There's no virtue in being proud and lonely. If he's the love of your life, Mary, you should take him back. There is nothing that can't be forgiven.'

I grabbed a piece of kitchen roll and attacked the table,

desperate for occupation while I coped with this development. We never had conversations like this; we never discussed love, or sex, or happiness, or feelings. I couldn't start now. And what would I have said, anyway? Was Leo the love of my life? That sounded too romantic, too idealised to reflect the relationship we had. And too final – because if he was the love of my life, what was I supposed to do with the rest of it?

'It's not about forgiveness,' I said, scrubbing at a sticky ring on the table, until the paper disintegrated and my knuckles grazed the wooden surface. 'It's about biology. I don't have a penis. Leo's not coming back.'

I regretted my crudeness when she flinched and turned to the back door. She had been trying to help, in her way; the sentiment had been good, even if I didn't want it.

'Are you going anywhere nice?' I asked, as she opened the door.

'To a folk club, to hear a band playing. The Fergus Brothers or something like that.'

'The Fergus Brothers? That sounds Irish.' It sounded like the sort of thing my dad used to make us listen to. I couldn't believe she would want any reminder of him on a date with her new boyfriend. Even the idea was making her flushed.

'It's Scottish, I think. But I'm sure they'll play a variety of music.'

'Mum?' She paused again, not quite out of the kitchen. 'If you ever want to bring your friend round, we'd be happy to meet him. I promise we won't scare him away.'

'Let's see how it goes,' she said, and pulled the door tight shut behind her.

Over two weeks passed before I heard anything from the Archers, weeks where the minutes dragged by. I checked my phone for emails or missed calls so often that my touch screen could have had me prosecuted for harassment. Leo proved just as impatient, contacting me several times a day to see if there was news. He hadn't been so attentive when we were married; it was disheartening to be so relentlessly pursued only as a proxy for a woman dead for 150 years.

The call eventually came first thing one morning, when I was barely home from the school run, and I answered with bad grace, assuming it would be Ava demanding that I go back with the vital piece of homework that she'd forgotten despite my dozen reminders that she needed to pack her bag.

'Is that Mary Black? Bridie Archer here.'

'Hello? Did you enjoy the book?' So much for playing it cool. I'd never learnt how to play hard to get.

'We've read it.' Not quite what I'd asked, but I supposed it was progress. 'Can you call in?'

'Yes, of course, when were you thinking?'

'Twelve o'clock. We shut up shop for thirty minutes to have our dinner. We'll see you then.'

Bridie put the phone down without waiting for a response. I flew round to Audrey's and caught her trying to assemble the ironing board using one hand, two feet, and her chin.

'What are you doing?' I snatched the ironing board off her and stuck it back in the cupboard, then stood in front of the door to prevent any further raids. 'I told you I'd do your ironing.'

'I know you did, Mary, but Ethan did it while he was here, and now he's gone there hardly seems enough to bother you with.'

Ethan had moved to Waterman's Cottage a few days ago, after we'd agreed that Audrey was managing well one-handed. It was odd without him. I knew he called in every day, but it was strange not to see him in the garden, or setting out on a jog, or taking Audrey out somewhere.

'It doesn't matter if it's only two hankies and a vest, you're not to go near this ironing board again, okay?'

Audrey laughed.

'I wouldn't dare disobey when you're looking so ferocious, my darling. Goodness, I thought it was only Ethan who could make you lose your temper, and stop being so capable and efficient. Divorce suits you.'

'You want me to be incapable and inefficient?'

'Oh yes, why not? I want you to let go and be yourself.'

How had we strayed onto this treacherous ground? Audrey had a glint in her eye that suggested she would push me further given half a chance. She wasn't getting that chance from me. I hauled myself back.

'I'm sorry, but I won't be able to take you to physio later. Do you mind if I book a taxi for you? I hate to let you down, but I've had a call from a bookshop and they want to discuss Leo's book at lunchtime today.'

'Then you must go, and don't worry about me. You can't do everything and be everywhere. But ring Ethan first. He might be free to take me.'

'Won't he be working?'

'Oh, he only fiddles with the internet, he can do that anytime.' I had to smile at this dismissal of Ethan's work; I didn't really understand what he did, but he owned a successful international business, so I guessed it must involve more than messing about on Google. 'I need a lover, like your mother. It would solve so many problems – as long as he has a car! I wonder where I could find one?'

I was still laughing when Ethan answered the phone.

'What's tickling you, Mary Black?' His voice curled into my ear like a warm breeze. 'If it's a who, not a what, don't tell me. It's too early in the day for gory details.'

'It's Audrey.'

'Has she said something outrageous?'

'Doesn't she always?' I smiled at Audrey, who was now sitting down looking deceptively innocent. 'Would you be free to take her to physio later? I was supposed to do it, but now I have a meeting about Leo's book.'

'What time?'

'Two.'

'Sure, no problem.'

I marvelled again at how easy everything was with Ethan.

He did what you asked: there were no hoops to crawl through, no tightropes to cross, and no obstacles to negotiate. He had all the makings of a perfect husband, if only he could discover a sense of loyalty: it was his fatal flaw, as I had seen for myself at school, and by all accounts nothing had changed since then.

'When are you coming round?' he asked, interrupting my thoughts.

'Round where?'

'Here. To the cottage. For a house-warming.'

'Are you having a party?'

'No, I meant . . .'

Whatever he meant was lost under Audrey's squeal.

'A party? A house-warming party? What a marvellous idea. Tell him we can discuss the plans this afternoon. Maybe I'll find a lover there!'

'She said . . .'

'I heard. Please don't make me hear it again.' He sighed, but I could tell he was still smiling. 'So I'm having a party? Well, the first invitation goes to you. If I have to entertain a bunch of horny geriatrics, you're going to be right there at my side.'

Chapter Fifteen

In comparison to previous visits, my welcome at Archer's bookshop was positively lukewarm – pleasing progress. Bridie locked the shop door behind me, turned the sign to 'closed' and ushered me down the passage at the back into a room that appeared to function as living room, dining room, and kitchen in one.

A round table covered by an intricate lace cloth dominated the space, but was carefully positioned to allow wheelchair passage all round. The table was set for three, and I had been sitting in my allocated seat for barely thirty seconds before Bridie placed a bowl of steaming vegetable soup and slices of margarine-slathered white bread in front of me.

'So you've read the book?' I said, determined not to waste a second as we were clearly on a deadline. 'What did you think?'

Bridie glanced at her mother, but the old lady was too busy slurping soup with surprising gusto to reply.

'It was better than we thought, I'll grant you that,' Bridie said. 'Your husband has a soft spot for our Alice, that was plain enough.'

'More than a soft spot. He adores her. So do I. This book was a pure labour of love for both of us.'

'You?' Mrs Archer looked up from her spoon, narrowed eyes glittering at me like tiny slivers of onyx. 'What did you do?'

It would have been quicker to say what I didn't do, but discretion had to come before speed.

'I'm Leo's research assistant, so I helped with the background material and with a first edit. I . . .'

'You wrote it.' Mrs Archer didn't let me finish. She jabbed her spoon at Bridie, splattering soup across the tablecloth. 'I knew. There was a woman's hand all over it. Didn't I say a man couldn't have understood the half of it? Can't fool me.'

Clearly not, but it was more than my life was worth to admit it.

'Really, it's Leo's book . . .'

Another loud slurp shut me up.

'Tell her,' Mrs Archer said to Bridie, twitching her head in my direction. 'Tell her about Grandma.'

'Grandma?' I put down my spoon and leaned forward, hoping that we were getting somewhere at last.

'Mum's great-great-grandma,' Bridie said. 'She worked for the Hornby family, as a housemaid.'

'Who was it?' I asked. I pushed my bowl away, all thought of food forgotten. 'Mrs Coombs kept a record of them all. There was Mabel, Ellen, Florrie . . .'

'Florrie Betts,' Bridie said. 'She worked at the Hornby house for five years, then moved with Alice when she went to live with her sister, Elinor. Alice put in a word, she thought that highly of Florrie.'

'That's amazing,' I said. More than that – it was a miracle. Alice had never married, and had spent four years living with her sister's family as Elinor's health was poor. When Elinor died, Alice had returned home and remained a spinster until her own death ten years later. Those four years with Elinor were a mystery: we had no diary and only a handful of letters. All we knew was that on her return home, she had written her final novel, which she described to friends as her 'heart's work', but it had never been found.

'How do you know so much about Florrie?' I asked. 'Do you have letters from her, or did she keep a diary?' It was surely too much to hope for, but I still held my breath. A look passed between Bridie and her mother. Mrs Archer nodded.

'Fetch the box.'

Bridie opened a door through which I could see an iron single bed, and came back in a moment carrying a blue, metal strongbox, secured with a padlock.

'Not that one!' Mrs Archer screeched, spinning her chair round as if to block my view. 'In the drawer. The black one.'

Bridie returned with a much smaller box, the size of a conventional jewellery box. She put it down on the table and I had to sit on my hands to stop them yanking it open. Bridie lifted the lid, and I peered in and gasped. The first thing I saw was a folded sheet of paper, yellowed with age, covered in handwriting that I knew as well as my own.

'A letter from Alice!' I could have kissed them both, notwith-standing the dribble of soup on the old lady's chin. 'May I look?'

Mrs Archer nodded, and so I washed my hands and, with infinite care, took the letter out and unfolded it. I scanned the contents: no revelations, nothing to cast light on her secrets, but it was so wonderful to hold anything new from Alice that I wouldn't have cared if it had been a list of the most popular vegetables of the day. There were a few more letters underneath, a sketch of a pretty young girl, and a gold chain with a simple cross hanging from it.

'That's Florrie,' Bridie said, indicating the sketch. 'Alice sent it to her with one of those letters. And the necklace was a gift when Florrie married. There's a letter about that too.'

A clock on the mantelpiece above the blazing gas fire chimed the half hour.

'Time to open up,' Bridie said. She picked up the box to put it away again.

'Can I just take a picture?' I already had my phone out. 'Leo will be thrilled to see this.'

'You'll have to be quick.' Bridie gestured at the clock, and I took a few quick pictures, although it was unlikely one minute's delay in opening was going to lose them custom. I wandered back onto the street in a haze of excitement, and didn't even realise until I was halfway home that I had failed to persuade them to stock even a single copy of Leo's book. But it hardly mattered. I had discovered a new aspect of Alice's

171

life, a friendship with a housemaid that we'd known nothing about, and some items that her hands had once held. And if the small black box contained such treasure, what might there be in the blue box that was precious enough to need a padlock?

It was no surprise that the sun cracked the flags on the evening of Ethan's house-warming party; he had always lived a charmed life, and even nature couldn't resist smiling on him. Much to Ava's disgust – she was wearing ridiculous shoes, bought under the supervision of friends, not me – we strolled through the village and down the lane to Waterman's Cottage: me, Mum, Audrey, Jonas, and Ava, a merry little band despite the shoe grumbles. How could we not be? It was a glorious June day, lush with the sort of rare warmth that allowed us to shake off our cardigans, and that we normally had to travel many miles south to discover. It was almost the summer holidays, and we were going to a party. Even Mum had been caught smiling, and had told me I looked nice. The evening couldn't possibly not go well.

A few early birds had already staked a claim on the wine and food when we arrived. I couldn't see Ethan, but assumed he wouldn't mind if I stowed the children's bags in one of the spare bedrooms – they were going home with Leo after the party, to save him a journey next day. I nipped upstairs, dumped the bags, and emerged on to the small landing just as Ethan came back down from the master bedroom. His hand landed on my waist as we stumbled to avoid a collision.

'What are you doing lurking outside my bedroom, Mary Black?'

'Oh God, you're drunk already, aren't you? You're not going to try to seduce all the ladies from the village, are you?'

'Not all of them.' He leaned forward and teased my cheek with the softest of kisses. He was wearing that delicious floral aftershave again. 'You're looking exceptionally lovely tonight.'

Whichever lady he picked didn't stand a chance. The smile, the twinkling eyes, the laughing charm, the muscled body that lay under particularly well-fitted clothes, the way he could make you feel as if he had waited his whole life to spend that moment with you – it was irresistible. As a teenager, I had seen countless girls fail to resist it, and it had only become more potent with age. Even I, who knew well what a meaningless performance it was, felt a momentary enchantment steal over me at the pressure of his hand against my waist – a weird and totally inappropriate reaction, as if he were a man and not Leo's brother, my teenage sparring partner, and the world's biggest flirt.

'Behave,' I said, stepping back and wriggling to dislodge the hand. 'Don't waste your blarney on me. You've not changed, have you?'

'And neither have you. You don't look any different now than when we were teenagers and you were the hottest girl in school.'

I shook my head.

'I'm beginning to wonder if you're going to stay on your

feet long enough to greet the rest of your guests. Is there any alcohol left?' I headed down the stairs.

'There's Prosecco in the fridge. I've been saving it for special people.'

I paused mid-flight, and turned back, hands on my hips.

'Don't tell me. I'm on water, right?'

'Wrong. I bought it for you. You can have your very own bottle if you like.'

I made do with a glass, to start off with, and we wandered out into the garden, where most people were gathering in tribute to the gorgeous evening. The cottage sat in the centre of its plot, and extensive lawns wrapped around the house; the front lawn looked out across the reservoir, which sparkled like molten silver in the evening sun.

'Are you sure you don't want a lodger?' Audrey exclaimed, as we joined her, Mum, Jonas, and Ava, who had barely progressed beyond the front gate. 'I'm very well house-trained, and I'd be so quiet you'd think you had a mouse!'

Her joyful laugh was enough to contradict her words.

'Hello, Mum.' Ethan kissed her, then stepped back and looked her up and down. 'You look beautiful.'

'Is it very naughty of me to agree?' Audrey gave him a twirl. 'It's all down to my darling Mary, who blow-dried my hair. Hasn't she done the most marvellous job?'

Ethan smiled at me, and I braced myself for a sarcastic comment but none came.

'Aren't you going to offer us some bubbles?' Audrey said.

'Irene, we'd like some bubbles, wouldn't we?' Poor Mum had no chance to answer. 'Four more glasses please, Ethan.'

'Four?' I repeated. 'I don't think Jonas and Ava . . .'

'Oh Mary, live a little! One glass of wine won't do them any harm. Leo and Ethan have been drinking since they were twelve.'

'Is that supposed to reassure me?' I said. Ethan laughed and I shrugged, determined not to give him any more cause to call me beige. Perhaps I should live a little, if this was life: standing in the sunshine, with my favourite people, drinking Prosecco. It was certainly better than watching Friday-night TV with only Dotty for company.

'Come on, Ava, you can help carry the glasses.' Ava followed Ethan without a second's hesitation, but I was relieved to see that when she came back out she was carrying a glass of Coke in one hand.

'That stuff is disgusting,' she announced, handing a glass of the disgusting stuff to her brother. They wandered off to find someone more interesting to talk to, and Ethan chatted for a few minutes, until he suddenly trailed off and stared over my shoulder.

'You brought a date?'

'What?' I turned and saw Owen walking down the lane. 'Yes, I invited Owen. I didn't think you'd mind.'

'I didn't know it was still going on. You've not mentioned him, and Ava hasn't grumbled for a while.'

The truth was that not much had been going on recently.

After Breastgate, we had lapsed back into meeting for dog walks, where I could be sure that nakedness wouldn't be an issue, and I had avoided any contact closer than the occasional brush of lips. I knew I couldn't go on like that forever, and this party had seemed like a perfect chance for us to take another step in the safety of a crowd. I waved at Owen, uncomfortably conscious of Ethan's gaze boring into the back of my head.

'Who is it? Is it Leo?' Audrey moved to my side. 'Oh no, it's not. Leo has a shirt just like that, doesn't he? Such a lovely shade of blue. Is this a friend of yours, Mary?' She gasped, and stared at me. 'Did Ethan call him your date? Do you have a boyfriend?'

I waited for her to be pleased, to say how marvellous it was, but she simply carried on looking at me with a rather perplexed, almost sad expression. She perked up when Owen joined us and I made the introductions, but she still only managed a subdued smile of greeting. What had happened to the instruction to live a little?

Ethan didn't stay for more than a minute before going off to speak to other guests, and Audrey trailed after him. Conversation with Mum was desultory, to say the least, and I could have cheered when I saw Leo's car pull onto the drive – until he got out of the car, and revealed that he was wearing an identical shirt to Owen.

Leo and Clark came over and we all kissed or shook hands in a civilised way.

'Do you remember Owen Ferguson?' I said to Leo. 'He once taught Jonas art.'

'Yes, yes, of course,' Leo said, in a way that meant he didn't remember at all.

'This is awkward, isn't it?' Owen smiled and gestured between himself and Leo.

'Is it? Oh, because of Mary? Yes, I suppose it is. I know I've no right to object, but it will take some time to adjust to her being with someone else.'

'I meant because of the matching shirts.'

'Ah, yes!' Leo laughed, and looked down at his chest. It didn't surprise me that he hadn't noticed: I would put ten pounds on the fact that Clark had picked his shirt for him tonight. 'One more thing in common.'

We needed Audrey to shatter this awkward moment, but she was now on the far side of the garden, and my mum could only stand by looking po-faced: she had as little desire to hear about my sex life as I had about hers. Clark saved the day by dragging Leo away to get a drink, swiftly followed by Mum.

'Is this a sign of progress, Mary, that you've introduced me to your mother?' Owen asked, putting his arm around my waist.

'Either that or I'm trying to scare you off.'

'It would take more than that.' He squeezed my waist, and I responded by resting my head briefly on his shoulder. He was a good man, and I was lucky that he had been so incredibly patient with my dithering. 'Although the look that Ava's giving me is fairly terrifying.'

Ava was in a huddle with Chloe, Daisy's daughter, alternatively scowling in our direction and collapsing into giggles.

'Ignore her,' I said. 'I don't know how you put up with being surrounded by teenagers all day. How can you breathe when the air is so thick with hormones?'

'Even hormonal teenagers need good teachers.'

Ah, the serious, worthy answer, as I would have expected; Owen was an admirably dedicated teacher, and never joked about his job. In fact, any joke from him was rare, and more precious because of it. He didn't spend his life laughing, talking in riddles and messing about like some other people around here. Like Ethan, to pick a wholly random example, who was currently doing what looked like an impression of a baboon to the delight of a couple of small children.

'Hello!' Daisy tottered over the grass towards us, a glass of wine in her hand – not the first of the evening by the looks of it. 'Is that champagne? Where did you find that? I could only find normal wine.' She waved her glass to illustrate the point, and most of the contents sloshed out onto the grass. 'Bugger.'

'I'll get you another,' Owen offered. 'Is it in the house?'

'In the kitchen.' Daisy waited until Owen was out of earshot. 'Is that a new dress? It's very daring for you. We don't normally see so much of your cleavage. Is this for Owen's benefit?'

'No, for mine.' Owen had already seen quite enough of my cleavage. 'I thought I deserved something new.'

It had been a bargain in the sales in Clitheroe: a skater-style dress with a flared skirt in a mossy shade of green, quite unlike anything I'd worn for years. And that was the point: trying on the dress in the shop, I hadn't seen a middle-aged divorced mother of teenagers in the mirror. I had simply seen me. How could I resist such a miracle dress?

A cannon of laughter shot across the garden from where Ethan was entertaining a group of guests.

'Is he seeing anyone?' Daisy asked, nodding her head towards Ethan.

'Probably any three or four knowing him. Are you interested? In Ethan?'

'Come on, it's not so surprising, is it? Look at him!'

I did: my eyes swivelled his way quite against my wishes. Of course he was handsome, it was ridiculous to deny it: tall, athletic, dirty blond hair, and eyes the colour of the reservoir in full sun. No, I'd never been blind to it. But. There was an enormous but.

'He's Leo's brother!'

'Well, yes, I suppose it is weird for you, but if you weren't related to him you'd have noticed that he's gorgeous. We had a good chat a few weeks ago when I was babysitting. He's funny. Interesting. What sort of women does he like?'

'Anything with breasts, I imagine.' Daisy's face fell, and I immediately felt rotten. Why shouldn't she like Ethan? It had nothing to do with me. 'His first wife was stunning,' I said. 'She had perfect shiny black hair . . .'

'Sounds closer to you than me,' Daisy interrupted.

'Hardly.' I laughed. 'She was born in China, but her family emigrated when she was a baby and she'd grown into a ballsy New Yorker.' I shuddered: I'd met her a couple of times and found her terrifying. It was a mystery what Ethan had seen in her. 'She was petite,' I added, nodding towards Daisy's small frame. 'And his second wife was blonde.'

'So it's not hopeless?'

'He'd be lucky to have you.' Daisy brightened and I resisted the urge to give her a warning. Perhaps he could be loyal if he found the right woman – and why shouldn't that woman be Daisy? I glanced over at Ethan, and he smiled back, a huge warm wide-lipped smile, travelling across the length of the garden and losing none of its dazzle. Daisy would be lucky to have him, I thought – and immediately turned away, horrified by a surge of something that had no business to be surging.

It was a lovely party, every bit as enjoyable as I'd hoped. There was a great turn out from the village, and everyone seemed happy and intoxicated by the plentiful alcohol and the foretaste of summer that this beautiful weather offered. Ethan must have extended an open invitation to the villagers, because I couldn't for the life of me imagine why he would have invited the Misses Tippett, two elderly sisters from my meals on wheels run. And yet there he was, in deep discussion with them – well, they were talking; Ethan's mouth wasn't moving from its rather fixed grin. He saw me and waved. It was tempting to leave him drowning, but I took pity and wandered over.

'Hello!' I interrupted their twittering with my own Prosecco-fuelled chirpiness. 'What do you think of the house? Do you remember it from when a real waterman lived here?'

'It's very fancy inside,' Doreen said. 'Very modern.'

'We didn't like the bedroom,' Doris added. 'Those glass panels above the bed. The noise would have me up all night when it rained, with my bladder the way it is.'

I hid my smile behind my glass, as Ethan's eyes registered his horror that his bedroom had been invaded.

'It wouldn't suit me, living here,' Doreen continued. 'It's an unlucky house; just you ask them that did all this fancy work. But I hear you've not had much luck with marriage anyway, so perhaps it won't do you any harm.' She nodded at Ethan. 'Strange, though. You're a handsome lad, the image of your father.'

'And Mary's the image of *her* father,' Doris said. 'Better behaved, mercifully, or else . . .'

She was silenced by a sharp nudge from her sister.

'No chicken this week.' Doreen wagged a knobbly finger at me. 'We've had it for the last three weeks. Any more and we'll be laying eggs!'

They scuttled off, heads bent low together.

'Who the hell are they?' Ethan asked. It was impossible not to laugh at his bewilderment.

'Don't you remember the Misses Tippett? They've lived in

Stoneybrook forever.' My smile faded a notch. I'd lived here forever too – was I going to turn into the Miss Tippett of my generation, without even a sister to keep me company?

'But I didn't invite them! They're gatecrashers!'

I giggled.

'Should we call the police?'

'Can you rugby tackle them while I ring?'

'Why can't you? You're the sporty one.'

'I'm the heavier one. I might kill them.'

'But it would look much less suspicious if you're seen jumping on ladies. You're known to make a habit of it.'

'Not women that old!'

'So you say, but they were curiously familiar with the inside of your bedroom.'

'Oh God! How can I ever lie in bed again without thinking of leaky bladders?'

And that was it. It wasn't even that funny, but Ethan started laughing, and I was caught up with it, and couldn't stop, until my eyes were streaming and I had to bend over to ease the stitch in my side. I hadn't laughed like that for years – had forgotten how good it felt to let go, be silly for a while, allow all the stress and the sensibleness to be replaced by a fizz of euphoria that left me so light I could have floated away.

'I've missed this.' Ethan rubbed my shoulder. His fingers caught the back of my neck and his touch seemed to sear every inch of my skin. I straightened up, panic and shock weighing me firmly back down. Ethan was still smiling broadly, thankfully oblivious to my reaction. Over his shoulder I saw Owen watching.

'I need to go.'

'You don't need to do anything.'

But I did, I really did. I needed to do anything that would cut through this odd, intimate web that had wrapped around us with such silky soft strands that I hadn't noticed it forming; anything that would stop me dwelling on how much I had missed this too. I practically ran towards Owen, grabbed hold of his arm and anchored myself to his safe, reliable presence until the unwelcome stirrings subsided.

As the sun began to meander behind the trees, streaking the sky with swathes of orange and gold that turned the reservoir into molten embers, Ethan lit lanterns and candles around the lawns for those who remained outside. Some of the guests had moved inside, to be nearer to the food and drink; some had wandered – or staggered – home, including Mum, who had admitted with much self-consciousness that she was expecting a visitor.

Sanity restored, I joined the Blacks, delighting in the company of my favourite people; even the presence of Leo and Clark had become easier, with time. But Audrey was still below par, and I couldn't leave it be.

'In three weeks, we'll be packing for St Ives,' I said, trying to cheer her. 'I'm looking forward to it, aren't you?'

The arrangements had been finalised for the holiday. I would go down for the first three weeks with both mothers and the children; Leo and Clark would spend the last two weeks with Audrey, Jonas, and Ava.

'Yes, my darling, I think it will do us all good to get away.' As I'd hoped, Audrey smiled with most of her usual brightness.

'Let me know if you'd like me to take you shopping before we go.' I turned to Jonas and Ava, who were sitting on the grass, sharing a pair of ear pods, adding, 'And you two need to sort out anything you want washing.'

Ava shrugged one shoulder. Jonas pulled out his ear pod.

'Don't worry about me,' he said. 'I'm not coming.'

'What do you mean? Not coming where?'

'St Ives.' Jonas spoke slowly, as if to an idiot. And perhaps that was right, perhaps I was being an idiot, because for a mad moment I thought he'd said he wasn't joining us on holiday, the holiday we had all enjoyed together for the past ten years. 'I'm moving in with Dad over the summer.'

'Dad? Moving in?'

Ava pulled out her ear pod and jumped up.

'You're leaving me with her? All summer? You selfish . . . ape's arse!' she yelled, and stomped off across the lawn.

Jonas looked baffled by all the fuss. Leo gave me an apologetic smile, because he'd known – of course he'd known. They must have plotted and planned this during all those weekends without me. How could they?

'But Dad and Clark are spending two weeks in Cornwall. Will you come home then?' My heart lifted a little. I'd misunderstood. Jonas didn't want to come to Cornwall, that was all. I would only be without him for three weeks – a horrendous prospect, but not as bad as the eight weeks I had originally feared.

'No, I'll stay in the flat. I've got a summer job in a café. It's cool, Mum. I'll move back when school starts.'

Cool? I wasn't the slightest bit cool; in fact, I was boiling with so much fury and despair that I thought I might erupt at any moment. I couldn't find my brave face this time, couldn't smile and be calm and capable and pretend that this was okay. It wasn't okay. I didn't want Jonas to go. I wasn't sure I could bear for him to go. I had already lost Leo. How much more did I have to lose?

But as I trembled, terrified that I couldn't keep myself together for a second longer, a hand brushed mine: a strong, warm hand, offering comfort, and I grabbed it and squeezed it tight. It squeezed back, and even in the depth of my anguish, I felt a rush of hope. Owen was here. This was what mattered in a man: not the heady excitement of a searing touch and tingling skin, but a firm, reliable hold when I needed it. I looked up at the owner of the hand, ready to smile my thanks, and encountered Ethan's sympathetic gaze.

I was sitting on the grass embankment overlooking the reservoir, watching the moonlight skate on the surface of the water, when someone flopped down next to me. Faint notes of jasmine mingled with the night air.

'Penny for them,' Ethan said.

'I'd be ripping you off if I gave them for free.'

'A trouble shared?'

'Is a surefire way to lose friends. Have you finished with the idioms?'

'Don't buy a pig in a poke?'

'What? That doesn't even make sense.' But I couldn't help laughing at his absurdity. Ethan leant towards me and bumped his shoulder against mine.

'Do you want me to have a word with Joe?'

My laughter died.

'No. There's no point. I won't stop him doing what he wants.' My breath stuttered as I tried to hold back a sob. 'I know he's seventeen, and in a year he'll be going off to university. But I thought I had that year. Losing alternate weekends was hard enough. But the whole summer? And where will it end? Will he stay with Leo for every school holiday now?'

'He'll be too busy revising for his exams. This is just a summer thing.'

'But summer's the worst – it's two months! And what's next? Ava would leave tomorrow if she could. Am I going to be left with only Dotty and a garden full of poo?' Ethan laughed, sending vibrations up and down my arm. 'How could Leo do this? Haven't I been reasonable with him, more reasonable than he could have expected?'

'Yes. But if Joe asked to stay with him, he probably didn't think he could say no. You'd have done the same.'

'I might have known you'd be on his side.' I shuffled a few centimetres along the grass, breaking contact with Ethan.

'His side? God, Mary, you've no idea . . .' He stopped, put his arm around me, and pulled me back. 'I'm on Joe's side, that's all.'

I knew that I should break away; that this was a terrible idea, especially after my confusion with the hand-holding. But I had plenty of excuses ready to explain why I didn't. It had been a tough night. I needed comfort. Ethan was here, offering it. So I relaxed against his chest, and as his heartbeat quickened beneath me, mine calmed and slowed. And it was odd, because I had never expected this from Ethan. The brothers were totally different. In my mind, Leo had always been the pair of granny shoes: comfortable, the right choice for long haul – so comfy that it was easy to forget you were wearing them. Ethan was like a pair of scarlet four-inch stilettos –fantastic-looking but impractical over any sort of distance. And yet here he was, showing his granny-shoe credentials, while Leo displayed his scarlet side with Clark. Who would have thought that Ethan was so good at this? Peace stole through my veins.

But as we sat by the water, with the sky turning ink blue over our heads and casting the trees into silhouette, and with the occasional sound floating across the lane from the cottage, peace wasn't the only thing flowing through my veins. Only a thin wisp of cotton shirt lay between me and Ethan's chest. His breath was warm in my hair, his arms tight around my body. The scent of jasmine was doubly bewitching in close proximity. The feelings I had resisted all night were stirring again, in a way they hadn't done for a long time, and however much my head was shrieking that this was wrong – that this was Leo's brother – my body was high on Prosecco and redis-covered desire and would not listen to sense.

I eased away from him, slowly, trying to give no clue that something was wrong, because he must never find out about this momentary aberration: he would either be horrified or think it so hilarious that he would tease me about it forever, and neither seemed a good option.

'It's getting late,' I said, being as mundane as I could to break the atmosphere. 'Quite nippy too,' I added, laying it on thick. 'I think it's time to go.'

'If that's what you want.'

I stood up and looked across at the garden of Waterman's Cottage. Not many people were still outside. Jonas and Ava were in the thick of a group of teenagers; Owen was talking to Daisy; Leo and Clark were holding hands, barely speaking, and yet it was hard to imagine a couple in closer communion. I hovered at the garden gate, wondering where I belonged in all this. Love on one side, me on the other. Who wanted or needed me?

'What's the matter, slowcoach, are you so cold that you're frozen to the spot?' Ethan poked at my shoulder. 'Don't stand there looking ornamental and blocking my way. I need to start turning the lights out or this lot will be expecting breakfast.'

He brushed past me to open the latch on the gate, and desire flared again. That spurred me into movement. I dashed into the garden and headed straight for Owen and Daisy.

'Everyone's leaving now,' I said. Leo and Clark were rounding up the children, and I knew they were driving Audrey home too. 'Will you walk me home?' I asked Owen.

'Of course. Daisy?'

'It's okay, I've cadged a lift. These heels weren't made for walking!'

She wobbled to prove her point, but I suspected the alcohol had more to do with that than the heels. We said our goodbyes – I clung to Jonas for far too long, as if he were leaving now for two months not two nights – and I set off back up the lane towards the village with Owen. He was quiet, but I was fine with that: it was a comfortable silence. Leo and Clark weren't worried about not speaking, were they? I reached out in the gloom and took hold of Owen's hand, and clung on to it all the way home.

We reached the house and Owen hesitated at the top of the drive. The streetlights through the village stopped at Audrey's, leaving the road to fade away to blackness beyond our house. We stood on the periphery of the pool of orange light, so that whilst I could see Owen's figure, I couldn't make out his expression.

'Would you like to come in?' I meant for coffee – real coffee, not euphemistic coffee – but Owen hesitated in his reply, shifted his weight from one foot to the other, and generally gave off such awkward vibes that I realised I needed to be clearer. But as I opened my mouth, ready to ask if he wanted a drink, I wondered why I was still holding back. Mum's friend was staying the night; Leo and Clark were besotted with each other; Daisy was planning an advance on Ethan. Why should I be on the wrong side of the garden gate? Owen was a good, kind man. I mustn't lose him too.

I stepped forward and kissed him, trying to harness those stirrings I had felt earlier, and put as much passion into it as I could. He responded, but not as emphatically as I'd hoped. I needed to be clearer, make him understand beyond doubt what I was offering. I could do this, couldn't I? I wasn't actually a virgin or an idiot, even though, right at this moment, I felt like both. Closing my eyes, I trailed my hand along Owen's chest and down to the fly of his trousers.

'You could stay, if you wanted,' I whispered. My heart raced as the evidence that he did want to pressed against my hand. But then he pulled away so swiftly that I was left like an abandoned waxwork, with one hand in the air, where it had been round his neck, and the other in a cupped position down below.

'I need to get back for Lucilla,' Owen said. My hands dropped. His dog? He was rejecting me for his dog? She was a nice enough dog, but still . . . Humiliation settled over me like a second skin.

'And I don't think it would be a good idea, tonight,' Owen added. 'Not really what you want. Those complications haven't gone away, have they?' He popped a brief kiss on my cheek. 'Goodnight, Mary.'

Chapter Sixteen

'Do you need a hand?'

Without waiting for a reply, Ethan hurdled the hedge between our gardens with impressive agility for a man approaching forty. I wished he would stop doing that. He could stand still and look fitter than most of the men in the village, without having to demonstrate his athleticism at every opportunity. It was exactly the sort of annoying thing he used to do as a teenager, and proved how little he'd changed since then. Although he hadn't possessed quite so many firm muscles in those days . . .

'I can manage,' I called, turning my back on him and approaching my car. I realised my mistake at once. Obviously, in hindsight, it would have been better to unlock the car and open the boot before staggering over, laden down with a box full of books so huge that my arms felt like a chimpanzee's

I tried to balance the box between my chest and the side of the car to free one hand, but before I could search for my keys, Ethan frisked me as if I were a criminal and extracted them from the pocket of my jeans.

'What are you doing?' Ethan opened the boot and whisked

the box off me before my body had even started to process that his hand had been in an area reserved for intimate acquaintances. 'Stop molesting me!'

'Why, what will you do if I don't stop?' He laughed and nodded towards the open boot. 'Bash me over the head with your shovel?'

'It's for the snow. You've probably forgotten, but we get a lot of it over here.'

'It snows in New York too, but not in summer, and I've never needed to carry a shovel around.' My head filled with a picture of New York in the winter, stolen straight from films and TV: of a whitewashed Central Park; people in bobble hats ice-skating at the Rockefeller Center; Christmas lights reflected on sidewalks covered in crisp snow. I had tried to persuade Leo that we should visit Ethan one Christmas, but it hadn't been a good time. Now it never would be.

'And what's all this?' Ethan rested the box on the lip of the boot, and rummaged in the rucksack that was next to the shovel. 'Torch, blankets, water, snacks . . . All very sensible precautions.'

His smile was on the right side of amused, not mocking, but I couldn't help wondering if he saw the bag as further proof of how colourless my life was. The girl who cartwheeled naked across the garden wouldn't have packed an emergency severe weather bag. When had I settled for a life of efficient, capable dullness?

'Where are you going with this?' Ethan peered into the box. 'Off to more bookshops to flog Leo's book?'

'No, it's the annual meeting of the Alice Hornby Society today.' Ethan looked blank. 'Every year we hold a day of talks, discussions, and readings, and all the Society members are invited. People have been known to come from America,' I added, when Ethan still didn't look as interested as I thought he should. 'It's a big day.'

'It sounds it. Are you giving a talk?'

'No.' I removed the shovel and rucksack from the boot. Perhaps it would be safe to store them in the shed for a couple of months. 'Leo always gives a talk, and then we have a couple of guest speakers.'

'Why not you? You know as much about Alice Hornby as he does.'

'But Leo's the professor. He has the name.' Ethan opened his mouth as if to argue again, but I stopped him. 'Do you want to stick that box in the boot? I've lots more to bring yet.'

I'd intended to dismiss him, but instead of taking the hint, Ethan followed me into the house, where a stack of bags and boxes waited in the hall.

'All this?' I nodded. There was a lot more than usual, because of the new book, and Leo was normally here to help shift it all. 'I'll help. And I'd better come with you to unpack at the other end. We'll take my car; there's more room.'

'You can't.' I wasn't used to dominant behaviour in this house; Leo had nominally worn the trousers, but only those I'd chosen and put out for him. 'It's by ticket only.'

'Then I'll have to gatecrash.' He laughed. 'If the Misses Tippett can get away with it, I'm sure I can. I'll bring the car round.'

He strode off, but then stopped in the doorway and turned back.

'I didn't think. Is your teacher friend coming to help?'

'No.' I bent over and made some quite unnecessary changes to the contents of a bag so that he wouldn't see my face.

'How are things going with him?'

'I'm really not comfortable discussing my sex life.'

'You have a sex life with him?'

'No!' Since my sexual wiles had crashed and burned on the night of the party a couple of weeks ago, I had barely seen Owen. I had been a coward and deliberately changed my routine for walking Dotty so that I was unlikely to bump into him. What was I meant to say to him now? Apologise for groping his private parts? I wasn't clear whether I still had any sort of relationship with him, let alone a sexual one. Or what he had meant by complications. My life couldn't be more straightforward. More *beige*.

I glanced at Ethan, hoping he wasn't giving me a sympathetic look; I doubted if his sexual wiles had ever been rejected. But it wasn't sympathy hovering over his face. I didn't know what it was, but he certainly wasn't feeling sorry for me.

'Is it still too soon?' he asked. 'After Leo?'

'Maybe.' Or maybe not. After all, Owen had turned me down this time, despite explicitly clear signals that I was willing to move on.

'Or maybe he was your rebound. Now you've got it out of the way, and you can move on to a proper relationship, one that might last. What do you think?'

'I think you should spare me the pop psychology.' I picked up a handful of bags and approached the door. 'When you've tried to live without someone you've loved for over twenty years, I might listen to your advice. Until then, stick to what you're good at and move those boxes.'

The meeting of the Alice Hornby Society took place in the grounds of the beautiful Georgian house where she had been born, and had spent all her life save for the four years staying with her sister's family. We were lucky: the house still belonged to her sister's descendants, and they were enthusiastic patrons of the Society, generous with their money, time, and property. I had first approached them ten years ago, when the Society was newly formed as a charity and had no more than two dozen local members. At that point, they had allowed us to meet in their drawing room, an extraordinary treat to be surrounded by walls that had once sheltered Alice, and to stand in the window and see the same view that she had so evocatively described in her diary.

As the Society had grown, our annual meeting had expanded to include lectures on Alice, her work, and life in Victorian times: today a culinary historian was attending with explanations and samples of the type of food that Alice would have eaten. We now met in a marquee in the garden, all paid for by Alice's family, but every year a lucky few were allowed inside the house. This year I had bent the rules and allowed non-members to attend, and to enjoy the house tour: the Archers had been the obvious choice, and I had been thrilled when Bridie had finally accepted the invitation.

I had an ulterior motive, of course. I hoped that if they saw how committed we were to celebrating and respecting Alice, and if Leo could charm them with his expertise and enthusiasm, they might agree to show me what was in the secret blue box. I'd wasted hours wondering what it might be, and what could be valuable enough to need locking up, and I could only think of one thing: it had to be the diary for the years that were missing, and that would tell us more about Alice's final book, and maybe even what had happened to the manuscript.

My grand plan started badly. As soon as I arrived with Ethan, I could tell that Leo was in one of his rare bad moods, the sort that usually only surfaced when something Brontë related came out at the cinema or on TV, or made it onto the book bestseller lists. He pottered around the garden like a teddy bear with a sore head, showing none of the gentle charm that had made him such a popular speaker in previous years. I'd told him that the Archers were attending, and primed him to do a five-star job of making them welcome, but when they eventually arrived he was nowhere to be seen.

'Hello! I'm so glad you could come! Isn't it a gorgeous day!' My voice was too high, my smile too bright, and my exclamation marks were like thrusts of a knife, so it was no wonder that Mrs Archer recoiled in her chair.

'It'll rain by nightfall,' she said. She lifted her chin and sniffed. 'It's in the air.'

'Is it?' I sniffed too, but all I could detect was an overpowering smell of mothballs and peppermint, which I suspected was due to Mrs Archer rather than impending rain. 'Would you like to come over to the marquee? There should be time to grab a cup of tea before the talks begin.'

'I'm here to see the house,' Mrs Archer said.

'I thought we could show you around the house during the first break . . .'

'I want to see the house.'

I looked at Bridie, but she shrugged and offered no support. She was probably glad to have a breather while her mother ran someone else ragged.

'Fine,' I said. 'I'll just need to find Leo . . . Oh, here he is!'

'Do you have my welcome speech, Mary?'

'I emailed it to you on Wednesday.'

'I can't find it. Have you brought a spare?'

Of course I had, and I pulled it out of my handbag.

'Leo, this is . . .'

But he didn't wait for me to make the introduction. He snatched the speech from my hand and headed back to the marquee. Mrs Archer gave a loud sniff, which I could tell by the expression on her face had nothing to do with the weather.

'I'm sorry,' I said. 'Leo's about to give the welcoming address, so he's preoccupied. Would you like to come and listen and then we'll do the tour?'

This didn't turn out to be my brightest idea. Talking about Alice usually transformed Leo, but something was off today. His beautiful voice sounded flat, he fluffed lines and ruined a joke with poor timing, and he showed as much enthusiasm as he might have done for yet another adaptation of Jane Eyre. I wanted to push him out of the way and give the speech myself; either that or torture him slowly. Perhaps even both. How many hours had I wasted, telling him how important it was that today went well? Half the audience were fidgeting, including Bridie and Mrs Archer.

'Shall we do the house tour now?' I grabbed the handles of the wheelchair and slipped out of the marquee, ignoring the alarmed squawk that came from amid the blankets. I pushed it all the way to the front door of the house, then stopped. Three stone steps led up to the front door. How had I overlooked that? I'd wanted this day to be a Rolls-Royce job. As things stood, we were barely scraping the level of a Reliant Robin.

I glanced around the garden. Everyone else was inside the marquee, enduring Leo's talk – everyone except for Ethan, who was lolling about on a tree stump, laughing into his phone. It didn't look important laughter. I ran across the lawn.

'I need you! It's an emergency!'

'You don't know how long I've waited to hear you say that, Mary Black.'

He switched off his phone. I thumped him.

'Stop being an idiot. We've no time for all your nonsense. I need to get Mrs Archer and her wheelchair into the house. Will you help?'

'Two ladies need me? How can I resist?'

Between us we managed to lift the wheelchair up the steps and into the house, where the owner showed us round; luckily the spacious Georgian proportions allowed the wheelchair to go through doorways and turn around without difficulty. Ethan tagged along on the tour, and helped lift the wheelchair down a couple of steps into the kitchen, where Mrs Archer gave a few more of her infamous sniffs: approving ones this time, I was sure, as it must have been incredible to be in the room where her great-great-grandmother would have spent so much time.

Usually the tour continued upstairs, to see the room that had belonged to Alice, but I doubted that even four of us would manage to lift the wheelchair so far. Ethan caught me looking up the stairs.

'Do you need to go up?' he asked.

'We can't.'

'Didn't your mum ever tell you there's no such word as can't?' He smiled and in one smooth move, bent down and scooped Mrs Archer into his arms, and carried her up the stairs.

'I've got legs! I can stand!' she squawked as we all reached the landing. Ethan put her down.

'She could have mentioned that before,' he whispered to me.

'Where would be the fun in that?' I replied. Because judging by the glimmer in Mrs Archer's eyes, and the unusual colour in her cheeks – not to mention the way she latched onto Ethan's arm for support – her ride upstairs had been more fun than she'd had in a long time. 'Another conquest,' I murmured. 'You're irrepressible. Is there a woman in the world you haven't won over yet?'

'Maybe.' He grinned as Mrs Archer tugged him towards a bedroom. 'But I'm working on it.'

I wondered who he had his eye on now. Could it be Daisy? I hadn't heard how her plans to woo Ethan were progressing. There was no time to ask, as by the time we finished the tour, I had to dash off to the marquee to chair a panel discussion on whether Victorian writers had any relevance to today's readers. The poor academic we'd drafted in to argue that Alice and her contemporaries were out of date and should be forgotten stood no chance against this crowd, and appeared so drained that I had to bring the food historian on early, to whet our appetite for lunch with her pictures of lavish feasts and samples of Victorian cooking.

I had hoped that Leo would try to speak to Mrs Archer over lunch, but Ethan claimed the chair I was saving, and when I saw the old lady smile for the first time, I couldn't regret the substitution. Leo's mood hadn't noticeably improved since I'd arrived, even though the day was undoubtedly a success, and I'd sold lots of signed copies of the autobiography.

'What's wrong with Leo?' I asked, when I wandered outside with my cup of tea, and found Clark lurking behind the marquee, reading the BBC news on his phone; clearly Leo hadn't brainwashed him into adoring Alice Hornby yet. 'This used to be his favourite day of the year, more than Christmas. Is he feeling ill?'

'Not ill. Guilty, I think.'

'Guilty?' I'd forgotten Clark's habit of frank speaking. 'What about?'

'You. Last year you organised this together. This year he hasn't been around, so you've had to do it all yourself. You've even had to rope in Ethan.'

Organising this together was stretching the facts, but I let it go.

'Is that why he's in a bad mood? Because Ethan's here? He's an extra pair of hands, that's all. I had a lot of boxes to bring.'

'It's not about Ethan. It's the reminder that you don't have anyone else to turn to. You're on your own. Leo blames himself for that.'

It would be hard for him to blame anyone else.

'So you're saying he won't be happy until I find someone else? I can't help that. Moving on isn't always an easy thing to do.'

I was thinking of my disastrous attempts to move on with Owen, but perhaps Clark assumed I was having a dig at Leo, as he studied me for a moment before answering.

'Would it really be moving on?' Clark spoke gently, but something in his tone burrowed into my head and fixed my attention. 'Or letting yourself fall in love for the first time?'

I was about to object – I loved Leo, and Clark had no right to suggest otherwise – but the words faltered on my tongue. This was a bizarre conversation to be having with my husband's fiancé, but perhaps it took an outsider to see the truth. I had always loved Leo, but I had never *fallen* in love with him, not in the way I had read about in countless books, Alice's included. Was it as simple as that? Had I been looking at this all wrong? I had been afraid that by moving on I might lose something: the connection with Leo that had supported me for so many years. Should I be thinking instead of everything I might gain?

'Tell me what it's like,' I said. 'How does it feel to be in love?'

'I can't. It's not something I feel, it's something I am. You can't describe how it feels to have blood running through your veins. It's just there, a part of you, and you wouldn't exist without it. For me, that's what it's like being with Leo.'

My relationship with Leo had never been like that. But I wanted it – I wanted the love that Clark experienced. I wanted someone who loved me just as I was: whether I cartwheeled naked or packed emergency winter kits; whether I agreed with them or argued over every detail; whether I was making food for old people or snapping for no reason at my mother.

'How did you get so wise?' I said.

'Too many relationships that weren't that sort of love.' He winked. 'But let's not tell Leo about those.'

Bridie and Mrs Archer stayed longer than I expected, and didn't leave until they'd enjoyed a substantial afternoon tea. They hadn't mentioned the secret blue box all day, and so I accompanied them to their car, determined they wouldn't get away without me probing.

'Have you enjoyed the day?' I asked, as we headed towards the drive, where they had been given special parking privileges.

'It's been interesting,' Bridie said. From an Archer, I took that as high praise. I had seen how fascinated they had both been by the Victorian food, and the Alice souvenirs I had brought with me.

'You can see how much we love Alice. We want to know everything about her. Would you consider showing me what other mementoes you have from Florrie?' I decided to come straight out with it. 'Will you tell me what's in the blue box?'

They didn't reply, and I thought I had pushed too soon and blown my chance. But as we reached their car, Mrs Archer leant forward in her chair.

'Who was that fella?'

'Which one?'

'The one with the smile. Him that's too handsome for his own good.'

'Ethan?' I didn't know why his was the first name that popped into my head at Mrs Archer's description; except that he did have a fairly memorable smile, one that could have melted both North and South Poles with one twitch of the lips. 'He was with us on the tour of the house?'

'Aye, that's him. Know him well, do you?'

'Yes. He's Leo's brother.'

Mrs Archer's hand emerged from her blankets and grasped mine, her thin fingers closing over my skin like twisted roots clinging on to the earth. She studied my face, and obviously found something there, because she nodded her head twice.

'Then happen you'll understand.' She nodded again. 'I'll think on it.'

It was as much as I could have hoped for, and as Ethan drove me home later, I was happy that the day had gone well; that despite the division in our personal life, Leo and I had still managed to put together a good day for the members of the Alice Hornby Society.

'What?' I asked, as from the corner of my eye I caught Ethan turn to look at me again. 'What's the matter?'

'You were fantastic today.'

I let out an exasperated sigh.

'Okay. Fantastically bad? Bossy? Annoying?'

'Fantastically fantastic.' He looked at the road again, but was smiling what Mrs Archer would call the smile. 'I've never seen you at work. You know more about Victorian literature than I probably know about every subject put together. And even I began to get excited when you showed us Alice's lace collar.'

I laughed, but I wasn't modest enough to deny it. Of course

I knew my subject: I had spent years researching it, with the guidance of one of the best teachers. Recognition was too rare for me not to grasp and cradle it when it came.

'It was a good day,' I said. I relaxed back into the passenger seat and stretched out my legs into the foot well, savouring the luxury of Ethan's rented car.

'You look happy.'

'I think I am. No, I am. I discovered something today. I'm ready.'

'Ready for what?'

'To fall in love.'

Ethan looked at me for so long that the car behind us had to parp its horn twice before he noticed that the traffic lights had changed to green.

'Who with?' he asked, as he pulled away. 'The teacher?'

'Maybe.' The car accelerated, jerking me forwards. 'Maybe not. It might be with someone I know, or it might be with someone I meet in future. It might happen next week, or in ten years from now. The point is, I want it. I'm looking forward to it.'

'Really?' He glanced my way. 'Are you sure?'

'Positive.' I poked his arm as it came between us to change gears. 'Don't go shooting me down, wondering who would be mad enough to love me, okay? Be kind. This is exciting.'

He smiled, a smile so dazzling that I imagined I would still see the imprint of it if I closed my eyes.

'It certainly is.'

Chapter Seventeen

Our summer holiday didn't start on an auspicious note. Thick grey clouds and a sharp wind gathered to wave off our little convoy: me, Ava, and Dotty in the lead, Mum and Audrey in the second car, and Daisy and Chloe bringing up the rear. Heavy rain started to fall before we had left Stoneybrook, and pursued us doggedly all the way down the motorway from Lancashire to Cornwall, until we pulled up outside the rental house.

Arriving here was always one of my favourite moments of the year. The house itself was gorgeous: a sprawling whitewashed cottage set on a quiet lane in Carbis Bay, a couple of miles from St Ives, not quite on the cliff edge but close enough that the sea was visible over the tops of trees and houses. We had met the owners years ago, and had negotiated a perfect arrangement whereby we rented the house for the summer, while they escaped the crowds and travelled. We were effectively house-sitting for them, and the mutual convenience was reflected in the price – five weeks here for less than we would have paid for two weeks abroad.

But the house represented more than a bargain. Something happened to us when we came here, something magical: away from home, and work, and school, we shook off our stresses, and grumbles, and disappointments, and became ourselves again. Leo smiled more; Jonas talked more; Ava moaned less, and I relaxed and felt more like my old self than at any other time. Less dull. Less *beige*.

But it could have hardly felt more different this year as I dashed up the path to the front door, knowing that this would be our last summer here, and that our last summer here as a proper family had already gone, slipping by without fuss or fanfare. The house looked the same, and as I stepped inside it smelt the same – of beeswax and fresh bread, with a lingering undertone of dog; but the magic was missing.

'This place sucks even more in the rain,' Ava said, dragging Dotty inside but conveniently leaving all the suitcases and bags for me to bring in. 'Why can't we go to Spain or somewhere hot like a normal family?'

She let go of Dotty's lead, and Dotty scampered off round the house, searching for the owner's dog that she could smell on the furniture. Excited barks came from upstairs; Dotty wasn't allowed up there, as Ava well knew, but I bit my tongue. This holiday was as hard for her as me; probably worse, as I still loved her however badly she behaved, while Ava hated me however well I behaved.

'Isn't it marvellous to be back!' Audrey followed us in, bringing a little dose of sunshine with her. 'An all-girls holiday!

Won't we have fun! We should have a spa day if we can find one, and get rid of all those winter blues.'

It would take more than a facial and some nail varnish to buff away the blues I'd been through this winter, but I smiled and agreed. Ava was busy glaring at me as if there was only one thing she wanted to get rid of, and it was more Black than blue.

'Where are we sleeping?' she asked, an unmistakeable challenge in her voice.

'I thought you and Chloe could share the room in the attic.'

'Without a bathroom?' She couldn't have sounded more horrified if I'd offered them a room with no beds.

'There's one right at the bottom of the stairs.'

'Which room are you in?'

'The usual.'

'But how is that fair? We're the only ones sharing a room, so we need the biggest. You should have the small one as you're on your own.'

Ava cocked her head to the side, and her eyes shimmered with a curious mix of excitement at her own insolence, and fear that she may have gone too far. Audrey squeezed my hand.

'I don't mind the top floor,' she said. 'I used to love sleeping under the eaves and hearing the rain dancing on the roof slates. It will make me feel quite young again.'

'No, you can have your normal room.' I smiled as brightly as I could manage. 'Ava's right. She and Chloe can have the master bedroom, at least until Leo and Clark come.'

Ava wandered away to claim her prize, no doubt disappointed that I hadn't argued about it. I thought I heard a murmur of 'little cow' from Daisy's direction, but when I turned her way, her lips were as still as if they were playing musical statues.

'I couldn't face another argument,' I said, giving an explanation, though no one had asked for one.

'Giving things up is all part and parcel of being a mother,' Mum said. 'You're lucky it's only a room.'

As opposed to a whole house, I supposed she meant, like she'd given up for me and Leo. Although, to be fair to her, she'd done it with extraordinary good grace, and hadn't until this moment tainted the gift by making us feel guilty. Did she now think that with Leo gone, and the children likely to leave in the next few years, I didn't need the big house anymore?

'I'm sorry,' I said, sounding snippy but unable to prevent it, 'if you ever felt you had to give up anything for me.'

'Like I said, mothers make sacrifices every day,' she replied. 'Some small, some big, and most of them unacknowledged. We show we care in a thousand ways, even if we can't say it, or our children don't want to listen.'

And with this bizarre speech, she patted me on the shoulder and went off to find her room.

No one wanted to cook after the long journey, so we strolled down to a hotel in Carbis Bay for dinner. We were a surprisingly merry little group as we drank our wine and watched the waves creep up and down the sand; Audrey and Daisy were rarely stuck for words, and even Mum relaxed enough to smile when Audrey teased her about having left her mystery man behind.

Audrey and Mum walked the girls home after the meal, leaving me and Daisy to finish the wine on our own.

'I've often wondered how you could bear to go away with the parents,' Daisy said, as we settled down in comfy chairs in a conservatory bar overlooking the beach. The beach was deserted except for a middle-aged couple who wandered hand in hand by the water's edge, dodging the waves. 'Now I see the benefit. Is this what you and Leo used to do? Hide out in the bar until the kids were asleep?'

'No, we never did. Leo wasn't keen on spending the night in a pub. He was happy to stay at home.'

'Were you?'

'I . . .' It wasn't something I'd thought about. It was the way things were. When we were together, we read or watched TV, talked about Alice or the children – what difference would it have made having those conversations in a bar rather than at home? But as I watched the couple on the beach, ten or fifteen years older than me and yet acting like teenagers as they laughed and raced away from unexpectedly fast waves, I wondered why Leo and I had never done that, and whether it might have made a difference if we had. Perhaps a change of scene and time alone would have broadened our conversation, made us talk about who we really were and what we wanted. Perhaps then Leo's defection wouldn't have been such a surprise.

'When I fall in love,' I began. Daisy laughed.

'Will it be forever?'

'I hope so. But it will also be like that.' I waved my glass in the direction of the beach. The couple were now sitting on the sand, the man with his arm around the woman, her head resting on his shoulder. They weren't talking, just being together.

'Sweet, isn't it?' Daisy sighed. 'I know we're meant to be all feminist and say we can manage on our own, and we don't need a man. But it's rubbish. I don't want to manage on my own. I want companionship like that. I want someone to put the bins out when it's raining. I want someone to pour me a glass of wine when I've had a bad day. I want *someone*, you know?'

I nodded.

'I can't watch anything funny on television,' I said. 'I hate the sound of my own laughter echoing around the empty room.' I divided the remains of the wine between our glasses, and clinked mine against Daisy's. 'Here's to finding love and companionship.'

'Love and companionship.' She smiled. 'Talking of which, did you say Ethan was in New York for a few days? When does he get back?'

I choked on my wine, and my chest burned as the alcohol trickled into my lungs.

'Ethan?' I repeated, when I recovered enough to gasp out a few words. 'Are you serious about him?'

'No harm trying, is there? We could see if we have anything in common. He might be glad of the company with you lot down here for the summer. You wouldn't find it weird, would you?'

'Weird?' I echoed. 'No. Why should I?'

'Because he's practically your brother. But that wouldn't make it awkward, would it? You never know, if things went well, we could be sisters! And I see what you mean about Audrey. If mothers-in-law must exist, they should all be like her.'

I gazed out of the restaurant's picture windows. The clouds that had threatened us all day had thinned at last, and the sky was painted with glorious bold streaks of yellow, pink, orange, and blue as the sun set beyond the headland towards St Ives. But the beauty of the sky was in stark contrast to the ugly thoughts in my head. Audrey was mine. I didn't want to share her, even with Daisy. And as for Ethan . . . I closed my eyes and took a few long breaths to ease the sudden racing of my heart. I didn't want to share him either.

Daisy could only stay with us for a week. Her boss, the MP, used the parliamentary summer recess to interfere in local issues, and needed all his staff on hand to identify and arrange photo shoots about causes that would look good on his website and newsletter, and that he would promptly forget come autumn. Chloe would remain in Cornwall for another two weeks until I could bring her home.

Daisy's departure spoilt the dynamics of our group. Ava and Chloe were thick as thieves, getting up to all sorts that they shared on Instagram but not with me. Audrey and Mum were closer this summer than they had been in the past, as Audrey's weak wrist still restricted what she could do, and Mum delighted in being a martyr and sacrificing her own plans to help Audrey, even when no help was required. So that left me, the odd one out, unwanted by the young pair and unwanting to tag along with the old one. I had never had so much free time on holiday – never had so much free time at all. Was this a foretaste of how my life was going to be in a few years' time, when Jonas and Ava had both left home? One day of it was great; two days were tolerable; by the third day I was going out of my mind – so much so that as I lay in the garden, simmering in the glorious sunshine, my skin prickled and I could have sworn I was being watched, even though the others had all gone out.

'Sleeping in the day, Mary Black? You need to cut down on those boozy lunches.'

It was a sorry day when I was so desperate for company that I imagined Ethan was here. I reached over to pick up my book from the floor – it had slipped out of my hand, though I absolutely hadn't been sleeping – and caught sight of a pair of shoes by the garden gate. My gaze travelled up and over a pair of jeans, a T-shirt, and a face that undoubtedly belonged to Ethan.

'Are you real?'

'Certainly am. Why, were you dreaming about me?'

He grinned and I rallied.

'It's too delightful a day to be having nightmares.'

He laughed and walked towards me across the lawn, leaving a holdall behind him.

'What are you doing here?'

'I've come on holiday. Mum said there was an empty room, and invited me to fill it.'

Audrey? She hadn't mentioned it to me. I should have been cross – if my mum had done this, I would have been furious – but oddly, my first thought was to be glad. Company! Someone my age to talk to! I may even have smiled – until Ethan plonked down on my sunlounger, pushing my legs aside with his bottom. Then my burgeoning pleasure at seeing him turned to horror as I realised how *he* was seeing *me*. This was a girls' holiday, which gave us a degree of laxity that we might not have enjoyed with men around. My bikini, much like me, had seen better days, and no longer fitted as securely as it once had. At my age, if I lolled on a sunlounger, random bits of my anatomy lolled too. And Ethan didn't even have the decency to look away.

I sat up, whipped out the towel I was lying on, and threw it over me. Ethan laughed.

'Spoilsport. Do I have to remind you that I've seen you naked?'

'Please don't.' I tucked the towel under my arms. 'Over twenty years and two children have happened since then.'

214

'There doesn't look much difference to me.'

'You shouldn't be looking! Bugger off, and save your twaddle for someone who wants it. I thought you were in New York?'

'I flew back on Friday. Everything is going well, and they can manage until October.'

'October?'

'When my six-month sabbatical ends.'

I'd forgotten about that. Was he halfway through his time already? It had rushed by – and yet, in some ways, it felt as if he'd been here forever. It was hard to imagine going back to the days when he was on the other side of the Atlantic, not leaping over the hedge from Audrey's house or luring me into his cottage for a cup of tea when I was taking Dotty for a walk around the reservoir.

'You're definitely going back?' I asked. That would scupper Daisy's plans, and perhaps I ought to warn her before she set her heart too firmly on Ethan.

'I have to. But whether I stay is another question.'

'And the answer no doubt depends on a woman.' Perhaps Daisy had a chance, after all. 'Anyone I know?'

Ethan shifted on the lounger. The tint of my sunglasses enhanced every colour, making his eyes an extraordinarily rich blue. But when he lifted my sunglasses away from my face, his eyes looked no different, dazzling straight into mine.

'I had a drink with Daisy last night.'

'Did you?' Despite the heat of the sun, and the warmth of

Ethan's buttocks pressed against my thighs, a chill slithered through me. 'Hang on. Last night? And you're here today? Don't tell me you slept with her and ran away?'

'Of course not. We had one drink.'

'One?' I repeated, risking dizziness with the speed of my U-turn. 'What's wrong with her? She's gorgeous and funny and smart. And a woman, which I thought was all that mattered to you. Since when did you get so fussy?'

'Since always. She's not the right woman.' He fiddled with the edge of my towel. 'Don't go fixing me up with any more of your friends. If I want you to be involved in my love life, I'll ask, okay?'

Chapter Eighteen

Ethan's arrival transformed our holiday. He effortlessly charmed Mum and Audrey, was cool with Ava and Chloe, and knitted us all back together as one group. We had grown lazy over the years, rarely venturing out further than St Ives, but for Ethan it was all new, and he dragged us out to places that we hadn't been to before, or that had changed so much since our last visit that it felt like our first time. It was the best holiday we'd had for ages, and however much I rejected the thought – that was so disloyal to Leo – it wouldn't go away.

Even simple pleasures, such as going to the beach, something Leo had never been keen on, sounded fun when Ethan suggested it. I couldn't remember the last time we had spent a day on the beach, and certainly couldn't remember Mum ever coming with us. But when we woke up to a cloudless sky and burning sun, and Ethan bounded down to breakfast with a cry of, 'Let's go to the beach!', we all dashed round gathering up chairs and towels, balls and books, and enough food and drink for an army, as if it was the greatest adventure of our lives.

Dared by Ethan, Chloe and Ava were the first into the sea, shrieking with horrified delight, and reminding me that my little girl still lurked somewhere beneath the attitude and the indecent bikini. Ethan soon followed, stripping off his T-shirt and plunging straight into the water in a way that made me shiver to watch. I peered over the top of my book from time to time, drawn by the squeals and laughter.

'Isn't he marvellous with them?' Audrey asked, catching me watching. They were throwing an inflatable ball around, and it looked as if the girls were deliberately missing Ethan by miles so that he had to swim to fetch it. 'I know it was naughty of me, but aren't you glad I invited him?'

I was – until my book was snatched out of my hands, and icy water dripped onto my legs.

'That's enough reading,' Ethan said. 'Teenagers turn evil when mixed with sea water. I need back-up.'

It was lucky that I was wearing my sunglasses, because my eyes must have dangled out of their sockets at the sight in front of me. Ethan was wearing nothing but a pair of wet beach shorts that clung to him in eye-catching fashion. Water trickled from his hair, down his neck, and across an unbelievably well-defined chest. Was that a real six-pack? I'd never seen one in the flesh, and certainly not so close that with one twitch of my arm I could stroke my finger along those grooves . . .

'Earth to Mary. Are you asleep again?'

The chest loomed far too close as Ethan leaned in and poked my shoulder.

'Get off!' I batted him away, inadvertently swiping the six-pack as I did. My cheeks blazed. 'Shouldn't you have more clothes on?'

'I'm on the beach. What do you expect me to wear? Waders and a cagoule?'

That sounded an excellent idea, preferably teamed with a balaclava to hide the smile.

'There are impressionable young girls about. You look too . . .'

'Too what?'

It was a good question. All sorts of words were racing through my head, none of which I wanted to admit to by letting them out of my mouth: hunky, attractive, sexy. God help me. Was this the effect of sunstroke or had I gone mad?

'Too male,' I said, flapping my hands about as if I were being attacked by midges. 'Too James Bond.'

I really wished I hadn't said that when Ethan shook with laughter, sprinkling me with more water. He held out his hand.

'Come on. You can be Ursula Andress.'

I hated being cold and wet, but as anything would be better than continuing this conversation, I ignored his hand and stood up. Turning my back on Ethan – as if that would magically prevent him seeing me – I pulled off my shorts and T-shirt.

'What the hell is that? I know you like all things Victorian, but isn't a vintage bathing costume taking it too far?'

'I bought it last year,' I said, trying to muster some dignity while I folded my clothes in a tidy pile. It was my public swimming costume, designed to be serviceable and to cover up as much of me as possible. It was nowhere near as bad as Ethan was implying and, to my mind, infinitely better than the scrap of bikini he'd caught me wearing before.

'From an antiques shop? I'm surprised you didn't demand a Victorian changing hut too. Watch out! I can see your ankles.'

Laughing, I walked down to the sea – running would have highlighted my wobbly bits – and paddled in deep enough to cover my ankles.

'Not far enough.' Ethan waded past me, shaking his head. 'Up to your knees, at least.'

I shuffled forwards, but stopped as a gigantic wave sloshed against my thighs, numbing my legs.

'One more step.' Ethan offered his hand again, and this time I took it, as I had lost all sensation of having legs below the level of the water. I didn't know how Ava and Chloe could bear being so far out, bobbing about up to their waists with occasional waves splashing over their shoulders. Ethan needn't think he could cajole me out that far . . .

With one tug on my hand, Ethan pulled me over and I fell forward into the sea. My head went under the water, and for a second I flailed as the shock and the cold numbed my reactions; and then my face crowned the water again, the sun burned into my hair, and two strong hands grasped my waist and lifted me back onto my feet.

'Bastard!' I shrieked, pummelling his chest. I shivered as the breeze skated over my damp skin. 'What did you do that for?'

Ethan laughed, and pulled us both down so that our shoulders were under the water. His hands were still securing my waist, and our legs tangled.

'Because sometimes, Mary Black, you have to stop thinking about things and take the plunge.'

Time cranked to a halt. The world shrank to this tiny space, less than a metre square, in which I was aware only of the scent of coconut sun cream and the sensation of swirling water massaging my skin, the sun's rays stroking my face, and Ethan's fingers curling around my back. The cries of the seagulls, the shrieks and the laughter of children, were muffled as if an open window had been slammed shut, and all I could hear was Ethan's words – or more than that: a whole different message that seemed to come from his eyes rather than his voice. And the sea around us suddenly felt so hot that it could have poached an egg in seconds.

'Mum! Mum!' Ava's call filtered into my mind, and the weird moment dissolved. Reality rushed back in, chasing away my wild imaginings. I swam over to her, savouring the freedom of coasting through the fresh water. Ethan overtook me and as I stood up I caught him high-fiving the girls.

'What's going on?' They all collapsed with laughter. 'Was this a trick to get me in the water? Did you not need help?'

'You're such a sucker,' Ava said. She was smiling at me, which was a rare event, so I didn't take offence at her words.

221

'You can read anytime,' Ethan added. 'We thought you needed rescuing from being boring.'

'Boring?' I wasn't going to forgive that however much he smiled. Grabbing the beach ball, I hurled it at Ethan, hoping it would clobber him on the head and knock that smile away. I should have known better. The combination of his athletic prowess and my lack of it meant that the ball was an easy catch for him.

'Piggy in the middle!' he yelled, and tossed the ball over my head to Ava, who in turn threw it over to Chloe. And so began a series of games, races and competitions, mostly at my expense, during which I saw Ava laugh more than she had probably done in the last three years, in my company at least. At one point she even clung with her arms round my neck, her slippery little body trying to wriggle on top of mine as if I were a surfboard, exactly as she had done in the public swimming baths when she had still been my adoring little girl. We hadn't been so close in months, physically or emotionally. And I couldn't help thinking that I had Ethan to thank for this. These precious moments wouldn't have happened if he hadn't joined our holiday. Our three weeks would have slipped away, one beige day after another; and instead here we were, living a day that sparkled and shone with colour.

I had hardly registered the knock on the door before it opened and Ethan walked in.

'What are you doing?' He was the last person I expected

or wanted to see in my bedroom. 'I could have been getting dressed.'

'I know. Curse my rotten timing.' He grinned, and I looked away, towel-drying my hair for the second time in a bid to hide my face. Two minutes earlier and he would have found me in my bra and knickers, and how would we have ever moved past that? Saggy underwear seemed so much more intimate than a bikini. 'Come on. We're going out for breakfast.'

'Breakfast? Surely no one else is up yet?'

'No one else is invited.'

I folded the towel in half, then quarters, then eighths.

'I can't do that,' I said, when the towel defied my efforts to tidy it any further.

'I need to take Dotty for a walk and make breakfast for everyone.'

'No, you don't. The mothers can cope – and if they can't, two teenagers certainly can. They won't come to any harm if you take one morning off.'

He held the door open, waiting for me to go through, and before I knew what was going on, we had crept out of the silent house and were on the coast path walking towards St Ives. It was a gorgeous bright morning, and the sun was burning off the early sea mist, revealing spectacular views across to the bay of St Ives in one direction and Godrevy Lighthouse in the other. Even after ten years of holidaying here, I wasn't tired of this view.

'Where are we going?' I asked, as we walked down the hill towards Porthminster Beach.

'Here.' Ethan indicated the Porthminster Beach Café. 'There can't be a better spot, can there?'

He led the way inside, straight through the cheery white-washed main restaurant and onto the terrace. It was busy here, but the waitress led us to the one empty table for two in the prime spot on the front row, directly above the sand.

'You have the devil's own luck,' I said, as we took our seats at right angles to each other, so we could both face out to sea. 'Fancy one of the best tables being available just as you turn up.'

'An amazing coincidence, isn't it?' He grinned, in a highly suspicious way, but he was looking down at his menu so I couldn't read his eyes.

We gave our orders: poached eggs on sourdough toast for me, and a stack of pancakes with maple syrup and bacon for Ethan.

'Pancakes? You really have turned into a native New Yorker, haven't you?'

'Only where food is concerned.'

'So you haven't entirely lost your heart to America?'

'My heart never left Lancashire. Coming home has made that clear.'

I was about to make a joke – he'd been through so many women over the years that it was a wonder he had any heart left – but he looked up, and my flippant words withered, and I fussed about pouring tea instead.

'You must love New York too, to have stayed so long. Is it exactly like we see on TV and in films?'

'It was hard to believe it was real, at first. You turn a corner and step onto a movie set. You should have come to visit. I'd have loved to show you around, the famous sights and the secret ones.'

'We couldn't come,' I said, and though I tried hard not to sound wistful, I failed. 'It was never the right time. And there's no way we could have afforded it.'

'I offered to pay.'

'Leo wouldn't have accepted.'

'I know. That's why the year before last I went ahead and bought the tickets. October half term – I checked the dates with school. The kids would have loved the Halloween parade. I couldn't believe it when you still didn't come.'

'I didn't know.' I put down my tea cup. If Ethan was telling the truth – and instinctively I knew he was – where did that leave Leo? 'Leo never mentioned it. He can't have known. Did you post the tickets? They must have got lost.'

'Leo knew. We talked about it.'

An inflection in Ethan's voice on the word 'talked' suggested it hadn't been an amicable discussion. But it still made no sense. An all-expenses-paid trip to New York? Leo wouldn't have turned that down, not when he knew how much I would have loved to go.

'There must have been a misunderstanding. Leo wouldn't have kept that a secret.'

'It's not the biggest secret he's kept from you, is it?'

I gripped my cup between my hands, and held them there even when the heat of the contents spread and tingled along my skin.

'Sorry.' Ethan's finger traced a line down the back of my right hand, so now both sides tingled. 'It still annoys me that you didn't come. Would you really have liked to?'

I nodded.

'I love it here,' I said, indicating with my hand the sweep of the fine sand in front of us, now filling with families, and the sea beyond that stretched until it became indistinct from the sky. 'But occasionally it would be good to experience places and not just read about them.'

'You must have been on holiday somewhere else.'

I shrugged, and leant back as our breakfasts arrived.

'The odd weekend in the Lake District. A wet weekend in Wales.' I stabbed an egg with my fork, and the runny yolk bled over the toast. 'Never abroad. Jonas and Ava have travelled further on school trips than I have. I've not been abroad since I came with you to France.'

'When we were fifteen?' Ethan laughed, his whole face lighting up with the memory. 'That was a fantastic holiday. You were hilarious. *Oui, ça va, merci.*'

It had been my stock response to every French person I'd met, and had become the running joke of the holiday. Ethan was right: it had been a fantastic two weeks. Audrey and Bill had rented a gîte in the Dordogne to celebrate Leo's A level results and his place at Oxford. They had invited me too, and I had squeezed in the middle of the back seat of their car, one thigh pressed against Leo, one thigh pressed against Ethan, for the long drive down there. Leo had spent most of the fortnight pre-reading for his English degree in the shade of a walnut tree in the garden. Ethan and I had borrowed a couple of bone-shaking bicycles and ridden through the country lanes in the sunshine, stopping only to picnic on baguettes, Brie, and beer stolen from Bill, and to wash off our exertions in the river. The whole holiday had been a delight from start to finish, and by the end of it I was more in love with the Blacks than ever, and determined that I would be part of their family one day.

After breakfast, Ethan dragged me down to the beach, and we wandered along the water's edge, shoes dangling from our hands. A rogue wave splashed over my feet and I shrieked. Ethan grabbed my hand.

'Run!' he shouted, and he towed me along, splashing through the shallows until we reached the end of the beach, where we collapsed onto the sand, laughing. I lay back, basking like a seal, trying to get my breath back without obviously panting.

'There are places in the world,' Ethan said – of course, there was no sign of him labouring for breath – 'where the sea is as warm as a bath, and you can dive below the surface and see creatures of shapes and colours that you wouldn't believe are real. There are mountains only a couple of hours away, where you can sunbathe at the bottom and ski at the top, even in the middle of summer. There are igloos made of glass where you can spend the night watching the Northern Lights cascade overhead. There are . . .'

'Enough,' I said. 'Those places might exist in your life. They don't in mine.'

Ethan turned his head towards me.

'They should. They could.'

How? I wanted to ask. What was I supposed to do with real life and real responsibilities while I gallivanted across the world enjoying myself? But I couldn't say it, not to Ethan. What did he know about responsibility, about putting your own wishes aside for the sake of others? He would dismiss me as beige for even thinking about the obstacles.

Ethan's phone buzzed and spared me answering. He checked the screen and stood up.

'Come on,' he said, holding out his hand. 'Time to go back.'

He hauled me up, making a great show of straining as if I were heavy, and teasing a smile out of me despite my best efforts to resist. We strolled back to the cottage, and I headed straight to the kitchen, anticipating that I would need to clear up. But instead of a pile of dirty pots, the first thing I saw when I walked in was a banner reading, 'Happy Birthday!' hanging over the sink, and the four guilty faces of Audrey, Mum, Ava, and Chloe; five faces if I counted Dotty, who had a habitually guilty expression.

'Surprise!' Audrey cried, with a feeble echo from the others.

She stood up and came over to give me a kiss and a hug. 'Happy birthday, my darling. Have you had a wonderful breakfast?'

'Yes, I . . .' I turned to Ethan. 'You knew? You were in on this?'

'He was the chief instigator.' Audrey gave me another squeeze. 'We wanted this year to be different.'

This first year without Leo, she meant, and my heart ached with gratitude. I had blocked out all thought of today, dreading how odd it would be, and that without Leo no one might even remember, as Mum wasn't known for making a fuss. And yet already it had been one of the best birthdays I'd had for years. I smiled at Ethan.

'Of course I know when your birthday is.' He kissed my cheek, and I thought he was going to leave it at that, but he pulled me in for a long hug too. 'Happy birthday, Mary.'

I pulled away – the faint scent of his floral aftershave against his sun-warmed skin was worryingly addictive – and Mum and Ava both wished me a happy birthday. Ava handed over an envelope.

'Here's your present.' Before I could open it, she continued. 'It's a voucher for a day at a spa, with treatments and lunch. We're all going. Gran's driving,' she added, pulling her face.

'All of us?' I glanced at Ethan. 'What are you having done?'

'All the girls,' he clarified. 'I'm looking after Dotty. I don't mind,' he said, as I opened my mouth to voice a protest – a half-hearted one, because the thought of a few hours being pampered was irresistible. 'Now off you go, and don't come back until you're so relaxed you can barely hold yourself vertical.'

On that basis, I'd never see the cottage again. But several hours later, after I'd been pummelled and plucked, scrubbed and scented, I was so relaxed that I oozed rather than walked back in to the house. As I wafted past the dining room, Dotty woofed a greeting, and I peered round the door. Ethan was sitting at the table, frowning at the screen of his laptop. He was wearing dark brown glasses that I'd never seen before. He looked up and saw me, and removed the glasses.

'I didn't know you needed those,' I said. He pulled a face.

'The punishment for a lifetime spent staring at a screen. Old age is breathing down my neck.'

'They don't make you look old. You look . . .'

He tipped his head, waiting for me to finish, but I smiled and let the sentence drop. He looked a different Ethan: a serious, thoughtful, reliable Ethan – someone I wasn't familiar with.

'Are you okay, Mary? You look spaced out.' Ethan shut his laptop and stood up. 'Have all those fancy oils made you crazy?' He leant forward and sniffed me. 'You do smell delicious.'

Crazy? The oils must be hallucinogenic, because for a bonkers moment, with Ethan's face and lips skimming my neck, lust whooshed up inside me like the flames in a gas fire. I stepped back, rubbing my forehead with the heel of my hand to erase these horribly inappropriate thoughts.

230

'I hope you're not too sleepy,' Ethan said, picking something up from the table. 'Because I haven't given you my present yet.' My hand stopped rubbing and I goggled at him, inappropriate thoughts very much still alive. He held out some paper. 'Tickets for the Minack Theatre tonight. It's *Much Ado About Nothing*. That's okay, isn't it? Not Victorian, I know, but . . .'

'It's brilliant.' Here was a different Ethan again – hesitant, uncertain, and looking inexplicably worried. 'I love Shakespeare. Is it just the two of us again?'

'Well, no . . . I got tickets for everyone. I didn't think you'd want . . .'

'No, that's perfect!' My manic smile punctuated the sentence with at least five exclamation marks. 'Of course we shouldn't go on our own. Audrey's going to love this, isn't she? I'll go and tell her now.'

'She already . . .'

I was out of the room before he'd finished his sentence.

It was a fantastic night. After a pub meal, full of delicious food and laughter, we drove on to the Minack and took our places on the grassy stone seats. The stage hovered on the cliff edge, above Porthcurno Bay, such a glorious setting that I would have been happy to sit and watch the light fade over the sea, and not bother with the play. I changed my mind when the performance started: it was a skilful production, funny, touching, and irresistibly romantic in turn, and I cheered so loudly at the end that Ethan pretended to cover his ears, and Ava rolled her eyes at my embarrassing behaviour.

It had been a long day. Everyone vanished to their rooms when we arrived home. I stayed downstairs to let Dotty out and make a cup of tea. I thought Ethan had already gone up, but ran into him in the hall as I was on my way to bed.

'Have you had a good day?' he asked.

'It was great. Thank you, for breakfast, and for the theatre, and . . .' I shrugged. Just for being there, I could have added. The day would have been something entirely different without him. I had hardly thought about Leo, except when I had opened his card – *their* card – this morning. 'Thanks.'

'It was my pleasure.' And though it could have been just a glib response, I could see that it wasn't – in the half-light of the lamps casting shadows around the hall, his face shone bright with genuine happiness. 'Have you made your wish?'

'You remembered that?'

'I remember everything.'

Everything? I clutched my mug to my chest. He couldn't really mean everything, could he? There was one memory I had reassured myself he must have forgotten long ago.

'Was it the usual wish?'

I nodded, flicking back to the present day. Since the first birthday after my dad's disappearance, I had made the same wish – that he would come home. It was the first thing I did each birthday morning, before I got out of bed, and even thirty years on, I had spent a few moments making my wish and wondering if he was thinking of me today.

That had been my birthday wish this morning. But now I longed to be greedy, and have some more. I wished that this day would keep repeating on a perpetual loop, until I remembered no other past and feared no other future. I wished that Jonas was with us, and that time would pause so that we could stay here and live a life full of fun as we had done today. And I wished with all my heart that it had been any man but Ethan who had made me so happy.

'Keep faith, Mary. It might come true.'

'It can't,' I said, hardly knowing which wish I meant. 'It's impossible.'

'But that doesn't matter, does it? Sometimes the things we want are so fundamental a part of us that you can't let go, however long it's been, and however impossible it seems. You have to stay loyal to hope, because what else is there?'

He could have sliced open my heart and read those same words running through the centre. How did he know me so well, how did he understand? The grandfather clock in the hall struck midnight, and I fled up the stairs to bed.

Chapter Nineteen

By the third week of the holiday, we had become so used to Mum's mystery man sending her letters, gifts, and flowers – all of which were whisked away to her room in a hilariously furtive manner – that when she wandered in to the kitchen one morning, a Jiffy bag in her hands, Ethan nodded his head and winked at me, but no one made any remark – until Mum dropped the bag on the table in front of me.

'There's a parcel for you, Mary,' she said, managing to sound curious, disappointed, and disapproving all at once.

'Oh Mary, have you found yourself a secret lover, too?' Audrey asked, hooting with laughter. 'I hope he's as rich as a Sheikh and hung like a horse. Or do I mean donkey? Is there a difference? Irene?'

Mum flicked on the kettle, her stiff neck indicating that she wanted no part in this lewd conversation. Chloe and Ava sniggered in the corner. Ethan gazed at me from across the table, his customary smile absent.

'Of course I haven't,' I protested. 'I've no idea what it is or who it's from.'

I yanked at the flap of the envelope, but it was stuck down with at least half a roll of Sellotape, and I had to resort to hacking it open with scissors. I pulled out a sheaf of cheap, shiny copier paper, attached to which there was a compliments slip from Archer's Booksellers bearing the words, 'To Mary Black – strictly Private and Confidential. *For your eyes only.*'

I unfastened the paperclip, looked at the first sheet beneath it, and my lungs jammed halfway through a breath. It was a poor photocopy, but the paper was headed, 'Chapter One', and below it the page was filled with line after line of Alice Hornby's handwriting. I rifled through the pile, noting the increasing chapter headings, and reading the odd paragraph here and there. None of it was familiar. I knew Alice's books inside out, and these words didn't belong to any of them.

'Oh my God,' I said, finding my breath, and not caring that I sounded horribly like Ava. 'I think this might be Alice Hornby's missing novel.' I flicked to the last page, where the word 'End' had been written with a flourish. 'And it's finished!'

'Where's it come from?' Ethan's smile dazzled me across the table, probably a mirror image of my own.

'From old Mrs Archer. Remember the lady in the wheel-chair?' He nodded. 'This must be what she was hiding in the blue box – perhaps even the original manuscript. I hoped it might be more letters, or a diary. I never expected this.' I scooped up the papers and clutched them to my chest. 'This is the most fantastic thing ever. If this is real, it could change the face of Victorian literature. This is huge! I have to read it.'

'What, now?' Ava glared at me from the window seat where she was sitting with Chloe. 'You said you'd take us shopping in Truro today. You promised.'

'I know, and I'm sorry, but this is work . . .'

'Work?' Ava stomped over to the table and stood in front of me, one foot forward, arms folded, attitude to the fore. 'You don't work. You read a few books, make some phone calls, and send some emails for Dad. You're just selfish. You only ever do what you want to do.'

Even Audrey remained silent, apparently unable to think of anything to laugh about this time. I tried to tell myself that Ava didn't mean it – that these were sulky, careless words, flung recklessly, not with deadly intent – but the pain was the same when they landed, whether she had intended it or not. To have my whole life belittled and reduced to nothing, by the child I had cherished and adored since I had first stroked her tiny hand, was a unique kind of agony.

'That's not fair, Ava,' Ethan said. 'Your mum has given everything for this family. She works incredibly hard. She wrote most of the book your dad's just published.'

'How do you know that?' I couldn't believe Leo had told him, and I certainly hadn't.

'I've read it,' Ethan said. 'Your voice is on every page. It's a brilliant book.' He turned to Ava before I could follow that up. 'You can't waste this weather on shopping. An old friend from university runs a surf school up the coast towards Rock.

What do you say to you, me, and Chloe giving it a go? I'm sure we can find a teashop for the grans.'

'Cool,' Ava said, giving a one-shouldered shrug, but unable to stop an excited grin spreading across her face. She hurried away with Chloe, no doubt to make sure their hair and make-up were perfect before it was ruined by a drenching in the sea.

'Are you sure about this?' I asked Ethan. 'You don't have to take them out. I could save this for later.'

'Could you?' He looked at my chest. I was still hugging the pages to me. He smiled, and came around the table to squeeze my shoulder. 'Take the day to yourself, and read your book. I'm happy to help.'

He left the kitchen, and the sound of his footsteps drifted into the room as he ran upstairs. I turned back from the door and found both Mum and Audrey watching me.

'Isn't he lovely, Mary?' Audrey said. 'And so good with the girls.'

'He's Ava's uncle,' Mum said, giving a pointed nod in my direction as she emphasised that last word. 'Family. It's only right that he mucks in.'

'He's very kind,' I said, thinking that it was a suitably neutral response. But as both mothers sighed, I had an odd feeling that in some way I had managed to disappoint them both.

As soon as the house was empty, I took the photocopied manuscript to the living room, settled down with my feet up on the sofa, and a cup of tea at my side, started to read – and the whole day vanished. I loved all Alice's books, but this one was in another league. It was essentially a love triangle, involving two sisters and one man: the eldest sister and the man were pressured into an arranged marriage, although he was in love with the younger one, a feeling secretly returned. The eldest sister died giving birth to her third child, and the man moved away with his children. Though it was illegal in those days to marry your deceased sibling's husband or wife, the younger sister travelled around the country until she found him; and they finally lived as man and wife, though they couldn't legally wed.

It was a simple story – but the passion that throbbed in every word, the yearning of the younger sister who defied the law and convention to be with the man she loved, lifted it into something extraordinary. Every sentence was so full of heart, so drenched in raw passion, that it was more like reading the most intimate diary than a novel. But though it had an echo of Alice's life, it couldn't be autobiographical. We knew that Alice had returned to live with her parents when her sister died, and that the sister's husband had gone on to marry a woman ten years his senior. So how could Alice, a spinster and virgin as far as anyone knew, have described desire and longing with an intensity that made my own heart pound?

'Hey, have you been here all day? Mary?' I jumped as Ethan pulled my toes, dragging me back to Cornwall and the present. He picked up my full mug of tea from the floor and moved it to the table. 'This is completely cold. Have you moved since we left?'

'Yes . . .' I had, hadn't I? As if to answer the question, my stomach gave a muttering rumble. Perhaps I had been too caught up in the book to move. Ethan laughed, and pushing my legs aside, sat on the sofa.

'How was the surfing?' I peered past Ethan, but the room was empty. 'You have brought everyone back safely, haven't you?'

'It was fantastic. Ava and Chloe gave it a good go.' He smiled. 'They had to rush upstairs to sort their hair out. How was the book? As good as you hoped?'

'Better. It's amazing. So beautifully written. I can't wait to read it again and take my time over it.' I told him a brief outline of the story. 'This could be massive. The younger sister is such a modern heroine in many ways – defying convention and public opinion to fight for what she wants, and what will make her happy.'

'But it's only half a happy ending if they couldn't marry. It wasn't allowed in those days, was it? Thank God that stupid law has changed.'

'Since when did you know so much about family law?' Ethan shrugged and rubbed at a patch of dried sand on his leg. 'Anyway, I think we're both proof that marriage doesn't guarantee happiness.'

Ethan looked up.

'What happened to falling in love and the great new adventure?'

'Nothing's happened yet.'

'Really? Not even a teeter?'

'No.' But it seemed that my body was determined to contradict everything I said, because as Ethan gazed at me, forget-me-not blue eyes like magnets drawing me in, my heart galloped; not so much teetering, as already mid-flight. It was Alice Hornby's fault: all that passion and longing had stirred me up, made me dissatisfied with being alone. There was nothing more to it than that, nothing deeper. All the same, when Audrey wandered in, it felt like someone had thrown me a rope.

'Have you had a good day?' I asked, trying to sit up, but Ethan was leaning against my legs and I was stuck.

'Marvellous. I was almost tempted to have a go myself.' Audrey hovered by an armchair. 'Am I interrupting something interesting?'

'No.' I managed to shift my legs at last, and nudged Ethan with my knees. It wasn't meant to hurt, but he looked unusually grumpy as he stood up. 'We were talking about this book.'

'Have you read it already? You are clever. And is it what you hoped?'

'Yes, I think it really is Alice's last novel. The handwriting and the style are right, but we'll need to see the original, go through the provenance, and have it authenticated.' I stroked the top page, excitement replacing more unwelcome feelings. 'I can't wait to tell Leo. This is going to make his year. His decade, probably.'

'Leo?' Ethan stared over at me, from where he was now perching on the arm of Audrey's chair. 'You're going to tell Leo?'

'Yes, of course. He's been looking for this book for years. Why wouldn't I tell him?'

Ethan reached forward and picked up the compliments slip that had been attached to the manuscript.

'For your eyes only,' he read, tapping the paper for emphasis.

'That doesn't mean I can't show it to Leo,' I said. 'We'll work on it together.'

'Why? This is your discovery. You deserve the credit for it.'

'And I'm sure Leo will give me credit.'

'Like he did on the biography that you clearly wrote for him? Where was your name on that? You weren't even in the acknowledgements.'

The thin sheets of the manuscript crumpled under my fingers. That wound hadn't scabbed over, even after all these months. I had written the first draft of the acknowledge-ments, and obviously hadn't included myself. I had passed the draft to Leo to check before sending it to the publisher. He had tweaked it, moving a few names up the pecking order, but hadn't included mine – nor was the book dedi-cated to me. It was only after the book was published that I saw the dedication: 'To Clark – for showing me how to be myself.'

'Things have changed, Mary,' Ethan said, in a softer voice. 'You need to think about your own career now, and stop

241

taking a back seat to Leo. Why can't you be the one to publish this book, and do whatever you need to do with it?'

My slouching ambition sat up straight, and waved an eager arm high in the air, desperate to be the one to do it. I would love to edit this book, to tighten up some of the passages and to remove a few clunky phrases and repetitions that I was sure Alice would have changed if she'd revised the book again. I'd love to launch it on the world, to parade it around the country, and to see Alice finally take her place alongside the other great nineteenth-century writers. But it was impossible.

'I couldn't do that to Leo. He's waited his whole life for this. I couldn't be so disloyal.'

'Disloyal?' Ethan stood up, shaking off Audrey's restraining hand. 'Do you really think Leo is so scrupulous about being loyal to you?'

That was a low blow, and I swung my legs to the floor, so that I could glare at him properly without cricking my neck.

'You don't need to remind me about Clark. Leo fell in love. I'm not going to punish him for that.'

'I'm not talking about . . .'

'Ethan, my darling, will you help me with something in my bedroom?' Audrey spoke over Ethan, and stood up, linking her arm in his. 'One of the drawers is so stiff that I may have to turn my underwear inside out tomorrow if I can't open it.'

'Hang on,' I said, also standing up. 'I want to know what Ethan was going to say. Are you claiming that Leo has been disloyal before Clark? Prove it. If you're saying that Leo hasn't

242

been faithful to me, tell me when. I want the places, dates, and names.'

I stared at Ethan, holding his gaze, challenging him to finish what he'd started. My blissful day had shattered within the space of a few minutes. I held my breath, hardly knowing what I wanted him to say. There was no right answer here. If he gave me the details I'd asked for, proved Leo's infidelity went further than I knew, I'd be devastated. If he didn't – if it was all a petty lie, cooked up to cause trouble as part of the ongoing discord between Ethan and Leo, regardless of the pain it might cause me – then Ethan wasn't the man I thought he was either. One of the brothers was about to sink in my estimation, but which one would it be? Which would be worse?

Ethan opened his mouth. Audrey squeezed his arm. He let out a gushing sigh, so strong that it could have blown out a room full of candles, shook his head, and walked out, with Audrey scurrying after him. And there I had my answer to both questions, and flopped back down on to the sofa as unexpected, unwanted disappointment flooded my heart.

I could hardly believe our three weeks in St Ives were over; it had rushed by, until the last few days – until, within the space of a few seconds, I had realised that I thought more of Ethan than I should, and more of him than he deserved.

We were an odd group, on that final Saturday morning. Mum was as chirpy as I'd ever seen her, as she loaded up her car, seemingly thrilled to be returning to her mystery man. Audrey bombarded us with cups of tea, unable to appear too sad at our departure when she was looking forward to the arrival of Leo. Ethan was quiet, as he had been ever since our showdown: not sulking – he wasn't the sulky type – but not his usual sunny self either. Frustration clung to him as tightly as his T-shirt, but in a far less attractive way.

My own feelings were torn. I'd arranged to meet Jonas for lunch in Manchester tomorrow, and couldn't wait to see him, but leaving Ava behind for two weeks would be horrendous. Not that the impending separation bothered her; she was more upset that Chloe was leaving than that I was.

'I'll miss you,' I said, catching her in a hug. She stiffened and arched backwards away from me, so it felt like I was embracing a bendy plastic ruler that might snap at any point. 'It will be odd at home without you.'

Without anyone – I would have the house to myself, apart from Dotty. It would be a taste of the future, of when Jonas and Ava had moved on to university, or to their own houses. I tried to focus on the positive: my time would be my own; I could do whatever I wanted. So why couldn't I think of a single thing I wanted to do?

'It will be different here without you,' Ava said, and I smiled – it was as close to a compliment as I'd had from her in a long time. This holiday had worked wonders for our relationship, thanks to one person in particular. 'For a start, we won't have to watch your attempts to flirt with Uncle Ethan anymore.'

'What?' That jerked me out of my complacency. 'I've not flirted with anyone!'

'It's disgusting,' Ava said, flicking her hair over her shoulders and sneaking a quick look at herself in the mirror. 'A teacher was bad enough, but this is worse. I mean, he's Dad's brother. It's weird.'

I looked at Mum for back-up, but I should have known better. Her lips were so tightly pursed that it was impossible to believe she wouldn't have to spit out a mouthful of pennies before speaking.

'It would have been better if he hadn't come,' she said, folding her arms. 'You're clearly feeling needy and have latched on to the only man around. I didn't bring you up to act like a floozy, Mary. The poor man probably can't wait to get away.'

'A floozy?' With my history, it was hard to imagine a more ill-fitting description. 'So it's okay for you to have a man, but not me?'

'Not that man,' Mum said.

'And it's different with Gran,' Ava added, pouting in my direction. 'She needs a friend at her age. She won't be, like, having sex.'

'Oh, won't she! She's having a lot more of it than I am. Either that or they indulge in naked knitting in her bedroom.'

'Mary!'

I ignored Mum's admonishment, but did feel a twinge of guilt when Ava's face dropped in horror. Perhaps this hadn't been a suitable conversation for my teenage daughter to hear

245

– even if the teenager daughter was probably a lot more worldly-wise than I was.

'Urgh, you old people are just disgusting,' Ava said, moving her sunglasses from the top of her head to cover her eyes again, presumably so our gruesome, decrepit bodies couldn't offend her vision for a second longer.

'This sounds fun, what am I missing?' Ethan wandered in to the kitchen, and glanced between the three of us. He needn't look at me – torture wouldn't drag out of me what he had missed. I was fairly sure that Mum's lips would be all but sewn up too. Unfortunately that still left us with a blabby teen.

'You don't want to know,' Ava said, and I could tell her eyes were rolling behind those dark lenses. 'Mum and Gran are comparing their sex lives. It's the grossest thing ever.'

'Well . . .' Ethan began, but for once even his legendary teen-taming skills let him down. He caught my eye, and pulled a stricken 'rescue me' face. I laughed, and Ava let out an almighty huff and stomped out, slamming the door behind her.

Leo had new holiday clothes: the scruffy chinos and polo shirts he brought out every summer had been replaced by stylish shorts and a T-shirt, and he was wearing flip-flops despite years of acting as if they were the footwear choice of the devil. With a trendy pair of Tom Ford sunglasses covering his eyes, his transformation was complete: there was nothing left of the man I had married, and in his place stood the man who was going to marry Clark. I watched from the upstairs-landing window as Leo took Clark's hand and led him across the lawn, to the point where a gap in the trees revealed a swathe of the bay. Everything about their body language marked out their contentment, their complete rightness for each other, and this time it didn't hurt as much: my response had downgraded from pain to a sort of wistfulness that I thought I could probably live with.

I hurried downstairs and out into the garden. Never mind the view – I had something much more exciting than that to show Leo.

'Leo!' I shouted, tearing across the grass, wads of paper flapping in each hand. 'Look what I have!'

Leo and Clark turned away from the view, and both took a step back as I hurtled towards them: clearly I resembled a charging heffalump rather than the graceful gazelle of my imagination. I skidded to a sweaty, panting stop in front of them.

'Hello, Mary.' Leo brushed a kiss on to my cheek. Clark, valiantly overcoming his initial recoil, managed to force himself near enough to give a passable show of an air kiss. 'Is there an emergency?'

'No. Well, yes, in a way.' Leo lifted his sunglasses, as if I might make more sense unfiltered. 'This arrived a few days ago.'

I thrust the papers into his hand. He lowered the sunglasses again – they must be prescription lenses, as he was practically blind without them, something I'd been glad of as my body aged – and glanced down at the tatty pages. His reaction was all that I'd hoped it would be. His hand shook as he lifted the top page, and glanced at the next and the next one after that. His smile grew with every word he read.

'This is it,' he said, and there couldn't have been more joy in his face and his voice if he'd been holding a winning lottery ticket worth fifty million pounds. 'After all this time, I think this is it. Has this come from the Archers? We've done it, Mary! We've found Alice's last work!'

He hugged me, the manuscript still tightly grasped in his hand. I squeezed him back, brimming with tears over his evident delight, and more than anything, because of that double 'we'. Ethan was wrong, and I was right: Leo wouldn't take the credit for this. It was our discovery. We would work on it together, and it would be a huge success. Alice deserved nothing less.

Mum had already gone, desperate, I presumed, to be reunited with her lover; the idea of what she would be getting up to this afternoon was almost enough to put me off the family lunch that Audrey had organised. Poor Audrey – not even at her most optimistic could she have called it a marvellous gathering. As if the strained relationships around the table weren't enough to ruin the festivities, Leo and Clark spent the entire meal photographing Alice's manuscript on their iPads, page by page, after I'd refused to leave my copy with them.

There was no time to linger after lunch – we had a six-hour journey ahead of us, if the traffic was kind. As soon as the last page of the manuscript was photographed, I tucked it into my bag, bundled Chloe into my car, and said my good-byes.

'Don't worry about Ava,' Audrey whispered, as I clung to her, wondering how I would manage without my daily dose of good cheer from next door. 'We'll have a super time. You need to concentrate on yourself for the next two weeks. Do get up to lots of mischief, and tell me all about it when I get back.'

I prised myself away reluctantly, assaulted Ava with a final hug, and headed over to my car. Ethan was parked behind me, and hovered by his car, ready to move it to let me out.

'Enjoy the rest of your holiday,' I said, sounding horribly formal, but sure no one could accuse that of being a flirta-tious statement.

'I'll only stay one more night. Leo won't want me hanging around.'

He smiled, but newly wary, I couldn't help dissecting his words for hidden criticism of Leo.

'What are you going to do on your own for two weeks?' Ethan asked. 'You should come round to the cottage. It seems daft for each of us to cook for one and eat on our own every night.'

It did seem daft, and my head filled with an image of lazing in the garden of Waterman's Cottage, laughing, drinking wine, and watching the sun gild the reservoir as it dropped behind the trees. It was far too appealing an image.

'I won't be on my own,' I said, opening the car door and stepping behind it, as if it were a shield. 'Daisy will be around, and I'm sure Owen will be too.'

'Owen?' A rare frown puckered Ethan's forehead. 'The teacher? You're going to see him again?'

I smiled and shrugged, which I hoped covered every possible answer but committed to none, and ducked down into my car, slamming the door shut in a manner I had inherited from my daughter. As I waited for Ethan to move out of the way so I could go, I thought about Owen. Was I going to see him again? I hadn't heard from him in weeks. Until now, he hadn't crossed my mind all the time I'd been in St Ives. But perhaps I should think about him. He was interested, eligible, and not a member of the family – all excellent recommendations. What more did I need? I drove past Ethan. He was leaning over his steering wheel, watching me through his windscreen. My heart fluttered, as if it was trying to tell me exactly what else I needed. But I'd had years of practice at ignoring it, and wasn't going to break the habit now.

Chapter Twenty

I dropped Chloe off at home first; she hugged Daisy with a level of enthusiasm that I could only dream of seeing in Ava after a two-week absence from me.

'She's been great,' I said, although Daisy hadn't asked; in fact, I had the strange impression that I wouldn't have been invited into the house if I hadn't been carrying Chloe's suitcase. 'What have you been up to?' I said, as I barged my way into the hall. 'You can give me some ideas about what I can do for the next two weeks.'

'I've been flat out. With work,' Daisy added, when I wiggled my eyebrows and grinned at her. She didn't smile back. 'You know what his lordship our worshipful MP is like in the summer. Time to remind the voters he exists and pretend he's interested in village fêtes and squabbles about parking on double yellow lines. It's been very dull.'

'At least you found time for a manicure.' I grabbed her hand. Her nails looked incredible, all glossy and pink, with sparkly flowers painted on each one. There wasn't a chip in sight.

'Just a ten-minute break.' Daisy pulled her hand back, and

self-consciously fluffed up curls that, now I examined her more closely, were blonder and silkier than normal. Her eyebrows were finely shaped too, and generally she had a well-groomed glow about her. I hoped that being childless for two weeks would work the same magic on me.

I stretched extravagantly, but Daisy didn't take the hint.

'I could murder a cup of tea,' I said, going for a less subtle approach.

'Sorry, of course you must be longing to get home.' Daisy squeezed past me and opened the front door. 'Thanks for bringing Chloe back.'

Short of marching into the kitchen and flicking on the kettle, I had little option but to leave.

'Is something wrong?' She'd barely made eye contact since I arrived. We'd been on excellent terms when she left St Ives, so unless Chloe had spent the last two weeks feeding back tales of me being a terrible hostess, I couldn't understand why this awkwardness had crept in.

'No, I'd just like to spend some time with Chloe. She's going off to her dad's in a few days.'

That sounded reasonable enough, except that Chloe had vanished upstairs within seconds of returning home, and the noise of her music now thumped around the house. If the last two weeks were any example, she would spend the night in her room, multi-tasking on at least three gadgets at once.

'Is this because of Ethan?' I touched Daisy's arm. 'I'm sorry that didn't work out as you'd hoped.'

'Ethan?' Daisy looked directly at me for the first time, surprise in her eyes. 'I'd forgotten all about that. What made you think of him?'

I wished I knew how to stop thinking of him. He had haunted my thoughts for pretty much the entire drive back from Cornwall – a very long time to have the same image trapped in my head. But there had been something about his expression as I drove away that I couldn't define or forget – something raw, something honest, which had dug into me and then opened up like an umbrella, so I couldn't pull it back out. I'd hoped that Daisy would distract me with gossip, but clearly I would have to resort to Plan B – alcohol.

The usual blue car was parked on the road as I pulled onto the drive, and I couldn't help envy Mum that her companion for the night didn't have a glass body and a cork head. As I switched off the ignition I caught a flash of dark hair in the window, before the curtains were yanked closed. I looked up at my house: heartless grey windows stared back, challenging me to blink first. The house bore a resentful air of having been left alone too long: empty, lifeless, unloved – the similarities didn't escape me.

I unfastened Dotty's seatbelt and pulled her onto my knee, kissing the top of her fluffy head.

'It's just you and me, Dotty,' I said, hugging her closer as she turned and licked my cheek. 'Just you and me.'

She whimpered in reply, and I couldn't blame her. I wasn't looking forward to the next two weeks either.

Lunch with Jonas brightened the next day. We met in a cosy old-fashioned pub in Manchester – his choice, and a good one, though I tried not to think about how my little boy knew the local pubs. While he wolfed down his food, as if he hadn't eaten for a month, I devoured the sight of him. It was a little over three weeks since I'd seen him, but already he'd changed. He had a lick of city varnish over him: his hair, glossy and black like mine, had a sharper cut; his clothes were new; he asked after Ava and the grans with genuine interest and more confidence than I'd ever seen. It was hard to believe that this handsome young man was mine – was the placid baby who hadn't cried when he was born, but had looked up at me with enormous blue eyes so clear and trusting that I had promised in that moment never to do anything to let him down.

He told me all about his job in a café, and very little about what he had been doing outside work, although the name Sam cropped up enough times to make me suspicious.

'Oh God,' I said, putting down my spoon and abandoning half my tiramisu. 'Are you trying to tell me something? Are you gay too? I mean,' I added quickly, folding my paper napkin into quarters and laying it down on the table, 'it's fine if you are, absolutely great, it doesn't matter to me at all.'

'Chill, Mum, you can cut the PC.' Jonas slid my plate over to his side of the table and tucked into the remains of my pudding. 'I'm not doing a Dad.'

Doing a Dad? Since when had Leo's actions become a verb?

'So Sam's just a friend?'

254

'No, Sam's my girlfriend. Sameira,' Jonas said, in the special tone he usually saved for my mum.

'A girlfriend!'

He sighed and pushed the empty plate away. There was a speck of chocolate on his cheek, but I let it be: a young man with a girlfriend wouldn't appreciate me licking my napkin and cleaning his face.

'I've been dating since I was thirteen. Dating *girls*.'

'Thirteen?'

Jonas laughed at my squeaky question.

'You can't disapprove. How many times have you told us that you were that age when you met Dad?'

And look how that had turned out! But of course I couldn't say that.

'There's no need for you to rush into anything though, is there? Take your time. Enjoy being by yourself. Try going out with all sorts of different girls, so if you ever decide to settle down, you can make an informed choice.'

'Cool. Permission to sleep around.' Jonas grinned. 'Most of my friends have had the opposite lecture.'

It wasn't exactly what I'd meant, and twelve months ago I'd have given the opposite lecture too. I didn't want him to leap into bed with every girl he met – if I could lock him in iron underpants until he was thirty, I would. But how could I hold up my life as an example for him to follow? I had to hope for a better outcome for him. If he ever decided to commit to one person, I wanted it to be a decision based on experience, with full knowledge of what other lives were available, and absolute confidence that he had chosen the one that would make him happiest. I didn't want him to ever have any niggles of 'what if'. He might not be as good at burying them as I'd been.

A terrifying thought jumped into my head.

'Ava doesn't have a boyfriend, does she?'

'Not that I've seen.' That was no comfort – she had a well-developed secretive streak. Like father, like daughter, as it turned out. 'Too busy pouting and giggling.' Jonas pulled a face. 'Sam might come with me to Dad's wedding, if she can get the day off work. You won't be embarrassing, will you?'

'Embarrassing?'

'Yeah, you know. Don't ask a million questions. Don't fuss.'

'I'll be on my best behaviour.'

It was only a few weeks now until Leo's wedding to Clark. I'd blocked it from my mind, years of practice standing me in good stead, until Leo had reminded me yesterday. Amongst the excitement of the Alice Hornby manuscript, he'd slipped into the conversation that the colour theme was red, as it was Clark's favourite colour. The two grooms and the other best man – an actual man, on Clark's side – were wearing red waistcoats and cravats, and they'd like me to wear red too. So after lunch with Jonas, my mission was to go shopping and find a fabulous red dress – and some heavy duty make up that I could layer on thickly enough to hide any emotion on the day.

The waitress cleared away our plates, and flirted with Jonas in a way that made me feel at best invisible, and at worst an ancient old crone. Would anyone ever flirt with me again? Had anyone ever flirted with me in the first place? It hadn't been Leo's style, but then, I'd latched on to him with such single-minded tenacity that he hadn't needed to make any effort at all. I stifled a pang of longing. How lovely it must be to be pursued, wooed; to be certain that someone had actively chosen you, rather than merely failed to resist your advances.

'Are you bringing Mr Ferguson?'

'Bringing him where?'

'Dad's wedding.' Jonas rolled his eyes, the one trait he shared with his sister. 'Are you still seeing him?'

'I don't know.' It had been more a case of him seeing me, and the memory of Breastgate still chilled me to my toes. But hadn't I vowed to give it another try? Perhaps not at Leo's wedding, though. It was too public. There would be too many curious eyes on me as it was, watching to see how I handled standing at Leo's side as he committed himself to someone else. I couldn't handle the scrutiny of being on a date as well.

'Don't worry, Mum,' Jonas said, pushing back his chair and stretching out his long legs. He was taller than me and Leo now, approaching Ethan's height. 'You'll find someone else one day. You're not that old.'

'Thanks.'

Jonas grinned.

'And you're near the top of the list of fit mums.'

'You have a list! That's disgusting!' I folded my arms and shook my hair away from my face. That done, of course I couldn't resist. 'Who's at the top?'

'Oliver Perkins' mum.' Jonas shrugged. 'Head and shoulders above the rest. Sorry.'

Head, shoulders and bust would be more accurate. Her enormous breasts defied gravity and bounced seductively as if operated by an invisible puppeteer. It was fair enough that she topped the list – but she was a stepmother, barely ten years older than Jonas and his friends. I was absurdly flattered to fall within the shadow of her bust, which only helped to emphasise how sad my life had become. Or had it always been this narrow, a series of flat stepping stones of small pleasures, rather than mountain peaks of delight? Something stirred in my chest. I didn't want to gingerly pick my way over stepping stones anymore. I didn't even want to climb mountains. I wanted to soar over them, until the sun burned my back, my lungs screamed for oxygen, and for once I felt truly alive.

Before I soared over mountains, though, it was time to drive through the rolling hills of Lancashire and visit the Archer's bookshop. I hadn't made an appointment this time, as there had never been a soul in the place when I'd visited previously. So it was quite a surprise when I pushed open the shop door and was greeted by the welcoming jingle of the bell and the curious gaze of five or six customers.

Mrs Archer was parked behind the desk, guarding the till, while Bridie circled round the customers, proffering an assortment of books.

'You're busy today,' I said to Mrs Archer, putting my tin of goodies down on the desk. I had made a fresh batch of scones this morning, and brought them as a thank-you, along with some Cornish clotted cream and strawberry jam.

'Witch,' Mrs Archer muttered. I looked over my shoulder, but there was no one else nearby. Did she mean me? What had I done to offend her now? I'd be taking the scones back home if she was going to be rude.

Bridie dashed over, pink-cheeked and flustered.

'We weren't expecting you,' she said, with marginally more warmth than her mother. 'We're rushed off our feet.'

The customers appeared quite happy browsing by themselves, but I nodded with what I hoped was a sympathetic expression.

'You're busy for a Monday,' I said.

'It's the Witch Festival,' Bridie replied. 'We're on the trail for drivers and walkers.' She thrust a leaflet into my hand. 'We've an extensive selection of books about the Lancashire Witches if you're interested.'

I wasn't, but at least it explained the muttering from the old lady – I hoped. Giving her the benefit of the doubt, I gestured at the tin.

'I've brought you some scones, and Cornish jam and cream.'

Mrs Archer manoeuvred nearer the desk.

'Fresh?'

'Of course. I baked them this morning.'

'Let's see them.'

I opened the cake tin and held the scones out for inspection. There were a dozen delicious golden scones, evenly baked and uniform in size. I'd laboured all morning to make them so perfect they could win prizes. Mrs Archer peered into the tin and sniffed.

'They'll do.'

I snapped the lid back on the tin. Checking that no customers were in earshot, I perched on the desk.

'Thanks for sending the parcel with Alice's manuscript. I can't tell you how exciting this is. We've been looking for the missing book for years.' I ploughed on, despite the wary faces in front of me. 'Do you have the original copy?'

'Aye, it were left to our Florrie, right and proper,' Mrs Archer said, beady eyes narrowed, challenging me to suggest otherwise. I wouldn't have dared.

'We've a letter to prove it,' Bridie added.

'Have you?' Another letter from Alice! How much more treasure was hidden away here? 'May I see it?'

Mrs Archer nodded at Bridie, who disappeared into the back and returned a minute later with a folded paper in her hand. I slipped on the gloves that I'd brought, just in case, and carefully opened it out and read it. It was a letter from Alice to Florrie, entrusting the manuscript to her care.

'*Guard this well,*' the letter said, '*for my heart beats on every* page. *Do with it as you wish, when I am gone, but until then, bury it deep and let no human eye cast a beam upon it. I will face God's judgement, but no other. You alone know what I have suffered over this work, and now there will be no more. I cannot write of happiness, when my soul no longer believes that such a state of being exists.'*

I wiped my eyes on my sleeve, and handed the letter back to Bridie. We'd known that the death of Alice's sister had affected her, and that she'd retired from society as well as from writing afterwards, but to see her grief set out in this letter was amazing and incredibly moving.

'What did you think of it?' Bridie asked. 'Alice's book. Is it any good?'

'It's the most beautiful, heartfelt, and satisfying of all her books,' I said. 'I loved it.'

'Good enough to publish?' Bridie glanced at her mother, who gave another twitch of a nod.

'Without a doubt.' I hesitated. This was exactly what I'd wanted to talk to them about today, so it was a huge bonus that they'd raised the issue first. But I had to be cautious. I wanted Leo and me to be involved with the publication; it would mean the world to both of us. I couldn't risk scaring the Archers off now. 'Is that what you'd like? For the book to be published?'

'If we could get a bit of money out of it, it would help,' Bridie admitted. 'Help us keep going here a bit longer.'

'Enough to see me out,' Mrs Archer added, surprising me

with a gummy grin. 'Bridie can do 'owt she wants with the place then.'

I explained that we would need to take the original manuscript and have it authenticated, which brought on a few more sniffs even though I was at pains to emphasise that it was routine and not a slur on either them or Florrie.

'And once it's been authenticated, we can look for a publisher,' I said. 'It may need some editing too, just to tidy up a few inconsistencies and repetitions.'

Mrs Archer pulled her blanket round her shoulders and shook her head.

'No changes,' she said. 'No muck. None of that wet-shirt malarkey. It is as it is, and it mun stay that way. Tell her, Bridie.'

'We don't want any shades of smut adding,' Bridie said, and she actually wagged a finger at me – quite unnecessarily, as I didn't know any smut to add, even if I'd wanted to. 'That's not what Alice is about.'

'I know, the book doesn't need that at all. The passion and the longing are intense and powerful enough without any sex. I promise you can trust us to look after Alice.'

Chapter Twenty-One

The first week on my own dragged by. The weekends without Jonas and Ava hadn't prepared me for this endless stretch of hours that needed filling. There was no shape to the day; time was marked only by meals, and I looked forward to them with undeserved joy. My outstanding work for Leo was completed in a day when I had no other distractions. I volunteered to do extra meals on wheels shifts to cover holiday absences, but that only filled a few extra hours on a couple of days. I needed a project, I decided, when by Friday Dotty had taken to hiding when she heard me pick up the lead for yet another walk. So I popped to the nearest DIY shop and bought some cans of paint, and set about transforming my bedroom. It was time to make it mine, and erase the ghost of Leo.

I worked through the day, humping furniture around and stopping only to let one coat dry before applying the next, and couldn't believe it when the front door bell rang and I saw it was after seven. I dashed downstairs and opened the door. Ethan was standing on the doorstep clutching a Booths' bag for life to his chest. His jeans and T-shirt were soaked, and water dripped from his hair and trickled down his face.

'Is it raining?' It had been fine when I'd last let Dotty out into the garden.

'Either that or a gang of yobs have attacked me with heavy duty water rifles for the last five minutes.' He smiled. 'Can we discuss the weather when I'm inside and not experiencing it first hand?'

Reluctantly I stepped back and let him in.

'It wasn't raining when I set off,' he said, putting down his bag and taking his shoes and socks off in a way that suggested he was planning on staying. 'I'd just reached the village when it started lashing it down and I had to run. I hope this has survived.'

He prodded at the bag with his big toe.

'What is it?'

'Chilli. I made too much, so I thought I might persuade you to share it.' He opened the bag and we both peered in. The chilli clearly hadn't benefitted from the run: it had escaped the casserole dish and globules of it were splattered all over the inside of the bag. Ethan laughed. 'You're tempted, aren't you?'

I tilted my head and found two amused eyes perilously close to mine. I straightened up.

'Not at all,' I said. 'You'd have been better using Tupperware.'

'You see, Mary, if you hadn't been avoiding me all week, you could have taught me some practical things like that.' He smiled, and I looked away. I had avoided him, ignoring his calls and pretending not to see him when he'd waved at me in the village while I was delivering meals. 'Talking of practical things, what are you up to? Is that paint on your cheek?'

He reached across and wiped my cheek with his thumb.

'I've been painting my bedroom,' I said, chucking the words at him as if they were weapons to hold him off. 'It seemed a good time when everyone was away. It was time for a fresh start.'

'A fresh start?' Ethan rubbed some water off his neck. 'Why, are you expecting a visitor in there?'

'I wasn't expecting a visitor at all,' I replied, staring at him pointedly.

'You've got me whether you want me or not.'

What could I say to that? My hall had never seemed so hot, so small, or so thrumming with tension. Or was it just me? I clung to the practical.

'You'd better borrow a towel,' I said. 'There are some in the airing cupboard in the bathroom.'

He jogged up the stairs, leaving a trail of drips behind him, and I picked up his bag of chilli and took it into the kitchen. I emptied the casserole dish into the bin, filled the sink with soapy water, and washed it, scrubbing at the sticky bits with fierce determination. If only I had a scourer to wipe away the unwanted thoughts in my head.

I was rinsing the bowl, splashing cold water everywhere, when Mum gave a cursory knock on the back door and toddled in.

'Are you busy, Mary? I wondered if you were free to come over . . .'

Before she could finish, Ethan wandered in through the other door.

'Your bedroom looks great,' he said, before noticing Mum. 'Hello, Irene.'

Mum stared at him. I stared at him. He was still bare-footed, but now bare-chested too: standing in my kitchen, wearing nothing but a pair of jeans, rubbing a towel over his damp hair. Though he'd worn less on the beach, it was different here – more intimate, and with more impact when everyone else was fully dressed. My kitchen had never seen a sight like this before. And what a sight! He was a truly beautiful man. He knew it. I knew it, despite my best efforts not to. And every woman in the world knew it too – I had to remember that, before my imagination swept me away, persuaded me that there was something more meaningful in his behaviour than his usual teasing charm. Even if he hadn't been Leo's brother, my children's uncle, I couldn't allow myself to fall in love with this man. He could never be loyal, could he? I had known him too long to believe it. One day he would receive a better offer and leave, just like my dad had left Mum and me; just like Leo had left me. I doubted I could survive it a third time.

'Can I stick my T-shirt in the tumble dryer for ten minutes?' Ethan gave his hair a final rub, and dropped the towel over the back of one of the kitchen chairs. 'I'd borrow one of Joe's, but it might be a tight fit.'

266

Of course it would be a tight fit. Jonas was a typical lanky teenager. Ethan had the body of a man, and a chest that was broad and muscular, and that would be solid and warm to the touch. Touch! Why was I even thinking such a thing? I stepped forward and snatched the T-shirt from his hand.

'I'll do it. Why don't you go and watch TV? I'll bring it when it's ready.'

He nodded and wandered off to the living room. His back was almost more attractive than his chest: the deep groove of his spine trailing from wide shoulders to a narrow waist, practically inviting a finger to trail down it.

'Mary? Mary!' I turned back to Mum. 'I hope you know what you're doing.'

'I should do. I've used the tumble dryer about a million times.'

'You know very well that's not what I meant.' Mum picked up Ethan's abandoned towel and folded it – a scarily familiar action. 'People will talk.'

'About me using the tumble dryer?'

'About you carrying on with Ethan. Replacing one brother with another, in a matter of months . . .' She touched my arm – a scarily unfamiliar gesture. 'I know it's hard being on your own, and I'm not blind to why you might be tempted. But think of the consequences . . . The children have had enough upheaval with their father turning homosexual. And now their uncle might become their father? What if it all goes wrong?

267

You'll tear this family apart. You have to give him up, for the children's sake.'

'There's nothing to give up. Ethan would never think of me in that way. He still treats me as the slightly aggravating girl-next-door, ripe for teasing. Don't read more into it. He was caught in the rain tonight, that's all.'

'That's far from all. I know you better than you realise.'

'And I'm better at resisting temptation than you realise.'

'I hope you're right.' Mum looked at me, worry lines deeply scored across her forehead. 'The survival of this family could depend on it.'

Ethan's T-shirt was still damp after a quick spin in the tumble dryer, but I returned it to him anyway: the sooner he had his clothes on, the better. I found him sprawled on the sofa, an adoring Dotty at his side.

'Has Irene gone?' he asked.

'Yes.' Gone without ever explaining why she had come over. I wondered what she'd wanted to talk about. It was too late now – I wasn't following her home and subjecting myself to another lecture.

'Have you eaten?' I shook my head. Ethan jumped up. 'Great. Let's go to the pub. It's the least I can do after the chilli disaster.'

'It's fine. I'll grab a sandwich.'

'After a day's painting? That's not enough. Come on.' He was already nudging me out of the door. 'I'm starving. If you're not ready in ten minutes I'll come up and drag you down.'

I was back in five minutes, having changed out of my painting clothes, and resolutely refused to put on any make-up or perfume. This wasn't a date. I didn't need to make any effort. I was only going along with the idea because . . . Well, I couldn't really think of any convincing reason, other than that Ethan wasn't going to give up, and if he was determined to keep me company, it would be better in the pub than home alone. Surely Mum couldn't argue with that?

The rain had stopped, but dampness hung in the air, and we hurried to the closest of the village pubs, the Hale & Hearty. The pub was in a gorgeous position overlooking the pond on the village green, and was a quirky-shaped building, rising and falling in different storeys, like an athletes' podium. I hadn't been in the pub for years, as even with a glut of babysitters to hand, Leo had preferred to stay at home. I hadn't minded. The place reminded me too much of my dad. He had been a regular here, out with the boys every Friday night, and sneaking in at other times too. It had been our secret: he would tell Mum that we were going to the village play area, but after a few goes on the swings and the roundabout, we'd end up in the Hearty. I would sit on my stool, clutching a lemonade with bendy straw, watching the customers flock around, listening to conversations I didn't understand, and knowing that I had the funniest, handsomest, most popular daddy in the world.

Ethan's smile chased away the ghosts that flapped around

me as I hesitated outside. He held the door open and I stepped in, coming to an abrupt halt as I slammed into a fug of noise, cooking smells, and warm air. The place was packed, every table occupied as far as I could see.

'What's going on?' I asked, as heads swivelled in our direction then away again, as if we were the wrong arrivals at a surprise party.

'There's a band on tonight.' Ethan pointed to a poster on the back of the door. 'I didn't realise. Do you want to stay or come back to the cottage?'

'Stay.' I didn't have high hopes for a band called Status Hoe, but I was sticking with my theory that there was safety in numbers, and even terrible music would distract me from memories of a certain naked chest.

We squeezed our way between the crowded tables to the bar, which ran in a long straight line across the three-storey section of the pub. There were a couple of young women serving, but an elderly man approached to take our order. I recognised him at once as Frank, the landlord who had been in charge in my dad's day.

'Well, aren't you the sight for sore eyes, Mary love,' he said, looking me up and down and beaming at me. 'We've not seen you in here for donkey's years. I take it you'll be wanting more than lemonade nowadays?'

'Red wine please.'

'No bendy straw?'

I smiled and shook my head. Ethan ordered a pint, and as

Frank bustled off down the bar to find an open bottle, he lowered his head to speak in my ear.

'What did he mean that you've not been here for years? Not travelling the world is one thing, but could you not even have made it to the local pub? Did Leo never take you anywhere?'

I spun round, hackles ready to rise.

'Don't start criticising Leo again.'

'I'm not. But you were meant to have a rich and fulfilling life. He promised . . .'

I turned back to the bar, ignoring whatever Ethan was saying. Something had caught my eye as I spun round. I scoured the packed shelves, past the dozen or so bottles of speciality gin, past the Amontillado collection and the Jack Daniels, past the group of vile coloured spirits which I presumed I was too old to drink . . . and then I saw it on the bottom row, in a prime position as if it were frequently used and so needed to be on hand. I clutched the thick brass rail that ran across the front of the bar.

'Mary? What's wrong?'

Ethan put his hand over mine, and rubbed my white knuckles with his thumb.

'My dad,' I said. 'That's his special Guinness tankard behind the bar. He brought it over from Ireland. He said he could taste the craic when he used it.'

Frank put our drinks down on the bar.

'The tankard? Aye, it is like Eamonn's, you're right, love.

But this one belongs to one of our regulars.' Frank picked up the tankard and moved it into a cupboard. 'These drinks are on the house. It's grand to see you again, Mary.'

'Sure you're okay?' Ethan asked.

I nodded, though I wasn't really. My house no longer reminded me of Dad – it was Leo who haunted me there. But this place hadn't changed since I had last visited and my dad was everywhere.

I hadn't noticed that Ethan had slipped his arm round me until it was jerked off as the elder Miss Tippett squeezed into a non-existent gap between us.

'What are you doing to our Mary?' she asked, bristling in Ethan's direction. 'Isn't it about time you were heading back to America? *Over familiar*,' she mouthed, leaning in towards me.

'I'm here for a few more weeks yet.'

Ethan smiled, undaunted by the bristling.

'Weeks?' I repeated. 'Have your six months almost gone?'

'Four of them.' He grinned. 'Will you miss me?'

I would – I couldn't deny that my first reaction was disappointment. He had slipped back into our lives as if he'd never been away, and I couldn't think what life would be like without him. Or perhaps I could – it would be dull and predictable and beige. Much like the last twenty years, a devilish little voice whispered in my head.

'Have you met your mother's fancy man yet?' Miss Tippett asked, turning her back on Ethan. 'I heard he's never away.'

'He seems keen, but I've not been introduced yet.'

'I'll have a word. It's time.' She shuffled off towards the table where I could see her sister and a few of the older residents, but then looked back. 'And we'll have none of that sweetcorn next time. Plays havoc with my bowels.'

'I'm in danger of knowing more about her bodily functions than mine.' Ethan passed me my glass of wine. 'Why is Irene being so secretive? Is there something wrong with him? Have you not seen him at all?'

'Only a glimpse of dark hair in the window.'

'Not grey? Well there's your answer. She has a younger man. Perhaps she needed the stamina of youth to help her make up for lost time . . .'

'Stop it!' I laughed. 'I don't want to hear any lurid speculation about my mum's sex life.'

'Spoilsport.' He smiled, and I marvelled at how easily he had shaken me out of my gloomy mood. What would I do without him? 'Shall we sit down? We could squeeze onto the table in the corner with the group from Foxwood Farm.'

With his hand on my back, Ethan steered me over to the table. The Foxwood Farm group were here tonight to support the band, as Beryl the cleaner was married to one of the members. My heart sank a little at that news, expecting that we would all have to pretend the music was fabulous even if it felt like our ears were being stabbed with razor blades. But no pretence was necessary. It didn't look promising when a bunch of middle-aged men in gardening clothes shambled on to the makeshift stage, but as soon as they started playing and singing, the crowd was hooked.

They were well into their third song, an inventive reworking of a Madonna classic, when Daisy walked into the pub. I hadn't seen her since dropping Chloe off at the weekend, and I rose from my seat.

'There's Daisy,' I said and waved to get her attention through the crowd so she could join us. She didn't notice me, too busy laughing and talking to someone behind her. 'Oh, there's Owen.' This was going to be awkward – I couldn't imagine Ethan was going to welcome him to our table. I was committed now, though, and carried on waving. Daisy turned and looked at me – just at the moment that I realised she was holding Owen's hand.

I sat down with a thump on the bench. Ethan shifted beside me, as if he'd half risen to see what was going on, and then swore. He reached down and grasped my hand.

'You didn't know?'

I shook my head.

'Were you still . . .'

'Obviously not.' I hadn't seen Owen since my return from Cornwall. I'd sent him a text, to let him know I was back, but when he hadn't replied I assumed he must have gone away. How ridiculously vain to imagine that he had been waiting for me all this time! I ducked my head, humiliation weighing heavily on my shoulders. What a middle-aged fool I was.

Ethan squeezed my hand and I looked up to find Daisy at my side.

'Mary, please can I speak to you?' Her voice quavered, and tears swam in her eyes. I nodded and followed her to the ladies', the only quiet place we could find.

'I'm sorry,' Daisy said, as soon as the door was shut behind us, and she had checked the cubicles were empty. 'You must think I'm a total bitch.'

'How long have you been seeing him?'

'Only since I came back from St Ives. It's early days. It might not even work out. He might discover I'm boring as hell, like James did, and ditch me for an exciting young trollop with knockers the size of rugby balls . . .'

Tears were trickling down her cheeks by this point, and I couldn't bear it. I pulled her into a hug.

'He won't. Owen's not like that.' Daisy sobbed again, and I kicked myself for reminding her that I'd spent enough time with him to know that. 'You know, don't you, that nothing serious ever happened between me and Owen?'

She nodded, and popped into one of the cubicles to fetch some toilet roll, which she used to mop her eyes and blow her nose.

'I would never have stolen him if I thought you were genuinely interested. But you didn't seem that keen. You showed more interest in Ethan than in Owen!' She gave a shaky laugh, which I couldn't return. Was that true? I would have to be more careful. 'When we spoke in Cornwall, about what we wanted from a relationship, you didn't mention Owen at all. I honestly thought it was over. So did Owen.'

'It's fine,' I said. 'It was over.' No need to tell her that I had tried to rekindle it. Owen clearly hadn't told her about my text, and neither would I. 'I hope it works out for you.'

Bizarrely, that set Daisy off again.

'Don't be so nice to me. You have every right to be furious. And after Leo as well . . . I feel terrible doing this to you for the second time.'

'Owen was a rebound thing, that's all, just to get used to the idea of dating again. It wouldn't have developed.' I said the words to make Daisy feel better, but they worked on me too. Was that the truth? Had I never stood a chance of falling in love with Owen? Too late to find out now. But my lack of heartfelt disappointment was enough of an answer. What was wrong with me? If I couldn't fall for a straightforward, decent man, what hope was there? I was in danger of sobbing more than Daisy.

Someone came into the bathroom.

'Let's tidy you up and go back,' I said. There was nothing more to say. I wasn't going to argue with Daisy. Losing one best friend was unfortunate; losing two within the space of a year was unthinkable. 'Was he there?' I asked, remembering Daisy's odd behaviour last time we met. 'Was he at your house when I dropped Chloe off?'

'Yes. I'm sorry. I didn't want you to find out like that.'

'Because as Leo has already proved, finding out in public is so much better . . .' It was too soon for joking. Daisy's newly restored face crumbled again. I squeezed her hand. 'It's a relief. I thought I must have done something to upset you.'

Our sentimental hug was ruined by a Niagara Falls of urine splashing into the toilet bowl. We giggled and returned to the pub, Daisy joining Owen while I found my seat next to Ethan. He studied my face but said nothing – a response so unexpected, but so perfectly in tune with what I wanted, that those pesky tears prickled my eyes again, threatening to spill.

We stayed in the pub until closing time, long after Daisy and Owen had finished their drinks and gone, with an awkward nod in my direction.

'I'm walking you home,' Ethan said, and I didn't argue. I wasn't afraid of the dark, or of being on my own, but his chatter would distract me for a while longer from thoughts of Owen, and what a mess I'd made there. My imagination had leapt forward through time, and crashed into giant obstacles. What would happen if he married Daisy? How could I go on seeing her, knowing that her husband had been on intimate terms with my breasts?

'Do you want coffee?' I asked, as we passed Mum's twitching curtains and reached my front door. Ethan checked his watch.

'Better not. I'm meeting the village running group at eight in the morning for a 10k run.' There was a village running group? I'd lived in Stoneybrook my entire life and not discovered that. Ethan shifted so the light above the front door left him in shadow. 'I'm sorry that tonight wasn't the fun I'd planned. The chilli, the teacher . . .'

I sensed rather than saw his shrug.

'It wasn't your fault.'

'He was never good enough for you. Do you want me to challenge him to a duel? I reckon I could have him.'

I laughed, but the sound turned into a sob. It had been an emotional night, and Ethan's kindness finally caused some rogue tears to fall.

'No duelling necessary,' I said. 'My honour and my heart are quite intact. And how can I be cross with him for preferring Daisy? She's gorgeous, and warm and kind.'

'But she's not you, Mary Black.' And Ethan reached out and wiped a tear from my cheek, leaving a trail of fire in its wake before he walked away.

Chapter Twenty-Two

Life returned to normal. Audrey and Ava arrived back from Cornwall; Jonas came home. And I shut my mind to the memory of Ethan's touch on my cheek, and to the knowledge that with every passing day his time in England was running out.

PTA meetings started again: we had a busy time ahead, preparing for the annual bonfire and fireworks display. Owen and Daisy appeared together as a couple at the first meeting; she had offered to sit on the opposite side of the room from him, to save my feelings, but I'd assured her that wasn't necessary. I was dreading the gossip, but it was best to get it over with so we could concentrate on more important matters.

'I see Daisy Flood has had a busy summer,' Marissa, the PTA chair, said as soon as Daisy and Owen had left at the end of the meeting. I'd stayed to tidy up – too capable and efficient for my own good sometimes. 'Fancy her walking off with Mr Ferguson! I always thought him such a steady man, although I suppose he is an art teacher.' She said this with a significant lift of her eyebrows, as if for 'art teacher' I should mentally substitute 'sexually amoral hippy'. 'And you and Daisy used to be such good friends!'

'We still are.' I carried a rattling tray of mugs over to the staff room sink. 'I think they make a lovely couple.'

'And what about you? Seeing anyone at the moment? We'd be happy to have Ava for a sleepover if you need a night alone.'

'Thanks.' Ava would murder me if I ever suggested that. 'But she spends every other weekend with Leo so I have plenty of time alone.'

'Once a fortnight is enough, is it?' She tilted her head and patted my arm, apparently sympathising over my sexual inadequacies. 'That was an impressive piece about Leo in *The Times* at the weekend, wasn't it? What a coup for him! And what rotten luck for you that he made the discovery after you'd divorced. I imagine it will be a lucrative find.'

I'd been busy scrubbing tea stains off mugs, with only half an ear on Marissa's conversation, but this made me turn round.

'Leo was in *The Times*?'

'Didn't you see it?' Marissa's glossy red smile was so wide that her lips almost met round the back of her head. 'Oh, you must read it, Mary. I'm surprised he didn't tell you. He said it was the high point of his career. Don't you do that little bit of work for him anymore? You must come and join our spa and yoga days if you're at a loose end now.'

My end could never be loose enough for that to be an option, but I forced a polite smile, rushed through the rest of the washing up, and hurried home, desperate to check the computer. How could Leo have appeared in the newspaper without me knowing? I dealt with all the publicity side of things for him. And yet there it was. I used Leo's password to sign in to *The Times* online, and soon found the piece that Marissa had been talking about.

I read it three times before I could believe what I was seeing. Leo had given an interview about the discovery of Alice Hornby's lost manuscript, and how, having read it, he had no doubt that it was genuine. It was a lively, well-written piece, and Leo's enthusiasm and excitement rose off the page as if the article was presented in 3D. But he didn't mention me, or my part in this discovery, and however hard I tried, I couldn't blame journalistic inaccuracy or misreporting. Leo had claimed the discovery as his – he had cut out my role entirely. And though I didn't care about the fame, the disloyalty carved a hole right through my heart.

But there was worse even that that. Leo had spoken of the passion and the sexual tension at the core of the story. The journalist had run with the idea and reached another galaxy: the phrases 'bodice ripper' and 'sexed up' were used, and Alice was described as a 'frustrated spinster satisfying her sexual fantasies on the page'. It was horrendous, and exactly what Mrs Archer had feared would happen. If the Archers saw this article, they would never trust us to publish the book.

I tried to telephone Leo but he was on voicemail, which was probably for the best, because what would I have said? He was a master of words, but none that he could conjure would undo the damage he had done here. And I was far too worked up to consider my words as carefully as I should. I sent him an email, simply saying, 'Can we talk?' and waited for a response.

A knock on the window interrupted my brooding. Mum mee-mawed at me to let her in.

'The door was locked!' she said, with totally misplaced outrage.

'It was meant to keep out unwanted visitors.'

'Is this a bad time, Mary?'

'Whatever gives you that idea?'

'You look like you've just lost a brutal wrestling match. Twice.'

Well, that told me – but it wasn't a bad summary of how I was feeling. I sighed. It wasn't Mum's fault. I had spent my life blaming her for most things, but I couldn't hold her responsible this time. 'Do you want a cup of tea?'

'No, I'm not stopping.' Mum clutched her hands in front of her chest, as if she were praying. 'I wondered if you could pop round tonight.'

'What for? Is something wrong?'

'No. Only I thought it might be a good idea for you to meet my . . .' She stumbled over her words, and twisted her hands. 'My friend. Meet him in private, before Saturday.'

'Saturday?'

'Leo's wedding.'

I'd forgotten. Oh, I'd known it was coming, but in all the

anguish of the last hours, cursing and hating and crying over Leo, it had slipped my mind that on Saturday I would have to stand at his side and be his main supporter, smile and wish him happiness in his new life without me. How was I supposed to do that after this second betrayal, now I knew he was cutting me out of his working life too?

'Oh love, I'd no idea you were still hurting over him.' Mum pulled a tissue from up her sleeve and dabbed at my cheeks. And there it was again – the flash of a mum I had known, but who had vanished along with my dad. 'You need to be strong, Mary. However bad the pain is, you mustn't let the children see it. They are all that matters.'

I nodded, because she was right. However cross I was with Leo, I couldn't let Jonas and Ava pick up on it, or make them think he was anything less than perfect. I would bottle up gallons of pain to protect them. For their sakes, I would have to deal with this further rejection from Leo as I had done the first: by hiding my own feelings and trying to keep everyone else happy. What choice did I have, with the wedding only a few days away?

'Forget about tonight,' Mum said. 'It's not the right time. Do you want me to stay, or would you rather be on your own?'

'On my own,' I said. 'Thanks.'

But it wasn't true. There was one person I wanted to be with; someone who could support me by holding my hand; who could laugh me out of the thickest gloom. But he was away in London, and I couldn't have him even if I wanted him.

It was twenty-four hours before Leo called back.

'Sorry, Mary,' he said, his voice pitched high with excitement. 'I missed your message. We were caught up in an eleventh-hour flower crisis, but disaster has been averted, and we will have our table centrepiece after all.' He laughed. 'You wouldn't credit the extent of the minutiae.'

I could hear noise in the background, domestic sounds – the clink of glass and the bang of pans, and I imagined Clark in their luxury kitchen, preparing their evening meal. My house was quiet: Jonas and Ava were both out with friends, and the only sound came from Dotty as her collar clanked against her water bowl.

'I have done the whole wedding thing,' I said, hating myself for being jealous, and hating myself more for not being able to disguise it. Leo didn't notice.

'Not like this,' he replied, and he muffled the phone as he presumably spoke to Clark. 'I hope you're not about to confront us with another problem. Do tell me that you have something red to wear?'

'Yes, of course.' I had the dress. Now I just needed the courage to wear it. The shop assistant in Selfridges had sussed me as a naive shopper as soon as I stepped off the escalator, and had taken me perhaps too literally when I had tentatively told her that I wanted something fabulous. It had turned out that her definition of fabulous involved expanses of bare flesh and figure-hugging scarlet fabric. She and two of her colleagues had assured me that I would turn every head, and I had a horrible fear that they might be right.

'It's not about the wedding,' I continued. 'It's about the article in *The Times*.'

'Did you see it? What did you think? I thought it was an excellent piece. I've received numerous calls about it. This has caused a stir, exactly as we hoped.'

'But Leo,' I protested. He sounded delighted – not a hint of guilt or apology. 'You didn't tell me you were going to the press.'

'There was no time. I heard a whisper about a new biography of Anne Brontë. There's a move afoot to raise her profile, and elevate her to the same level of fame as her sisters. I had to strike with the Alice news first, you must see that.'

I could see only one thing, and I wondered how I had been blind to it for so long. When I latched on to Leo as a lonely thirteen-year-old, I must have placed voluntary blinkers over my eyes. How else had I missed this selfish streak in Leo? Despite my good intentions not to stir trouble before the wedding, I couldn't let this go by unchallenged. It hurt too much.

'You didn't mention my involvement in the article. You made it sound as though you'd discovered the manuscript. Why did you do that? Are you planning to work on it without me?'

'Good Lord, no.' Leo laughed, seemingly oblivious to the

pain in my voice. 'I can't do it without you, Mary. You are the wheels that keep this whole operation moving. Nothing has changed.'

Not for him, maybe. My feelings weren't so straightforward. I should have been reassured: we would carry on working together, which was what I wanted, wasn't it? So why wasn't I happy? And there was still one huge problem Leo was overlooking.

'We don't have permission from the Archers to publish the book yet,' I pointed out. 'And if they've seen it described as a sexy romp, they're unlikely to give permission.'

'You'll persuade them to do the right thing. I have the utmost faith in you, Mary. Love to the children, and we'll see you all on Saturday!'

Leo and I married on a sunny July afternoon, not long after I had completed my degree. Leo's father gave me away, in the absence of my own dad. Bill and I walked to the church in the village on our own; then after the ceremony, Leo and I led a procession back to what would from then on be our house. The fence panels were lifted from between the back gardens, and the guests, mostly villagers and Leo's academic friends, milled around the lawn, enjoying a cold buffet that Mum and Audrey had prepared. It had all been over by seven o'clock, and Leo and I had spent the evening helping tidy up.

Leo and Clark had chosen a very different affair for their big day. Their wedding was taking place in a country house hotel in Cheshire: a nuisance for us Lancastrians to reach, but convenient for Clark's family, their mainly Manchester-based friends, and for access to the airport the next morning. After their ceremony, the guests would enjoy the traditional sit-down wedding breakfast, followed by dancing until midnight. Close family were staying the night – just as well, because there was no way I would be able to see the day through sober.

Ethan collected Audrey first thing in the morning; his laughter filtered into my house even through the double glazing as they chatted outside. I'd expected that Mum's gentleman friend would drive her, but when I arrived back from dropping Dotty off at the dog minder's, Mum was busy loading her own car, and for once the blue car was nowhere to be seen.

'I'm going to follow you,' Mum called over. 'I don't know Cheshire.' She made it sound as if we were venturing into the Amazon jungle. 'Mind you drive slowly.'

'Okay.' As if I ever did anything else. 'Why are you driving? I thought your friend would have offered.'

'He's not coming.' Mum didn't look at me. 'He's not well.'

'That's a shame.' I assumed they'd fallen out, given Mum's shrewish expression, but had no intention of asking. 'I was hoping to meet him at last. I'm sorry I didn't manage to come round the other evening.'

'He's keen to meet you too.'

So perhaps they hadn't fallen out, and he really was ill.

'Are you sure you should still come? Do you need to stay and look after him?'

'No. We agreed that I need to go and look after you.' Mum slammed down her boot, emphatically ending the conversation. 'Knock when you're ready.'

It was late morning when we drove through elaborate wrought-iron gates and along a twisting drive to the hotel. I pulled up on the crest of a bridge so that we could have a proper look, as it was a stunning setting: the hotel was situated on a large meander in a river, and with an artificial lake at the front, it gave the impression that the house and gardens were floating on their own island.

Jonas peered through the windscreen and whistled.

'Are we posh enough to go in there?'

I smoothed the hair back from his face.

'You're the son of a professor. You can go anywhere. I don't mean now!' I yelled as Ava hopped out of the car. She took a selfie, posing and pouting with the hotel in the background, and returned to the car. 'You're not going to do that all day, are you?'

'Yeah,' she said, shaking her head – a mixed message that I translated as 'stop asking such inane questions'. 'Everyone wants to see the photos. It's cool. No one else at school has been to their dad's gay wedding.'

'You won't take any of me, will you?'

'No one's interested in you, Mum.'

The hotel was equally magnificent inside, all thick carpets, chandeliers, and wood panelling. Leo was waiting for us in the entrance hall.

'Perfect timing,' he said, kissing me and Mum. It still felt odd to have been downgraded to the same level of relationship as my mother. 'There's an early lunch in the drawing room if you're hungry.'

'Oh! I brought sandwiches,' I said, indicating the cool bag hanging from my shoulder.

'It's up to you,' Leo replied. 'If you need more time to get ready I'll have someone show you to your room.'

'No need! I'm sure there'll be more than enough time after lunch.' I glanced at my watch, inwardly flinching, and wondering which bit of my preparations I could miss out. 'Is Clark joining us?'

'No, we're being traditional and not seeing each other until the ceremony.'

'Lovely!' I smiled, but it was a woefully inadequate effort next to Leo's excited beam. Something else to squeeze in to my preparations: I would have to practise a better smile, so I didn't look like a jealous old witch. Feeling like one was quite bad enough.

'Isn't it marvellous to have all the family together again?' Audrey cried, as we followed Leo into the drawing room. She kissed us all enthusiastically, even managing to catch Ava. 'I love weddings!'

'Very kind of your boys to give you so many, then,' Mum said. Thankfully Audrey laughed.

'They are good boys, aren't they? But I won't be happy until this one finally settles down.' Audrey linked her arm with Ethan's, and squeezed it. 'And you too, Mary. There's no reason why you shouldn't try again.'

'Urgh, gross.' Ava pulled a horrified face. 'Don't encourage her, Gran. We don't want her hunting around school for more teachers to flirt with.'

'Did it not work out with the teacher you were seeing, Mary?' Leo asked, taking a vol-au-vent.

'No.'

'Daisy nicked him,' Ava explained.

'Let me have a word with Clark later. I can think of two or three single men coming to the wedding who might be suitable.'

'Not gay ones,' Mum said. 'She's been there, done that.'

How was I supposed to survive a day of this? I wished the carpet pile were even thicker so I could sink down and let it close over my head. But an even better solution arrived. Ethan nudged my arm, smiled down at me, and held out a wine glass. Perhaps the day would be bearable after all.

I was ready to go downstairs, and wishing I'd had the foresight to arrange to meet Audrey, so I didn't have to emerge alone, when there was a knock on my bedroom door. I smiled in relief, and hurried over to answer it as fast as I could in my ridiculously ambitious heels. It must be Leo. I should have known that he would think of me. Of course we should arrive together – I was his best woman, wasn't I? In fact, I should probably have collected him, but it was such a topsy-turvy day that I supposed I could be forgiven.

I opened the door and Ethan was standing on the other side – but no ordinary Ethan. Ordinary Ethan was outrageously handsome. This Ethan was dressed in full black tie with a scarlet cummerbund, smelt like an intoxicating summer garden, smiled at me with a smile that stopped my heart, and was quite simply the most beautiful man I'd ever seen. I grabbed the door handle. That second glass of wine at lunch-time had been a terrible mistake.

We stood and stared at each other for so long that we might have missed the wedding before either of us noticed. But eventually Ethan whispered, 'Mary,' and I stepped back to let him in.

'Crikey,' Ethan said, looking around the messy room. 'Is this what the real Mary Black is like behind closed doors?'

I could have kissed him for the normal remark, and for breaking the strange atmosphere – if kissing wasn't exactly the sort of thought I was trying to avoid.

'Well, you know what they say about ducks.' He looked at me blankly. 'Serene on top, frantic paddling below the surface.' I laughed, verging on the hysterical. I had no idea what I was babbling about.

'Serene isn't the word I'd have chosen.'

'Go on then.' I just about resisted putting my hands on my hips. I was feeling more myself by the second. 'Spit it out. But it had better not be anything about mutton and lamb . . .'

Ethan smiled.

'You are breathtaking, Mary.'

I hadn't expected that. I hadn't expected this surge of warmth that spread through me either, that probably flushed my skin the same shade as my dress. Far from taking anyone else's breath, I seemed to have lost all my own.

'Are you sure it's okay? I have to stand up in front of everyone, at Leo's side, with Clark on his other side. I couldn't bear people to look at us and think it's no wonder he changed . . .' I was babbling again, but couldn't stop. 'And I haven't even had time to do my hair. I was going to put it up, try something elegant . . .'

My hair was in its normal style, hanging straight and loose on my bare shoulders. Ethan reached out and stroked down its length, twisting the end round his finger. I froze. What was he doing? And why was he looking at me like that – not like I was the childhood friend he had teased for years, but as if . . . I hardly knew what. No one had ever looked at me that way before.

'Your hair is perfect. Don't change a thing.'

There was a loud knock on the door, and I jumped back, wobbling on my heels. Ethan put his hand on my waist to steady me – it had quite the opposite effect – and then answered the door.

'What are you doing in here?' Mum's strident voice blasted in from the hall. 'Isn't this Mary's room?'

Mum didn't wait for a reply, but barged in past Ethan.

'Gracious, Mary, what are you wearing?'

She must have been shocked if she had overlooked the state of the room to focus on me. She reacted as though I were wearing nothing but a see-through basque. In fact, I was almost entirely covered up, in a full-length satin dress, with an off-the-shoulder neckline – admittedly cut very low – that clung to my body as snugly as cling film then fell in graceful folds from below my bottom.

'I think it's an amazing dress,' Ethan said. He winked at me from behind Mum's back. 'Although I'd love to know where you're hiding the rings.'

I laughed.

'The other best man has those. And it's not that bad, is it?' I asked Mum. Perversely, her disapproval was making me warm to the dress.

'Not if you want to be talked about. Has Leo seen it? Something simpler would have been more appropriate. You're not the bride here.'

That knocked my smile away.

'Do you really think I can forget that?'

'No, Mary, I'm sorry. I wasn't thinking.' Mum patted my hand. 'Chin up, love. Are you ready to go down?'

'Yes, but I didn't know if Leo might come . . .'

'Leo's been downstairs for ages,' Ethan said. 'That's why I'm here. I thought you might not want to go down on your own.'

'Very kind, I'm sure,' Mum said, while another warm surge ran through me. 'But I'm here now. Why don't you escort Audrey?'

'Already done.'

I looked from one to the other. Was I supposed to choose between them? Mum, with all her faults, was still Mum. And Ethan, with all his faults, was still . . . Well, I wasn't ready to think exactly what he was. Not today, when my emotions were as close to the surface as the blue veins running across the back of my hand.

'Can't I have you both?'

Ethan smiled, Mum sighed, and we all headed to the wedding together.

It was far and away the most romantic wedding I'd ever attended. The elegance of the arrangements was never in doubt with Clark at the helm: he could probably have made me stylish if I'd let him. But the jubilation, and the tenderness and the intimacy . . . no amount of money or taste could have manufactured that.

I tried my best, but comparisons were inescapable. Leo hadn't written a sonnet for me as part of our wedding vows; he hadn't cried when we exchanged rings; he hadn't said, in his speech for me, that it was the happiest day of his life. There had been no first dance for us. Stranded on the end of the top table, next to Clark's father, who clearly had no idea what to say to me, I watched as Leo brushed off the last few emotional links between us. Best friends, I had thought when we first separated: we were best friends, and that could withstand anything. But here he was, surrounded by new friends

– and with a new best friend, husband, and soulmate. My role as best *woman* was a demotion in my status that I had failed to recognise until now; a swansong to the relationship we had shared.

And I should have been sad – and in a way, I supposed I was – but sadness wasn't my overwhelming feeling. It was as though I'd turned the final page on a book I'd loved reading, but had then seen a vast library from which I could choose my next adventure. Or at least, I might be able to choose, if I could shake off Mum. She'd clung to my side like a third arm ever since the meal ended; goodness knows what she thought I was going to do if she left me alone. But in the end, age and a bout of cystitis saved me. Mum couldn't resist the call of the bathroom, and I escaped through the French windows and into the garden.

A knot of smokers huddled immediately outside the doors, and I wandered past them, through a formal rose garden illuminated by the lights radiating from the hotel. A gravel path marked out by Victorian-style lanterns led the way through a cluster of trees to an arbour where a stone bench overlooked the river. Moonlight picked out the occasional ripple in the water.

Footsteps crunched the gravel, and I expected them to pass on – and yet it was no surprise, really, when a figure sat down on the bench beside me.

'Was Irene a bodyguard in a former life?' Ethan asked. 'I was worried for a while that you might be stuck together. But now she's let you out here on your own. You're not thinking of throwing yourself in, are you? This suit was expensive, and if I have to jump in to rescue you, I'd like some warning so I can take it off first.'

'It's okay. I came here for some peace, that's all. Your suit is safe.'

A lantern above the arbour cast Ethan's face in soft focus. He smiled.

'This reminds me of our summer in the Dordogne. All we need are two bicycles and some cheap beer.' He laughed. 'Fancy a skinny dip?'

'I did not swim naked!'

'No, I could never tempt you, could I?' He bumped his arm against mine. 'How are you bearing up?'

'As well as can be expected? The copious supply of champagne has certainly helped.'

'Mary . . .'

'Don't you pity me as well. I've had enough of that. I mean, it's not as if he's dead. He's happy, and that makes me happy. And we'll still be working together. Everything is fine. Fantastic. Fabulous.'

I may have protested too much; Ethan shifted on the bench.

'I saw the article in *The Times*. About Leo's discovery.'

I jumped up. I hadn't wanted to think about that today; hadn't wanted to let my niggling resentment sour the occasion.

'Why did you have to bring that up? Couldn't you resist saying I told you so?' My voice was rising with every word, fuelled by too much champagne. 'I can't believe you're still being disloyal to Leo, especially today.'

'Disloyal?' Ethan stood up. The lamplight sprinkled his hair with gold. 'When have I ever been disloyal to Leo? For God's sake, what more could I have done for him? I let him have everything.'

He stopped abruptly.

'What do you mean?' I demanded.

'Nothing.'

Ethan stepped back, out of the light, so I could only make out his shape standing by the arbour, and hear his rapid breathing. I waited, but he didn't say anything more. But there was more. There had always been something more between Leo and Ethan than the usual sibling rivalry. This was the closest I'd ever come to finding out what it was, and I needed to know. I'd closed my mind to too much, for too long.

'When we were in Cornwall,' I began, my voice sounding surprisingly steady and clear in the twilight, 'you said something about Leo not having always been loyal to me.'

'Clark,' Ethan said. 'I was talking about Clark.'

'No, you weren't. You were going to say something else until Audrey stopped you. I want to know what it was.'

'Let's not have this conversation now.'

'Yes, let's have it now. When could there be a better time? Leo has irrefutably moved on today. What harm can it do, whatever you have to say?'

'I'm not going to hurt you.'

It was too late. Those words were enough. I'd poked at the fire and the flames had caught my fingers. He knew something, something more than Clark – and I couldn't let it drop.

'I need to know.'

'No, you don't. It can do no good now. Don't ask me, Mary.'

I grabbed his hand, worming my fingers around his clenched ones.

'Who else can I ask? I'd rather hear it from you than find out from anyone else. Tell me. Please. I need you to do this for me.'

The silence stretched, and I thought he wasn't going to say anything, until he let out a sigh of frustration.

'Ask Leo. If you're sure you want to know, ask him who he celebrated his First with in Oxford.'

A cool breeze ruffled my hair, lifting it from my shoulders, but it was nothing compared to the chill spreading through me. I don't know what I'd expected, but it wasn't this – not something that might slice through the roots of our relationship.

'No,' I said. This simply couldn't be true. 'What are you implying? Leo didn't sleep with another woman at Oxford. I know he didn't.'

'Probably not.' Ethan squeezed my fingers. 'But do you really think that he turned forty and decided to be gay out of the blue? Without any previous experience?'

I snatched my hand away from Ethan's.

'Are you telling me that Leo had a homosexual relationship in Oxford?'

'I'm not telling you anything. Don't do this, Mary.'

'And you knew? You knew this before I married him, and said nothing? How could you?' I shouted, forgetting where we were, careless of who might hear. I should have been shocked by Leo's disloyalty – but all I could focus on was Ethan's. 'I suppose he asked you to keep it secret and you went along with it, without giving me a second thought.'

'You're wrong.' Something in Ethan's body language changed, and he moved closer. 'I gave you a lot of thought. I wanted to tell you, more than you know. But you loved him. You relied on him. So yes, I kept his secret. But I didn't do it for him.'

'Then who, for me? You think you did it for me, letting me marry a man who was unfaithful and gay?'

'Letting you marry the man you were in love with.'

'Love? What do you know about love? It's never been more than a five-minute wonder for you.'

'Five minutes?' Ethan's voice cracked. 'I've been in love with you for over twenty years!'

'But . . .' It came out as little more than a croak. My world was spinning, and it had nothing to do with the champagne. Was he serious? Ethan was in love with me? 'But I was with Leo.'

'I know.' Ethan moved into the light, so I could see every word on his face as he spoke them. 'There was one glorious evening when I thought you might choose me, but you didn't. I had to stand at the top of the aisle and watch you walk towards me, so beautiful in your wedding dress, and listen to

299

you exchange wedding vows with my brother. I had to be godfather to the babies I wished were mine. I tried to make my own life, while all the time hearing about and seeing photographs of the life I wanted. So I know plenty about love. It's year after year of jealousy and pain, without ever being able to hope it might end. But it's part of me, and I can't go on pretending that it isn't.'

I kissed him – because it was the most romantic thing anyone had ever said to me, even on my own wedding day. Because the anxiety on his face tore at my heart. And because he was Ethan – and above everything, because I wanted to. One brief, perfect kiss, pressed against his lips, and then I drew back.

His eyes, centimetres away, were fixed on mine. We were both completely still, completely silent, barely breathing. And then we both moved forward, he caught me in his arms and kissed me. And I *knew*. The thing that Leo had found with Clark – the insatiable connection between them – I understood what it was. It was *this*.

I shivered as the wind blew across my shoulders and chest. I was sitting on Ethan's knee, on the bench. I had no idea how long we'd been there. I had no idea of anything – except that my body had never felt like this before. Sensation had chased away sense. I wanted more.

Ethan raised his head from my breast and kissed my lips.

'You're cold. Let's get you inside.'

'Let's go upstairs.'

Ethan pulled up the top of my dress, gathered me into his arms, and rested his forehead against mine.

'Oh Mary,' he said, and my name on his lips was as seductive as any caress. 'Ask me that tomorrow when you've not had a difficult day or drunk so much.'

But that was no good. Tomorrow I would be me again – the beige housewife and mother of two, not this scarlet woman who was kissed beyond reason by a gorgeous man. Tomorrow my heart would pump with ordinary blood, not passion. Tomorrow I would be efficient and capable, seeing obstacles where now I saw dreams.

I held Ethan's hand, and half dragged him back along the gravel path and in through the French windows. And there the warm, muggy atmosphere brought back sense more effectively than any cold shower. Ava glared at me from across the room; Leo stared, his smile missing for the first time that day. Mum, waiting by the windows, grabbed my arm, forcing me to break the contact with Ethan.

'Oh Mary,' she said, and her unconscious echoing of Ethan somehow made this worse. She adjusted the neck of my dress. 'What have you done?'

Oh God. What *had* I done?

Chapter Twenty-Three

I hid in my room the next morning until Jonas banged on the door and shouted for me.

'We thought you might be dead,' he said, grinning at me with no hint of concern when I opened the door. He wrinkled his nose. 'You do look like you might be. You shouldn't drink so much at your age.'

I hugged him, overcome with relief that at least one member of the family seemed unaware of my antics last night. If only alcohol was all I had to regret.

'Steady on,' he said, wriggling away after giving me a half-hearted hug in return. 'Are you okay to drive us back? Ava's kicking off about missing her riding lesson if we don't leave this second.'

'I'm ready.' Jonas took my suitcase and I picked up the dress bag from where it was hanging on the front of the wardrobe. I'd abandoned my dress on the floor last night – most out of character – and when I'd hung it up this morning I could still smell traces of Ethan's aftershave lingering on the fabric. 'Has everyone else gone?'

'Dad and Clark have gone. Dad waited for you as long as he could, but they had to catch their plane.'

'Did Dad want me for something?'

'Dunno.' Jonas wheeled my case along to the top of the stairs. 'He looked rough too. I think he was having a go at Uncle Ethan about something.'

'Ethan?' I stopped. 'What was that about?'

Jonas shrugged and headed off down the stairs. I followed more cautiously, dreading who I might run into, but when I reached the entrance hall Mum was there on her own, looking like a ferocious bulldog.

'About time too,' she said. 'There's no time for dawdling in bed. I need to get back and Ava's been waiting outside for ten minutes.' She sighed. 'You've not had a good night, have you?'

'Not the best.' I clutched the dress bag to me.

'I knew that dress would be trouble.' She shook her head. 'But there's no use in crying over it now. Most people were drunk enough by that point that they didn't notice. You were lucky, this time.'

I followed her out to the car park. Ava, Jonas, and Audrey were waiting by my car. Ava turned her back as I approached: she hadn't spoken to me since I'd returned to the wedding with Ethan last night. At least Audrey smiled.

'Haven't we all had the most marvellous weekend?' she said, coming forward to kiss my cheek. 'I haven't enjoyed a wedding so much in years.'

She appeared to be serious – another one, clearly, who had

missed my grand entrance with Ethan. Just as well: when I'd popped to the bathroom, under Mum's armed guard, I'd been horrified at my appearance. My hair was a mess, my chest and cheeks flushed, my lips a dark shade that no lipstick could match – but my eyes gave me away more than all the rest. They were wide and bright, still shining with desire so that I hardly recognised them as mine.

I unlocked the car, but wasn't fast enough. Ethan strolled across the car park in our direction. I tossed the dress bag on to the back seat, wishing I could crawl in after it. What if he mentioned last night? What if he kissed me? What if he didn't – did he regret what we'd done? Never mind that I regretted it; it would be unbearable if he did. And how were we supposed to act normally now, in front of Jonas and Ava, Mum and Audrey? Maddening though she so often was, Mum was right about this. It would affect the family – it already had.

'I see Lazybones has made an appearance at last,' Ethan said, stopping at Audrey's side. Two more steps and he would be near enough to kiss me, but he didn't take them. 'She missed a stunning breakfast, didn't she, Joe?'

'Awesome sausages.' Jonas nodded.

'That's one thing I miss in New York. The proper English sausage.'

'You'll have to take some back with you,' Mum said. 'Not long now, is it?'

'Three weeks.'

Ethan's eyes flickered in my direction at last. I leaned against the car. Three weeks! How could his time here have vanished so quickly? I didn't know whether to be glad or distraught. Glad, I supposed, given his behaviour this morning. How little must last night have meant to him if he could stand there so calmly and talk about sausages?

'Are you ready, Mum?' I asked, as if I hadn't been the one keeping everyone waiting for hours. 'We'd better head off if we're to make it back for Ava's riding lesson.'

Ava got into the car with a huff – an improvement on silence. At this rate, she might grunt at me by bedtime.

'Safe journey, my darlings, and we'll see you all soon!' Audrey said. Mum was already in her car, reverse lights lit, waiting to go. I opened my driver's door, and glanced back at Ethan. From behind Audrey's back, he smiled, the way he had smiled at me last night, and he carried on smiling until I could no longer see him in my mirrors.

The answering machine was flashing with a message when we reached home.

'It's Bridie Archer.' It was lucky she said that – I wouldn't have recognised the posh telephone voice. 'We need you to come as soon as possible.'

That was it – no hello or goodbye, and no hint of what they wanted, although it wasn't hard to guess. I'd been on tenterhooks since Leo's article was published, dreading that they might see it, but also convincing myself that it was highly unlikely they would. As if I didn't have enough to worry about, having alienated half my family and fallen for the ultimate ineligible man; now we might lose the chance to publish Alice Hornby's last book too. What had happened to my neat and orderly life?

Once Ava was installed at the stables for the afternoon, I busied myself with the boring jobs – washing, ironing, cleaning the fridge – anything to recapture normal existence, and forget the alternative life I had glimpsed the previous night. But when the front door bell rang, I knew at once who it would be. Sure enough, Jonas soon padded into the kitchen, with Ethan close behind.

'Didn't you hear the bell? Ethan's here,' Jonas said, clearly thinking my hearing and sight were both impaired. 'Hangover,' he muttered as he passed Ethan on his way back upstairs. 'Watch out.'

I stuffed things back into the fridge, abandoning my usual order, concerned only to avoid looking at Ethan.

'Will you take those rubber gloves off, Mary?'

I paused.

'Why?'

'Because I don't want you to think I have a fetish when I kiss you.'

'You weren't so keen to kiss me this morning.'

I shoved my head into the fridge, but it was too late to be cool. What had I said that for? Hadn't I decided, after a miserable, sleepless night, that I mustn't think of Ethan that way?

Must never again remember how he had turned me inside out with his kisses?

Ethan drew me away from the fridge and pulled off the rubber gloves.

'I was very keen to pick you up and carry you back to my room. But I didn't think you'd want me to do that in front of everyone.' He placed a gentle kiss on my lips. 'I'm an expert in hiding my feelings. Don't forget I've had twenty years of practice.'

This was no good at all. Every time he said things like that, or touched me, or kissed me, my heart skipped, my skin burned, and I lost control. I had to conquer it, and until I worked out how to do that, I had to avoid Ethan.

'I need to take Dotty for a walk,' I said, bending to tickle her head in apology, as I knew the dog-sitter had already taken her out this morning.

'Okay.' Ethan went out into the hall and I relaxed. 'Joe, we're taking Dotty for a walk,' he shouted up the stairs. 'See you later.'

'Fine,' Jonas called back – little traitor.

Mum's net curtains danced as we walked down the drive, and for a second, I thought I saw a large figure behind them, and a shiver crawled down my spine. The usual car was parked on the road.

'Does that belong to your mum's boyfriend?' Ethan asked, pointing at it.

'I think so,' I said, recoiling at the word 'boyfriend' and all it implied. Was this how Ava had felt about me and Owen? Perhaps we weren't so different after all. 'I haven't met him yet.'

'I'm sure I've seen it around the village. The driver was a big man, dark hair, about Irene's age. So not a toyboy.' He laughed. 'Actually, he looked like . . .' He studied me and smiled. 'I may be slightly obsessed. He looked like a nice man.'

'I hope so. Mum deserves to be happy again.'

'So do you.' He stroked my arm, and I cursed to myself for walking into that one. We carried on towards the village, Ethan talking and me trying and failing not to laugh, until we passed Daisy's house. Daisy and Owen were approaching from the opposite direction, Lucilla trailing along behind like a sulky teenager.

'Hello!' I cut across Ethan's story about an elderly hotel guest who had wandered into the wedding reception by mistake – his impression of her trying to find the bride to apologise was making me giggle like a toddler. 'What are you two up to?'

Daisy immediately looked guilty and wandered away from Owen to talk to me.

'Sorry,' she said, lowering her voice. 'Is it awkward to see us together? We're trying not to be too obvious.'

'What?' It took me a moment to work out what she meant. 'No, it doesn't bother me in the slightest. Be as obvious as you like. Within the bounds of public decency.'

Daisy smiled, but faint lines of anxiety still marked her

forehead. I didn't know what more I could say to reassure her. That kissing Ethan last night had made me forget Owen existed? That any other man existed. That life beyond him existed.

'How are you?' Daisy asked, scrutinising my face more closely than I'd have liked. 'It was Leo's wedding yesterday, wasn't it? What was it like? Please tell me it was totally camp, with sequins and feather boas, drag queens and songs from the musicals.'

'That would have been fun, but not very Leo. It was tasteful and romantic, and they looked blissfully happy.'

'Poor you.' Daisy hugged me. 'No wonder you look rough. That must have been horrendous.'

It should have been horrendous: watching the man I'd relied on for twenty-five years marry someone else; finding out that he might have been unfaithful to me before Clark – although I was struggling to believe that was true. But there had been nothing horrendous about those minutes in the garden.

I glanced over at Ethan. He was talking to Owen, which was an unnerving sight. There were three men in the world now who had intimate knowledge of my breasts, and two of them were standing here chatting – about what? Yesterday's football results? The weather? How saggy my boobs were? It didn't bear thinking about.

'Are you taking Lucilla for a walk?' I asked, shouting so that Owen would hear too. 'Do you want to join us?'

'We've just been,' Owen said.

'And James is bringing Chloe back soon,' Daisy added.

That scuppered my grand plan to avoid time alone with Ethan. I looked over at him, and he smiled, with so much affection shining from his face that I wondered how I could have missed it before. Hiding his feelings? He might as well have a neon pink sandwich board strapped on him, announcing the news. Daisy turned and followed my gaze.

'Mary?' I could tell at once that she had noticed the way Ethan was looking at me. The shock was stark on her face before she tried to brush it away with a weak smile. But I'd seen it, and it confirmed everything that I had told myself a million times last night. If my best friend was scandalised by the hint of something between me and Ethan, what would the rest of the world think?

'You know where I am if you need me,' Daisy said. She touched my arm, confusion flickering across her face. 'Come round if you want to talk. About anything.'

I nodded, and we carried on with our walk, taking the footpath that skirted around the edge of the village and through the fields behind Foxwood Farm. It was one of my favourite walks, as within a few hundred metres all civilisation was lost from view, and there was nothing to be seen but a jigsaw of fields, and the blunt-ended Pendle Hill looming over us in the distance. I paused on the step of a stile to soak it all in – the solid familiarity of it, such a contrast to the unfamiliar feelings that were raging inside me.

'This is amazing.' Ethan lifted me off the stile and swung

me round, lowering me to the ground with a kiss. 'You've no idea how much I've wanted to do this – just to be with you, and hold your hand, and be normal.'

He took my hand, but I pulled away and carried on tramping along the well-worn track through the field. This wasn't *my* normal. This was terrifying.

'I'm sorry about last night,' Ethan said, striding through the rough grass at my side. 'It wasn't great, was it?'

'Wasn't it?' My stupid, treacherous voice trembled, and I couldn't look at Ethan. It was bad enough that he regretted it enough to apologise, but the damning verdict on my kissing skills brought tears to my eyes – tears that shouldn't be there. But how could I stop them? My good resolutions were swept away with one huge wave of emotion. He thought last night was 'not great'. I thought it had been wonderful.

I concentrated on Dotty, trying to blink away the tears, but only succeeded in pushing a few down my cheeks.

'Mary?' Ethan pulled me round to face him. 'Don't be an idiot. Of course the kissing part was great. Incredible.' He kissed my eyelids, and the damp trails down my cheeks, with such unmistakeable tenderness that I was close to crying again. 'But the situation wasn't as perfect as I'd have liked – the timing, me blurting it all out, getting carried away in a hotel garden . . . After waiting twenty years, I should have come up with something better.'

It had been perfect to me, but I held my tongue, because I mustn't encourage him – or encourage myself.

'It doesn't matter.'

'It does to me. I wanted it to start right.'

'Wanted what to start?' I stepped back, out of reach of his lips. 'What do you think is going to happen now? That we kissed so I'm going to up sticks and move to New York? It won't work.'

'I'll move back.'

'And what then? Will you move in with me, and slip into the gap left by Leo? Sit on his chair at the table, drink coffee from his mug? Sleep with me in the bed I shared with your brother, filling the dent he made in the mattress?' I paused on top of the next stile, and looked down at Ethan. It would be so easy to fall in love with him; impossible to *be* in love with him. 'Have you thought about how weird that would be?'

'Yes. I've had years to think about it. I know it would be weird. But if that's what it takes to be with you, I'll do it.'

I jumped down from the stile.

'And if you did, what would people say?' I dragged Dotty away from a fascinating pile of sheep droppings, and down the hill to where the path followed a stream. 'Can you imagine the reaction?'

'What reaction? We're not living in Alice Hornby's day. It's not illegal. It's not against any religious laws. I don't care what anyone else thinks.'

'But I do.' I stopped and looked at Ethan, because I needed him to understand. 'You've become used to New York, and life on a massive scale. It's different here. I've spent my life in Stoneybrook, and everyone knows me. I'm the girl whose father vanished into thin air one day while she was at school. I'm the woman whose husband turned gay. All that was hard enough to deal with in the public eye. Now you want me to be – what? The woman who moved in her husband's brother, six months after her divorce? I can't go through it all again, for what might turn out to be nothing but a few great kisses.'

'A lot of great kisses. And love. And happiness. We could be incredibly happy, Mary. You know it.' He trapped my gaze. 'You've always known it.'

It was true. I had known it, since we kissed. Not the kiss last night; our *first* kiss. Because there had been another one, many years ago, before I married Leo. A kiss that had come from nowhere, in the middle of a public firework display on Ethan's birthday, one glorious crisp autumn night. A kiss that had been more thrilling and more terrifying than any I'd shared with Leo. And yes, in those moments I'd realised there was a whole dimension of happiness beyond the one I knew; but there was a galaxy of pain there too. I had made my commitment, and nothing could make me let Leo down by breaking it.

We crossed the stream over the narrow, single plank bridge. Ethan trailed behind me, and I could sense his frustration blowing towards me on the wind.

'There's only a handful of people whose opinions matter,' he said, catching up as the path widened. 'Forget everyone else.'

'Mum and Ava are against it. Leo doesn't even like me talking to you, let alone anything else. And Audrey . . .' What would she think if I simply swapped one son for the other? 'I couldn't bear to damage my relationship with Audrey. I need her.'

'Mum loves you. She wants us all to be happy.'

'But for how long would we be happy?' I turned and looked at him. The wind ruffled his hair, and my fingers longed to join in. 'All the disruption, all the gossip, all the problems with the family we would have to face – and what if it all went wrong? You have a terrible track record. You've always flitted from one girl to the next, with no staying power. I didn't let a great kiss sway me twenty years ago, and I mustn't let another one sway me now. What if this is just an amusement because you had to come back home for Audrey?'

'God, Mary, haven't you listened to me at all? I came back for Mum. I stayed for you. I would never let you go.'

He was too quick for me. He grabbed my hand, pulled me to him and kissed me so thoroughly that I thought he might literally never let go. But I had to wriggle away. This was temptation, not persuasion. I couldn't allow it to change my mind.

'I can't do this,' I said. 'I can't think about this now. Everything's turning into such a bloody awful mess . . .'

I stomped away, not before Dotty had made her own contribution to the mess by rolling in a patch of muddy leaves.

'What's bothering you?' Ethan would not be shaken off. 'Tell me.'

'Apart from you?'

Ethan laughed, and the sound calmed me, and punctured the tension that had blown up between us. He wasn't just an extraordinarily attractive man and an exceptional kisser; he was a friend too.

'I found a telephone message from the Archers this morning,' I said. 'I've been summoned to see them.'

'Isn't that good? More Alice Hornby talk over tea and biscuits?'

'It didn't sound like a friendly summons.' I sighed. 'I have a horrible feeling that they might have discovered Leo's article.'

'Is that a problem? Won't the publicity help sales if you publish the new book?'

'If they've seen Leo's plans to sex up the book, I don't think they'll let us publish it at all.'

My voice wobbled, and Ethan caught me in a hug: a perfect, friendly hug, offering comfort not passion. It was exactly what I needed, and I leant my head against his shoulder.

'If they don't want Leo to be involved, you know what you have to do, don't you?' Ethan's words rumbled against my hair. I shook my head. I didn't want to hear it. 'You have to do it without him.'

'But . . .'

Ethan stepped back so he could look at me.

'No buts. I know you're going to tell me that you couldn't

be so disloyal.' That was exactly what I had been going to say. He knew me better than I realised. 'Wouldn't it be worse to let the book be forgotten, or be published by people who didn't care so much? You have the talent, and the passion. You can convince the Archers that you're the right person to do it.'

I could have kissed him for that – for making me feel, in that moment, that I could do anything. If I could sell myself as well as he sold me, I would have nothing to worry about. As a kiss was out of the question, I took his hand and gave it a quick squeeze before we carried on walking home.

'I won't come in,' Ethan said, as we reached the top of my drive. He handed over Dotty's lead. Despite the shadow I could see at Mum's window, despite everything I'd said, and despite the last ten minutes of convincing myself that I shouldn't invite him in, a hollow of disappointment opened in my chest. 'I do understand why you're finding this weird. I've had years to get used to the idea. You haven't. If you need time to work it out, without pressure from me, that's fine. I can wait a little longer.'

I nodded, though I wasn't sure which bit I was agreeing to. What was there to work out? And how much time did I have? He was going back to New York in less than three weeks. Three weeks to make my decision . . . But I'd made it, hadn't I? Three weeks to stick to it.

'But as you're working it out, remember this. We're not

defined by our relationships with other people,' Ethan said. 'I'm just a man, and you're just a woman. I love you, Mary Black, and I hope you might love me. Nothing matters beyond that.'

Chapter Twenty-Four

It wasn't a promising start when the Archer's shop bell jammed as I pushed open the bookshop door. There was no friendly jingle to welcome me this time, and seeing the antagonism on Bridie's face, I half suspected the bell had been sabotaged on purpose, ready for my arrival.

'Mum!' Bridie called, keeping an eye on me as I advanced through the shop. 'She's here!'

Mrs Archer wheeled in from the back room. I clearly was no longer welcome there.

'Hello! I've brought you some parkin,' I said, opening my cake tin and putting it on the desk. If I'd had any thoughts of using it as a bribe, it didn't work: Mrs Archer peeped into the tin, sniffed, but didn't take a piece.

'Too late for soft-soaping,' she muttered. 'We've seen it. Bridie!'

Bridie moved back to the desk and took a page of newspaper out of a drawer. It was Leo's article: his publicity photo gazed up at me, with eyes that were steady, serious, and utterly reliable. Or so I'd thought. Totally opposite from the laughing, mischievous blue eyes of his brother . . . But I mustn't think of him. I'd spent two days not thinking about him. If only the nights were as easy to control . . .

'We didn't give you permission to talk about the book,' Bridie said, tapping the article with an accusing finger. 'For your eyes only, that's what we said when we sent it to you.'

'I know, and I didn't show it to anyone else!'

'He's seen it!' Bridie's finger stabbed Leo in the face.

'But that's Leo. He had to see it. He's the expert.'

'We thought you were too, with your book and your Society and all that.'

'I . . .' I hesitated. I had spent years deferring to Leo – but oddly, Bridie's complaint was one of the best compliments I'd ever received. I *was* an expert, not only in Alice Hornby, but also in Victorian literature as a whole. It had simply never been my role to stand up and be counted as an expert. I was like those members of a curling team that scrubbed furiously at the ice with a brush, so the puck could glide smoothly to victory. It was the way we'd always worked.

'Leo's the professor,' I pointed out. 'I'm not.'

'He could be the Lord High Duke of Lancashire for all we care. All we wanted was someone who understood Alice and would have a bit of respect for her book.'

'We do.'

Mrs Archer drove forwards and gestured at the newspaper cutting.

'Sexed up!' she grumbled. 'Bodice ripper!'

Her outraged expression probably matched my own when I'd first read the article.

'Don't take any notice of that. It's journalistic nonsense. Leo wouldn't have used the term bodice ripper. It derives from America in the 1970s and . . .' I stopped. Neither Archer appeared interested in the etymology of the phrase, though I could have talked about it at length.

'It's not what Alice would have wanted. She didn't trust her book with our Florrie for this to happen. That book was special. Personal.' Bridie glanced at her mother, who twitched her head in what looked like a warning. 'Anyhow, we've been on the Google internet and there's a chap who's an expert on the Brontës and that sort of time period. He could do it. He's at Oxford.'

'So was Leo.' And as he'd proved, it was no guarantee against idiocy. A horrible suspicion occurred to me. 'It's not Lucas Flynn, is it?'

'Professor Flynn,' Bridie corrected. Touché. 'Have you heard of him?'

Heard of him? More than I could ever have wanted. He was one of the leading experts in all things Brontë, and so as far as Leo was concerned, Flynn was his arch-enemy in the literary world. They had an annual spat over something or other. If Leo knew that Flynn might be the one to edit and publish Alice's manuscript . . . I couldn't let it happen. And I heard Ethan's voice, loud and clear over my shoulder, giving me a tender prod.

320

'Let me work on the book,' I said. 'I had nothing to do with this article. I was as shocked as you when I saw it.'

'Then why did you let him see the book?' Bridie asked.

'Because I thought he would view it the same way I did. We've been a close team until now. And I really think he became over-excited and the journalist put her own spin on it.' The Archers were frowning again. I was losing them. I had no choice: either I threw Leo overboard or we both sank. 'But you're right. This isn't the way the book should be treated at all. Yes, it's a passionate story, and bold for its time, but romance is at the heart of it. Alice has written the most extraordinary story about the power of love, and how much you would be prepared to give up for it.'

The frowns had gone, and Bridie exchanged a glance with her mother.

'So you would be willing to do it without him?' Bridie flicked the newspaper.

'Leo may need to be involved in authenticating it, but apart from that, yes. I'd be willing to edit the manuscript and get it ready for publication – assuming I can find a publisher who would take me on.'

I could see from their faces that they weren't persuaded.

'Forget that,' I said. 'I'm not *willing* to do it. I would love to work on this manuscript. It's the most beautiful, magical, moving story I've read for years. The public need to read this book and understand what an amazing writer Alice is: how she can catch you up from the first page and not stop squeezing your emotions until long after you've finished the last one. I want to be the person who launches this book. I want to do it for Alice.'

The words flowed out without me even thinking of them. I needed the Archers to see how committed I was, and that my enthusiasm was genuine, and heartfelt. I looked from Bridie to Mrs Archer: they weren't smiling, but their expressions had softened considerably since I walked in. I was close to persuading them; and now my flickering guilt over ditching Leo was replaced by naked determination. I *had* to persuade them. I couldn't bear anyone else to touch Alice's words but me.

'You might want to do it,' Bridie said, 'but how do we know you're the right person for the job?'

'Because I understand Alice. I know her books and her diary and her letters inside out, and I know what she would have done with this book if she'd tried to publish it in her lifetime.' Bridie gave a slight shrug, as if to point out that anyone could know all that. I needed more – and the words came again, my heart taking control of my tongue. 'And because I understand this book more than anyone else can. I know what it's like to love someone you shouldn't . . . when it seems wrong and impossible and hopeless . . . because that's the situation I'm in.'

I sat down on the edge of the desk. What had I said? My heart answered again: nothing but the truth. Of course I loved Ethan. I always had, on some level – a level I had done my best to ignore. But it had deepened over the last few months, since his return to Lancashire – since I had been reminded how well we connected, how he made me laugh, how life sparkled when he was around. It wasn't simply attraction, as I'd tried to tell myself; not just the embarrassing lust of a recently divorced woman. It was way beyond that. I'd told Ethan that I was ready to fall in love, but I had never imagined that *he* would be the man I fell in love with. And there lay a problem: because my head still told me this was wrong, a risk I couldn't and shouldn't take. Lust would have faded, or been replaced; but not love. How was I supposed to live with this?

Mrs Archer manoeuvred around the desk and pulled up in front of me. To my surprise, she reached out from her blankets and put a bony hand on mine.

'The man who carried me,' she said. My face must have mirrored my confusion. 'At the Hornby day,' she added.

'Ethan.' I nodded. I'd forgotten that. It had stuck in Mrs Archer's memory, judging by the twinkle in her eye, and no wonder. I couldn't forget my time in his arms either, despite my best endeavours. 'My husband's brother.'

'Ex-husband, isn't it?' Bridie asked. I nodded, hoping that she would say that made a difference – made it perfectly acceptable, not weird at all – but she said nothing. Then she looked at her mother. 'Tea, Mum? And shall we have some of this parkin?'

'Just a bite.' Mrs Archer drove towards the door to the living area. She turned back and stared at me. 'Come on.'

'Does this mean . . .' I hopped off the desk. Was I forgiven? Were they going to trust me with Alice's manuscript after all?

Mrs Archer sniffed.

'I'll think on it.'

Ethan was frustratingly true to his word, and didn't call round to see me. He came close one day: I saw him vault over the hedge from Audrey's, making my heart soar with him, but Mum arrived home and interrupted whatever he planned to do. Another morning I opened the front door and found a hedgerow bouquet – creeping thistle and chickweed bound up with a piece of string – lying on the doorstep. A slip of paper tucked under the string read simply, 'For Mary x', in writing that I knew well. I smuggled it up to my bedroom, and arranged the flowers in a jug beside my bed, so they were my first and last sight of the day.

I couldn't go on pretending. What I'd said to the Archers hadn't been a sales pitch, any old flannel that I'd tossed out in the hope of persuading them to let me work on Alice's book. And now I'd acknowledged the truth, it had spread and grown so quickly that I couldn't fit it back inside its box. I longed to be with Ethan. Countless times I picked up my keys, determined to go to Waterman's Cottage and . . . what? Tell him that I loved him? And my mind would play out the next few hours, the kisses, the laughter, the delirium, the blissful hours we might spend in that bed, with the clouds racing above our heads . . .

But my imagination stopped short within hours. I couldn't see what would happen beyond that. There was a gaping hole where the future should be, and it terrified me. I believed that Ethan thought he loved me now, but I'd seen it too many times before to be confident that it would last. Too many girls at school had cried in my ear, hoping that I would convince him to give them another chance. I'd watched him bring home a different girl almost every university holiday. And then there were his two brief marriages and the count-less relationships Leo had told me about in-between . . . Ethan wasn't cut out to be loyal; and I wasn't cut out to risk being left again.

I did my best, but my distraction leaked out over other areas of my life. Leo, infuriatingly chipper after his honey-moon, pointed out two references I'd missed in an article I'd written for him. The Tippetts complained that my carrots were too crunchy for their teeth and the chicken was like eating sandpaper. Jonas spent most of his time in his room. Only Ava appeared happy, mainly because I was too caught up with my own life to notice what was going on in hers. Our rela-tionship had rarely been sweeter.

'Goodness, I think Mary must be away with the fairies!' Marissa's laugh cut into my thoughts, and I was dragged back to the dreary staff room and the PTA meeting. I ought to be concentrating: this meeting was about the annual bonfire and fireworks display, an event I always arranged, but at the first hint of toffee apples and wood smoke my memories had whisked me away. My cheeks felt as hot as if there was a real bonfire in the room.

'You will be here, won't you?' Marissa asked. I tensed, sensing trouble in her voice and smile.

'Of course.' I'd run the event for the last eight years. It was my moment, and one of the biggest fundraisers of the year. There was no way I would miss it.

'Only I heard that you may be jetting off to New York soon.' Marissa's smile glittered. I grabbed the chipped 'World's Best Teacher!' mug I'd been given and sipped the cold dregs of tea, trying to stop my heart battering against my chest. She had to be talking about Ethan ... but how did she know anything about him? How had a rumour spread already? My gaze flicked to Daisy, but it was unworthy of me: Daisy appeared as startled as I was.

'It's typical of you to be so efficient in your choice, Mary,' Marissa continued, 'so you won't have to go through the rigmarole of changing your name on documents.' She laughed. 'Is this it now? There's not a third brother waiting in the wings for when you grow tired of this one?'

'Don't be such a bitch.' Daisy jumped to my defence, waking up some of the quieter members of the PTA. 'Mary's not like that.'

'Oh, I don't blame her,' Marissa said. 'We'd all like a younger man if we could get one.'

'He's older than me!'

Too late I realised what a rookie mistake I'd made. Marissa

couldn't have looked more delighted if I'd whipped out a one-way ticket to New York and waved it around the room with an exuberant 'ta-da!' It was all Ethan's fault: Leo had never taken over my head and driven away all sense like this.

I tried to sneak away after the meeting, but Daisy was as nimble as a fox when she wanted to be, and caught up with me as I strode along the corridor to the exit.

'Are you okay, Mary?' she asked – which I interpreted as a polite version of, 'What the hell's going on?'

'Great.'

Daisy abandoned the indirect approach.

'You're not going to New York, are you? With Ethan?'

'Of course not!' I stopped at the head of the grand flight of stairs that led down to the ground floor. The school had been built as a magnificent country house, and it was impossible not to imagine all the elegantly gowned ladies who had once descended these stairs, ready to float around the ballroom and fall in love. When the school was empty, like this, the ghosts of hopes and dreams shimmered in the air. Mine too.

'What would you think if I did?' I couldn't resist asking. 'Not go to New York. I mean if I did do – anything – with Ethan?'

'By anything, are you including . . .' Daisy tipped her head to one side a couple of times. I nodded. 'Blimey.'

'What?' I started down the stairs as some of the other parents headed our way. 'You think it's too weird, don't you?'

'Well, yes. But that's because when I divorced James, one

327

of the advantages was losing the mother-in-law. I would never have wanted her in that role again. And frankly, James' brother has the looks and the manners of an enraged bull, and I would rather lock myself in a suit of armour than risk him touching any part of me. Ethan's different.'

'I know.'

Daisy shot me a curious look, and when we reached the bottom of the stairs, she grabbed my arm and steered me into the nearest classroom.

'Are you serious?' she asked, studying my face. 'Has anything already happened?'

'No.' I wilted under her searchlight gaze. 'Not much more than kissing.'

'And did it feel weird?'

'Not at the time. Afterwards . . . yes. He's Leo's brother!'

'But they're not twins, are they? You wouldn't even know they were related by looking at them or talking to them.'

That was true. I knew in my own mind that my attraction to Ethan wasn't a pathetic attempt to cling on to a part of Leo. But would other people see that?

'Be honest, Daisy. If I were in a relationship with Ethan, what would you think?'

'That you were very lucky?' She smiled. 'Don't tell Owen I said that.' She squeezed my hand. 'If it made you happy, I'd be thrilled for you.'

A little bud of hope unfurled in my chest. Was it possible? Could this work?

'But it wouldn't be easy,' Daisy continued, and that little bud shrivelled. 'There are some people in Stoneybrook who are only too ready to be scandalised. There's bound to be gossip. And if you're seriously thinking of doing this, you have to be sure that it's for keeps. This is going to turn your family upside down. You can't do that for a fling.' She squeezed my arm. 'Only you can decide whether he's worth it.'

It had taken a while, but the owner of the bookshop in Bickton, who I had met after Leo's and Clark's dinner party, had finally agreed to stock the Alice Hornby biography, and invited Leo over for a signing. It was a joint event, and he shared the floor with a local historian and a debut novelist of historical romance set in Victorian times. Despite his initial reservations, it had been well attended, the books had sold, and I had even signed up two new members to the Alice Hornby Society.

The only downside to the morning had been Leo's insistence on mentioning the new manuscript, an unauthorised addition to the short speech I'd prepared for him. I hadn't had chance to tell him about my latest visit to the Archer's bookshop: it wasn't something I could raise over the phone, and Leo had all but given up coming home to work in our shared office. I still didn't know whether the Archers would let me be involved with publishing the book, but as either way they had ruled Leo out, I couldn't put off telling him any longer.

We'd both parked our cars beside the town park, and as it was a dry but breezy day, I suggested we could take a walk through the park before going home.

'A walk?' Leo checked his watch. 'I'm not sure . . .'

'It's important.'

We wandered into the park, and Leo bought us coffee from a vending cart.

'I suppose they must have told you,' he said, as we followed the path to the left, in the opposite direction to the playground. 'Good. I believe they hoped I'd do it for them.'

'Told me what?'

'Jonas and Ava have asked to stay over the Christmas holidays.' Leo looked at me and sighed. 'They hadn't mentioned it, had they?'

'No.' I gulped my coffee, feeling the scalding progress of the liquid down my throat.

'Jonas is hoping to work in the café again.'

'And Ava?'

'Yes. She first raised it in St Ives, but I expected the idea to wane once she was home.'

Knowing Ava, the idea had probably blossomed when she came home and had to endure my company again. What had I ever done to these children to make them want to abandon me at the first opportunity? And at Christmas too . . .

'What about Christmas Day?' I stopped in the middle of the path, and a wiry Jack Russell terrier collided with my legs. 'Are they spending that with you too?'

'No, they can't. Clark and I have booked a restaurant with friends.'

So much for my vague imaginings that we might have a joint Christmas like last year.

'What will Audrey do?'

Leo gave me the patient frown he always used when one of us had said something dim.

'She'll join you as normal, won't she?'

Of course she would, if she wanted to. Christmas wouldn't be Christmas without Audrey, and her silly hats, and hoots of laughter at the most appalling cracker jokes. But how could Leo describe it as normal? How easily he had moved on from his last Christmas as a married man to his first. And how differently he was behaving the second time around, putting time alone with Clark before family. Perhaps we should have done that when we married – insisted on carving out our space as a married couple, instead of going on as if things had hardly changed, save for a shuffle in who lived where. Would it have made a difference if we had moved away, taken time to become ourselves and experience life on our own? But we would never have had that time. Jonas was born within a year of our marriage, earlier than I had planned, but Leo had been desperate to start a family. I had adored him for understanding how much I needed a family of my own.

A skateboarder whizzed past, and I had to step out of his way, almost tripping over Leo's foot. He steadied me and smiled, the reassuring smile that I had relied on for so long.

'What did you want to talk about, Mary, if not the children?'

'Alice Hornby's manuscript.'

Leo's smile brightened. I could hardly bear to look at him. I had no idea how he would react to the news. I wanted to believe that he would understand, and support me, but Ethan had sewn doubts in my head that I couldn't entirely shake out.

'Can we proceed?' he asked. 'My agent has already sounded out three or four publishers who are interested. We may even have a bidding war!'

'The Archers haven't decided yet.'

'Would it help if I met them again? I'm sure you will have tried your utmost, but perhaps they need to hear from me.'

'That won't help.' There was no easy way to say this, so I blurted it out. 'They don't want you to be involved.'

'Why ever not?' Leo stared at me, blatantly nonplussed. 'Have you explained who I am? My credentials? They can't have understood, Mary. You must try again.'

'They don't care about any of that. They saw the article in *The Times* and didn't like it. They won't let Alice be sexed up.'

'Oh, that was the journalist being sensational!' But there was a tell-tale colour on Leo's cheeks that told me it wasn't all down to the journalist. He'd known exactly what he was doing, maximising the publicity. He was too clever not to have known. 'What do they intend? To bury the book again and let no one see it?'

'No.' I glanced at him, weighing up the best way to approach this. 'They looked on the internet and found details for Lucas Flynn.'

'Flynn?' Leo stopped walking and goggled at me, his cheeks mottling to deep purple. 'No,' he said, and it seemed a struggle to even manage that much. 'No.'

His reaction was even worse than I'd expected. What was it about Flynn that riled him so much? They'd been at Oxford around the same time, shared a love of literature – they ought to have been friends, not rivals.

'There is an alternative,' I said, shamelessly exploiting the moment. 'They might let me edit and publish the book.'

'You?' It wasn't quite the same tone he'd given to 'Flynn' but I detected an unflattering degree of surprise in the word.

'Yes, me. Who else, after you, has such a comprehensive knowledge of Alice? And I'm not totally ignorant of what it takes to create a book fit for publication.'

That hit home, as I'd intended. Leo walked on, and I could see the battle of his thoughts scarring his face. I knew him too well not to understand what he was thinking. Finding and publishing Alice's lost work had been one of the chief ambitions of his life. And now the miracle had happened, and the public would finally be able to read it – but only if he stepped aside. What would be the greater torture for him? Seeing someone else work on the manuscript, or allowing it to be lost to the world for another generation?

I said nothing, and let him struggle with his thoughts, while the path led us past an old-fashioned bandstand and a graf-fiti-covered skateboard park. A few teenagers were flipping and jumping at horrifying speeds, but otherwise the park was quiet except for dog-walkers. My hand felt oddly empty without Dotty's lead.

'You're right, Mary,' Leo said at last, when I had begun to think we would return to our cars without exchanging another word. 'If the Archers have determined against me, it will have to be you. The manuscript must be published. It's too impor-tant a piece of literary history to lose. Lucas is not the man for this. You must persuade the Archers to let you edit it.'

Relief buoyed me so high I could have floated across the park. It was the answer I'd wanted to hear. Not because I needed his permission to pursue it – I would have done that anyway – but because I needed to know that Leo was, despite everything, the man I had always thought him to be.

'Thank you,' I said, and I threw my arms round him and hugged him. 'I knew you'd support me.'

'Of course.' Leo squeezed me back, briefly. 'Better you than Flynn. The Archers need never know that I'm helping in the background.' He pulled away. 'Why did you have any doubt?'

'I didn't really, it was just something Ethan mentioned in St Ives . . .'

'Ethan?' Leo frowned. 'What did he say?'

'It doesn't matter now, just some nonsense about you not always being loyal to me . . .'

My hand covered my mouth. It was an involuntary action:

if I'd acted consciously, I would have covered my eyes, so I didn't have to see the truth hovering on Leo's face. A series of rapid blinks, the raised colour, the sudden short breaths all told me what I'd been reluctant to believe. And I thought back to Leo's wedding – the conversation before the kiss – the bit of the day that I'd blocked out, in my usual fashion, and pretended hadn't happened.

'How did you celebrate in Oxford, Leo, when you found out you'd got a First?'

'Mary . . .'

I sat down on the nearest bench, brushing a Greggs' paper bag to the floor and sending pie crumbs scattering across the path. This wasn't true. I wouldn't believe it. Leo would not have done that to me. Oh, but he had – the guilt and apology clung to him like smoke fumes and echoed in his voice.

'You had sex with someone in Oxford.' I looked up, then put my head in my hands; it felt too heavy to hold up. 'Or was it more than one? Was it going on the whole time you were there?'

'Only one. Only once.' The bench wobbled as Leo sat down beside me. 'And not sex, as such. It was a man – a student.' I said nothing. 'I've never slept with another woman. I've never wanted to.'

'It makes no difference!' My shout disturbed a mother passing by, and she pushed her pram to the other side of the path. 'I don't care if it was a man or a woman. We had something pure and innocent. We weren't like other people. When we married, I believed that we had only slept with each other, and that would be true for our whole lives. It was perfect loyalty. But none of it was real. You ruined us.'

I pulled my jacket tighter across my chest, but shivered all the same. Perhaps it made no sense that I was more distraught about an old infidelity than the one that had ended our marriage. But it felt like our past had been rewritten, and our history was crumbling like a sandcastle constructed with too-soft sand. The Leo I'd thought I was marrying – the reliable, safe, loyal Leo, the man I had chosen – had never really existed. And though I tried to hold back the question, it wouldn't be silenced. *Would I still have chosen him if I'd known?*

'I tried to live up to your idea of perfection, but it was impossible. I have faults like everyone else. Sometimes the need to be myself was inescapable.'

'Infidelity isn't a fault, it's a choice! And so is loyalty.'

'And where was your loyalty when you kissed my brother?'

The flash of temper came from nowhere – a side to Leo that I had never seen before.

'We're divorced!' I said, feeling absurdly guilty all the same. 'What does it matter now?'

Leo stiffened.

'You mean you kissed Ethan recently? The opportunistic bastard. The ink on the divorce papers is barely dry.'

'Dry enough for you to have a new marriage certificate!'

I stood up, huffing out short, angry breaths, and had stomped a few metres away before the significance of what

Leo had said occurred to me. He hadn't known about the kiss at the wedding – his reaction had proved that. So if that wasn't the kiss he had meant . . . There had only been one other. I turned and looked back. Leo had risen from the bench, and was standing, arms folded, watching me. The wind was blowing his hair, messing it up so he resembled my Leo, not the polished stranger that Clark had created. And yet he felt unfamiliar – a man tight with anger and secrets, whom I barely recognised at all.

I walked back to him.

'How long have you known?'

'Always.'

And with that, the past made sense. So much was explained: the hostility between Leo and Ethan; the reason why I had never visited New York, or even known that we'd been invited there; Leo's insistence that I change my choice of university so I could live at home near him instead of going away to Durham with Ethan. I needed time to think through all today's revelations, but one fundamental thing jumped out already. Now I understood Leo's odd behaviour when he returned home after graduation, when I feared that he would leave me; his hasty proposal was stained with guilt, not love.

'Did Ethan tell you?' I asked.

'Surprisingly, no.' I felt a prickle of relief; I had wondered whether Ethan had betrayed me to make mischief with Leo. 'Or not immediately.' Leo took my hand. 'What has he been saying to you, Mary? That he's been loyal for twenty years, waiting for you? Don't let him fool you. He had his chance. We discussed what to do about the situation. The choice was his – and he decided to let you go.'

Chapter Twenty-Five

'Mary, my darling, are you sure you're well enough to go?' Audrey slapped her hand against my forehead, checking my temperature. 'You look peaky.'

It was kind of her to say so. The truth was that I looked appalling, my hair dry and limp, my eyes puffy and bloodshot, and the end of my nose red and flaky due to constant abrasion from a tissue. Over the last few days I must have cried all the tears I'd held back, growing up. It was a wonder that we hadn't ended up swimming round the house like goldfish. But what else was I meant to do when my past had been turned inside out, and my future had soured before I'd even decided if I wanted it?

'I have to go,' I said, attempting a smile. 'Leo's agent is too busy to mess around. There may not be a second chance if I cancel.'

'There may be no first chance if you turn up looking so maudlin. You should be happy! This is a marvellous opportunity. You need to buzz and sparkle!'

I wasn't convinced I'd ever buzzed or sparkled in my life; and if I had, the days were long gone. But Audrey was right:

I did need to brighten up before my meeting. I had so much to be bright about: the Archers had finally telephoned and agreed to let me work on the publication of Alice's book. Leo had called his literary agent, and persuaded her to see me. This was exactly what I'd wanted. I should be thrilled. And I was, for sporadic flickers of time, until I remembered, and sadness bowled me over again.

'Have you no time for make-up?' Audrey persisted, scrutinising my face. 'Some blusher? And perhaps with some clever eye shadow those dark circles could look like a fashion statement rather than a disaster.' I shook my head. 'I wish you had let Ethan go with you! He would have laughed those shadows away.'

I didn't reply, and busied myself with setting out Dotty's bowls on the kitchen floor. I was only going to London for the day, but it would be a late night, and Audrey had agreed to look after Dotty and to feed the children when they returned from school.

'You need to talk to him, Mary.' The stern note in Audrey's voice made me glance up. In many ways, she was the negative image of Mum: soft and warm on the outside, but with a hidden core of steel, rarely seen but more powerful for that. 'This time next week he'll be back in New York, and who knows when we'll next see him!'

As if I weren't aware, almost to the second, of how much time there was left! I filled Dotty's bowl with biscuits, and stroked between her ears as she immediately dived on them.

'He'll pitch a tent on your lawn if you keep on avoiding him!'

It was about the only thing he hadn't tried yet. The notion of giving me time had faded away under a deluge of increasingly bewildered texts and emails. Gifts appeared on my doorstep every morning, thoughtful, sweet gifts that carried shared memories with them: a bottle of the beer we had drunk together in France as teenagers; a cupcake decorated to look like a bonfire; a postcard of a girl cartwheeling. He had rung the doorbell on numerous occasions while I had lurked out of sight, refusing to answer. I'd had years of practice at avoiding issues and people I didn't want to face: I should have worked for MI5 with my skills.

'He's terribly upset, my darling, that you won't see him.'

'I don't know what to say to him.'

'Then you must listen to your heart, Mary.' She stroked my hair back from my face, and kissed my cheek. 'You must let it have a voice at last.'

It was past ten o'clock when I arrived home, exhausted by a day spent sitting on trains and negotiating the busyness of a city that couldn't have been more different from my quiet village life. It had been a good day; Leo's agent had agreed to take me on as a client, and hadn't minded at all that the book wouldn't be the steamy novel that Leo had suggested. She loved my ideas, and the whole story behind my move from being in Leo's shadow to making one of the most important literary discoveries of the decade. In fact, at times, it felt that she was as keen to promote me as much as Alice, but I was sure I could dissuade her from that. It was impossible not to be buoyed by the knowledge that at last my work would go out in my own name.

The light was on in Audrey's sitting room when I let myself into the house.

'It's only me,' I called, pushing open the sitting room door. Audrey wasn't there. Ethan was sprawled on the sofa, apparently asleep, one leg dangling on the floor, one arm around Dotty who was spread-eagled across his chest.

Before I could retreat, Ethan opened his eyes and smiled at me. His movements disturbed Dotty, who tried to sit up, but slipped against his shirt and ended up on her back, a mass of flailing legs and fur. Ethan placed her gently on the floor before he stood up. Listen to my heart, Audrey had said to me that morning, and in that little act of kindness to my dog, I heard my heart loud and clear. I loved him.

'You look shattered,' he said, meeting me where I still hovered by the doorway. He didn't kiss me – a relief and a disappointment, all in one twisted mess. 'How did it go?'

'It was great. I've signed a contract to work with Leo's agent.'

'Your agent.' Ethan hugged me. 'That's fantastic news. I knew you'd do it. You're an official academic, like you always wanted.'

That had been my dream a long time ago. I had wanted to complete my degree and work at the university, as Leo had done. But an early marriage and a swift baby had shelved that dream. Instead of following in Leo's footsteps, I'd lurked in his shadow, invisible. No more.

Ethan drew back his head, still holding me, and his eyes met mine. If I'd expected or hoped for desire, I was disappointed. He was uncertain, for possibly the first time in his life, and it endeared him to me even more. I pulled away.

'Where's Audrey?'

'At your house. Ava needed the printer for her homework.' He glanced at his watch. 'They must have decided to stay over there.'

If it had been anyone else, I'd think I'd been set up, but Audrey wasn't like that. She wasn't the interfering type, or not beyond the words of encouragement she'd given me this morning.

'I'd better go home.' I turned to leave, but Ethan grasped my hand.

'Mary, wait.' His thumb grazed the back of my hand. 'Have you thought any more about what I said? I have to go back to New York in a few days. I can't avoid it. I need to know whether I'm staying there or . . .'

He let it hang, but I didn't need that 'or' spelling out. I knew full well what that 'or' involved, and my skin burned as the thought of it filled my head.

I sat down, perched on the edge of Bill's chair. I had lived so much of my life in this room, in this house, from the moment our new neighbours arrived. I had rushed in here, dragging Leo by the hand, to announce our engagement – to share my delight in becoming a proper member of the Black family. I had drunk a toast in here on my wedding day; brought my babies here first to show them off to their grandparents; held Audrey in my arms on the sofa over there when she had struggled to cope with Bill's sudden death. I was part of the fixtures of this house as much as the bookshelves in the alcoves, and the oak fire surround on the chimney breast. But my place here was secured by being Leo's girlfriend, his wife, his ex-wife, and the mother of his children. How could my role segue into that of Ethan's *something*, without sending ripples through all our lives?

'I've spoken to Leo,' I said.

'Right.' Ethan sat on the sofa again, a baffled frown creasing his forehead.

'I asked him what happened in Oxford.'

Ethan's eyes didn't leave mine.

'Did he tell you?'

'Yes.'

He half rose, and suspecting he planned to come over and comfort me, I held up my hand to stop him.

'Does it matter now?' he asked.

'Yes! Because even though we're divorced, I had the memory of something good, something solid – some sense that the last twenty years had a meaning and a purpose. But now I wonder whether any of it was real. And the absolute worst of it is, I can't help asking myself whether I would still have married him if I'd known.'

'Oh God, Mary, don't say that. Don't do that to me.' Ethan put his head in his hands.

We didn't speak again for a few minutes. Dotty wandered over and licked Ethan's hand, resting her front paws on his knees, before settling down on top of my feet.

'Leo's not the only guilty one, though, is he?' I said. Ethan looked up. 'Leo knew all the time about us. What we did.'

'It was a kiss. It hardly compares . . .'

'It's worse! I was engaged to Leo! He said you discussed it. Why would you tell him? Was it just a way of making mischief?'

'Of course it bloody wasn't!' Ethan jumped up, and Dotty raised her head and gave a low growl. He sat down again. 'We didn't have a discussion. It was a blazing row. I asked him not to marry you – or at least to tell you the truth, and let you choose for yourself.'

'What? When?'

'A couple of weeks before the wedding.'

I'd known nothing about it, hadn't suspected a thing. How could my wedding have been in jeopardy, without my knowledge?

'What did Leo say?'

'He said no. He wouldn't call it off, and refused to tell you.'

'And so, what? You said okay and walked away? Leo was right. You claim to have loved me for twenty years, but it's nonsense. You can't have loved me enough. You let me go.'

Ethan stood up and wandered over to the fireplace. There

was a photograph on the mantelpiece of Leo and me on our wedding day – so young, so happy, or so I'd thought. And yet two weeks before, Leo had been negotiating with his brother about whether that day should happen or not. Ethan stared at the picture, tension fixing his shoulders.

'He told me you were pregnant.'

'What?'

'Leo refused to call off the wedding because he said you were pregnant.'

'But I wasn't!'

'I know.' Ethan looked at me. 'I worked that out when Joe was born eleven months later. What was I supposed to do by then?'

I flopped back in my chair. The past had shifted again. I couldn't believe that Leo had lied – but seeing the distress on Ethan's face, as he relived those times, I couldn't doubt it either. And now Leo's eagerness to have a baby so quickly after our wedding took on a whole new slant. I'd believed it was a sign of commitment. Instead, it was to make good a lie to his brother. The shape of my life had been plotted and manipulated by these two men. And had either of them, at any point, paused to ask what I wanted?

'Wasn't I worth fighting for?' I asked. 'Did you not want me with another man's child?'

'It wasn't just any man though, was it?'

'So the brothers closed ranks and did a deal between themselves? I'm not a commodity. I was never yours to trade, and not his either. How do you think it feels to find out that the last twenty years weren't the life I thought I'd chosen, but a ramshackle, fragile thing, hung together with secrets, lies, and a grubby pact?' Ethan tried to speak but I was on a roll, and didn't stop to listen. 'Thank God for Audrey, that's all I can say.'

'Mum? What about her?'

'She's the one member of your family who has been true and loyal, and put me first – the only one who seems to realise that I'm a human being with real feelings. At least I can still rely on her. She would be horrified if she knew all this.'

Ethan didn't answer. The lines on his face deepened, the footprints of the thoughts travelling through his head. Then he came and knelt beside me, and took my hand.

'Forget the past. I'm here, I'm now, and I love you. Is that not enough?'

'No. Words aren't enough if they're not supported by actions. My dad told me he loved me every day. On the day he left, he called me his Mary-bear, and said that he loved me more than anything in the world. But he was gone when I came home from school, and I never heard from him again. I've no idea if he's alive. He doesn't know if I am. He doesn't know I married or that he has two amazing grandchildren. Words of love mean nothing if they can't be trusted.'

'Don't do this, Mary.' Ethan squeezed my hand. 'It's our time. It has to be.'

'It's not. It would be wrong – wrong in every way, and most of all, wrong for me.'

'Tell me you don't love me.'

Listen to my heart, Audrey had said – but how could I, when it was in a million tiny fragments? All I could go by was my head, and that was telling me to end this now, before I could be hurt even more. But looking into Ethan's face, where grief replaced the usual smile, tears dulled eyes that were normally so bright and full of fun, I couldn't imagine how there could be worse pain than this. Of course I couldn't tell him that I didn't love him. But nor could I risk the consequences of telling him that I did.

I leaned forward and kissed his forehead, breathing him in for the last time.

'Have a happy life in New York,' I said, and then I picked up Dotty and left.

Chapter Twenty-Six

It was important to me that the Archers should feel part of the adventure with Alice's manuscript as much as I was, and so after signing with the literary agent, I invited them out to lunch to celebrate. They weren't keen, but eventually I found a wheelchair-friendly pub within ten minutes of their village, with a menu they approved of – proper Sunday lunch with mash and homemade gravy – and they graciously succumbed to my invitation. I asked Audrey along to make up numbers and to keep conversation and laughter flowing, but ten minutes into our journey, I began to think the unthinkable and wonder whether Mum might have been a more cheerful option after all. Audrey gazed out of the car window, in utter abstraction, responding to me in monosyllables, and she hadn't said 'marvellous' once.

'Is anything the matter?' I asked, reaching across the car to touch her leg when she failed to answer for the third time. 'Would you rather I took you home?'

'Of course not. I'm here to support you, my darling.' She rustled up a smile. 'I shall be brimming with gaiety when we're there.' The smile drooped. 'One message to say he'd arrived, and that's all, in a week! I don't suppose he . . .'

'No.' I didn't need to ask who she meant. Ethan had returned to New York a week ago. I'd heard nothing from him since I walked out on him at Audrey's house. I missed him more than I'd expected. His departure had created a gigantic sink-hole in my life, wide and deep and impossible to ignore. Who knew that an absence could be every bit as solid, every bit as disruptive as a presence?

Audrey sighed. Aware that she was studying me, I kept my gaze steadily on the road ahead.

'I know your father hurt you a great deal, Mary, but you must be careful not to bottle up your feelings too tightly. One day someone may believe your act that you don't care.'

I glanced at her in astonishment, but she had turned her head towards the side window again. It was the closest Audrey had ever come to criticising me, and an initial flare of resentment didn't last long. She was right. I prided myself on my ability to block out my feelings. How else had I endured Leo's defection, and sailed through a record-breakingly quick divorce? How else was I surviving Ethan's absence? If I was surviving it. The days weren't so bad: if I kept busy, kept moving, I could go for an hour or more without thinking about him. The nights were a different matter. Then I had too much time to wonder about what I had done, and to wonder how different my life would have looked now if I could have brought myself to say yes.

As promised, Audrey did perk up over lunch, although

knowing her so well, I could tell it was a veneer of her usual liveliness, not the real thing. It was a good enough show to amuse the Archers: although at first they had appeared overwhelmed by Audrey's exuberance, it was impossible not to love her, and within half an hour I'd even spotted a hint of gum as old Mrs Archer was lured into smiling. Then she turned her glittering eyes on me.

'How's it with that fella of yours?' she asked through a mouthful of mashed potato.

A couple of peas dived off my fork and made a break for freedom across the table. I was tempted to follow. What had made her ask that now? Perhaps it was my fault: I'd introduced Audrey as my friend, fearing that the 'ex-mother-in-law and rejected future mother-in-law' introduction might bring on exactly this sort of question.

I coughed and drank some wine, and generally made a show of not having heard the question.

'Mary?' Audrey asked, when I'd run out of things to do. 'You didn't tell me you had a boyfriend.'

Wide-eyed and droopy-mouthed, she looked so woebegone that I rushed to reassure her.

'I don't! You'd be the first to know if I did. Audrey is my ex-husband's mother,' I explained to Bridie and Mrs Archer. I hoped that they would have the tact to let it drop. They didn't.

'Ooh.' For a moment I thought Mrs Archer was choking, as the noise gargled in her throat. 'And mother of t'other.'

'The other?' Audrey repeated. Three pairs of curious eyes fixed on me.

'Ethan.' My heart knocked so loudly at the sound of his name that I was sure Audrey must be able to feel the vibrations through the settle we were sharing. 'Bridie and Mrs Archer met him at the meeting of the Alice Hornby Society in July.'

'He carried Mum up the stairs,' Bridie said. 'It made Mum's day!'

'He's always been a kind and lovely boy.' Audrey sighed and put down her fork. 'I miss him terribly.'

'He's not dead, is he?' Bridie asked.

'No.' Not even my exemplary blocking skills would allow me to stuff my face with Sunday lunch in those circumstances. 'He's returned to New York, where he lives. He was only here on a long holiday.'

'But I hoped we might have been able to persuade him to stay,' Audrey added. 'He slotted back into our lives so beautifully, almost as if he'd never been away, didn't he, Mary?'

'Hmm.' I didn't want to be reminded how well he'd slotted into my life, or how it was my fault that he hadn't been persuaded to stay.

'I'm sorry to hear it.' Audrey murmured her thanks, although Bridie had been looking at me when she spoke. 'Mum?'

Mrs Archer stared at me, in an intense and frankly terrifying way. It would have put me off my roast beef if my misery hadn't already managed that.

'Aye, happen she needs to see it.'

Urged on by this mysterious uttering, Bridie reached into her Cath Kidston shopper, which had been sitting on her knee like a spoilt lapdog throughout the meal. She pulled out a thick, A4 envelope and handed it across the table to me.

'How marvellously mysterious!' Audrey exclaimed, perking up and mercifully moving on from talk of Ethan. 'What is it, Mary?'

I didn't reply, because I was drawing out a pile of paper — the same cheap shiny paper that Alice's manuscript had been copied on. Turning the pages print side up, I recognised Alice's handwriting, but it wasn't the closely packed writing full of crossings-out that I was used to from her manuscripts. This was a flowing, neat script, divided into dates . . .

'This is Alice's diary!' I checked the first date again, hardly believing what my eyes were telling me. 'This was written later than anything that's been published so far. This is all new.' I looked across at Bridie. 'Did Florrie have this too?'

Bridie nodded.

'It starts a couple of weeks after her sister's death, and goes on until she finished the last book. There's no more after that.'

'Can I take this and read it?' I didn't wait for an answer: they would have to kill me to prise it from my fingers. 'Do you want this to be published too? If the diary is about Alice writing her last book, it would be fantastic to launch them at the same time.'

353

'Read it and see,' Bridie said, glancing at her mother. 'It's personal.'

'Read it and think,' Mrs Archer added, in her usual mysterious way.

Luckily the children were with Leo for the weekend and not due back until after tea, so as soon as I arrived home, I let Dotty out into the garden – I don't think she minded missing a walk, as it was pouring with rain – and settled down to read the diary. I had studied Alice's diaries in detail, and expected to find more of the same: beautiful, stylish prose, full of warmth and wit, and clearly written with an eye on possible publication. It told Alice's life, but wrapped in silk and ribbons, with always a layer between the reader and what really lay beneath.

This diary was different. It was beautifully written – I don't think Alice could do anything else – but there was no silk or lace to cover up the truth. Bridie had said it was personal, and it was – personal to the extent that every thought, good or bad, was recorded here, leaving Alice exposed. And the truth was exposed too. I had thought Alice's novel was heartfelt and the emotion so raw that it was like reading a diary, and now I understood why. Alice had been in love with her sister's husband, just like in the book, and he had asked her to go away with him and live as man and wife.

But as I already knew, Alice's story didn't have the same happy ending that she gave her characters. Alice rejected her brother-in-law and returned to her parents, and he eventually married a widow to be a mother to his children. I cried so much as I read the last pages of the diary that the paper crinkled and began to tear in my hands. And then I read one of the final paragraphs, and my breath caught because it felt as though Alice was reaching out through the pages and speaking just to me.

'*Oh, that I had my chance again, and that my courage were as brave as my imagination! What should I care for the opinion of the world? My conscience would be my only judge, and love my only master. Why should anything matter, but what is in our hearts? Seize happiness, happiness at any price!*'

I thought I must have imagined it when Jonas mentioned Ethan's name later that night – as if my head was so full of him that he had leaked out.

'What?' I said, spinning round to look at Jonas. He glanced up from his iPad and managed not to roll his eyes, though I expect he was tempted.

'Do you know when Ethan's coming back? There's going to be a half marathon around the village in March, and I thought he'd be up for it.'

'Can Dad not do it with you?'

Now he did roll his eyes.

'Dad couldn't run 1k. I can pre-register now if you think Ethan will be back.'

I could feel Ava's eyes boring into me.

'He's not coming back, unless he pops over to visit Gran. He still lives in New York.' I struggled to keep my voice and expression neutral. 'This summer was just a holiday.'

I'm not sure my neutrality was coming across, because Jonas gave me a sympathetic look – the sort of look I should use on him when he had trouble with girlfriends, not the other way round.

'I'll email him and ask,' he said.

'No . . .' But he sloped off upstairs before I could say any more, leaving me with one more thing to worry about. What if he did email Ethan? What if Ethan thought I'd asked Jonas to do it? I turned off the television and picked up a book instead, hoping it might prove a better distraction. Ava was still watching me over the top of her phone.

'Are you going to New York?' she asked, after five minutes of silent glaring, during which time I'd read the same page twice without having a clue what it said.

'No!' I put down the book. 'Why would you ask that?'

'Because it's what people at school say.' Ava tossed her hair over one shoulder. 'That you've been having a thing with Uncle Ethan for months and that you'll move over there to live with him.'

'And you believed it?'

'Why not?' She shrugged. 'He's not going to choose here over New York, is he? And Dad moved away without giving me or Joe a thought, so why wouldn't you? You're both as selfish as each other.'

'Selfish?' My screech woke Dotty, and she whimpered and scuttled over to Ava's feet. 'How dare you call me selfish? Everything I've done for the last twenty years has been for Dad, or Jonas, or you and the grans.'

'Like when you went down to London to see that agent? Which of us was that for?'

'Once! That was one thing I've done for myself, and even that's not entirely for me, because if I earn any money, what do you think it will be spent on?' I started counting on my fingers. 'Mobile phone bills, horse-riding, internet, Netflix, your clothes and make-up, stuff for Jonas, a possible holiday next year if there's anything left . . . I'm hardly going out every night having fun, am I?'

'Er, Mum?'

I barely registered Jonas, who'd come back downstairs; my blocked feelings had burst open like a breached dam.

'I have no life beyond this house, but I didn't mind, because I wanted to make you all happy. So no, I haven't been having any sort of thing with Ethan. I turned him down because I thought you would all be against it and I didn't want you to be talked about. But if the gossip has spread already, and you hate me whatever I do, I wish I'd accepted him after all!'

I dropped my head to my knees, covered my face with my arms, and cried. What was I doing? I couldn't shout at Ava like this. She might act like a bolshy young woman, but she was only a child – my child, the one I should love and protect, not screech at. I'd failed as a daughter and failed as a wife.

Being a mother was all I had left, and now I'd failed at that too.

The sofa cushion shifted beneath me.

'It's okay, Mum,' Jonas said, and he put his arm across my back and patted my shoulder. That made me cry even more. It was my job to comfort him, not the other way round.

'So you do fancy Uncle Ethan?' Ava asked.

'I think it's a bit more than that,' Jonas replied.

'It doesn't matter.' I raised my head and wiped my cheeks. 'I shouldn't have said anything.'

There was no way Ava would leave it at that.

'Did he ask you to move to New York?'

'No.'

'Then what?'

'He offered to move here.'

'Here? Here as in England, or here as in this house?'

'Either. Both.'

For a moment the confident mask slipped, revealing the young girl she had once been, wary of the unknown but unwilling to admit it. I crossed over to her chair, perched on the arm, and kissed the top of her head before she could recoil.

'I'm sorry I shouted.'

'Fair's fair,' Jonas interrupted. 'She shouts at you often enough.'

'You don't need to worry. No one is moving into this house.'

'It's Dad's house . . .'

'He's not coming back, Ave.' Jonas perched on the other chair arm. 'He's married to Clark.'

'I know, but . . .' Ava's chin wobbled as she tried to hold in her tears. 'We hardly see him now. And when we do, Clark's always there, or Dad's always talking about him. He's not *ours* anymore.'

She lost her battle, and the tears rolled down her cheeks, though she swallowed her sobs and tried to pretend it wasn't happening. Is this what she had been doing, all these months? Bottling up her feelings, just like I did? I pulled her into my arms and she melted against me.

'Is that what you were bothered about? Why you objected to the idea of Owen and Ethan?'

I felt Ava's nod against my chest.

'I don't want you to change too,' she mumbled into my jumper. I squeezed her tighter.

'Dad hasn't changed. He's still yours. He loves you both as much as ever, but he loves Clark too. You can stay with him as often as you want, and you have the Christmas holiday to look forward to, don't you?' It tore my heart to say it, but what choice did I have? 'And I promise you I won't ask anyone to move in here.'

'No need to go that far, Mum.' Jonas grinned at me over Ava's head. 'You're not past it yet. I think we can probably cope with you having a sex life.'

'Urgh, gross,' Ava said, but she lifted her head and smiled.

'And if Gran's still at it, I don't see why you shouldn't be,' Jonas added.

'Urgh, gross,' we all chorused, and laughed.

The following Thursday I woke up to find an email from Ethan in my inbox. Three breakfasts, two hours, and one fresh batch of cherry scones later, I still couldn't bring myself to even touch the phone again, let alone open the message.

Why was he contacting me now? I hoped it had nothing to do with Jonas and the disclosures at the weekend – but who knew with these sneaky Black men? Manipulation and secrets were second nature to them, and I had no reason to suppose Jonas hadn't inherited the family traits. Then I told myself to stop being so egotistical. It was probably nothing to do with me at all – it was much more likely to be a favour for Audrey, and purely because I was her neighbour. So I opened the email and read it.

Mary,

If I'd paid attention in Mrs Todd's English lessons I could have wowed you with the poetic words you deserve, but I only have my plain ones. I can't give up. I miss you. There are eight million faces here but yours is the only one I want to see.

No one else laughs at my jokes like you do. No one smiles at me like you do. No one has ever filled my head and my heart like you do.

Come to New York. You said you've always wanted to visit, and it's a great time to see it in the fall. Your ticket is booked – see attached. No excuses!

There's one condition. You have to meet me on Brooklyn Bridge at 7 p.m. on 30 October and take me for a birthday drink. It's only fair – I bought you break-fast on yours.

There's a whole colourful world out here. Come and see it. Come and see it with me. Why should we both live half a life when we could have one amazing one together?

I'll be waiting. You wouldn't stand me up on my fortieth birthday, would you, Mary Black?

Ethan

Smiling, I clicked on the first attachment. It was a flight ticket from Manchester to New York, booked in my name, for 29 October, less than two weeks away. Another link opened the website for a boutique hotel in Greenwich. And then, as if by magic, as if he had somehow been waiting for me to open the first one, a flurry of new emails arrived from Ethan. They contained a series of photographs of New York landmarks, some iconic, some undoubtedly chosen for me: the Empire State Building; the literary walk in Central Park; Times Square; The New York Central Library. At the end came a picture of Brooklyn Bridge. 'So you know what to look out for.' Ethan had written on this message. 'Tempted yet?'

I'd been tempted before he bombarded me with all the images. I longed to see these places, but I longed to see him more. Scrubbing away my tears, I put down the phone without sending a reply. What could I say? How could I disappear to New York, at a moment's notice? The children would be at home for half term. I had the bonfire and fireworks display to organise and attend. There might be a colourful life waiting for me in New York, but there was a black-and-white one here, full of mothers and children and dogs and responsibilities that I couldn't abandon. Especially not for a man who had once abandoned me.

I couldn't avoid it any longer. Mum had invited me round for dinner and made it clear that nothing less than imminent death would be an acceptable excuse – and probably only then if it were something contagious. Jonas and Ava had cunningly invented homework assignments and revision sessions that would take them to friends' houses, which meant that I would be the sole gooseberry at the feast. Mum wasn't in the habit of inviting us over, and to be fair, her garage conversion hadn't been designed with dinner parties in mind. This had to be the big 'meet the boyfriend' moment, the last thing I was in the mood for with Ethan's email from yesterday still sitting unanswered in my inbox.

I'd told Mum that I would be out until five, and dinner was scheduled for seven, but in the end a headache drove me home early and it was barely three when I pulled onto the drive. It was bad timing: Mum was disappearing through her front door, and a man stood at the boot of her car, lifting out a handful of Booths' carrier bags. He was tall and stocky, and thick black hair dotted with grey crept over the collar of his coat. He closed the boot and took a few steps towards Mum's door, kicking his right leg out as he walked in a peculiar half limp.

My heart pounded, making me suddenly dizzy. I'd seen that walk before. I'd seen it countless times, in real life and in my memories. How could there be two men who walked like that?

I slammed the car door and stood on the drive, too dazed to move. The man turned round.

'Well, would you look at you now, Mary-bear!' he said, and affection thickened a voice I had longed to hear again for years. 'Aren't you a grand sight for your Daddy's eyes?'

Chapter Twenty-Seven

The front door banged shut behind me, and I fell to my knees on the hard tiles of the hall floor. This wasn't real. This couldn't possibly be real. That man standing outside on my drive – the man who walked like my father, spoke with his accent, and in every way resembled an older version of my father – couldn't possibly *be* my father. Could he?

I bent over, hugging myself, and rocking backwards and forwards. My eyes stung but no tears fell. My heart had recognised him even before he'd turned around, before he'd spoken. But where had he been for the last thirty years? Deep down, I had thought he must be dead – that nothing else could have kept him away from me, however badly he had fallen out with Mum. And yet here he was, unpacking groceries, as if he had never been away. What was going on?

Dotty scratched on the kitchen door, whimpering to be released, and the sound brought me back to my senses. I let Dotty out and stomped over to Mum's garage, barging through the front door without knocking, and into the lounge. Mum and her boyfriend – my father – were standing in the window, arms round each other. They turned as I walked in. Mum's face was tight and pinched; his shone with such joy that it temporarily distracted me. But I couldn't be distracted. I had to know everything.

'Where did you go? That day when you walked me to school and kissed me goodbye – what happened? Why were you not there when I came home? Where have you been for every single day since then? How could you abandon me like that when you knew, you must have known, how much I adored you?'

'Mary-bear . . .' He moved away from Mum, his arms outstretched as if he intended to hug me, but I stepped back, and crossed my arms against my chest.

'Stop it. Don't Mary-bear me. That's what you called me when I was a child. I'm not a child any more. That's what happens when you disappear for over thirty years. You missed me growing up. You missed me going to university, getting married, having children, getting divorced. You chose to walk away from all that, from whatever future waited for the eight-year-old me, and you don't get to walk back in now.'

'Oh Mary, as if I'd have ever made a choice to leave my little sweetheart . . .'

'You must have done! Unless you were locked up some-where and unable to escape . . .'

I hadn't meant it as a serious suggestion, but Mum glanced at him sharply, and he nodded.

'Sit down, Mary,' she said, but I shook my head.

'No! Just tell me what's going on.'

'Your father was sent to prison. That's why he didn't come home.'

I sat down, sinking onto the dralon armchair as if my legs had been kicked from under me – and along with them, another little piece of my history.

'That's not true,' I said. My daddy in prison! It was impossible. Everyone loved him. He couldn't have done anything wrong. 'He left because of you.' I stared at Mum. 'You drove him away, always shouting at him. I heard you. He couldn't bear to be with you.'

'You've got that wrong, Mary. I loved your mammy with all my heart.' He took Mum's hand, and led her over to the sofa. Mum's face softened as he looked at her, in a way that shook up my memories. I had seen them like this before – their younger selves, holding hands, laughing, happy. How had I forgotten that? 'We never had a cross word until I was an eejit and got myself into trouble. And then she only shouted at me because of what it was going to do to you.'

I glanced over at Mum. The pinched expression had gone, as had the frown that had pulled her eyebrows together for as long as I could remember. Could I have been wrong about her? Had I blamed her for years, when really she had been grieving for a lost husband every bit as much as I had grieved for a lost daddy? How much pain must I have caused her, rejecting her when I was all she had left, hating her when she had done nothing wrong?

'But how did I not know?' I asked. 'There must have been

publicity. Was it not in the newspapers?' Could I have found the answer to his disappearance easily if I'd searched for him on the internet? I'd never done it – too proud to look for him, if he didn't want to find me. 'Did people in the village not know?'

'Yes, they did,' Mum replied. 'But I spoke to everyone I could, and asked them to keep it a secret, for your sake. And they kept their word, didn't they?'

I nodded, but I was mentally raking back through the past. I could no longer remember the details, but the impressions had never left me: of conversations silenced as I walked in; of glances exchanged over my head; of sympathy that I had shaken off, unwanted. I had shrunk into myself, hating being an object of gossip, a hatred that had dogged me throughout my life. It had never crossed my mind before that it might have been well meant. I couldn't imagine my proud, private mother going round to her neighbours one by one and begging for their secrecy. And they had given it, and kept the secret all these years. How much regard must they have for Mum to have done that? The same Mum that I belittled at every opportunity. Shame burned in my heart.

'Did Audrey and Bill know?' I asked. I couldn't bear the idea that Audrey could have known a secret of this magnitude and hidden it from me; I needed to know that out of all this mess, there was one person left that I could trust.

'No, only people who lived in Stoneybrook at the time.'

Amid my own relief, I noticed the sadness flash across

Mum's face. She must know how much I loved Audrey, couldn't have missed how much more time I spent with her than with my own mum. I tried to imagine how I would feel if Jonas or Ava did that to me, and I failed – even tiptoeing to the perimeter of that idea was so painful that I had to draw back. I looked round this room, as if seeing it for the first time: living room, dining room and kitchen all squashed into one, hardly bigger than a prison cell itself, but accepted by Mum without hesitation for my sake. Every available surface was crammed with photographs of me – on my own, with Leo, with the children. Mum's love was evident everywhere, if only I'd been willing to see it.

'What did you do?' I said, turning to my dad. 'It must have been serious to have been in prison for so long. Did you kill someone?'

'Ah Mary, I was so drunk I could hardly remember then, never mind now. I'd been out celebrating St Patrick's Day in Manchester, and enjoying the craic, but somehow a fight started, punches flying everywhere, and the next thing you know there's a fella lying on the floor bleeding, and the ambulance and police showed up. All but three of us had run away, and the landlord was happy to point the finger at us. The wee fella had fallen and banged his head, and died a month later. Involuntary manslaughter they called it. I couldn't tell you whether I laid a finger on him or not, and that's the truth.'

My stomach heaved. How could the perfect daddy I'd worshipped ever have been guilty of this?

'And you were sentenced for thirty years for that?'

Mum jumped up.

'I'll make us some tea,' she said. Dad followed her to the other end of the room, where amongst the boiling of the kettle and the clatter of spoons and mugs, I could hear a whispered debate going on. Mum was waving her hands in the agitated way I knew well, and Dad took hold of them and kissed each in turn, before pulling her into his arms. The gesture was so affectionate, so gentle, that I understood one thing clearly: whatever he had done in the past didn't matter to them. He was neither wholly good nor wholly bad – exactly the same as the rest of us. Mistakes could be regretted and forgiven. And despite the shocking events of this afternoon, my thoughts strayed again to the email I had still not answered, and someone else who perhaps I should learn to forgive too . . .

Mum thrust a mug into my hand, and sat down again opposite me. Dad loitered at her side.

'The prison sentence wasn't thirty years,' Mum said, rushing out the words as if they were burning her tongue. 'It was ten.'

'Ten? But that means . . .' I put down my mug before my shaking hands could spill the contents. I looked at my dad, holding his gaze. 'You were released when I was eighteen?'

'I was.'

I felt like I'd been tricked. I'd assumed he'd been let out this year, and come straight home to Mum. I'd been ready to forgive, to accept that he hadn't really abandoned me. And perhaps he hadn't, when I was eight. But when I was eighteen . . .What possible excuse could he have for that?

'Why didn't you come back then?'

'I decided . . .' Mum began, but Dad interrupted.

'We agreed, Reenie. Tell her straight.'

'We agreed it would be better if he didn't come back. You were at university, doing well. You were engaged to Leo, and he had a bright academic future ahead of him – an early professorship, that's what everyone said. You were settled and happy, as far as I could tell. What would have happened if your convict father turned up and the old story was raked over again? I couldn't have stopped the gossip a second time. What would it have done to Leo's chances to have a former prisoner for a father-in-law? There was too much to lose.'

'Not as much as there was to gain!' What might I have done – what decisions might I have made – if my dad had returned then? If I had known that I had never been abandoned, and that it wasn't necessary to choose a safe life to avoid it happening again? 'Where did you go?'

'Back to Ireland, to do building work for your Uncle Terry. It was all the job I could get.'

'And you knew where he was?' Mum nodded. I swung back to Dad. 'And did you not even want to see me before you left?'

'I did. I saw you and your man go off cycling together, and I saw that your mammy was right. You were happy, so full of

370

love, laughing and joking like we once had – exactly what I wanted for my Mary-bear. I wasn't for risking that.'

Cycling? I had never cycled with Leo, only Ethan. But I couldn't dwell on that now.

'And one glimpse was enough for the next twenty years?'

'Who do you think converted this garage, Mary?' Mum interrupted. I shrugged, thrown by the random question.

'Some builders . . .' I stopped, thinking back. It had been a team of Irish builders. I hadn't paid them much attention. One hint of that accent and I had avoided the building site at all costs.

'It was your Uncle Terry's men. Did you never wonder how I could have paid for it? How I could have paid for anything, when I didn't work? Your dad and his family have supported us all this time.'

'You were here, working on the garage?'

'I was. It had to be the best, for your mammy.'

I couldn't believe it. My dad had been here, under my nose for months, and I hadn't noticed. Had I lived my whole life wearing blinkers?

'If you knew I was getting married, could you not have come to the wedding?'

'I did, and it shattered my heart to see my Mary-bear given away by another man.'

He was in tears, my big strong daddy, and how I managed to hold back my own I'll never know. Mum held his hand and he rested his head against hers, and in that moment, I realised how selfish I was being. This wasn't all about me, and never had been. These two people had given up their love, their lives, to do what they thought was best for me. But they had been wrong. It was the ultimate kindness, and the ultimate mistake.

'You shouldn't have done it,' I said. 'I wouldn't have cared how much gossip or trouble there was. I would never have wanted you to be unhappy or apart.'

'If you love someone, you love them, however long or far apart you are,' Dad said. 'I had faith we'd be together one day.'

'Nothing you do for your children is ever a sacrifice,' Mum said. 'You should know that.'

She looked at me steadily, and I knew what she was referring to. She meant Ethan – comparing our situations, assuming that I had given him up to avoid complications and difficulties for Jonas and Ava. She was wrong – that wasn't the only reason, and probably not even the main one. But far from persuading me that I'd done the right thing, as I returned her gaze, noticing the glow of love about her, the way she clutched my dad's hand, the softness of her smile – the transformation into the mum of my early memories – I wondered if I'd made a mistake. This was the mum I should have had throughout my life, not the bitter, lonely one. This was the sort of mum I wanted my children to have.

'I know that I would rather you had been happy. And that I might have been happier if you had been. Perhaps the best thing I can do for Jonas and Ava is to teach them not to be afraid to grab a piece of happiness, whatever obstacles are in the way.'

'Perhaps you're right.' Mum sighed. 'You must do what you think best. Your dad and I will be here to support you, whatever you decide to do.'

'You're back for good?' I asked Dad.

'As long as Reenie can stand me.'

Mum laughed – a rare sound, and one I had half thought extinct.

'Why now?' I had a sudden panic that this was too good to be true – that one of them would disclose a terminal illness that had brought them together for their final days. 'What's changed to bring you back?'

The answer, when it came, surprised me.

'Leo,' Mum said. 'Now you're divorced, his career can't be damaged by any gossip about us. And . . .' She hesitated. I knew how uncomfortable this must be making her. 'Your dad has wanted to come home for years, and I wouldn't let him. When he asked again this year . . . I simply couldn't think of a reason to say no.'

Jonas and Ava greeted the arrival of a long-lost grandfather with curiosity swiftly followed by indifference when they realised he didn't have any scars, tattoos or other stereotypical attributes of a gangster. They seemed more baffled by the change in Mum: they were used to one laughing and one serious gran, but to find that they had practically swapped roles overnight took some getting used to. Mum wasn't quite at the stage of calling everything marvellous, but it was surely only a matter of time.

I had no idea whether I thought it was marvellous. Life had banged me over the head with so many surprises this year that I was struggling to come to terms with another. Of course I was thrilled that my dad was alive, and that he had never truly abandoned me. But the irony was inescapable: because I believed I'd been abandoned, I chose Leo; and because I chose Leo, my dad had stayed away. It felt as if I had spent my whole life being pushed along a road in a direction chosen by other people, stopping and turning only when they dictated I should. When was I going to choose my own path?

I had never felt so alone as I did during those first days of my dad's return. I wanted someone to talk to about it all, to explain how I was feeling and try to make sense of my muddled thoughts. I wanted someone to hug me and tell me that it would be okay. I wanted someone to sit with me and say nothing. And though Leo had filled that role for twenty-five years, it wasn't him I wanted now. I needed Ethan.

The days crawled by, and every day I read his email, and every day I closed it without replying. I had turned him down once, emphatically and agonisingly so, and what had changed since then? Nothing, I argued to myself: he was still exactly who he had always been. But then I thought of Alice Hornby, who had given up her chance of happiness because of fear of public opinion, and regretted it throughout her life. I thought of Mum and Dad, and how in trying to do the right thing they had made so many people unhappy. So perhaps my attitude on that had changed; but my fear hadn't. It made no difference that now I knew Dad hadn't deliberately left me; by his own admission, Ethan had. The memory stilled my fingers every time I started a reply.

Two days before the flight was due to leave for New York, Audrey marched into the kitchen with what I could only call a determined air. I was relieved to see it. She hadn't been herself lately – quiet and serious, more Leo than her usual Ethan.

'Sit down, Mary,' she said, pulling out a chair and steering me into it. 'We need to talk about half term.'

'Okay,' I said, baffled but going along with it, as Audrey was displaying her rare steely side. 'Do you want to do something?'

'Why aren't you going to New York?'

I hadn't expected that.

'You know about New York?'

'Of course I know. Ethan rings me several times a day to ask if there's any sign of you packing.'

'Does he?' My heart did an unauthorised little somersault. 'So . . . you know . . .'

'Everything.'

'Everything?' I repeated, hoping it was a typical Audrey sweeping statement.

'Everything,' she said firmly, meeting my gaze. 'Including the kiss at the bonfire on Ethan's birthday, the kiss at Leo's wedding, and all that went before and after.'

That was a pretty comprehensive everything.

'How long have you known?'

'Since the beginning. Mary, my darling, I spent hours with all three of you, watching you grow up. How could I not know?'

I leant my elbow on the kitchen table, and rested my head on my hand. This was not a conversation I would ever have chosen to have with Audrey. What must she think of me – have thought of me for all these years?

'I'm sorry,' I said. 'I never meant to betray Leo. It was . . .'

Audrey took my free hand and held it between hers.

'You loved them both, in different ways. I understand that. And you chose the one you needed at the time. I understand that too. But what I don't understand, having spent the summer watching you bloom as I always knew you could, is why you haven't shown any signs of catching that flight in two days' time.'

She made it sound so simple – so simple that it was clear she didn't know everything after all.

'I'm not going to New York.'

'Oh Mary, whatever can be stopping you?'

'The children . . .'

'Can stay with Leo.'

'Dotty . . .'

'Can stay with me, or Irene.'

'The school bonfire . . .'

'Daisy can take charge of that. Really, if those are your only objections, what are you waiting for? He won't let us make any fuss about his birthday, because all he wants is to see you. He's loved you for years.'

'But he didn't love me enough. You don't know everything. You don't know what they did. They discussed me like I was a piece of furniture, and agreed which of them I should be with. And Ethan was happy to walk away.'

Audrey's grip on my hand tightened.

'He wasn't happy, my darling, far from it. And he didn't walk away.' She squeezed my hand again and then let go. 'I sent him away.'

Slowly I sat back in my chair, and looked across the table. Audrey was sitting there – my lovely Audrey, the mother I had wished for, the friend I had counted on for so long. Her thick silver-blonde hair was piled into the usual messy bun, loose strands caressing her neck; watery blue eyes, a paler version of Ethan's, gazed into mine. She looked the same – so how could she be saying something so odd?

I didn't speak, and waited for her to explain.

'What could I do?' she asked, twisting her wedding ring round her finger. 'You were all so young. I loved you all equally, and how could I choose between you? Either two of you could be happy, or none at all. I did my best. I picked the two that I thought needed each other most. I adored my fragile little

Mary from the first moment that Leo brought you here, so desperate to find security and stability. You needed Leo, and he needed you too, especially after his wobble in Oxford when he was so confused about who he was. So my poor sweet Ethan, the strongest of you all, was the one to lose out.' Tears rolled down Audrey's cheeks, leaving lines etched in her face powder. 'He wanted to fight for you, Mary, and I wouldn't let him. I arranged for him to have a home and a job with a friend of mine in New York, and bought him a one-way ticket. He didn't choose to leave you, my darling. He chose to be loyal to his brother and to me.'

She really did know everything – even, it seemed, Leo's liaison in Oxford. And perhaps I should have been furious: the one person who I thought was innocent of secrets and manipulation had in fact played the major part. But all that trailed in the footnotes beyond the headline news: Ethan hadn't chosen to leave me. Loyalty wasn't a clear cut, black-and-white thing: it came in all forms and shades, sometimes solid, sometimes shifting, and sometimes conflicting. Perhaps I could trust him, after all . . .

'It's too late,' I said, jumping up and sending my chair crashing to the floor. 'My passport is probably years out of date. I don't even know where it is.'

'I do!' Audrey opened the middle drawer of the dresser and held up my passport. I stared at her. She smiled. 'We needed the details for your flight and for the visa waiver. All you need to do is pack, and go to the airport.'

She waved my passport at me, tempting me. But before I could take a step towards it – or away – Jonas and Ava burst through the kitchen door.

'Hi, Gran.' Jonas let his bag fall to the floor where he stood, and grabbed an apple from the fridge. 'What's for tea?'

'What's going on?' Ava, always the more astute when it came to atmosphere, looked between me and Audrey.

'I need to speak to Uncle Ethan.'

'Cool,' Jonas said. 'Is he back?'

'No. He's in New York.'

Ava glared at me.

'You said you wouldn't go to New York.'

'I said I wasn't moving there, and I'm not. It would be a visit, nothing more.'

'Promise?'

'Promise.' I kissed the top of her head, and took it as a good sign when she didn't jerk away.

'Is Uncle Ethan coming back with you?'

'I don't know.' I looked round at three of the people I loved most in the world. I couldn't help myself: their opinion mattered. 'What would you think if he did?'

'I think it would be the most marvellous news,' Audrey said, and she hugged me, thrusting my passport into my hand as she withdrew. 'But you will always be a daughter to me, my darling, whatever happens.'

'Jonas? Ava? You don't think it would be too weird?'

Jonas tossed his apple core into the bin.

'Dad is married to a man. Gran is married to an ex-con. Nothing that happens round here can surprise us anymore.' He grinned at me. 'Go for it.'

I looked at Ava, my heart fluttering with hope and fear. If she objected . . .

'Fine,' she said, and shrugged. 'But I want a present from Tiffanys. And a Little Brown Bag from Bloomingdale's. And . . .'

The rest of her list was lost in a blur. I was going to New York . . .

Chapter Twenty-Eight

It was years since I'd visited Leo at work, but the classic Georgian mansion at the heart of the university, surrounded by ugly concrete tower blocks, had hardly changed since I'd been a student here myself. Students swarmed past me, anorak hoods up to ward off the rain, backpacks bulging with books, and the sight whisked me back twenty years; it was almost a shock to see a middle-aged Leo approaching, not the ambitious young fellow I was remembering.

'Mary!' he said, noticing me at last as I stood in his path. He bent to kiss my cheek and our umbrellas collided. 'What are you doing here? Is something wrong?'

'No, I just need to talk to you.'

I could have phoned him last night – Audrey, with her typical zeal, urged me to ring him so the plans were final and I couldn't back out – but it wasn't a conversation I could imagine having over the telephone. It needed to be face to face. He deserved it.

He led me round to a squat grey building, and up in the lift to the top floor, where his corner office provided views of traffic in Manchester city centre and of a busy railway line.

It was a stark contrast from the mellow stone and spires of Oxford that he had once hoped for. For a long time, I had felt guilty that marrying me, and my refusal to move away from Stoneybrook, had held him back, and denied him his dream; but not anymore. He had lived exactly the life he had chosen. Now it was my turn.

I prowled round his office while he made us coffee, soaking in the familiar touches: books we had bought together; books we had written together; numerous little pieces of junk that the children had made him for various Fathers' Days and birthdays. I could draw a dot-to-dot around the room, tracing the progress of our life together through the objects on display. The trail ended on his desk, where a photograph of me and the children, on our last holiday as a family in St Ives, stood side by side with a picture of Leo and Clark on their wedding day.

'Happy times,' Leo said, coming up behind me as I studied the family photographs. He handed me his Emma Bridgewater 'Dad' mug, keeping a tatty plain one for himself. The instinctive gesture prodded at my heart, reminding me of a lifetime of kindness he had shown me: so many kindnesses, that I knew, without any further thought, that if placed in the balance they would outweigh even the heaviest mistakes of his youth. He had done me wrong; but he had done me right a million times over to make up for it.

'Are you busy over half term?'

'Not especially. Clark has no more holiday allowance left

until Christmas, so I expect I'll carry on with the book about Victorian writers. Your notes are invaluable, as always.' Leo smiled. 'You didn't come here to discuss holiday plans.'

'Actually I did. I need you to have the children to stay with you, from tomorrow.'

'Of course. Are you . . .' He hesitated, drank some of his coffee. 'Am I allowed to ask? Are you going away?'

'I am.' He pushed his glasses up his nose. He knew what I was going to say; I could see the truth dawning over his face, frown lines spreading out like the sun's rays. 'I'm going to New York.'

'Ah.' Leo wandered over to the window and leant against the glass, his head turned to the street below. The wet road amplified the sound of the traffic, and car horns blared as impatient commuters tried to get ahead. 'I suppose you're here to ask for my blessing.'

'No.' He turned back to me. 'I don't need your blessing, or anyone else's.'

'But you are going to Ethan?'

'Yes. I'm going to talk to Ethan, and then I'm going to decide what happens next. But if the what happens next involves Ethan coming home – involves me having a relation-ship with Ethan – then I know you won't like it, but you have to accept it, just like I accepted Clark. No squabbles from the past are going to harm this family.'

'It isn't a question of not liking it. It never has been. He's my brother. Of course I love him, and want him to be happy.

You too.' Leo took hold of my hand and led me over to the squashy red velvet sofa we had chosen together more years ago than I could remember. 'The truth is, that the idea of you being with Ethan is terrifying.'

'Why? Do you not think we would be happy?'

'On the contrary, I fear you would be too happy.' He traced the space on my finger where my wedding ring had once been. He had a new ring now, a thick platinum band, shining evidence of his love for Clark. 'Because seeing you happy together would make me wonder what life you might have had if I hadn't stood in your way: where you would have gone, what you might have achieved. And it would make me wonder whether you regretted the life you shared with me. You gave me everything, Mary, made me everything I am. I couldn't bear it if you regretted a moment of it.'

I remembered thinking at Leo's wedding to Clark that he had never cried over me. Now he did, and the sight of it filled my heart with so much affection for him that it washed away the stain left by the recent revelations. I didn't care that he had betrayed me in Oxford; I didn't care that he had lied to Ethan by telling him I was pregnant. It didn't matter – because I didn't regret my marriage to Leo, and I never would. I couldn't regret anything that had brought me Jonas and Ava; and I couldn't regret it for my own sake either. I had been a lost, discontented teenager when Leo arrived in my life, and he had given me a purpose, a family, stability, and contentment. He had given me everything I needed back then. Audrey had made the right judgement: Leo and I had been meant for each other at the time. But that time was over.

'No regrets. You saved me, Leo. You were my anchor when I needed one. I wouldn't be me without you.'

I leant forward and hugged him; the last time, perhaps, that it would be appropriate to do that. I rested my head on his shoulder, soaking it with tears, and tried to convey in that embrace all the gratitude, forgiveness, and love that I felt for him.

'But it's time to sail away now,' Leo said.

I nodded.

'It's time to try.'

He kissed the top of my head in farewell.

'Safe journey, my darling Mary.'

Could I say that New York was one of my favourite places in the world, when I had never previously travelled further than France? My heart was lost at the first sight of a yellow cab and never properly settled down. It was all so gloriously, overwhelmingly mad: everything was twice as bright, twice as noisy, and a hundred times more vibrant than I had expected. I had never been anywhere so alien – in contrast with my quiet village life – and yet so familiar. So many times I turned a corner and recognised a place and then had to do a double-take, because this wasn't a film or a photograph. It was real. I was actually here, in New York. And I was here in New York to see Ethan. And then . . .

But I couldn't think about that. He might not even be there.

It only occurred to me as I sat in Central Park, watching the tourists, joggers, and horse-drawn carriages pass by, that in all the last-minute rush to come here, I had forgotten the most important thing. I hadn't replied to Ethan's email, and hadn't told him I was coming. What if he assumed my silence was a rejection and didn't turn up? I toyed with my phone, considering sending a reply now, but decided against it. If he was as loyal as he claimed, he would be there. And if not . . . I blocked that alternative from my head.

It was ten to seven when my cab dropped me off at City Hall, and the driver pointed the way to the pedestrian access to Brooklyn Bridge. I stared at it for a few minutes, legs too paralysed by fear to move. Swarms of people headed on and off. I'd had no idea that it would be so vast, or so busy. It looked like it stretched half a mile across the river . . . How did I know where he would be? What if I missed him in the crowd? What if he hadn't arrived yet? I pushed my legs forward, one anxious step after another, onto the wooden boards that formed the pedestrian walkway. What if he wasn't coming at all? And then, as I hesitated again, wondering if I had the nerve to do this after all, the family group I had been shuffling behind moved to one side to take a photograph, and there he was, leaning on the railing, gazing over the traffic below and down into the water, and my heart pummelled my chest so strongly that it felt as if it might escape and literally, as well as metaphorically, go to rest in his hands.

The breeze ruffled his hair and he straightened up and

turned so he was looking right at me. The lights on the bridge shone down on his face, and it was like watching a child see Father Christmas for the first time: the wonder and delight were instinctive and consumed every part of him. He hadn't known I was coming, and I was glad. I wouldn't have missed this moment for all the world. It told me everything I needed to know, and dismissed every doubt.

'You're here,' he said. 'You actually came.'

'Of course I did. I was sent a free ticket to New York. I'd be a chump not to take it.' I smiled. 'I can go if you like . . .'

'Don't you dare!' With lightning reflexes he grasped my waist, picked me up and spun me round. 'I've waited too long for this.'

'What do you mean?' I glanced at my watch as he lowered me to the ground, hands still round me. 'Bang on seven o'clock, exactly as instructed. I'm not late.'

'Of course you're not, my perfect, efficient Mary. But I've been here since six.'

'Doing what?'

'Hoping.'

'Oh, that's an excellent answer. How long did it take you to come up with that?'

'Twenty years, on and off.'

'Well, I suppose you always were sporty rather than academic, weren't you?'

He laughed and pulled me closer.

'Are you only here to see New York?'

'I've always wanted to visit.'

'I know. So come here.' He steered me over to the railing and stood behind me, an arm on either side protecting me. 'Look, there's Manhattan to the right. Amazing, isn't it?' I nodded. 'And over to the left, there's Brooklyn, and somewhere in the middle of those lights is where I live. And look straight ahead, and you can see the Statue of Liberty.' He pointed.

I turned round to face him.

'And what if I look this way?' I asked.

'There's me. Just a man who loves you and who still can't believe you're real.'

I reached up and stroked the side of his face.

'Totally real, and totally here.'

He grasped my hand and led me along the bridge.

'Last time we met . . .'

I squeezed his hand and interrupted him.

'I was an idiot. You were right. Forget the past.'

'I can't. Not if you think you can't trust me.'

'I can. Audrey explained. Why didn't you tell me?'

'That I left because my mum told me to? Sure, that would have impressed you. And I couldn't harm your relationship with Mum. I know what she means to you.'

I'd wondered if that was his reason – if he had, in his own way, been showing loyalty again, even though it had acted against his own interests.

'Has Audrey told you the latest news?' I asked. 'About Mum's boyfriend?'

'Yes.' He looked at me. 'But don't worry. I still love you even though your father's a convict.' He laughed. 'I don't care about anything but you. Although I suppose I do care a bit. But only because it's such a romantic story of love surviving through the years that you might think it eclipses mine.'

We had reached a stone turret on the bridge. Ethan stopped.

'I love you, Mary. Tell me you've reconsidered. You can't have come all this way to turn me down again.'

'But are you sure? You'd be getting the worst part of me – the horrible old age part.'

Ethan held both my hands.

'I'll take it. I'd take it a thousand times. I'll fan you through your hot flushes. I'll buy your incontinence knickers. I'll brush your glorious hair when it's turning grey. I'll iron your elasticated waist trousers. I'll be the most devoted nurse when your hips or knees are replaced. Our false teeth will sit side by side in tumblers beside our bed. I'll hold your gnarled old hand until one of us takes our last breath. And if it's you first, I promise I'll follow right behind. I won't ever let you go again.'

What could I possibly say to that? Nothing. Not a single word I'd ever read, in the greatest literature in the world, was adequate to describe how I felt. All I could do was kiss him.

'There's a problem,' I said at last, drawing away. 'I promised Ava that no one would move in with us.'

'That was unfortunate. Did Mum send me a birthday present?'

'Yes, I'd forgotten.' I rummaged in my bag, baffled by the abrupt change of subject, and pulled out a small box tied with a ribbon. I gave it to Ethan and he opened it and showed me a key lying inside.

'What is it?'

'The key to Waterman's Cottage.' He smiled. 'I've bought it. You like it, don't you?'

'I love it. But why . . .'

'Because this time I was never going to give up.' He kissed me. 'We can go at your pace. I'll live there, and you can stay as often as you can. And one day, I hope you and Joe and Ava will move in with me. Because this is serious, for the rest of our lives. And just so you're quite clear what my intentions are, I'm not going to rest until you are, in every way, *my* Mary Black.'

'I love you,' I said. Words failed me again: I had cherished them my whole life, and now when I needed them, they simply weren't adequate to explain. Love: four letters weren't enough to describe how utterly happy I was to be here with him, how the idea of a life with him was like looking through a kaleidoscope and seeing a shimmering swirl of colour ahead.

'Hallelujah! She says it at last.' And this time, when Ethan kissed me, it was different: all caution and uncertainty gone, replaced by confidence and passion that twisted round my soul and bound me more surely to him by the second.

'Why did we meet here?' I asked, when I drew away a fraction to breathe.

'It's one of my favourite places in New York. And it seemed a sort of crossroads. I was going to offer you a choice. Go that way . . .' He pointed towards Manhattan. 'And I can deliver you safely back to your hotel, back to the life you know. Or you can come the other way, come home with me to Brooklyn and see what my life is – what our life could be.'

The hotel he'd chosen was beautiful – the poshest place I'd ever stayed. It was bound to be ridiculously expensive. The capable, efficient Mary Black would never waste money and leave it empty.

I pulled out of his arms and glanced both ways along the walkway. It was relatively quiet – a few pedestrians, but no cyclists to get in the way.

'Hold this,' I said, shoving my handbag at Ethan.

'I don't think it matches my outfit . . .'

I gave him a final kiss and stepped away.

'Mary . . .'

I stretched up my arms. I had no idea whether I could still do this, but I was determined to try. I leaned to the side, propelled myself over and performed three perfect cartwheels. The world rushed past my eyes, a dizzying display of light and colour, mesmerising in its beauty.

I looked back at Ethan. Manhattan lay behind him, and my past life with it.

'What are you waiting for?' I called.

'I'm not waiting anymore,' he said, and taking my hand, he led me home to Brooklyn.